10-2

Praise for #1 *New York Times* bestselling author
Sherryl Woods

"Sherryl Woods writes emotionally satisfying novels about family, friendship and home."
—#1 *New York Times* bestselling author
Debbie Macomber

"Woods is a master heartstring puller."
—*Publishers Weekly*

"Woods…is noted for appealing, character-driven stories that are often infused with the flavor and fragrance of the South."
—*Library Journal*

Praise for *New York Times* bestselling author
Lee Tobin McClain

"Lee Tobin McClain dazzles with unforgettable characters, fabulous small-town settings and a big dose of heart. Her complex and satisfying stories never disappoint."
—Susan Mallery, #1 *New York Times* bestselling author

"[An] enthralling tale of learning to trust…. This enjoyable contemporary romance will appeal to readers looking for twinges of suspense before happily ever after."
—*Publishers Weekly* on *Low Country Hero*

With her roots firmly planted in the South, #1 *New York Times* bestselling author **Sherryl Woods** has written many of her more than one hundred books in that distinctive setting. Her Chesapeake Shores books have become a highly rated series success on Hallmark Channel and her Sweet Magnolias books have recently been released as a much-anticipated Netflix series. Sherryl divides her time between her childhood summer home overlooking the Potomac River in Colonial Beach, Virginia, and Florida's east coast.

New York Times and *USA TODAY* bestselling author **Lee Tobin McClain** read *Gone with the Wind* in the third grade and has been an incurable romantic ever since. When she's not writing angst-filled love stories with happy endings, she's probably Snapchatting with her college-student daughter, mediating battles between her goofy goldendoodle and her rescue cat, or teaching aspiring writers in Seton Hill University's MFA program. She is probably not cleaning her house. For more about Lee, visit her website at www.leetobinmcclain.com.

#1 *New York Times* Bestselling Author

SHERRYL WOODS

NOT AT EIGHT, DARLING

**HARLEQUIN
BESTSELLING
AUTHOR
COLLECTION**

**HARLEQUIN®
BESTSELLING
AUTHOR
COLLECTION**

Recycling programs
for this product may
not exist in your area.

ISBN-13: 978-1-335-40623-1

Not at Eight, Darling
First published in 1986. This edition published in 2021.
Copyright © 1986 by Sherryl Woods

The Soldier and the Single Mom
First published in 2017. This edition published in 2021.
Copyright © 2017 by Lee Tobin McClain

This edition published by arrangement with Harlequin Books S.A.

For questions and comments about the quality of this book, please contact us at CustomerService@Harlequin.com.

Harlequin Enterprises ULC
22 Adelaide St. West, 40th Floor
Toronto, Ontario M5H 4E3, Canada
www.Harlequin.com

Printed in U.S.A.

CONTENTS

NOT AT EIGHT, DARLING

Sherryl Woods

Chapter 1

The only sound in the hushed, cavernous television studio was the increasingly rapid, evidently angry tapping of Barrie MacDonald's pen against the metal top of a makeshift conference table. Then, as a dozen people looked on in anxious and surprisingly silent anticipation, she dropped the memo she'd been reading, peered over the top of her oversized glasses with indignant brown eyes and spoke in a voice that, she noted proudly, was quiet and controlled. It was not at all like the scream of pure frustration she wanted to unleash on poor, unsuspecting Kevin Porterfield.

"Kevin, dear, did you read this?"

The young man gulped nervously. "Of course, Miss MacDonald."

"Then you know how utterly absurd it is," she said softly. She actually sounded calm. Amazing. "I will not add a sheepdog to the cast of *Goodbye, Again*, just because some crazy demographic study shows that kids like sheepdogs."

Several members of the cast gasped as eyebrows lifted toward the ceiling in a disgusted, what-did-you-expect expression. Others simply giggled. If the memo hadn't sounded so incredibly serious, Barrie might have laughed herself. Instead she managed an expression she hoped would put the fear of God into this...this Yuppie who was still wet behind the ears and who was staring at her now with a look that teetered between misery and smug satisfaction. It was actually a rather amazing combination, and she wondered for a fleeting second how he managed it. If he could do it on command, he might make a decent actor.

"But, Miss MacDonald..." he began again.

"That's all there is to it, Kevin," she interrupted firmly. "End of discussion."

"But, Miss MacDonald, I'm afraid Mr. Compton was adamant. The show has to have a dog. The research shows that dogs..."

"I know what the bloody research shows, Kevin," she said, her voice beginning to rise toward a less-than-serene screech, despite her best efforts to control it. She took a deep, relaxing breath—precisely as she'd learned in her stress reduction class—and added more gently, "If the research showed that viewers liked ax murders, would you expect me to put one of those in each week, too?"

Kevin looked at her indignantly. "Of course not."

"Then don't talk to me about research. Have you read the script for this show, Kevin? We are talking adult situation comedy here. We are talking relationships. Funny, sophisticated relationships. We are not talking dog food commercials."

Poor Kevin turned absolutely pale, but Barrie was not about to relent and let him off the hook. She had created *Goodbye, Again*. It was her statement about the transitory nature of romance, about her values. There was an awful lot of her in the single, independent, fiesty heroine. Each time Karen Devereaux spoke, Barrie felt as though it was an echo of her own thoughts. *Goodbye, Again* had been born of her beliefs, and she had spent three long, agonizing years trying to get it on the air. She was not about to let these mindless, research-oriented twits destroy it on the first day of production. If she gave in on the dog, next week they'd want to add kids, and the week after that her lead character would be married and pregnant, and there would be a whole disgustingly cheery episode revolving around diapers and baby food. Well, they could take their blasted market research and stuff it!

Aloud, she said none of this. Exercising what she considered to be Emmy Award–winning restraint, she murmured pleasantly, "Now you run along and explain that to Mr. Compton, dear. I'm sure he'll understand."

"Understand what?"

The question, asked in a low, velvet-smooth tone, came from the back of the studio. It was exactly the sort of warm, soothing, sensual voice that radio stations liked to have on the air in the wee hours of the morning to stir the imagination of their female listeners. Despite her instinctive, sinking feeling that the voice belonged to Michael Compton, Barrie's own heart lurched at the seductive sound. Then it had a far more sensible reaction. It slammed against her ribs in sheer panic.

Michael Compton, the recently appointed network vice president for programming, was a man who reportedly dissected into tiny, insignificant pieces the people who dared to question his orders. Barrie wondered how much of her conversation with Kevin he'd overheard. Not that she'd change a word of it, she thought stoutly. It would just be nice to know exactly how much trouble she was in.

She had to admit that the man's timing was impeccable. "Just when I've got the battle under control, the enemy general has to show up with reinforcements," she muttered resignedly under her breath.

She should have anticipated something like this. The day had not gone well since the alarm clock had jarred her awake at daybreak. In fact, on a scale of one to ten, it ranked somewhere on the minus side of the ledger. First she had inadvertently washed one of her new soft contact lenses down the drain, leaving her to choose between blinking nearsightedness or the huge old rose-tinted glasses that made her look a bit like an owl. Then her hairdryer had sparked and sizzled to an abrupt halt, leaving her frosted ash-brown hair to dry naturally to a curly tangle, rather than the smoother style she preferred. Her windshield wipers had broken in the middle of a downpour, and she'd had to creep along the L.A. freeway, arriving at the studio an hour late. And finally, she had snagged her new hose as she was getting out of her sporty fire-engine-red Sentra in the parking lot. The run had made its way from her ankle to her thigh in less time than it had taken her to utter a satisfying string of obscenities under her breath.

"Apparently I'm on a roll," she said dryly as the man whom she assumed to be Michael Compton stepped out of the shadows and strolled confidently to the temporary office set of *Goodbye, Again*, where Barrie and the cast were assembled. They had been rehearsing the premiere episode when Kevin had wandered in with the latest memo from the network.

"Well, Miss MacDonald," the man said, a hint of amusement twinkling in his eyes as he perched on the edge of the conference table right next to her. One very solid, very tempting thigh was mere inches from her fingertips. "Exactly what is it you're so sure I'll understand?"

Barrie's gaze shifted reluctantly upward into dazzling blue-green eyes. She studied the square jaw and the determined set to his mouth and gulped. Perhaps a dog wouldn't be so bad, after all. He could stay in the bedroom and bark occasionally. That ought to keep everyone happy.

What in God's name am I thinking of? she snapped back mentally. I will not have a dog in this show!

Staring him straight in the eye, she said coolly, "We were just discussing your memo, Mr. Compton."

"About the sheepdog."

"Yes. I'm not sure you've thought this through," she began cautiously, wincing as his eyes hardened and bored into her. Mincemeat. This was definitely a man who made mincemeat out of his adversaries. She rushed on, anyway. If she was going to commit professional suicide, she might as well go out fighting. "I mean these people live in a thirty-five-story condominium in the middle of Manhattan. What would they be doing with a sheepdog?"

"That's something else we need to talk about," he said.

Although he spoke softly, there was no mistaking the authoritative tone. A warning signal flared in Barrie's brain, and she prepared for the next wave of his absurd, ill-conceived game plan to destroy her show.

"I don't think a condominium is quite the right environment," he explained.

"Oh? And what would you suggest? A vine-covered cottage with a white picket fence?"

He grinned, and her own lips defied her by twitching upward in an involuntary response. "That might be a little extreme," he agreed. "I was thinking more along the lines of a town house."

Barrie considered the idea thoughtfully. She was not above making some small compromises. "Maybe it would work," she said slowly. "One of those nice brownstones on the East Side, perhaps."

"Umm..." He shook his head. "Not exactly."

"What, then?"

"I was thinking of one of those town house developments. You know, with a swimming pool, tennis courts, sailboats, that sort of thing."

Barrie's eyes widened incredulously. The man had obviously come up through the ranks from sales. He had the creative mentality of an accountant.

"In Manhattan?" That distressing screech was back in her voice, though it had been weakened considerably by her absolute dismay.

"Well, we probably would have to move the location of the show. Maybe Marina del Ray or Santa Monica."

At that, her mouth dropped open, and her glasses slipped to the tip of her pert turned-up nose. "You've got to be kidding!"

"What's wrong with that? It worked for *Three's Company.*"

To her thorough astonishment, the man seemed genuinely puzzled. In fact, he looked downright hurt that she hadn't liked his suggestion.

"That's what's wrong with it," she explained as patiently as she could, considering her desire to deliver a primal scream that would shake the studio. "It's been done. I don't want to copy another series. *Goodbye, Again* is going to be fresh, different, contemporary. It's going to give viewers something to think about."

She glared at him defiantly. "It is not going to be an endless parade of bikini-clad bodies jiggling to the Jacuzzi."

"You think that's a bit too sexist?" he wondered aloud with apparent innocence. While she held her breath and waited, he seemed to consider her strenuous objection carefully. "Maybe you're right. Of course, if we put a couple of guys in there…"

"Forget it!" Barrie's shout echoed as she slammed her fist down emphatically. To her utter chagrin it landed squarely on his thigh. The damn muscle felt like granite. It felt, in fact, wonderful. However, she warned herself dryly, this was no time to get caught up with the feel of the man's physique. She had an important point to make. Several of them, in fact. "No bikinis! No swimming pools! And no sheepdog!"

A deep, rumbling laugh suddenly erupted from Michael Compton's chest. Barrie's hand twitched nervously where it had come to rest on his leg, and she yanked it back, looking at him as though he'd suddenly gone mad. The cast tittered uncertainly.

"You're wonderful, Miss MacDonald. Absolutely priceless," he said when he'd regained his composure. "I like a producer with spunk. I want my people to stand up for what they believe in."

His people? Spunk? Barrie's indignant roar dwindled down to a low growl as she stared at him, first in blinking confusion, then with slowly dawning understanding. "You were teasing me, weren't you?" she accused.

"Me?" The attempt at innocence failed miserably. There was far too much of a twinkle in his eyes.

"Yes, you."

He nodded contritely, though his lips continued to twitch with amusement. "I'm afraid so. I couldn't resist."

"You don't want me to move the show to Los Angeles?"

He shook his head.

"You don't expect me to spend five minutes per episode in a Jacuzzi?"

"Nope."

"You're not really asking for a sheepdog?"

"Well…"

"Mr. Compton," she thundered.

He smiled at her. Slowly. Winningly. It was a smile that belonged on the cover of an album of romantic ballads. "Okay, you win. No sheepdog…if you have dinner with me."

Despite the flutter in the pit of her stomach, Barrie refused to be won over. "Business conferences usually take place over lunch."

"I'm booked for lunch for the next month."

"I'll wait."

"I won't. If this show is going to go on the air in September—three weeks from now, in fact—we need to discuss it."

Barrie regarded him closely, one eyebrow lifting quizzically. "Mr. Compton," she began sweetly. "Are you blackmailing me into having dinner with you?"

"Miss MacDonald, do I look like I need to blackmail women into going out with me?" he inquired with entirely too much amusement.

Barrie surveyed him critically from head to toe and decided reluctantly that the amusement didn't stem from conceit. If anything, the man was probably being modest. Her gaze traveled slowly from the neatly trimmed thick brown hair and twinkling blue-green eyes over broad shoulders and narrow hips that not even a depressingly businesslike navy blue suit could disguise. The Kirk Douglas dimple in his chin and the square jaw only added to his aura of sex appeal. To top it off, he apparently had charm, and he definitely had power, both potent aphrodisiacs.

No, she decided with an unconscious sigh, this man would not need to resort to blackmail. Women probably lined up hoping for a chance to have him as an escort. Her glance swept over the cast of *Goodbye, Again*. Although they all seemed to be nervously awaiting her decision, disgustingly the women also appeared to be panting. Any one of them would probably kill to trade places with her.

"Well?" he taunted. "Are you going to take me up on this opportunity to discuss your future at the network?"

"Don't rush me. I'm thinking," she retorted, deliberately ignoring the ominous overtone of his question.

"If it takes you this long to reach a decision, Miss MacDonald, perhaps you've chosen the wrong career. Producers need to think on their feet."

"Perhaps I could become a network vice president," she suggested darkly. "They don't seem to think at all."

To her absolute amazement—and probable salvation—he laughed again. Her eyes widened as the hearty, unrestrained sound bounced off the studio walls. "Watch it, Miss MacDonald," he warned with a wink as he headed toward the door with Kevin trailing along behind him like an obedient puppy. "Casting has a huge sheepdog that would be just perfect for this show."

Barrie winced and took a deep breath. "Pick me up here at seven," she called after him.

With her glasses clenched tightly in her hand, Barrie couldn't quite see to the back of the studio, but Michael appeared to nod in satisfaction. "Six-thirty. My office," he called back as the door slammed shut behind him.

"Smart..." she muttered under her breath.

She hated men who had to have the last word. She especially hated men who had irresistible thighs.

Chapter 2

The studio was silent for exactly thirty seconds following Michael Compton's departure. Then all hell broke loose. Though Barrie would have liked to believe they were above it, the women immediately—and probably predictably— began debating the man's availability amid a chorus of heavy sighs. At the same time, the men's grumbling remarks about interference in the creative process by self-important pompous jerks contained more than a hint of jealousy. The writer of the opening episode muttered something about cretins under his breath, while he crushed empty Styrofoam coffee cups one by one. And Danielle Lawrence, Barrie's best friend and the director whom she'd chosen for the series' premiere, was ignoring all of it and smirking at her.

"What's your problem?" Barrie snapped.

"Nice looking, isn't he?"

"Who?" It seemed to be a good time to be deliberately obtuse.

"Who? Attila the programmer, of course."

"I didn't notice."

Danielle regarded her skeptically. "The woman who has taken a personal oath not to marry until she finds the perfect set of male thighs did not notice a man whose legs could have been carved by Michelangelo? I find that difficult to believe."

Barrie's eyes flashed dangerously. "There are other directors in Hollywood."

"But I'm good," Danielle retorted cheerfully. "I am also available, reasonably inexpensive, and I know all of your character flaws and love you, anyway. You can't top that."

Barrie sighed. "You're probably right, but could we drop the subject of Michael Compton for now? We have to go over this opening scene again. The pacing is all wrong."

An explosion of sound erupted just behind Barrie's shoulder. "What do you mean the pacing is all wrong?" Heath Donaldson hissed. "I've been writing comedy since before you were born. If you'd hired actors who knew how to deliver a line, the pacing would be just fine."

Barrie rolled her eyes at Danielle and turned around slowly. She put her arm around the short balding man who'd been huffing and puffing angrily in her ear. "Sweetheart," she began soothingly. "Your script is just fine. We all know you're one of the best in the business."

She lowered her voice to a whisper. "And you're right about some of the cast being inexperienced. But, love, you know they're just perfect for the parts. I think if you work with them and make just a few tiny adjustments to help them out, the opening scene will click right along."

Heath blinked back at her, and the fiery red that had

crept up his neck was fading away. He now looked a little less like a coronary waiting to happen. Barrie breathed a sigh of relief as he muttered more calmly, "Well, I suppose I could change a few lines just a little, tighten it up."

"That's it," Barrie said with exaggerated enthusiasm. "I knew you could do it. Why don't you and Danielle go over the first couple of pages of the script and see what you can come up with?"

For the next few hours Barrie felt like a firefighter who'd been asked to put out an entire county of brush fires with a pail of water. There was one crisis after another, none of them serious, but all of them requiring diplomacy, patience and a serenity she was far from feeling. The only possible advantage to a day like today, she decided, rubbing her throbbing temples, was that it had left her absolutely no time to work herself into a state over her impending dinner with Michael Compton.

At six-fifteen she sent the cast and crew home, touched up her makeup, took another stress-reducing deep breath that didn't do a bit of good and walked across the studio lot to the nearby network facilities. At precisely six-thirty she presented herself to Michael Compton's secretary, a cheerful woman with gray hair, rosy cheeks and sparkling, periwinkle blue eyes.

Mrs. Emma Lou Hastings looked as though she'd be perfectly at home in the kitchen making applesauce with an army of grandchildren underfoot. She also seemed like the type you could come to for motherly advice, Barrie decided, suddenly struck by the oddest desire to sit down and tell this perfect stranger that she was a nervous wreck because she was having dinner with a man who held the key to her future, a man who also had incredible thighs. She wondered what Mrs. Hastings would have to say about that.

Since Barrie kept her mouth clamped firmly shut, Mrs. Hastings only said, "You can go in now, Miss MacDonald. Mr. Compton is expecting you."

Barrie had started toward the door when the secretary added softly, "Don't worry, dear. He's really a very nice young man."

Very nice young man, indeed! Mrs. Hastings obviously didn't know that Michael Compton had virtually threatened to cancel Barrie's series unless she agreed to this dinner. What would she say about her nice young man if she found out about that? Barrie looked into her round, honest-looking face with the tiny laugh lines around the eyes and the encouraging smile and didn't have the heart to tell her. After all, she defended herself, could you tell a mother that her son is rotten to the core? Of course not. No more than she could tell Mrs. Hastings that her obviously well-liked boss was a thoroughly obnoxious louse who indulged in emotional blackmail.

Instead she smiled back. "Thanks," she said as she turned the brass doorknob and walked into Michael Compton's office. Grateful for any reprieve, she was delighted to see that he was on the phone. He looked up and grinned at her with that sinfully sensual smile of his and motioned for her to sit down. She selected the chair farthest from his desk and sank down, tucking her legs back in a futile attempt to cover the run that displayed a pale white trail of skin from her ankle up, disappearing at last under the hem of her beige linen skirt. Why hadn't she remembered the run earlier? She couldn't very well go tearing out of here now to buy new hose. Blast Michael Compton, she thought irrationally. Somehow this was all his fault.

She glanced over to discover that the object of her irritation was paying absolutely no attention to her. His head was bent to one side in order to keep the phone braced against his shoulder. If he did that long enough, he was going to have one heck of a neck ache, Barrie noted. She was torn between a perverse delight at the prospect and an even stranger desire to massage the soon-to-be-knotted muscles. She blinked and looked away, but, as though she'd been hypnotized, her eyes were drawn back time and again.

As Michael listened to his long-winded and apparently irate caller, he tapped a pencil idly on his huge rosewood desk. With his other hand he shuffled through a stack of papers, sorting them into two compulsively neat piles. Periodically he jabbed at another of the lit buttons on the phone, rumbled directives first into the receiver and then into the intercom on his desk. Two assistants scurried in and out, handing him papers to sign, waiting as he jotted notes on them, then rushing back out. A clerk from the mailroom came in with a half-dozen DVDs, piled them up next to his player and the bank of television monitors and left. Mrs. Hastings hurried in with several bulging file folders, dropped them into his In basket and picked up one of the stacks he'd just created. On her way out, she smiled sympathetically at Barrie, who'd begun to feel as though she'd fallen into the rabbit hole and wound up in the middle of *Alice in Wonderland*. Never in her life had she seen such perfectly orchestrated chaos. Never in her life had she felt so blatantly ignored.

"It won't be long, dear," Mrs. Hastings promised. "It's always this way at the end of the day."

Barrie glanced at her slim gold watch. It was seven-fifteen. She had suggested that Michael meet her at the studio at seven, but he'd refused and insisted instead that she meet him at his office at six-thirty. He was now forty-five minutes late, and Mrs. Hastings's reassurances to the contrary, he was showing no sign of quitting for the day.

Barrie waited and fumed. Eager to find any excuse for escape, she prepared herself mentally to rise as regally as she could with that blasted run in her hose and walk out of his office in a dignified protest of his imperious rudeness. Just as she started to stand, the phone clicked into place on his desk. He dropped the pencil, stopped shuffling papers, switched off the intercom and leaned back in his chair.

His pale blue tailored-to-fit shirt with his initials embroidered on the cuff emphasized his broad chest, his tapering waistline. His tie was loosened, his collar open at the neck to reveal a provocative amount of tanned skin and a shadowing of dark, tightly curled hairs. Eyes that now seemed more blue than green stared knowingly back at her. Barrie gulped and studied the pictures on the wall. They were modern splashes of bright, formless color. They were awful.

"So...Miss MacDonald," he said softly, seductively. "What do you think of my—" there was a suggestive hesitation that brought a guilty blush to Barrie's cheeks "—office?"

"I think the network overpaid the decorator," she responded tartly.

He grinned at her. "That's a rather dangerously blunt comment, don't you think? How do you know I didn't do it myself?"

"I've been in this office before. The pictures preceded you."

"Very observant," he noted approvingly, then added with a weary sigh, "I wish more people in this business would develop their powers of observation. It might improve the quality of the stuff that gets brought in here."

Barrie's brown eyes sparkled with excitement as she recognized a perfect opportunity. Heath Donaldson couldn't have scripted a better opening line for her. "That's what I want to do with *Goodbye, Again*," she said enthusiastically. "I want to create characters and situations that people will recognize. Relationships today aren't what they were when *I Love Lucy* went on the air. They're freer, more open. Women are less dependent on the men in their lives, married or not. They stay married out of choice, not necessity. How many families today are like the Andersons on *Father Knows Best*? We might wish they were, but, as the saying goes, wishing won't make it so. Today's world is more like Modern Family."

"So you want to force-feed reality, when what the audience wants is fantasy?" he challenged.

"No," she responded heatedly, so caught up in explaining her show so that he would understand that she once again missed the teasing glint in his eyes. "You're twisting my words around. You make reality sound like a dirty word."

As Michael rose and walked slowly around to where she was sitting, her breath suddenly caught in her throat, her argument sputtered to a halt, and she was immediately struck by the strangest sense of heightened anticipation. It was like waiting for a roller coaster to inch over the crest of its highest peak and fly down the other side. One knew something incredible was about to happen but had no idea quite how to prepare for it. Michael's impressive body towered over hers, sending out little electrical currents that seemed to head straight for her abdomen, flooding it with a pleasant warmth and a tormenting ache. Barrie's eyes were drawn to his, locked in a fiery awareness, challenging him to defend his statement.

"Actually, I like reality, Miss MacDonald," he protested softly, the velvet-smooth tone affecting her like warm brandy. It felt soothing and intoxicating. "In fact, I'm liking it more by the minute."

His charming, roguish grin brought a responding tilt to her lips. The man could obviously sweet-talk his way past Saint Peter at the gates of heaven. What possible chance did she stand, Barrie wondered a trifle desperately. She'd come here to have a serious discussion to assure the integrity of *Goodbye, Again*, and here she was melting like some damned stick of butter left out in the sun. Spineless. She was absolutely spineless.

"Mr. Compton, I thought you wanted to have dinner and talk about *Goodbye, Again*."

"I do."

"Well?"

"Dinner's on the way."

Barrie gulped. "Here?"

"Why not? It's more private than a restaurant, and despite the lousy artwork, the atmosphere isn't bad."

It is also entirely too intimate, Barrie wanted to shout.

So what? a voice shouted back. Intimacy is only threatening if you allow it to be. After all, the man has done absolutely nothing to indicate that he wants to seduce you. That was an idea that popped into your mind sometime between his thorough, unblinking survey and the soft, sensual smile that made your heart flip over.

Okay. So I'll force that idea right back out of my mind.

Right. The worst thing that could happen would be that he'd make a pass at you, and you'd file a sexual harassment suit.

No, she correctly, the worst thing that could happen would be that he would make a pass, and she would respond. She steeled herself against that embarrassingly distinct possibility.

"Dinner here is just fine," she said airily, taking off her glasses. Maybe if she couldn't see the man, his potency would be less dangerous. Of course, she also might miss the first signs of any planned seduction. She put the glasses back on, just in time to see a waiter wheel in a cart laden with covered silver dishes.

In less time than it would normally take her to scan the contents of her virtually empty freezer, the waiter draped a small table with a spotless white damask cloth, added an Oriental-style arrangement of tiny orchids, lit several tapered candles and set two places with heavy silverware and English bone china that Barrie recognized as one of the most expensive patterns on the market.

"I take it you didn't order from the commissary," she commented dryly.

He smiled back at her. "Wait until you see the food before making judgments, Miss MacDonald," he warned. "Isn't Hollywood known for creating atmosphere without worrying about substance? You could be in for a dinner of ham on rye."

"You don't strike me as the ham-on-rye type. Maybe bologna."

"Careful. That tart tongue of yours is going to get you in trouble yet."

"It usually gets me back out of it, as well."

"Perhaps it has...in the past," he taunted. "But you haven't come up against a man like me before, Miss Mac-Donald."

"How do you know that?"

"I'm one of a kind," he informed her with a wink as he sipped the wine and nodded approvingly to the waiter. "This is perfect, Henri."

"Bon appetit, monsieur."

"*Merci.*"

The waiter bowed graciously to Barrie and pushed the cart out of the office, leaving them alone.

"Well, Miss MacDonald," Michael said softly as he held out a chair for her. "Your dinner awaits."

Barrie sat down to a meal that was expertly planned, perfectly prepared and, despite Michael's warnings, quite obviously not commissary fare. It began with pâté and ended with fresh strawberries and thick, sweet Devon cream, each course a sensual delight.

Their conversation throughout was surprisingly light and witty. In fact, on several occasions Barrie had the feeling she was caught up in the middle of a briskly paced Noel Coward script. Never had she met anyone who could match wits with her so easily, who could make her feel so much like a woman while at the same time treating her as an equal. It was exactly the sort of relationship she hoped to create on *Goodbye, Again,* straightforward, intelligent, lively and provocative. Ah, yes, she thought with an unconscious sigh. Most definitely provocative.

As the meal ended at last, she was savoring one of the strawberries, slowly licking the cream from its sweet tip before taking the bright red berry into her mouth, when she noticed that Michael seemed fascinated with her lips. His eyes sparkled as he licked his own lips in unconscious imitation of her actions. Stunned by the obvious sensuality of his response and heady from the fine wine and the unexpected knowledge that she could stir him as he did her, Barrie almost involuntarily prolonged the moment, biting into the juicy strawberry with slow deliberation. A husky moan rumbled deep in Michael's throat, and at last he blinked and looked away.

My God, what am I doing? The thought ripped into Barrie's mind, and she practically swallowed the strawberry whole. She had been taunting Michael Compton, practically daring him to respond to her as a woman. He did not strike her as the type to back away from a challenge, and she had just presented him with a practically irresistible one. I must be out of my mind.

"About *Goodbye, Again*," she prompted in a voice that had a distressing quiver in it. Damn! All those acting classes, and she still couldn't hide her nervousness.

"Why don't we sit over here and talk about it?" he suggested agreeably, leading her to a sofa and then sitting down entirely too near to her.

She studied him closely and promptly projected her wayward thoughts onto him. "Is this the part where you tell me you'll cooperate with me, if I *cooperate* with you?" she asked, actually managing a lightly teasing tone, despite the fact that her blood was roaring in her ears like an erupting volcano. In anger? Or anticipation? She wasn't at all sure and, disgustingly, he only seemed to find her implication amusing.

"No. This is the part where I tell you what's going to happen to your series."

"And?"

"And you tell me you're a professional, and you can handle the changes I'm demanding."

Changes? Demanding? She had the distinct impression he had deliberately chosen those words just to unnerve her. Well, she was not too proud to admit—to herself—that he'd succeeded. For his benefit, she plastered an interested, calm expression on her face and asked quietly, "What did you have in mind?"

"For one thing, I've been taking a look at the fall schedule, and I don't think it's as competitive as it could be. In order to make it more effective, I'm going to move your show."

Barrie eyed him cautiously. "Yes?"

"I think it'll be perfect for the eight o'clock slot on Saturday."

All attempts at studied tranquility flew out the window. Barrie's protest began as a small grumble, but by the time it exploded from her mouth it was a full-blown roar of incredulous frustration. "Michael...I mean, Mr. Compton, no! You can't do this!"

"Oh, yes, I can," he said evenly.

Of course he could. She took a very deep breath and decided to appeal to his sense of logic. "I'm not sure you realize what a risk you're taking. You could kill the show. This program is targeted for young adults. Young adults do not watch television at eight on a Saturday night. Kids watch television at eight on Saturday."

"That's right. But I'm betting that the right show can keep some of those young adults hanging around home a little later. If it's good enough," he said slowly, throwing down the gauntlet, "they'll watch it while they get ready to go out." He paused to let that sink in, then added pointedly, "They watched Mary Tyler Moore on Saturday nights."

Mary Tyler Moore, indeed! That was TV history, not today's fast-paced world. Besides, they didn't even bring *her* back on Saturday night. Barrie's eyes were flashing, their usual soft brown shade glinting with sparks like flaming firewood. "Are you challenging me?"

He chuckled at her reaction. "You bet I am. Think you're up to it?" he asked softly, his eyes meeting hers with a question that had nothing to do with challenges and everything to do with romance and the very real male-female pull that had been playing tug-of-war with them since the moment they met.

A perfectly manicured, very masculine finger reached out to the tear in her hose and slowly traced the path it had taken from ankle to knee.

Barrie gasped softly. "Now we get to the part where you ask for my cooperation," she murmured shakily, fighting the heat that had swept through her at his touch.

He shook his head. "Not everything in this business comes down to sex."

She glanced down at his hand, which was still resting lightly, provocatively on her leg. "I wonder where I got the idea that it did?"

He chuckled and removed his hand. "Oh, I want you, Barrie MacDonald. I'm not about to deny it. I've wanted you since the first moment I saw you in that studio this afternoon. We're two of a kind, and I think we'd be very good together."

He paused to let his words sink in. Barrie gulped, wet her lips and waited breathlessly for what was to come. She couldn't have managed two sensible words had her life depended on it.

"But I won't ever ask anything of you that you're not prepared to offer," he promised in a voice that tantalized her with its rough huskiness. "And it will never have anything to do with *Goodbye, Again.*"

He paused again, and his blue-green eyes locked with hers. Finally, after several long seconds in which Barrie could feel each contraction of her pounding heart, he asked softly, "Do you believe me?"

Oddly, despite her thundering heartbeat and the wildfire that blazed through her, heating her blood to a glorious warmth, she did believe him. She believed she could trust him. She certainly believed he wanted her. And she also knew with absolute certainty that she'd better get out of there before she made him that offer he'd just sworn to wait for.

"I think I'd better be going," she announced firmly.

"Stay."

She shook her head. "I can't."

"Can't? Or won't?"

"Does it matter? I'm leaving."

"Okay, producer lady," he said quietly, surprising Barrie with his complete lack of anger, his ready capitulation. "If that's what you have to do. But I'll be in touch."

"I'm sure," Barrie said. "You'll probably decide you want that sheepdog in the show, after all."

"Now that you mention it..."

"Forget it, buster," she said emphatically, unable to prevent the small grin that tugged at her mouth and softened the effect of her vehemence. "Heath Donaldson is going to flip out when he hears about the time change. If I have to tell him to incorporate a sheepdog, as well, he'll quit faster than you can say demographics."

"In that case, I'll hold off on the sheepdog...for a few days," he said, his eyes taking on the sort of caressing, speculative masculine gleam that usually precedes a kiss.

"Good night, Mr. Compton," Barrie said firmly, ducking past his descending head.

"Good night, Barrie MacDonald." The words were softly spoken and tinged with tolerant amusement.

As she walked to the elevator, Barrie wondered idly what it would be like to hear those perfectly innocuous, ordinary words murmured in her ear as she fell asleep each night. Probably wonderful. She pressed the Down button and leaned weakly against the wall while she waited.

MacDonald, you are crazy. Certifiably insane! You are going to get yourself in over your head on this one yet. She shook her head. Going to? Lady, the water's already up to your eyebrows!

Chapter 3

The door to Barrie's tiny nondescript office crashed open at barely 8:00 a.m., and Danielle breezed in with a paper bag in one hand and her script in the other. She tossed the script into a chair, took two cups of coffee and two gooey sweetrolls from the bag and arranged them neatly on the desk, then sat down on the sofa with her jeans-clad legs crossed under her and stared at Barrie expectantly.

"Well?"

"Don't you ever knock?"

"Rarely," she retorted easily, obviously not the least bit put off by Barrie's grumpiness. "Why are you in such a snit? Didn't your dinner with the scrumptious Michael Compton go well?"

"Dinner was just fine," Barrie admitted honestly. "The problem came after dinner."

Danielle's gray eyes immediately narrowed. "Ohhh..." she began softly. Then her voice heated up angrily. "Why, the absolute gall of that man! Did he come on to you? File charges. That's what you should do. File charges. You can't let him get away with that."

"Whoa! You sound like an ambulance chaser. Do you have an attorney someplace who needs a case?" Barrie responded, chuckling at her friend's immediate rush to her defense. She reassured her, "It was nothing like that."

"He didn't come on to you?" Danielle's tone teetered between disappointment and skepticism.

Barrie's expression softened as she recalled in precise and blood-stirring detail Michael's almost casual advances, his seductive promises. "I wouldn't say that exactly," she admitted. "But it wasn't like what you meant."

"You mean you liked it."

"No, I didn't like it," Barrie said defensively. "I mean, it was okay. Oh, I don't know what I mean."

"He got to you, didn't he?" Danielle said triumphantly. "I knew it. I knew you wouldn't be able to resist those thighs."

"Damn it, Dani, it is not what you think!" There was an almost plaintive note in her protest. Michael Compton was the network vice president for programming, her boss, and that was all. It had to be. She was not going to let Danielle or her own skittering pulse rate tell her otherwise.

"Then what was the problem?"

"He's moving the show to eight o'clock on Saturday," she said in a rush of words, grateful to change the subject to one she knew would completely distract Danielle from her pursuit of the intimate details of her dinner with Michael.

Her announcement had the desired effect. Danielle was clearly shocked. "You can't be serious!"

"Oh, but I am. He thinks a really fantastic contemporary show can pull in a young adult audience. He virtually challenged me to prove *Goodbye, Again* is good enough to do it."

"And, of course, you fell right into his trap?"

"Trap? You mean did I agree to go along with him to get the series on the air? You bet I did," Barrie retorted heatedly. "I fought too long for this chance. I wasn't about to throw it away, just because the network pulled a stupid stunt like this. We can make the show work for eight o'clock."

"How?" Danielle sounded disgustingly pessimistic.

"By forgetting about the time slot and just doing a good television series. If it's funny at nine-thirty, it'll be just as funny at eight."

"Maybe on Wednesday, sweetie. Not on Saturday. On Saturday it had better be hysterical."

Barrie sighed. "So get Heath in here and start making it hysterical."

"That's your job. I'm only the director." Barrie glared at her, but before she could respond, the phone rang. When Barrie answered, she was greeted by the low, deep murmur of Michael's voice.

"Good morning, Barrie MacDonald." He sounded just as seductive this morning as he had on parting last night. Barrie's heart thundered loudly in her ears as she realized how easy it would be to become addicted to starting and ending her days like this.

"Good morning," she said calmly, unaware that her knuckles were turning white from clutching the receiver so tightly.

"Michael?" Danielle mouthed the name silently. At Barrie's nod, she grinned smugly, rose and tiptoed to the door. "I'll leave you alone," she whispered significantly as she waved cheerfully. Barrie had the oddest desire to strangle her.

"Barrie, are you there?"

"What?" she snapped, then softened her tone. "Yes, I'm here."

"Is everything okay?" He sounded genuinely concerned and somewhat puzzled.

"Everything's just fine, Mr. Compton. Why shouldn't it be?"

"You sound funny. And you're still calling me Mr. Compton. Are you upset about something?"

Barrie took a deep breath. "I am not upset...Michael," she protested tightly. "What do you want?"

"I want to see you."

"About what?" she asked cautiously.

He chuckled softly. "The usual," he taunted. "Do you always cross-examine a man who's asking you for a date?"

"I didn't realize that's what you had in mind," she said defensively. "We do have a business relationship, too, you know."

"Yes, I'm aware of that. It does tend to cloud the issue, doesn't it? Would you prefer it if I limited my professional calls to the workday and made my personal calls after hours?" he offered cheerfully.

Barrie promptly felt foolish and lightened her tone. "That assumes that both of us work predictable, normal hours. When was the last time you came in at nine and left at five?"

He paused for several seconds. "When I had the flu four years ago," he recalled at last. "I see your point. Where does that leave us?"

"I guess you'd better just state your business more clearly. For instance, you might suggest that we get together one evening for dinner and dancing. That is clearly a date," she explained.

"What if I ask you to go to a screening? Is that business or pleasure?"

"If you play your cards right, it could be both." Barrie heard the teasing comment as it came out of her mouth, and she cringed. She was asking for trouble, begging for it, in fact.

"Oh, really?" he said in a voice that suddenly lowered to a husky growl. "That sounds promising."

"Have any screenings lined up?" she taunted.

"Not for weeks."

"Too bad."

"How about dinner, then? I'll even cook."

"You're going to cook?" she retorted skeptically. "Is that the modern day equivalent of an invitation to view etchings?"

"Not in my case," he objected. "I take my skills as a chef seriously. I even have a food processor and a convection oven. So, how about it?"

"When?"

"Tonight."

Barrie gulped nervously. This was exactly the sort of contemporary fast-paced plunge-right-in courting she'd always believed in and had built into the concept for her series. No games, no promises, no commitment. Just dinner with a highly charged hint that passion was on the menu. So why did she want to shout that tonight was entirely too soon? Why did she have this persistent, nagging fear that men like this, men who swept you off your feet with a rush of attention, often dropped you in the dust just as quickly. It shouldn't matter one whit to her if Michael Compton walked into her life today and out tomorrow. In today's world you were supposed to shrug, say thanks for the memories and goodbye.

Barrie shivered. She'd gotten to be very good at good-byes. Her father had taken off more frequently than the flights from Los Angeles International Airport. Each time Barrie had watched her mother's reserves of strength crumble a little more. She had sworn she would never be in that position and that no man would ever matter that much. She had built up defenses that would have made the combined forces of the army, navy and marines proud.

With all that practice at self-protection, she could have dinner again with Michael Compton, she decided resolutely. Tonight or next week. It wouldn't make any difference. She was perfectly capable of keeping her emotions in check.

"Tonight's just fine," she said firmly, then wondered at the little thrill of anticipation that rippled along her spine. It was not the response of a woman who was indifferent. It was another clear-as-a-bell warning signal, and she was paying absolutely no attention to it. She had to be crazy.

In a tone that was suddenly brisk and businesslike, indicating that he was probably no longer alone, Michael gave her his phone number and his address in Beverly Hills. "I'll see you about eight, then. Call if you get lost."

Barrie had barely hung up the phone when there was a knock on her door. "Yes?" A messenger entered.

"Miss MacDonald?" Barrie nodded. "I have a package for you."

When the messenger had deposited the huge, beautifully wrapped box on her desk and left, she took the card out of the envelope.

"Enjoy these and think of me, just as I'll be remembering last night. Michael."

She opened the box and found two pounds of huge ripe strawberries, which had been dipped in a rich dark chocolate. Her mouth immediately watered, and her pulse rate fluttered as she recalled Michael's obvious arousal as he watched her eat those strawberries at dinner. She took one from the box now and bit slowly into it, savoring the sweet taste of the berry and the bittersweet taste of the chocolate. She closed her eyes. It was absolutely heavenly. It was also a provocative indication that Michael was interested in more than her skills as a producer and was determined to tantalize her with reminders of his more personal intentions. He might be a hard-nosed broadcasting executive, but he obviously had the sweetly seductive soul of a romantic.

Before she could linger too long on the dangers of that combination, Danielle and Heath burst into the office in the midst of an already heated argument. Melinda Ashcroft, who'd been cast in the series' lead role, was right behind them, her hands on her hips, her mouth pursed in her distinctive, sexy pout.

"Barrie, I cannot ask Melinda to play this scene the way it's written," Danielle protested, throwing the open script down on Barrie's desk.

"It just doesn't feel right," Melinda agreed in the low, husky voice that could probably lure men to jump off cliffs. "Karen would not do something like that."

"What do you know about Karen?" Heath snarled. "I wrote this part, and I say she would do exactly that; she would storm into Mason's office and confront him."

"In the middle of a business conference?" Danielle said skeptically. "Come on, Heath. Karen is supposed to be a rational, understanding woman. She is not going to jeopardize a big deal for Mason by screeching at him like a banshee in front of total strangers."

Barrie listened carefully to the raging argument, glanced at the script and then finally decided she'd better intercede before Heath's blood pressure went through the roof again.

Already the color in his neck was working its way from bright red to purple.

"Quiet!" she shouted to make herself heard over the uproar. Danielle, Heath and Melinda promptly fell silent and stared at her, obviously stunned by her emphatic, no-nonsense outburst. "That's better. Now would everyone please sit down, and let's discuss this like civilized adults."

The discussion lasted most of the morning, and much of it was far from civilized. Despite Barrie's best efforts to mediate, it seemed that her director, writer and the series' star were far too angry with one another to compromise. Finally she'd had about all of the bickering she intended to take.

"Okay, that's it," she announced decisively. "The scene stays. Karen wouldn't just sit back and suffer in silence."

Heath smirked triumphantly.

"However, Heath," she began, watching his smile fade. "I want you to tone it down slightly. Melinda and Dani are right. She might go barging into that office, but she would never blow up like that once she realized she was interrupting a business meeting. Maybe she'd pretend she came in for some other reason, or maybe she'd mutter something under her breath and leave. I don't know. You're the writer. Work on it. I want to see the new dialogue after lunch."

It was midafternoon before the rehearsal was back on track, and Barrie was determined to get one decent run-through before she let any of the cast off for the evening.

"Hon, I think we're wasting our time," Danielle told her at last. "Everybody's worn out. Why don't we call it quits and get on it again first thing in the morning?"

Barrie sighed and inquired wearily, "What time is it?"

"It's eight-fifteen."

"What? It can't be." She buried her head in her arms. "How could I do this?"

"Do what? What's wrong?"

"I was supposed to meet Michael for dinner fifteen minutes ago."

"And you forgot?" Danielle's voice was incredulous. "You had a date with the boss, and you've been sitting here worrying about props?"

"I haven't been worrying about props. I've been trying to keep you, Heath and Melinda from killing one another."

"Honey, don't you know that this was just a healthy disagreement among three rational adults?"

"Rational? Adults? You've got to be kidding. The three of you have been behaving like juvenile delinquents."

"That's just creative energy being unleashed," Danielle said airily.

"Well, why don't you use some of that creative energy to dream up an excuse I can give to Michael for being late?"

"How about the truth?"

"You want me to tell the vice president for programming of this network, who ultimately pays our salaries and decides whether we will be on the air longer than six weeks, you want me to tell him that I forgot about our date? Are you crazy?"

"I'm not the one who forgot the date with one of the most eligible bachelors in Los Angeles," Danielle reminded her smugly. "You did. You tell me who's crazy."

"I don't have time to stand here debating this with you. I'd better get myself over there before he burns whatever he's cooking. I have a feeling ruining his dinner would be an even bigger sin than forgetting it."

"You're going to his place? My, my!" The smug smirk was back.

"Don't say it, Dani, or I'll blame my delay on you. How do you suppose Michael would feel about that?"

"Okay. Okay. Get out of here," she replied with a laugh. "I'll send the cast home."

Barrie grabbed her purse and briefcase and headed for the door.

"See you in the morning," Danielle called out cheerfully, then added wickedly, "I can hardly wait to hear if those thighs are everything they seem to be."

"I do not intend to check out the man's legs," Barrie retorted indignantly.

"Right," she replied dryly. "You're only going over there to sample his favorite recipes."

"Exactly."

"Honey, the evening may start out with beef Stroganoff and asparagus vinaigrette, but I'll lay you odds that you're on the menu for dessert," she said with a wink.

"No way," Barrie insisted stoutly as she slipped out the door. But deep inside, where her stomach fluttered nervously and her blood sizzled, she wondered if she would have the strength to resist if Michael was really determined to have her.

Chapter 4

The drive from the studio into Beverly Hills, difficult under the best of conditions, had never seemed so long or the traffic so heavy. By the time Barrie was finally winding her way through the posh, unfamiliar neighborhood with its sculptured lawns and deceptively modest houses, it was already well after nine, pitch-dark, and virtually impossible for her to see the street signs clearly enough through those damned rose-tinted glasses to figure out where she was.

Terrific, she thought, as she peered vaguely through the windshield, then squinted at the address she'd scribbled down. Now she was completely lost in a tight-knit enclave not known for welcoming strangers. She was also just far enough from the nearest gas station to make the idea of backtracking to ask for directions thoroughly unappealing. Assuming that she could even figure out how to backtrack. She sighed and tried to resign herself to the possibility of spending the rest of her life roaming the streets of Beverly

Hills. Of course, she'd probably run out of gas or get picked up by the police long before that actually happened. And calling Michael and admitting she was thoroughly lost was not an option.

"Damn," she muttered in frustration as she pulled to the side of the palm-lined street and fumbled in the glove compartment for her map of L.A. Trying to hold the book so that she could read by the muted reflection of the streetlight, she finally found Michael's address. She glared at the map.

Of course his street was only one block long! She should have known he'd live somewhere so exclusive that it was barely on the map. However, it was only about a mile away and, barring any unexpected deadends—or restrictive gates—should be easy enough to reach if she just stayed straight about five blocks and turned left, then right, she decided at last.

As she crept along, squinting to read the street signs to locate the first turn, she murmured a silent prayer to the patron saint of lost souls to get her out of this fix, and quickly. Michael was going to be furious and, at this point, she wasn't any too thrilled about the situation herself. She hated being late almost as much as she abhorred being lost. The former made her feel guilty about her rudeness. The latter made her feel vulnerable, panicky in fact. And the combination was enough to send her fleeing home to burrow under the covers.

To top it off, she knew that this dinner had all sorts of hidden implications and dangers. Dangers best postponed for perhaps five or six years.

"I wonder if he'd believe that I developed a raging migraine that temporarily blocked out my memory and that I forgot all about dinner?" she asked herself aloud.

Not a chance, her conscience replied emphatically. He'd know you were being a coward.

It was probably fortunate, then, that before she could tell her conscience to go to blazes and then retreat to the security of her own bed, she found the street. After that it was an easy enough matter to find the address. There were only three houses on the whole blasted block.

It was nearly nine-thirty by the time she reluctantly walked up the palm-lined driveway and rang Michael's doorbell. When he opened the door, there was a worried frown on his face that altered into a tight, unwelcoming smile. Barrie shuddered. His mincemeat look was back.

"I've heard of being fashionably late, but don't you think this is overdoing it just a bit?" he asked.

The teasing question was light enough, but there was a hard edge to his voice that told Barrie he was really angry with her, far more angry than she'd anticipated he might be. Cautiously she put her hand on his arm.

"You really are upset with me, aren't you?" she said penitently. When he didn't respond, she rattled on nervously, "I don't blame you. I'm horribly late, but I was tied up at the studio working on the show longer than I expected. The traffic was awful. You know how that is this time of night. And then I got lost." She paused for breath and gazed at him hopefully. Nothing. Not even a blink of those blue-green eyes.

"Cell phone?"

"Dead."

She waited, then tried again. "Anyway, I'm sorry. Did I ruin dinner?"

He stood looking down at her for a moment, then shook his head and smiled. This time it was more genuine. At least he didn't look as though he planned to kick her back out onto the streets anymore. "Sorry. Of course not. I guess I was just afraid you'd changed your mind and decided to back out."

One eyebrow arched quizzically. That did not sound like the brash, self-confident Michael Compton whom Barrie had seen so far. In fact, there was an appealing vulnerability to the comment that intrigued her. "Are you serious?" she asked, still not quite convinced she had actually heard that insecure note in his voice.

"Well, you were more than an hour late," he retorted more lightly. He grinned at her then, and the vulnerability vanished, replaced by a more familiar cockiness. "Do you have any idea what it does to a man's ego to discover that an attractive woman is not nearly as anxious to see him as he is to see her?"

"I suspect your ego is doing just fine, Mr. Compton," Barrie replied sweetly. "On the other hand, I have been battling trucks on the freeway, lost on the streets of Beverly Hills and starving to death in my Sentra, while you nibbled on…" She looked at him impishly. "On what? Carrot sticks?"

"Mushroom caps stuffed with crabmeat."

Barrie sighed longingly as her mouth watered. She really was famished. She gazed boldly into his eyes and only barely resisted the urge to bat her long, dark lashes at him flirtatiously. "I don't suppose that if I apologized profusely for my tardiness I could talk you into sharing one or two of those with me?"

"That sounds like it might have some intriguing possibilities. Try it," he suggested, finally stepping aside to let her into the house. "I'm always open to an appeal from someone who's genuinely contrite."

"Don't press your luck, Mr. Compton," she flashed back.

"Don't you know it's dangerous to tamper with a starving woman? You promised me dinner, and all I've gotten so far is static."

Those blue-green eyes of his roved possessively over her. "There is a certain amount of electricity in the air whenever we get together, isn't there?" he murmured softly as Barrie flushed under the intensity of his gaze and tried not to notice how well his jeans hugged those muscular thighs of his.

"That wasn't what I meant," she countered, but there was a decided lack of conviction in her voice.

"Maybe not," he said, gazing at her doubtfully, a definite twinkle in his eyes. "But it's true. Maybe we should explore the idea a bit after dinner."

Barrie returned his gaze boldly at first but finally blinked and looked away. Dessert, she thought as a nervous excitement rippled along her spine. It was exactly as Danielle had suspected. He thought she was on the menu for dessert. She swallowed and faced him again. Maybe if she kept her mind on the appetizers, she wouldn't feel quite so panicky about dessert. "What about those mushroom caps?"

He grinned at her knowingly. "Coming right up. Why don't you go on into the living room, and I'll be right with you. What would like to drink?"

"A glass of wine."

"Red or white?"

"White. Are you sure I can't help with something?"

"Nope. I've got everything under control."

I'll just bet you have, Barrie thought. Men like Michael Compton always did. As she waited, she explored the living room with its comfortably overstuffed sofa and chairs in front of a blazing fire. The mantel and one wall were of a dark wood that gave the room a decidedly masculine feel. The darkness might have been oppressive, but the remaining walls had been papered with a light country French design, and French doors led out onto a brick patio that was softly lit by the moonlight. In the daytime those doors would let in plenty of sunlight, along with the sweet fragrance of the profusion of roses she could see blooming in every imaginable color from pale pink to bright red, from dazzling yellow to warm apricot. The bright turquoise of a free-form pool sparkled just beyond the edge of the terrace. It was simple and luxurious without being the least bit ostentatious, and Barrie had to admit that she was impressed by Michael's taste. His decor had a personal touch that she suspected was all his. She doubted that a decorator had been allowed near the place.

"Admiring the view?" his low, sensual voice whispered over her shoulder.

"It's lovely."

"I fell in love with it the minute I saw it. The previous owner had covered these incredible wood floors with some awful plush mauve carpet. He was also heavily into art deco with lots of pink and black. I practically had to close my eyes while I stripped the wallpaper."

"With your schedule, when did you find the time?"

"Late at night and on weekends. It took a while, but it was worth every minute. Besides, you have no idea how satisfying it is to rip up carpet and yank down wallpaper after a day of restraining every single urge to shred the imbeciles who parade through your office."

"If they're that bad, I'm surprised you bother to control yourself," she retorted.

"I am, too, sometimes," he admitted. "But I know one thing about this business. The person who's trying to sell you some perfectly impossible concept that makes you want to scream one day may develop a unique, innovative series later that could be number one. If you've been rude, he may take that idea to another network. I'm not about to take that chance."

"So you suffer in silence."

He shook his head. "I prefer to think that I'm diplomatic. I'd also like to believe I can create an environment that encourages their creativity, instead of stifling it. If there's a shred of talent there, I want to nurture it."

As he talked, he almost absentmindedly played with a strand of Barrie's hair, tucking it behind her ear, his fingers soft and gentle against the side of her face. Barrie trembled at the touch, her body so responsive to his nearness that she knew she wouldn't have a prayer of refusing him anything he asked of her unless she backed out of his reach now. She sighed but didn't move. She couldn't.

In *Goodbye, Again*, with so much potential passion creating a crackling tension between the characters, there would be no hesitation tonight, no regrets tomorrow. But this wasn't a script, and suddenly Barrie realized Michael Compton was leaping over her well-established defenses in a single bound. The realization that he might actually begin to matter to her was terrifying.

"Hey," he said softly. "What is it?"

Barrie blinked and gazed into Michael's eyes. Had he read her mind, sensed the troubling thoughts? "Nothing," she lied. "Why?"

"You had this far away expression on your face for a minute there, and you seemed so sad." He shook his head. "No. That wasn't it. More scared, maybe. Vulnerable."

Startled by his perceptiveness, she forced a shaky smile and a brave, teasing tone. "You're imagining things. Were you reading one of those melodramatic soap opera scripts before I got here?"

He studied her closely, as though trying to decide whether to pursue the subject. To Barrie's relief, he apparently decided to let it drop. "Nope," he responded lightly. "I was slaving over a hot stove. Are you ready for dinner?"

"Absolutely. I've never known a man whose culinary skills went beyond cooking steaks on a backyard grill."

He regarded her indignantly. "My dear, I'll have you know that the French Chef is my favorite TV heroine."

"She's a little tall for you, isn't she?"

"Ah, but those recipes! *C'est magnifique!*" He gravely touched his fingers to his lips and blew a little kiss into the air.

Barrie chuckled. "If she affects you that strongly, I'm surprised you haven't put those old episodes back on the air in prime time."

"Believe me, I've thought about it. Or better yet, can you imagine a whole situation comedy built around duck *à l'orange* and truffles?"

She appeared to consider the idea carefully. "Nope. Afraid not."

"Ah, Miss MacDonald, we must work on opening up your imagination."

He should only know, she thought dryly. Since meeting him just one short day ago, her imagination had been running wild, though admittedly the thoughts had very little to do with food or television. She'd had to fight to maintain her concentration during today's rehearsals for *Goodbye, Again*. Images of Michael had constantly popped into her mind. Images of the fire that blazed in his eyes when he looked at her. Even more disturbing images of the slim, athletic body, the rock-hard muscular thighs. In her mind, she had stripped him of his tailored jacket, his silk tie, his soft shirt and, finally, the slacks that hugged his hips and only barely camouflaged the strength of his legs. Her eyes had feasted on his masculinity, his potency, and she had trembled with a yearning so sharp that she'd thought for a moment the image was real.

And tonight it was. Or could be, if that was what she wanted. Michael was sitting across the table from her, and the shimmering candlelight paled in comparison to the bright flame of desire that burned in his eyes. Those unblinking eyes possessed her, cherished her, seduced her. Even as they dined on the delicious grilled salmon with dill sauce, his eyes told her his thoughts were elsewhere, in some special, intimate place where the two of them had become one.

Barrie's thoughts followed his, shared the intimacy, thrilled to the magic of his imagined touch. Unconsciously, she took a slow, provocative sip of wine, then ran her tongue over her dampened lips. Michael moaned and looked away, breaking the spell.

"Do you have any idea what you're doing to me, Barrie MacDonald?" he asked huskily.

If it was anything like what he was doing to her, she knew. But she also realized she had to deny it. To admit the truth would speed their relationship on a course from which there would be no retreat and that could only lead to disaster and pain.

"Barrie, I've told you before that I want us to be together," he said with straightforward honesty. "It was true last night. It's even more true tonight. You're an amazing woman. Intelligent, wise, funny, independent. The kind of woman I've always looked for but never found. And we're both mature adults. I understand your reservations, but we can handle this. We can keep our business and personal relationships separated."

It was a speech Heath Donaldson could have written, and it was spoken with absolute conviction, underlined with an undeniable urgency. If Barrie had read it in one of the scripts, heard it on the air, she would have believed it, would have thought desire and mutual respect were more than enough to justify a sexual relationship. The Karen Devereaux she had created for *Goodbye, Again*, had been patterned on her own liberated beliefs. So, she thought, why wasn't the sort of quick and easy intimacy Michael was suggesting enough for her tonight? Why was there this sudden empty feeling in the pit of her stomach?

The answer to that was easy and disturbing. She and Michael would be good together. Too good. A warm ache deep inside told her that with unerring, sizzling accuracy. But, for the first time in her life, she had a feeling it would not be nearly enough and that with Michael she would want much more, perhaps something that could never be.

Don't forget your promise, she reminded herself sharply. She had sworn all her life that she would never be as vulnerable as her mother had been. There would be no painful goodbyes for her, only breezy farewells. And to accomplish that, no one could ever get too close, especially not someone like Michael with whom intimacy would almost inevitably lead to emotional involvement.

To top it off, Michael held far too much potential power over her. Not only could he chop her heart into little pieces, he could control, even destroy, her professional future. The risks were tremendous.

Barrie shook her head. "Not a good idea," she said firmly, amazed at the strength in her voice, when she was so shaky and unsure inside. "In fact, I think I'd better be leaving."

"Running away?" he taunted.

"Of course not." She was merely retreating to get her line of defenses back into place. There was a difference, but she doubted if Michael would see it. She wasn't sure if she could explain it to him, either, so she didn't even try.

"Do you have work to do, then?"

"No."

"Then stay a little longer." His eyes pleaded with her. His words were softly, persuasively spoken. "Go for a walk with me."

She sensed his acceptance of her retreat and appreciated it, though she remained skeptical. "A walk?"

His eyes twinkled at her doubtful tone. "You remember walking. It's one of those quaint old customs that people used to indulge in before the advent of the automobile. It's very useful in getting from one location to another."

"Sounds intriguing. Did you have a particular destination in mind?"

"Nope. That's the wonderful part of walking. You just start out and go wherever your impulses take you."

Barrie regarded him cautiously. The suggestion seemed innocent enough, and surely his impulses wouldn't lead her into some sort of romantic trap in the middle of Beverly Hills. And it was a lovely night. The dry heat of midafternoon had given way to a cool, teasing breeze. The clear midnight black of the sky was dusted with silvery sparkles, and a full moon hung low over the mountains.

"Okay," she agreed finally. "Let's walk."

"Do you have a jacket with you?"

"No."

"Then I'll loan you one of mine." He pulled a bright blue windbreaker from the closet and draped it around her shoulders.

Barrie hugged the jacket to her and inhaled the intoxicating, woodsy aroma of his after-shave that lingered in the material. She felt almost as though she were wrapped in his arms, snug and protected. It was a dangerously pleasant feeling, an addictive feeling.

Prepared to walk briskly along, Barrie was surprised to find that Michael's pace was leisurely, and he'd meant what he said about exploring. As they passed each house, he told her brief, insightful anecdotes about his neighbors. Within minutes she had a clear image of the aging movie queen who never went out to pick up her morning paper without first dressing up and putting on her makeup, of the real estate tycoon whose legendary deals regularly made the business pages of the newspaper, of the couple whose regular marital spats—and subsequent reunions—were both colorful and noisy.

"And what do they say about you?" she teased. "I can just hear them, 'Oh, that Michael Compton is something else. Wild parties every week. A steady stream of starlets parading to the door. Why, goodness me, I don't know how the poor man does it. He must take megadoses of vitamins.'"

"Actually, I think they've been horribly disappointed. Not one single starlet has entered my front door, and our dinner tonight is the closest I've come to throwing a party."

"I don't believe it," she scoffed. "One of the most powerful men in television, and you paint a sad little scenario of a lonely, isolated existence."

"Hey, who said anything about lonely? I'm a very self-contained person. I don't need to be surrounded by people to have a good time. I don't need to have my ego stroked regularly just to keep functioning. In this business you can have a whole mob of acquaintances around anytime you want them, but I choose my friends carefully. They're people who genuinely like me for who I am, not because of the job I hold."

How ironic, Barrie thought, listening to Michael's thoughtful explanation of his chosen life-style. He was right. So many people would have given anything to be drawn into Michael Compton's inner circle simply because of his position at the network. Other producers—male and female—would have envied this closeness she was sharing with him, this apparent opportunity to further her career. Yet it was precisely because of his network position that she was having so much difficulty accepting him as a friend, much less a lover.

Suddenly he was tugging on her hand, like a child urging a parent on to sample the possibilities of some wonderful new adventure that had caught his eye. "Over here," he said, his eyes glittering with pure excitement.

"Where?" she asked. "All I see is a playground."

"Exactly. When was the last time you played on swings?"

"When I was much younger," she said. "In fact, well before puberty set in."

"Then it's about time you tried it again. You're getting jaded. You probably get your thrills from fancy roller coasters and flashy video games. You can't beat the simple pleasure of flying high into the darkness, trying to touch the stars."

Barrie looked at him curiously. What an amazing blend of seemingly contradictory traits had been packaged into Michael Compton's gorgeous body! A boy's excitement in innocent pleasures and the strong physical desires of a grown man. The self-assured strength of a natural leader and the gentleness of a lover. The quick, sometimes cynical mind of a hardened realist and the quiet, introspective soul of a romantic.

"Come on," he urged her. "Hop up. I'll push you to get you started. Ready?"

Barrie nodded and felt his hands firm and possessive on her waist, pulling her back until her body was against his. Just when she felt her nerves come alive with an unbearable tension, he released her, sending her flying forward. The climb high into the sky was exhilarating. The descent into his waiting hands was even more thrilling. With each release, she swung higher and higher until she was laughing at the sheer joy of the feeling, exulting in the rush of air against her cheeks, the breeze rippling through her hair.

"Having fun?"

"It's wonderful," she admitted, the words flying away on the whoosh of wind created by her arc through the sky. "I feel free, exactly the way a bird must feel when it soars away from the earth. Why aren't you doing it?"

"I'd rather watch you," he said, moving around to stand in front of her, just beyond her reach as her legs pumped to keep up the motion he had created for her. "You look like a little girl, all rosy-cheeked and happy."

Barrie caught an odd wistfulness in his voice. "Is there something wrong?"

He shook his head. "Not really."

"Not really means there is. You just don't want to talk about it."

"I just don't want to spoil the moment."

"Is what you were thinking about that serious?"

"Not serious exactly. I just wish you could relax with me the way you have out here."

"But I am with you."

"It's not the same, Barrie MacDonald, and you know it. I have the feeling you're afraid of me or of yourself. You're afraid to let yourself go with me, just the way you were before you climbed on that swing. But you did that. You took that risk. Why can't you take one with us?"

He stepped closer and caught her as the swing came forward, holding the edge of the seat, his fingers nestled so innocently against her thighs that she couldn't complain, yet so provocatively close that it was impossible for her to ignore them.

"Are you afraid of losing control? Is that it?" he asked gently. "Because I'm not trying to destroy your independence, you know. I don't expect you to yield to me because I'm a man and you're a woman. We're equals, Barrie. I respect your creativity, your intelligence, your spunk. Why would I want to change any of that, to make you less than you can be?"

Barrie sighed heavily. "You might not mean to, but that's what would happen," she said, her voice filled with years of pent-up bitterness. "I've seen it before. Two people get involved with the best intentions in the world, and pretty soon one of them is doing all of the giving, making all of the compromises. Usually it's the woman because men have no idea how to go about making concessions. It's *their* career that's important, *their* needs that must be met."

Her eyes flashed at him, filled with fire and challenge. "That's not for me. I've worked hard to get where I am, and no one is going to take it away."

Michael was shaking his head, and there was something in his eyes that she couldn't quite read. Understanding, maybe. Compassion. "I would never try," he said simply.

"You can't say that. You of all people. Not only could you ask it of me as a man, but you could demand it as my boss. Is it any wonder I'm terrified of getting closer to you?"

He sighed, and a great sorrow seemed to fill his eyes. He didn't even pretend not to understand. "No. It's no wonder.

I guess it's just going to take more time for me to prove to you that you have nothing to fear from me."

"Michael, don't even say that. You know that if you want to, you can and will order changes in my show. If it comes to that, you'll even cancel it. Don't tell me I have nothing to be afraid of. I have more to fear from you than any other man on earth."

Before he could say another word, she ran. Ran until her lungs were filled to bursting and her side ached. Then she walked the remaining blocks back to his house and got into her car. Her head was spinning with the words she had just hurled at him and with the terrifying awareness of their accuracy. She did fear Michael Compton's power. But more than that, she feared his sensuality and the damnable combination of wit, attractiveness and intelligence that lured her, taunted her body and mind in ways she'd never dreamed possible. She had a feeling there was more danger in that pull than she could even begin to imagine.

Chapter 5

The next day seemed to prove her point, demonstrating in graphic detail why any personal relationship with Michael would be sheer folly, why it could seriously jeopardize her career and play havoc with not only her emotions, but the very values—her values—that were at the core of *Goodbye, Again*. Barrie was sitting on the set going over the revised script for the opening episode with Danielle, when Kevin Porterfield came running in, his expression harried, his eyes shining with self-importance.

"Miss MacDonald, I have a memo for you from Mr. Compton. It's urgent," he announced breathlessly as he skidded to a halt in front of them. In his jeans, oxford cloth shirt and hand-knit sweater, he looked exactly like what he was: A very recent graduate of an Ivy League university film program.

Barrie tried not to show her irritation at the interruption. Ever since Kevin had been assigned to the show as network liaison, she'd had to remind herself she had once been his age and just as eager. She only prayed she hadn't been quite so pompous.

"I'm sure it is, Kevin. Put it on my desk. I'll look at it later."

"But you have to look at it now. It's about the first episode."

Barrie peered at him over the top of her glasses. "What about the first episode?" There was a dangerous edge in her voice.

Kevin avoided her gaze. He'd apparently detected the note of barely restrained antagonism and decided that any further involvement with the message might not be in his own best interests. "I don't know," he denied feebly.

Barrie didn't believe him for a minute. "Of course you do. I'm sure you read the memo on the way over here. Oh, never mind. Hand it over."

Her eyes skimmed over the terse, impersonal note, which was scrawled across a speed memo form: "Scene 3 in act 2 is entirely too suggestive for an eight o'clock show. Clean it up or take it out."

When she'd finished reading it, Barrie calmly shredded the memo into tiny pieces and spilled them onto the floor. "Okay, Danielle, let's get on with it."

Danielle eyed her warily. "That's all? That's all you're going to say? What did he want you to do?"

"It doesn't matter. I'm not doing it."

"But, Miss MacDonald…" Kevin began, a hint of desperation in his voice. He was apparently seeing his career go up in the smoke of Michael Compton's fiery outrage.

"Kevin, I am not changing one word of this show. Go tell that to your boss."

"But…but," he sputtered helplessly.

"You can't make poor Kevin do your dirty work for you," Danielle chided her.

"Why not? Michael sent him over here to do his."

"Ahhh. I see. That's the real problem, isn't it? You're mad because he didn't come over here himself."

Barrie glowered at her. "Correction. I am furious because he is trying to tamper with the integrity of my series. I don't give a hang who delivers the message."

"Right," Danielle said skeptically.

"Okay, so maybe that does tick me off," she admitted reluctantly. "But the point is that I have no intention of following his orders when they make absolutely no sense for the show. It's not my fault he put an adult sitcom in a kiddie time slot."

"Don't you think you ought to be the one to go tell him that? Work out some sort of compromise?"

Barrie looked at Danielle as though she'd grown two heads. "Do you actually think I should compromise on this?" she asked incredulously.

"I think you should at least listen to what the man has to say. Maybe he had a point."

Barrie's sigh teetered between disgust and resignation. Ever since college where they'd been roommates, Danielle had always appealed to the more rational side of her mind. Sometimes she hated Dani for it.

"All right," she grumbled. "I'll go over there." She stared at Danielle defiantly. "But I am not budging on this. He put the show on at eight o'clock. He's going to have to live with the consequences."

"No, sweetie pie. We are."

Barrie threw up her hands and stormed out of the studio, mumbling angrily to herself all the way across the parking lot to the executive offices. By the time she reached Michael's suite, she had worked up a full head of steam and formulated a diatribe that would make Michael's apparently overly sensitive ears burn. Too suggestive, indeed!

Marching past a startled Mrs. Hastings, Barrie ignored the secretary's frantic effort to restrain her and slammed into the inner office.

"Okay, Michael," she snapped, her brown eyes flashing sparks. "What's the meaning of this…this…"

Her outburst sputtered to a halt as she realized that she was staring into several astonished faces. "Oh, my…"

"I'm sorry, Mr. Compton," Mrs. Hastings apologized hastily from behind her. "I tried to stop her."

"That's true. She did. I just didn't listen. I didn't know," she muttered in embarrassment, wondering how the devil Heath had gotten Karen out of this situation in the script. If it hadn't been for Michael's ill-timed memo, she would have had a chance to read those new pages of dialogue and would have the words she needed to get out of this room gracefully. No, forget graceful. It was far too late. She just needed something to get her out of this room and into some kind of deep, dark hole.

Since words—hers and Heath's—escaped her, she merely backed toward the door, noting that Michael, the louse, seemed to be finding the situation incredibly amusing. At least he was grinning. She had a feeling, though, that there might not be a lot of humor behind that tight smile.

"Wait, Miss MacDonald," he said softly, though there was no mistaking the command in his voice. "Did you want something?"

Torn between embarrassment and still-seething anger, she shook her head mutely.

"You must have wanted something, Miss MacDonald," he repeated patiently. "I'm sure we'd all like to hear it."

Several faces watched her expectantly. She had to admit Michael was a master. He'd taken this lousy rotten moment and turned it to his complete advantage. "Later," she ground out between clenched teeth. "We can discuss it later."

"Why don't you wait outside, then? We'll be through here in just a minute." She heard the steely tone beneath the innocuous words. It was an order, no doubt about it.

Although the embarrassing incident had tempered her fury quite a bit, Barrie sat in the outer office and tried to nurse it back to health. It would never do to walk into Michael's office like some whimpering child, just because she had happened to make an absolute fool of herself.

"Would you like some coffee while you wait?" Mrs. Hastings asked kindly.

"No, thank you." With the state her nerves were in already, if she drank any more caffeine, she'd come completely unglued. She noted Mrs. Hastings's sympathetic expression and asked, "How furious is he really?"

"Well, it is an important meeting with some major advertisers," she began as Barrie moaned and hid her face. "But I wouldn't worry too much about it, dear."

"How can you say that? You said it was important."

"Yes, but you didn't let me finish," she said, her eyes twinkling. "Mr. Compton absolutely hates meeting with advertisers. I'm sure you provided a very welcome distraction."

"Right," Barrie said skeptically. "One of his producers comes barging in like a madwoman, and it absolutely thrills him to pieces. I'm sure it will do wonders for sales, too."

"Think of it this way, dear. It will break up the meeting early," she offered. Then, lowering her voice, she added with a conspiratorial smile, "I wasn't supposed to call in with a fake crisis for another half hour."

Barrie's eyebrows rose disbelievingly. So much for her desire to imbue Mrs. Hastings with saintly honesty. She was obviously, first and foremost, a loyal secretary. Barrie's lips twitched. "You were actually going to do that?"

Mrs. Hastings shrugged, but her blue eyes twinkled merrily. "I told you he hates meeting with advertisers."

Just then the door swung open, and the three men in their identical gray pin-striped suits were ushered out the door by a beaming Michael. Even without Mrs. Hastings's comments, Barrie would have known the heartiness toward them was feigned. As soon as they were out the door, his mouth settled into a grim line, and he faced Barrie. She thought she saw his lips twitching, but perhaps that had only been wishful thinking. His words were certainly curt enough.

"Now, Miss MacDonald, shall we try your entrance again? This time with a little less flamboyance."

Inside, he shut the door firmly behind them. Barrie had the oddest desire to ask that it be left open, so that Mrs. Hastings could be a witness when he decided to wring her neck. He walked back to his desk and sat down on the edge, waving her to a chair.

"I'd rather stand," she said stiffly.

"As you like. What's the problem?"

"I'm sure you know exactly what the problem is. I received your memo, which you didn't even have the decency to deliver yourself."

Blue-green eyes as hard as glass bored into her. Barrie winced. This was even worse than she'd expected. There was no warmth in those eyes, not even a flicker of the heat that had caressed her last night before she ran out on him. It was as though she were talking to a stranger.

Or to a boss, she reminded herself sternly. When was she going to learn to be more diplomatic? She sighed and thought probably never. She would always stand up for what she believed in, would always be thoroughly outspoken, and damn the consequences. The consequences right now did not seem to bode well for her future relationship—business or otherwise—with Michael Compton.

"I do not deliver memos," he informed her pointedly. "I write them."

Inwardly Barrie winced. Of course he did. They might have a personal relationship, but that certainly shouldn't imply that he should give her preferential treatment. She wouldn't even want him to. She sounded like a spoiled, petulant child.

"Okay, forget that. I don't suppose it really matters who delivers the memos around here," she conceded grudgingly. "The point is that I cannot do an adult situation comedy if you persist in tearing the guts out of the show."

For five minutes, as Michael calmly watched without a single change of expression, she paced around the office and argued passionately in defense of the scene he'd ordered cut. When she'd finally wound down, he said succinctly, "The scene goes."

Stunned by the finality of the comment, Barrie just stood and stared. "Didn't you hear a word I said?"

"Every one of them."

"And you're still determined to do this?"

"Yes."

"Then I don't know what you want from me," she said at last. "I don't know how you expect me to do this show."

"Tastefully, Miss MacDonald. I expect you to do it tastefully. You're trying too hard for sexy sophistication. There's too much glib chatter and cynical 'live it up in the fast lane' behavior. The audience will never buy it. They won't identify with it. Real people with deeply ingrained values don't act that way. That's as much of a fantasy as *Father Knows Best*. And you, of all people, should know it."

Barrie regarded him indignantly, her brown eyes flashing. "What do you mean?"

"You walked out on me last night, when you wanted to stay, didn't you?" Michael's eyes met hers, captured them, held them in a passionate duel.

"Who says I wanted to stay?" she fired back, the show momentarily forgotten.

"I do," he said softly, taking the few steps necessary to close the gap between them. His fingers trailed along her cheek, curved to cup her chin and remained there as his mouth descended slowly toward hers. Barrie's whole body tensed at the touch, fought against the feelings that were sweeping through her, proving his point. When his lips brushed across hers, the tender caress was like the offer of a blazing fire to someone who's been chilled by the night air. She moved irrevocably toward it, sought its comforting warmth. Her arms hung by her sides, her fingers curled into tight, angry fists. In her mind she saw herself pulling away, slapping his face, shouting at him that he was wrong. But deep inside, where that gentle kiss had set a wildfire blazing, she knew that it was a lie, knew beyond a doubt that she did want him, had wanted to stay with him last night, had left only to protect…what? Her lifelong vision of an unencumbered carefree future?

At last she forced herself to listen to her head, to the cries of danger, and moved away from him.

There was a glimmer of amusement in his eyes, a taunting satisfaction as she slipped out of his grasp. "I rest my case," he said softly.

"Oh, go to blazes," she snapped. "So what have you proved? That I'm attracted to you? Big deal. There's no accounting for the whims of hormones. What does that have to do with this scene? Last night…right now, that was about you and me, not Mason and Karen."

Michael smiled at her gently. "I'd say the similarity is pretty striking."

"Michael, this show is not about you and me. It's fiction. And I think the story needs this scene to move forward."

"I think we need that scene to move forward, too," he taunted. "But you don't pay any attention to me. Why should Mason have better luck than I do?"

Barrie stared at him incredulously. "That is the most peculiar bit of logic in support of censorship that I've ever heard."

"How about I'm the boss and what I say goes?"

"And what I believe doesn't matter?"

Suddenly Michael's lips formed a thin, very determined line. "Not in this case. No. I'm sorry."

"I see."

Without another word, Barrie turned and left the office, refusing to let him see the tears that glittered in her dark brown eyes. Her heart felt as though Michael had tap-danced across it. She'd had creative disagreements before. In fact, she had lost many of them. She should have been used to it. So why did this one hurt so much?

Because it had been so personal, because Michael had taken that scene and linked it to their relationship. He, too, had apparently recognized that she was Karen. That recognition made his criticism hurt all the more. It was as though he were judging her, saying that her sense of morality was wrong. But it was the way most liberated women felt today, wasn't it? She wrestled with that question all the way back to the studio.

The short walk had never seemed to take quite so long. Nor had it ever been quite so lonely.

Chapter 6

Barrie slowly pushed open the heavy door to the studio and went inside. She had never before felt so thoroughly and utterly defeated. The sight of Danielle, Heath and Kevin, seated in a tense, silent circle, didn't help. They were studying her expectantly, anxiously awaiting word of the outcome of her meeting. She knew that Danielle and Heath, at least, expected a victory.

"Well?" Danielle asked.

"The scene goes," she said tersely and marched into her office. Danielle immediately rose and followed.

"Want to talk about it?" she asked, closing the door.

"About what? We lost. End of report."

"Not about that. About whatever it is that has you looking as though you've lost your best friend."

Barrie looked at her oddly. "Is that how I look?"

"Exactly."

"Funny," she said, and there was a note of sadness in her voice. "That's how I feel, too."

Danielle studied her for several minutes. "You're not just upset because Michael insisted on the change, are you?"

"What makes you say that?"

"Because I know you. You're stubborn, and you stand up for what you believe in, but you usually concede defeat more gracefully than this."

"Okay. You're right," she admitted reluctantly. "There is more to it. Good heavens, Dani, I've worked on enough shows now to know that there will be changes. It comes with the territory."

"But those weren't your shows," Danielle reminded her. "Maybe your pride is on the line here."

"True, and that's part of it, I suppose. I love *Goodbye, Again* with my whole heart. I believe in it. But there's more to it than that."

Danielle appeared puzzled. "What more could there be?"

Barrie sank down wearily in the chair behind her desk. When she spoke at last, her voice was filled with frustration and pain. "Dani, he didn't even listen to me. I walked in there to try to discuss this rationally…"

"Rationally?" Danielle repeated skeptically.

Barrie grinned. "Okay, so I came on like an outraged fishmonger's wife. But I knew what I was talking about. I had perfectly valid arguments, and he paid absolutely no attention to them. He'd already made up his mind."

"Network programmers aren't known for their open-mindedness. That shouldn't come as a big surprise to you, either, and at least you tried."

"But this is Michael," she said plaintively.

Danielle's blond eyebrows arched quizzically over gray

eyes that were filled with sudden understanding. "And you're falling in love with him."

Barrie stared at her, openmouthed. "No! Never!" she snapped indignantly. "Don't be ridiculous. I hardly know the man."

"You know that he's strong, intelligent, funny, powerful and has terrific legs. If you ask me, he's what you've been looking for all your life. He may be the one man in the world who won't let you trounce all over him. Are you sure that isn't what this is all about? A last minute flurry of defiance before you take a tumble straight into his arms?"

"Danielle, for a woman who professes to be my friend, you have a very odd way of being supportive."

"I'm only trying to make you see the obvious."

"That I've fallen for Michael Compton?"

"Uh-huh," she said with a smirk. "Like the proverbial ton of bricks."

"You're crazy."

"If that's not it, then why does one little disagreement over the content of this show matter so much?" she asked smugly.

"Because it's as though he's rejecting me, my beliefs, my values. You'd hate it, too, if someone tried to make mince-meat out of your convictions."

"Of course I would," Danielle agreed readily enough. Too readily. Barrie waited for the kicker. Danielle grinned. "Especially if I happened to be in love with him and wanted his approval more than anything."

"I repeat," she said stoutly, "I am not in love with Michael Compton."

"Right," Danielle said dryly. "And I'm the world's sky-diving champion." She winked as she staged a perfectly executed tactical retreat. Her directorial sense of timing had never been better.

"See you on the set," she murmured as she closed the door with an emphatic click.

Barrie watched her leave, then shuffled the papers on her desk as she tried to figure out just why she felt so miserable. She refused to concede the possibility that Danielle might be right and that she could be falling in love with Michael Compton. That was too absurd to consider. True, he was all of those things Danielle had said, and more. He was sensitive and kind, and he challenged her in ways no other man ever had. He had even told her he wanted her to be the very best she could be. Not that she'd believed him. That was a line many men used, right before they asked you to give up something important. Good Lord, just look at what he'd asked her to do today.

Worse, his rejection of her arguments, his refusal to even really consider them, had seemed so arbitrary. That hurt even more coming from a man who permitted all sorts of violence and mayhem, to say nothing of some of the steamiest sex on television, after nine o'clock at night. On the other hand, she wasn't being permitted even the tiniest indiscretion, just because it would occur at 8:21. Where was the logic in that?

Not that arguing the point with him would do a bit of good. He had been pretty adamant, and she'd seen enough of his stubborn streak in the past couple of days to know it was a lost cause. They would just have to figure out some way to make the episode work without tearing the heart out of the show. Heath could do it, if he had to. He wouldn't sell out the show's integrity in the process, either.

But before she could think of a single tip to give him

to help him pull off that bit of magic, someone tapped on her door.

"Yes."

The door opened, and Michael peered in hesitantly, as though expecting a barrage of well-aimed missiles to greet him. "Still mad?"

Barrie glowered at him, though her blasted traitorous heart flipped over happily. She managed to keep an edge in her voice. "Furious. What are you doing here?"

"I thought maybe you'd like to go out with me tonight and forget about all of this."

Barrie shook her head in amazement. "You really are something. How do you manage to keep your personal life and your professional life in such tidy little separate compartments?"

"Practice," he informed her smugly. "Come out with me, and I'll give you some tips."

"Forget it. I have a script to revise, or have you forgotten?"

"Hardly. But you also have a perfectly competent writer to do it for you."

"We work as a team around here."

"Can't one member of the team take the night off?" he asked, perching on the edge of her desk and pulling two tickets out of his pocket. He waved them at her. "Box seats for the Dodgers against the Reds. It could decide who gets in the play-offs."

"A baseball game?" she asked incredulously. Was the man psychic? How had he known that it was the one thing that might tempt her? She could have refused the symphony, a play, or even a very romantic moonlit sailboat ride to Catalina. She could not resist baseball.

She eyed him warily. "How did you know?"

He grinned at her and, despite her best effort at resistance, her blood sizzled. "That you like baseball? I make it a point to get to know everything I can about my people."

"Danielle and her big mouth," Barrie muttered under her breath. Aloud she said only, "Okay, Compton. What time?"

"I'll pick you up at six. We'll have dinner at the stadium."

"The man who whips up gourmet meals in a flash is going to condescend to eat hot dogs?"

His eyes flashed, dazzling her with their amused glitter. "Peanuts and popcorn, too."

"What! No crackerjacks?"

"Be nice to me, and I'll get some for you," he taunted.

"I am never that nice," she replied haughtily.

"So I've noticed. See you at six."

"Don't you need my address?"

"I've got it," he said smugly. "Haven't you caught on yet? I know just about everything about you. For instance, there's this cute little birthmark…"

Her mouth dropped open. "Why you…"

His deep laugh rumbled through the office. "Careful, Miss MacDonald."

Barrie picked up her Rolodex and started to throw it at him but decided she was in no mood to pick up all those little cards if the thing flew apart. Besides, tonight would be soon enough to get even with him. He might have learned about her passion for baseball, but she doubted if he'd also discovered that her loyalties were with *her* home team, the Cincinnati Reds. She wondered if that mile-wide macho protective streak of his extended to saving one very vocal Cincinnati fan from the wrath of an entire Dodger crowd.

She grinned impishly. It was going to be a very interesting evening, and whatever happened was going to serve him right. As for that birthmark, she thought stoutly, hell could freeze over before he'd get to see that firsthand.

When Michael arrived promptly at six to pick her up, he didn't seem to attach any special significance to the fact that she was wearing a red-and-white pin-striped blouse with a pair of bright red walking shorts. He seemed much more interested in her slender bare legs, and for a fleeting instant she wondered if the shorts had been a bad idea. Nope, not in this heat, she decided firmly, ignoring his all-too-appreciative gaze.

They made the drive to Dodger Stadium in record time and were in their seats well before the first pitch was thrown. As soon as they were sitting down, Barrie reached into her purse and extracted a large button proclaiming her a member of the Rose Garden, a legacy from her grandmother. As she pinned it on her collar, Michael looked from the button to her perfectly bland expression and back again.

"Pete Rose?" he asked weakly.

"Of course," she responded casually as she reached back into her purse and pulled out a red-and-white Cincinnati banner. He seemed to turn pale beneath his perfect California tan.

"Why didn't you tell me?" he asked in a choked voice.

She beamed at him. "I thought you already knew everything about me."

"You think you're a real wise guy, don't you? You knew I had no idea you were a Reds fan."

"Does it matter?" she asked innocently. "I don't mind if you want to cheer for the Dodgers. Of course, it will be a losing cause."

"Like hell," he grumbled, getting to his feet. "I'll be right back."

"Bring me a hot dog, would you?"

He gave her a curt nod as he stalked off through the stands. Barrie chuckled as she watched him go. This was wonderful, even better than she'd anticipated. Michael clearly took his baseball very seriously. As she did.

While he was away, she read through the program and watched the players warm up on the field. Seeing the Reds in action again was like going back to her childhood, when she and her father had made the drive to Cincinnati's Stadium on his infrequent visits home. Those baseball games had been the only times they had connected, the only times when he'd even seemed to notice she was alive. Ever since she'd been in L.A., she had made it a point to go to see the Reds play at least once when they came to town. It always brought back one of the few good memories she had of her father, though try as she might, it couldn't temper the bitterness.

"Here's your hot dog." Michael's gruff words interrupted her reveries. When she looked up, she almost burst out laughing. He was wearing a blue Dodger cap and had the stick holding a Dodger pennant tucked in his belt to free his hands for the cardboard tray of hot dogs and beers.

"I see you're getting into the spirit of this," she taunted lightly.

"You bet I am. Maybe we should make a little wager on the outcome of this game, just to make it interesting," he suggested with a wickedly seductive little glimmer in his eyes.

Barrie licked her lips nervously. "Umm...I think it will be plenty interesting without that."

"Coward." There was a definite challenge in Michael's quietly spoken taunt, and there was no way Barrie was going to ignore it. She was too much of a scrapper.

"Okay, Compton. What's the bet?"

"If Cincinnati wins, I will take you to that benefit gala at the Dorothy Chandler Pavilion next week." He gazed at her significantly. "And if the Dodgers win, you'll come home with me tonight."

She shook her head adamantly. "Nice try, but that's no bet. You win either way."

He brushed a finger across her lips to silence her doubts. "So do you," he promised softly, setting off a series of tiny flutters in Barrie's abdomen. She opened her mouth to speak, but no words would come out. She licked her lips and tried again.

"How about letting me do the show the way I want to, if Cincinnati wins. That's a real bet."

He shook his head. "Sorry. No deal. I don't play games with my professional decisions."

Barrie sighed. "It was worth a try."

"How about my terms? Will you accept them?"

She glanced out on the field as if in search of reassurance that the Reds would not let her down and get her in even deeper with Michael before the night was out. Did she dare to accept a bet that might land her in his bed? Suddenly she grinned to herself. The bet said nothing about where she would sleep tonight. A loss by Cincinnati only dictated where they would go after the game. Even though Michael might have a very clear impression of what he wanted to happen when they got there, she was still perfectly capable of saying no.

Or yes.

She gave him a dazzling smile. "It's a deal," she agreed.

For the next three hours the battle lines between them had been drawn. Whenever Michael cheered for the Dodgers, Barrie glared at him. When she screamed for the Reds, he glowered back. On a particularly close call, they nearly came to blows.

"He was out by a mile," Michael shouted victoriously.

"Are you kidding?" Barrie grumbled. "You're as blind as the umpire. My man was lying across the base, while your guy was still fumbling around in the dirt for the ball."

"The umpire was right on it. He called him out."

"He needs bifocals."

"You're just a sore loser."

"I haven't lost yet, Compton. The score's tied."

"And the Dodgers are coming to bat."

"Big deal. It's the bottom of the batting order."

"They'll send in a pinch hitter for the pitcher."

"Who made you the manager?"

"It's the only thing that makes sense, especially in the bottom of the ninth."

The first batter walked.

"So what?" Barrie muttered at Michael's triumphant expression.

"I didn't say a word."

The second batter hit a sharp single down the right field line, sending the runner racing around second and into third base. Michael was on his feet, yelling his head off. Barrie was biting her nails.

"I am not going to get discouraged," she muttered under her breath. The game was not over yet.

"Come on, strike him out!" she shouted at the top of her lungs, her face flushed with excitement. The pitcher complied. "Way to go! Two more! You can do it."

She ignored the fiery disapproval in Michael's eyes and the glares of the fans around them. "Come on, baby. You can do it," she repeated defiantly. The next player struck out.

"Okay. You've done the worst of it. Only one more."

Michael was back in his seat, and now she was on her feet. "Strike him out," she urged.

The bat met the ball with a sharp crack that sent a shiver of fear tripping along her spine. She watched as the ball sailed high into center field. "It's an easy catch," she murmured softly. "Get it. Get it." The ball plopped into the centerfielder's glove, and she waved her banner triumphantly.

When she glanced down into Michael's face, she noted the unexpected amusement in his eyes. "What's so funny?" she asked curiously.

"You. I have never seen anyone who professes to such sophistication get quite so carried away at a baseball game."

She grinned back at him. "You've been doing a fair amount of shouting yourself."

He nodded sheepishly, as if surprised by the discovery. "That's true. I think you must bring out my competitive spirit."

"Either that, or you just want to win your bet."

He grinned at her. "There is that," he agreed. "We could call it off," he offered generously.

"Not on your life. I feel a victory coming on."

Cincinnati scored twice in the top of the tenth to Barrie's absolute delight and Michael's dismay. The Dodgers managed to put three men on base in the bottom of the inning before a relief pitcher came in and struck out the next three batters to end the game.

"So," she said, still waving her banner in triumph. "What night is that gala?"

"We'll discuss it later," Michael groused as they made their way to the car.

"Don't be a sore loser," she taunted him. "Even if I'd

come home with you, you wouldn't have gotten to first base."

"No pun intended?"

"Sorry. No."

"Are you so sure?" he wondered, studying her thoughtfully as they stood beside the car.

"I'm sure," she said softly.

He shook his head. "When are you going to admit that you want me as much as I want you?"

Giddy with her victory and the sheer fun of battling wits with Michael all evening, Barrie gazed up at him provocatively. "Oh, I'm willing to admit that," she said airily.

Michael sucked in his breath and stared at her. "You are?"

"Sure." She grinned at him. "I'm just not going to do anything about it."

Chapter 7

As the season premiere week for the network neared, Barrie's and Michael's lives became more and more hectic. They were both in heavy demand, she at the studio for rehearsals, he in the executive suite, where last minute programming decisions were being made from before dawn to well after midnight. Their contact seemed to be limited to quick late-night or early-morning phone calls that should have given Barrie the space she'd claimed to need.

And yet as the days passed by in a blur of activity, she instead found herself wanting more intimate contact, wanting to discuss the day's events in more detail, wanting even his most casual touch. Ironically, considering how she'd reacted to his previous comments about the show, she even found herself wanting more of his incisive, clear advice. And to her thorough dismay, just as Danielle had suggested, she also yearned for his enthusiastic approval.

What she didn't want anymore were dictatorial memos

and, to her relief, there weren't any. The final script for the first show had zipped through without a murmur of dissent, and the taping was scheduled for the next night, with the premiere episode to air the following week. Her simmering resentment of Michael's arrogant interference had faded without new edicts to fuel it.

In the meantime, there was the benefit gala to which he'd promised to escort her as a respite from their frantic schedules. It began to loom as a monumental turning point in their relationship. For the first time at a lavish, highly visible Hollywood function, she and Michael would be seen as a couple. She knew it would be the stuff people would gossip about the following morning and, as she dressed, she worried over her gown, her shoes, her makeup, even her underwear.

"You're being ridiculous," she muttered, as she tried to decide between two pairs of bikini briefs, one creamy white and mostly lace, the other silky champagne...what there was of it. "The paparazzi will not be taking pictures of your underwear."

It was a comforting thought, but it didn't help her make up her mind. When she realized that her choice would be the only garment, other than the sheer nylons, that she would be wearing under her slinky gown, she grew even more nervous and indecisive. She eyed the glittering copper-colored dress skeptically. The neckline was demure enough in front. It was the back that dipped low to the waist. There was also a provocative slit from the hem to just above her knees. The dress was stunningly sexy, enough to draw women's envy and to turn a man into a lustful beast, according to the saleslady. She humphed at the memory of the woman's own envious gaze. That should have warned her. This was no dress to be wearing with Michael. The man's sexual appetite was legendary, and he'd already made it abundantly clear that he'd like to make her his next meal. Why the devil was she tempting him to take the first bite?

Because some very perverse part of her obviously wanted him to, she told herself dryly. Her body had been sending very clear signals on that point, even when her mind was most vocal in its opposition. Right now her mind was telling her to get out some sedate little black dress, even as she was slipping the coppery designer gown over her head. Another victory for the hormones, she thought with a sigh as she gazed at herself in the mirror.

Her lips curved upward in a pleased smile. The elegant, glamorous woman who stared back at her was a far cry from the terrified teenager who'd left Ohio determined to break the bonds with her past. On the surface that girl had appeared to be afraid of her own shadow, but an inner resilience had driven her, had made her succeed in a profession in which all too many failed. Her shy smile had hidden a toughness that she'd learned from her mother. She had taken the early knocks in a highly competitive profession and turned them to her advantage, learning everything she could about television from anyone who had something to teach.

And, she vowed, she would learn from Michael, as well. When this infatuation of his faded, she would be left with something real, something more lasting than ephemeral love. Love was like a will-o'-the-wisp, elusive and fleeting. A career was tangible, something over which she had some control. She was neither cold nor calculating, but she was a realist. She would not let his dazzling, seductive promises distort her priorities.

For tonight, though, she had every intention of basking in his caressing gaze, of reveling in the warmth of his touch.

When she opened the door for him at last and saw his eyes light with a very masculine appreciation, she felt wonderfully special. To be sure, other women in Hollywood were more beautiful than she, but she doubted any of them had ever felt more alluring.

"You are…gorgeous," he said softly. "Let me see all of you."

As she spun around, he whistled. "I'm not sure I want to share you with the world. I think I'd like to keep you all to myself."

Barrie's laughter sparkled as brightly as the topaz and diamond earrings that glittered on her ears. "Oh, no, you don't, Mr. Compton. I won the bet fair and square, and we are going out on the town. I've never been to one of these fancy shindigs before."

"They're boring."

"How can a show that features some of the best actors, musicians, dancers and comedians in the country be boring?"

He cocked a brow at her. "My dear," he said as though greatly scandalized by her question, "no one goes to a benefit gala for the show."

"Oh?"

"Of course not. They go to be seen. We are a very generous people out here, but we want to be sure the whole world knows about it."

Barrie glowered at him and shook her head. "And you think my show is too cynical."

Michael smiled one of his soft romantic-album-cover smiles, and her pulse pounded. "Just watch when we get there," he suggested dryly. "You will see more jockeying for position than you've ever seen on the track at Santa Anita."

"You, of course, are just an interested observer of this

process?" she retorted lightly. "A sort of self-appointed social commentator?"

"Absolutely."

She grinned up at him and gazed pointedly in the direction of her driveway. "And that's why you rented the limousine?"

"I did not rent it," he responded indignantly. "The network provides it. I just rarely use it."

"I see," she said wryly. "Only on special occasions."

"Exactly."

She flashed him a dazzling, satisfied smile. "When you want to be seen."

He chuckled. "No, you little minx. When I want to have my hands free for the beautiful woman by my side."

Barrie's triumphant smile promptly faded as a flurry of butterfly wings stirred in her abdomen. "Oh."

"That's it? Just oh?" he taunted, mimicking her.

"I think that's sufficient. Besides, with my foot in my mouth, it's difficult to use too many words."

"You mean I've rendered you speechless? Quick, let's go while I have this tremendous advantage."

As they approached the car, the driver stepped out and opened the door for them. Barrie sank down onto the luxurious cushions and glanced around. "I think I could get used to this. Since you don't use it, do you suppose you could have someone start picking me up for work?"

"Sure," he said agreeably, then added casually, "If you leave from my place."

"Never mind."

"I had a feeling you'd say that," he said with exaggerated disappointment. "Too bad. How about a drink?"

He poured them each a glass of champagne. "To us," he said softly, tapping his crystal goblet against hers as he gazed unblinkingly into her eyes. It was as though he were willing her to repeat the toast, to vow with him that they were a couple with a future.

"To us," she murmured at last, unable to resist the power of that steady gaze, the implication of that simple toast.

When they had each sipped the bubbling wine, he took the glass from her. "And now, how about a kiss to seal it?"

"Seal what?"

"Our deal."

"Have we made a deal?" Barrie asked innocently, though her heart thudding against her ribs told her that they had.

He nodded. "You know we have."

He was close, so close she could feel the whisper of his breath against her cheek, feel the heat emanating from his body beneath the tuxedo that made him look even more dashing and desirable than ever. His eyes clung to hers as his hand reached out to skim across her breasts. Beneath the shimmering fabric they peaked into sensitive, aching buds.

"Do you know how I've longed to do that, Barrie Mac-Donald?" he whispered huskily. "You like that, don't you? I can see it in your eyes."

Barrie wanted to blink and look away, wanted to shutter her eyes against their apparent betrayal, but she couldn't. It was as though the softly-spoken, urgent words and his compelling gaze had hypnotized her. She would have done anything he asked of her. And he had asked for only a kiss.

She leaned toward him, closed the infinitesimal gap and touched his lips gently, praying for nothing more than a sharp tug of heightened awareness. Instead, it was as though a match had been struck and touched to dry tinder. Fiery, all-encompassing, ravishing. She felt herself pulled into his arms, felt his hands skimming down the bare curve of her spine, his touch alternately light and provocative, then rough and possessive. Both of them inflamed her. The innocent kiss he had sought was no longer innocent, had probably never been. He had known—as she should have—that once they were in each other's arms, the pent-up passion that had teased and taunted them would erupt into a full-fledged conflagration.

Barrie was pressed back into the cushions with Michael's body pressed against hers, his weight and warmth welcome rather than oppressive. Her hands had slipped inside the jacket of his tux, seeking bare flesh, but forced to find satisfaction in the muted suggestion of suppleness beneath the fine fabric of his shirt.

"I knew you would be like this," he murmured against her lips. "I knew there were fire and ice. So much sensuality.

"Ahh, Barrie." His tongue flicked against her lips, circled them, then penetrated the opening she gladly gave him. His hand found the opening slit in her dress, gently caressed her thigh, slowly reached upward. Barrie tensed with anticipation and, perhaps, just a hint of dread. The assault on her senses was already unerringly successful. How much further could she allow him to go before she would fall completely under his spell, give herself up to him and to these wonderful blood-stirring sensations?

A subtle cough saved her from having to answer that question.

"Sir, we have arrived." The disembodied voice came to them over the car's intercom.

Reluctantly Michael pulled away from her, his breathing heavy, his face suffused with unfulfilled desire. His hand remained where it had been on her inner thigh, and he caught her gaze and held it.

"I must be a mess," Barrie muttered, wanting to look away in embarrassment.

He grinned at her. "You look like a woman who has just been thoroughly kissed. The photographers will have a field day."

He started to climb out the door, which the driver had just opened.

Barrie grabbed his arm and held him back. "Michael," she whispered urgently. "I can't get out of here looking like this."

"Of course, you can. You look beautiful."

She looked at him oddly. "You really don't mind what people think, do you?"

"Why should I? I'm not ashamed of our relationship."

He gave her a penetrating look. "Are you?"

"No. Of course not."

"Then let's get out of here and prove my point about why all these people have come."

As they exited the car, flashbulbs popped, and several reporters asked Michael questions about the upcoming television season. He fielded them with absolute aplomb. He didn't even wince when one of the reporters asked, with a pointed glance at Barrie, if he thought *Goodbye, Again* would be given more than the usual amount of time to prove itself.

"I'm expecting great things of *Goodbye, Again*," he said coolly. "However, it will have the same chance that any other series has. If it's not working, I'll cancel it."

"What do you think about that, Miss MacDonald?"

Although she had flinched inwardly at the succinct reply, with outward calm she said, "I think that Mr. Compton is the vice president of the network. He'll do his job. I wouldn't expect any less of him."

"Bravo," he whispered in her ear, so that the reporters couldn't hear it. He ushered her out of their path and into the lobby of the Dorothy Chandler Pavilion, where a star-studded array of guests was sipping champagne and nibbling hors d'oeuvres at the preshow cocktail party.

They found a spot to themselves on the edge of the crowd and watched. Just as Michael had predicted, instead of avoiding the glare of the cameras, many of the guests seemed to be vying for an opportunity to be interviewed. It was all very subtle, but there was no mistaking the intensity of the competition. They giggled like a couple of kids as they took bets on who would win each of the battles.

Their pleasant role as observers didn't last long. As soon as people began to spot Michael and recognize him, they were caught up in a whirl of conversations. Although little business was discussed, Barrie recognized the participants and their underlying messages clearly enough. They were all using the brief social contact to try to cement their relationships with one of the industry's most influential men. And she couldn't blame them. It was a business that demanded that you snatch opportunity whenever or wherever you found it. Judging from their pointed, questioning glances in her direction, they were all envious of her presumed position of influence, all equally certain that she was taking advantage of it to secure the future of her series. She didn't like their assumption, knew it wasn't true, but she couldn't resent them for making it.

In fact, she thought with a soft chuckle, they should only know how little power she wielded over Michael. If they'd heard their arguments over *Goodbye, Again* or seen the changes in the script, they'd realize just how carefully Michael avoided any suggestion of impropriety. When it came to making decisions about the show, she could have been his archenemy for all the preferential treatment she received.

The rest of the evening was a blur of dazzling entertainment, sharp-witted conversation and tantalizing hints of passion. Michael never missed an opportunity to squeeze her hand or run his fingers down her spine. Even when he seemed totally absorbed in a provocative discussion with a business associate, his possessive touch burned her flesh, reminding her that he was thoroughly aware of her. Barrie couldn't have ignored such blatant signals had she wanted to. She knew beyond any shadow of a doubt that Michael Compton wanted her, desired her with a self-confident certainty that took her breath away.

But did he need her? She doubted it, doubted that he needed any particular woman as a lifelong companion and love. Surely he was the type of man who thrilled only to the chase, and admittedly, at the moment she was leading him on a merry one. Once the intrigue of that chase had ended, would he vanish, leaving her to nurse her pain as her father had so often left her mother?

Of course he would. Even now, though he drew her into the conversation, sought her opinions and listened respectfully, chuckled at her wit, she alone knew how easily he could turn on her, cut her down to size. When push came to shove, she felt her opinions didn't matter one whit to him.

They were both too strong-minded, too stubborn for this to work. Perhaps if their professional lives weren't intertwined, they would have been ideally suited. She could envision the challenge of late-night conversations during which they would hone their intelligence, spar over everything from the Star Wars arms race to the social satire of *Doonesbury.* She could imagine the passionate lovemaking that would be sparked by such lively debates, such diversity of opinion.

But that was the fantasy. The reality was something entirely different. The reality was Michael arguing with her over the actions of her characters, changing and distorting her dreams. The devastating possibility was that Michael would end up snatching her career just when it was within her grasp. She would hate him for that, even though she might understand it rationally. And it would destroy them.

She sighed as his fingers massaged the sensitive spot at the base of her spine. Her troubled eyes met his questioning gaze.

"What's wrong?"

"Nothing," she denied.

"Why don't I believe that?"

"Beats me," she retorted bravely. "I'm having a terrific time."

"But?"

She grimaced at his perceptiveness and his persistence. "But I think I'd better get home. Tomorrow's a busy day."

He grinned at her. "Do I sense a thank goodness at the end of that sentence?"

She gave an embarrassed chuckle. "Well…"

"It's okay. Sooner or later, you're going to stop running, Barrie MacDonald. And when you do, I'm going to be right there."

"Is that a threat?"

"Nope," he said softly. "A promise."

Chapter 8

As soon as the closing shot of the first episode of *Goodbye, Again* had been taped, and the audience's enthusiastic applause was nothing more than a fading echo in the studio, Barrie heaved a sigh of relief and slipped out of the control booth. It had gone reasonably well, far better tonight than during the previous night's dress rehearsal. The audience had been responsive, the laughs had come in all the right places, and Melinda had been absolutely superb as Karen Devereaux. Even if the show failed, she would emerge with a solid reputation as a talented comedic actress, a true television star. Barrie was sure of it.

"You were all magnificent," she praised as the weary troupe virtually collapsed in the vacated studio. "I think a party is in order. When we go on the air next week, I want you all to come to my place for a celebration bash. You deserve it. I think we're going to have a hit."

"Do you really believe that we can make it even in this

time slot?" Danielle asked quietly with a look of pure wide-eyed innocence.

Barrie's brows shot up in horrified disbelief. She wasn't particularly shocked by her friend's question, only by the fact that she had voiced it tactlessly in front of the others on what should have been their big night to celebrate. Now, instead of excitement, their faces suddenly registered uncertainty. It was one of the few times she had ever known Danielle to display such lousy timing. Barrie tried quickly to undo the apparently unwitting damage.

"I believe this show is intelligent, witty and unique," she said with heartfelt conviction, staring pointedly at Danielle as though daring her to disagree. "I'm convinced the critics and the audience will find it."

Her comment effectively silenced Danielle, but not Heath. "Assuming they aren't all out at the movies," he muttered bitterly, echoing Danielle's concern and reinforcing the depressing atmosphere.

"Don't think that way," Barrie chided him. "We are not going into this with a defeatist attitude. If we don't believe in ourselves, we'll never convince anyone else. Remember, *All in the Family* and *Hill Street Blues* weren't hits when they first went on the air, either. They took time to build an audience, and they did it by word of mouth and critical acclaim. We can do the same thing."

"Sure. But like you said yourself, first they have to find us," he retorted, oblivious to the increasingly dismayed stares of the exhausted and increasing appalled cast. But when Barrie glared at him, he finally caught on to the effect his words were having, especially on the younger members of the cast and crew who hadn't been around long enough to become used to the mercurial nature of working in television.

"Oh, all right. I'll shut up," he grumbled.

"Thank you," she replied with exaggerated sweetness. "Now stop worrying and get out of here, guys. We have a new show to work on beginning Monday."

Depressed by her admittedly ineffective attempt at a pep talk, Barrie started slowly back to her office.

"You're furious with me, aren't you?" Danielle said, walking along with her.

"No," she said tiredly. "Not really. I was surprised, but I'm sure you only said what everyone else was thinking. I suppose it was better to get it out in the open."

"I thought so," Danielle said. "They needed to hear that you still believe in them and in the show."

Barrie looked at her in astonishment. "You set me up, didn't you?"

Danielle grinned. "Something like that. I just wanted to be sure they got the message that no matter what happens in the ratings they've done their best, and the show really is great. I figured you're the only one they'd believe."

"I guess I ought to thank you."

"That would be nice, but I'll settle for your company at dinner."

Barrie shook her head. "Not tonight, Dani. I want to look over next week's script one last time."

"You sure you're not holding out for a better offer?" Danielle inquired hopefully.

"No. I just need some time to myself," she said vaguely. It was a flimsy excuse, but it seemed to satisfy Danielle, who left after giving her a quick hug and some sage advice about what she ought to be doing with the rest of her evening. As usual, it involved Michael and speeding up the snail's pace at which their relationship was progressing.

When she was alone, Barrie tried to push Danielle's

very explicit comments from her mind and to focus on the fact that her very first television series was about to go on the air. Her effort failed miserably. While thinking of her series' debut should have thrilled her, it had become so intertwined with her personal relationship with Michael that she was more confused than excited. She'd been trying all week to blame her odd sense of disorientation on the pressure of finishing the show, but she knew it was more than that. Thanks to Michael, she was on an emotional merry-go-round and had no idea how to get off.

But, instead of having time to think, no sooner had she settled down behind her desk than the phone rang. She knew intuitively that it was Michael.

"How did it go?" he asked without preamble.

"Are you asking personally, or do you want an analysis that will soothe a worried network programmer?"

"Both."

"The audience seemed to like it. The pacing was fine. Danielle did a superb job. The cast was terrific."

"And you? What do you think?" .

She hesitated, then finally admitted with total honesty. "I'm worried sick."

"Why?"

"You know why. You've put us in an impossible time slot."

"If the show's as good as you say it is, the ratings will be there."

"You know better than that."

"Barrie, if I didn't have faith in this show, I wouldn't have put it where I did," he said sincerely.

"Do you mean that?"

"Of course, I mean it. Why would you doubt it?"

"I thought perhaps you were making it your sacrificial lamb, because you figured it didn't have a prayer, anyway."

"Hey, what's this?" he said softly, the soothing tone like a balm to her opening night jitters. "What's happening to that upbeat, confident producer who keeps telling me how terrific her series is?"

"She's getting cold feet."

"Want to meet me tonight and let me warm them up?" he suggested huskily.

The invitation held an incredible appeal, an irresistible appeal, in fact, and not just because of Danielle's earlier nudging. She needed someone tonight, someone who would bolster her flagging spirits, someone who would make her feel warm and secure. She denied that what she really needed was Michael and that only he could make her feel that way. She still wanted desperately to believe that anyone would do.

"Why not?" she said boldly. She heard Michael gasp in surprise.

"Sure?"

"I'm sure."

"I'll meet you at your place in an hour, then. I just have a few things to wrap up here."

"See you," she said softly, a flutter of anticipation skittering along her nerves.

She threw the script into her briefcase, ran to her car and made the drive to Santa Monica in forty-five minutes. She barely had time to straighten up the living room, change the towels in the bathroom and freshen her makeup before Michael was ringing the doorbell impatiently. Fortunately, she had no time to reconsider her decision to let him come over, or she might have panicked. Instead she took a deep breath and opened the door.

"Hi," she said, struck by an unexpected shyness as she surveyed him from head to toe, taking in the perfectly tailored brown suit, beige shirt and pin-striped tie. Once more, she admired the way he always managed to look as though he'd just modeled for the cover of a magazine even after a fifteen-hour day. Only his thick brown hair was less than perfect. It was windblown, as though he'd driven over with the car windows rolled down to catch the cool breeze. It made him look healthier and more attractive than ever. She, on the other hand, felt limp and exhausted and suspected she looked it, as well. If he still wanted her after seeing her like this, she had a feeling she ought to grab him and hang on for dear life.

"Hi, yourself," he said, brushing a gentle, undemanding kiss across her lips and pushing a stunningly wrapped package into her hands. He barely looked at her.

"What's this?"

"A present," he said vaguely, prowling around the living room as though he'd been sent on a scouting expedition. He studied the titles of the books on her shelves, picked up the pictures she had scattered about, glanced out her windows. He even picked up her stack of unopened mail and thumbed through it. He did all of this without saying another word or even looking at her. Barrie couldn't decide whether to be amused or irritated.

"Are you searching for something in particular?" she finally inquired with exaggerated politeness. "Maybe I can help."

"What?" Michael asked distractedly, now seemingly absorbed by the cover story of a business magazine.

"I asked if you were looking for something."

"No, not really."

"Just hunting up more clues for my personnel file, then?"

He grinned at her sheepishly. "Nope. I think that's pretty well up-to-date."

Barrie looked at him oddly. "Michael Compton, are you nervous?" she asked incredulously.

"Me? Of course not," he retorted indignantly.

"You are, too. I would never have believed it."

"Open your present."

"Don't try to change the subject. Why are you so up-tight?"

Michael sighed and kept pacing. "It's your fault, you know."

"What's my fault?"

"You keep sending out these conflicting signals, so that I'm never quite sure from one minute to the next where we stand. Tonight on the phone I thought I got a very clear message, but now that I'm here, I'm not so sure. You seem distant again."

Barrie put the package down on the sofa and moved closer to him. "I'm sorry," she said softly. "Would it help if I told you that I haven't known from one minute to the next where we stand, either?"

"And tonight?"

She took a deep breath and gazed unblinkingly into his eyes. Tentative fingers reached up to touch his lips, caress the firm line of his jaw. His eyes darkened with passion at her touch, and a muscle in his neck twitched with the effort of restraint as he waited for her to speak.

"Tonight I want to be with you," she said honestly. "I need you. I need your warmth and your sensitivity and... and your loving."

"Oh, Barrie," he said, drawing her into his arms then and just holding her, letting her feel his strength, the power of his desire. Her head nestled into the curve of his neck, and when he whispered huskily of his need for her, the words ruffled her hair and sent tiny shocks tripping along her spine. His body trembled in her arms, and she realized for the first time how deeply she affected him. What's more, she realized how very much she needed him.

Her openness about her need, her commitment that whatever else happened tonight would be theirs seemed to remove some of the pressure. There was no urgency, only a deep sense of the rightness of this moment. They moved to the sofa and sat cuddled together and talked of their lives and dreams, of hopes and possibilities, of past adventures and future plans. They talked through the night and at dawn, with the sun streaking the sky with pale golden light, they made love, their passion gentled into something beautiful and tender, something that was totally giving.

Theirs was no fumbling first-time exploration. It was as though their bodies had been made for each other, as though they knew instinctively exactly how to please, where to touch, what to say, when to hold back.

For the first time in her life, Barrie found that she was unafraid of sharing herself completely and without reservation. And in that sharing she discovered a height of ecstasy never reached before. Michael's whispered words excited her, his touch against the satin of her flesh inflamed her, but more than that, his joyous release sent her own senses spiraling out of control. She gave herself up to an abandoned wantonness that provoked him, teased him and ultimately satisfied him beyond measure. Apart, they were strong and good and fiercely independent. Together, there seemed to be no limits to what they could feel, where they could soar.

"I just have one question, Miss MacDonald," Michael murmured huskily as they lay in each other's arms with sunlight dappling their flesh with a patchwork of brightness. "Why did we take so long to get here?"

"Because you're a gentleman," she retorted.

"I beg your pardon?"

"Most other men would not have been nearly as patient as you've been," she told him candidly.

He lifted himself to one elbow and gazed at her incredulously. One hand lay possessively on the curve of her waist, a curve he had explored in erotic detail during their lovemaking and now cupped with a lover's sure knowledge. "Are you telling me that if I'd thrown you over my shoulder and dragged you to bed, I could have avoided all those cold showers I took?"

She grinned at him impishly and wriggled under his roving fingers. "Probably."

Michael moaned.

"But," she added soothingly, "I would have hated you in the morning."

"Ahh. I see. And this morning?"

"This morning I am feeling so benevolent toward you that I might even consider fixing you some breakfast before you leave."

"Before I leave?" he repeated in amazement. "Woman, are you some kind of a sadist? I've been up all night. I need sleep. I don't need a cup of coffee, some toast and a long drive on the freeway."

She patted his shoulder. "You'll rest much better in your own bed."

"And you?"

"I'll rest much better in my own bed—" she paused, then added firmly "—alone."

"Why does that confuse me?"

Barrie shrugged. "It shouldn't."

"Are we back to playing games?"

She gazed at him with serious brown eyes. "Michael, I have never played games with you. I've told you from the beginning that it couldn't work between us."

Puzzlement suddenly filled his eyes. "Then what was last night all about?"

"Last night was about two mature adults who needed each other."

Confusion changed to hurt, then anger. "That's all it was for you? I don't believe it. You wanted me, Barrie. Me, Michael. Not just some willing male body."

Barrie winced at the accusatory tone, the underlying plea for an acknowledgment of caring that she wasn't prepared to make. Last night...this morning...had been special, but that didn't mean anything. She wouldn't let it. She would send Michael on his way and tug her defensive cloak back into place. It had slipped during the long, tender night, but she hadn't completely lost it.

"Michael, please," she begged softly. "Don't do this. I loved what we shared. I just don't want to magnify it all out of proportion."

Michael drew in a shocked breath, then exploded, "That is the most ridiculous comment I have ever heard in my life! You know we have something special between us, something the whole world searches for and hardly ever finds. Why won't you admit it?"

"I can't," she said simply. "It's not real."

Her cool words seemed to incense him. He grabbed her roughly and pulled her into his arms. His lips against hers were hot, demanding, his hands possessive, sure. Barrie felt yet another stirring of excitement, as flames licked through her. She tried to pull away, but he wouldn't release her. His body next to hers was on fire, his arousal pressing against her thigh with a powerful, tantalizing intimacy. A shudder of dismay seemed to rack his body and then, at last, he pushed her away, as though half-afraid of where his anger might lead. He looked shattered.

"Was that real enough for you?" he demanded, leaping out of bed and picking up his scattered clothes. He slammed the bathroom door shut behind him, and Barrie heard the shower go on. It seemed to pound down with the unrelenting fury of a storm. She couldn't bear listening to it another minute, imagining Michael's naked body standing under the harsh spray tense with outrage.

Barrie put on her robe and padded into the kitchen, her heart still thudding against her ribs. His violence hadn't really scared her. She had known instinctively that Michael would never harm her. But the depth of his anger had shaken her. A sophisticated male was supposed to kiss and say goodbye with calm acceptance. In fact, most of them were absolutely delighted to discover that their night's partner had no designs on their future independence. Why had Michael reacted so differently? Was it possible he actually cared about her?

She fumbled with the coffee maker with fingers made shaky by lack of sleep and tension. She spilled her first spoonful of coffee all over the counter and finally managed to get the machine working properly. By the time Michael came into the living room, she was sitting on the sofa, sipping a cup of very strong coffee. She looked up at him wearily.

He raked his fingers through his still-damp hair, the brown tendrils falling haphazardly onto his brow, giving him an appealingly boyish appearance. But there was nothing boyish or innocent about his anguish. "Please don't look at me like that," he begged contritely. "I'm sorry, I was furious, but I had no right to take it out on you like that."

Barrie returned his gaze with a thoughtful, unwavering look. "Maybe you did," she admitted at last. "Last night was important to you, wasn't it?"

"Of course it was important. I care about you. I've wanted to be with you for weeks now. Last night was just the way I knew it would be with us."

"Then I'm sorry if you thought I was demeaning it. I didn't mean to. It was special for me, too."

"Really?"

"Really." She paused, then added slowly, "But now I need some distance."

She looked up at him hopefully. "Can you try to understand that?"

He sighed, but nodded. "I can try, but you're not giving me many clues."

"I can't. I don't have it all straight in my head yet."

"Then I guess I'll have to wait."

"I'll call you later," she offered. "If you want me to."

"I want you to."

He gazed at her tenderly once again, the blue-green of his eyes shadowed with desire once more. "I'd better get out of here, or my noble promises won't be worth a hoot."

Barrie started to stand to walk him to the door. He waved her back.

"Don't move. I want to leave with the image of you curled up in the corner of the sofa like that. You look like a sleepy, contented cat."

"'Night, Michael."

"It's morning, love." He stood in the doorway for several long minutes, just staring at her, then smiled. "Sleep well."

After he had gone, Barrie opened the present that had

been left, forgotten, on the coffee table. It was a leather-bound copy of the script for the opening episode of *Goodbye, Again*. She clutched the thoughtful gift to her and tried to blink back her tears.

Michael's sensitivity, his touching generosity never ceased to surprise her. He was trying so hard to understand, but what he said was true. She wasn't giving him many clues, and he deserved them. It was even more than that. He deserved not just clues, but clear, straightforward answers.

She vowed to search her heart and find them for him.

For both of them.

Chapter 9

"What's he doing here?" Heath hissed as Barrie's front door swung open to admit Michael to the cast's already boisterous celebration of their premiere night.

"Shut up," Danielle muttered. "Barrie invited him."

"Nothing like bringing the enemy into the middle of your camp."

"Do you know a better way to disarm him?" she responded reasonably. "Besides, Barrie cares about him."

"Then she's crazier than I'd ever imagined," Heath snapped back. "The man's a… Oh, forget it. I'm going out on the patio."

"I think that's probably a good idea."

Barrie overheard the biting remarks, but she was too engrossed in greeting Michael to care much about the impact of his arrival on Heath and the others. She had known some of them wouldn't be overjoyed to have him here, but it was her party, and she wanted to see him, wanted to share this special night with him.

They had talked only a few times in the past week. Apparently he had taken her request for distance to heart and had given her all that she wanted. More, in fact. He hadn't called her once, waiting instead for her to call him. She'd never felt so lonely or abandoned in her life. After the decree she'd uttered only a few days earlier, she'd decided it was wiser not to try to figure out why she felt that way. As usual, though, Danielle had not been above offering a few pointed observations on the subject.

To Barrie's dismay, she was beginning to believe her friend might be right. At the very least, she had admitted to herself that she was clearly infatuated with Michael. Probably more than infatuated. Whatever label she stuck on it didn't really matter. The important thing was that she had decided to put aside her doubts, to open herself up to the possibilities of the relationship. No longer would she hold him at arm's length. Her newfound resolve gave a special warmth to her welcoming smile.

"I'm glad you came," she said, gazing up at him with brightly shining eyes no longer hidden behind glasses. Her new contacts had finally arrived, and she could actually see clearly just how spectacular he looked in his jeans and formfitting knit shirt.

Michael surveyed the gathering of hostile faces and grinned at her. "You're probably the only one."

"Ahh, but it's my party. I'm the only one who counts."

"You're the only one who counts with me, anyway."

"Let me get you a drink, and then you can mingle."

He feigned horror. "Mingle? With this crowd? They'll tear me to pieces. I thought you said you were glad to see me."

"I am. Very," she said softly, tucking her arm through his. "But I'm also the hostess. I have things to do."

"What things?"

She grinned at him and said airily, "Oh, you know. Hostessy things."

"Maybe I can help."

"Watch it, Mr. Compton," Danielle warned, coming up to wrap an arm around Barrie's waist. "She'll have you in the kitchen wearing a frilly apron and chopping up bits of disgusting raw chicken livers, if you're not careful."

"Chicken livers?" he repeated, eyeing Barrie skeptically. "Maybe I'll just stay here and talk to your talented director."

Barrie sniffed. "Oh, no you don't. You offered to help. Danielle abandoned me, just because I asked her to make a few little hors d'oeuvres."

"I did not sign on to touch that stuff," she said with an exaggerated shiver. "Ugh."

"You eat *that stuff*," Barrie reminded her.

"Of course. But that's after it's been wrapped around a water chestnut, surrounded by bacon and broiled beyond recognition. If I'd had any idea what it looked like in its natural state, I'd never have touched it."

Barrie laughed. "Okay, you win. You two enjoy yourselves. I'll do KP all by myself."

Michael and Danielle exchanged a significant look. "Does that sound like the wounded cry of a martyr to you?" he asked.

"Unfortunately, yes," she replied resignedly. "I suppose we both had better help, or we'll never hear the end of it."

The three of them worked side by side in the kitchen, finishing up the preparation of the appetizers and stirring the big pot of chili Barrie had made the day before. Michael kept adding chili powder whenever Barrie's back was turned. When she finally caught him at it and sampled the resulting spicy stew, her eyes watered, and she grabbed for a glass of ice water.

"What have you done?" she finally choked out between gulps of cooling liquid that did nothing to soothe her throat but pacified her need to do something.

"It needed a little oomph!" he informed her cheerfully. "Is it better now?"

"Better? It's lethal," she sputtered. "Do you realize that half those guests in there probably have ulcers already? This stuff will kill them."

Danielle dished up a spoonful and tasted it. "Umm," she said approvingly. "Barrie, what are you grumbling about? This is just right."

"Thank you," Michael said with exaggerated appreciation, then stared pointedly at Barrie. "See."

Barrie shuddered. "Okay, you two. I hold you responsible for calling the ambulances when those people start writhing on the floor."

"Don't mind her," Danielle told Michael airily. "She's always been a culinary wimp. In college she once complained to the cafeteria manager that the gravy was too spicy. Can you imagine ever calling that bland, awful glue too spicy?"

"That is not true, Danielle Lawrence."

"Well, it was something like that."

Danielle was not the least bit intimidated by Barrie's outraged protest. Her irreverent—and, according to Barrie, greatly exaggerated—tales of Barrie's college antics kept them all howling, until finally Heath and Melinda stuck their heads in the door to find out what was going on. They looked like two kids who were feeling left out of all the fun.

"Hey, you guys," Melinda said. "The party's out here.

You're not supposed to be enjoying yourselves over the drudgery."

"What drudgery?" Danielle asked with feigned perplexity. "I thought Barrie had come up with a new party game."

"In that case, who's winning?" Heath demanded.

"I think I am," Michael confessed. "I'm in here with two beautiful women all to myself."

"Maybe you should make it three," Melinda suggested with coy seductiveness.

"I think I'm in over my head with just the two of them, but what the heck," he responded gallantly. "Come on in."

"Actually I think you all should get out here," Heath interjected. "The show's coming on in just a couple of minutes."

In the living room everyone had gathered around the large-screen set by the time Barrie and Michael and the others came in. Barrie found a spot on the floor, and Michael sat right behind her. She leaned back against his chest, liking the comfort that broad, solid expanse offered her. One hand rested on his leg. His very muscular, very tempting leg. Her other hand kept creeping toward her mouth as she fought unsuccessfully against the temptation to bite her nails.

For the next half hour the group chuckled as they saw themselves on the air, laughing at Heath's clever dialogue and grinning as Melinda's Karen kept Mason decisively at arm's length, while taunting him with veiled promises. Barrie listened closely for Michael's laughter, cringed when it didn't come on cue, beamed with satisfaction when it did. As caught up as she was in the pride of creation, though, she knew there was something missing. It wasn't only Michael's tautness that told her that. She sensed it instinctively. There was a critical beat missing, some elusive ingredient that they would have to find if the characters were to blend perfectly.

At the end, when the others were congratulating each other, she gazed into Michael's face, saw the internal struggle he waged to find words that wouldn't hurt her, wouldn't hurt any of them.

"It was bad, wasn't it?" she asked softly, so the others couldn't hear.

"No." He shook his head. "It wasn't bad. The characters are good. The concept is good. The performances were great."

"But something's missing."

"Yes."

"Any idea what it is?"

"Nope. I can't quite put my finger on it."

"Neither can I."

He gave her a quick kiss. "Let's not worry about it tonight. Tonight we'll celebrate, and next week we'll take a look at the show more closely. I don't want us to throw a damper on your party."

From that moment on, it was as though *Goodbye, Again* hadn't even aired. Michael did his best to put the others guests at ease, to make them forget he was a network vice president. He showed them his warmth, his humor and, most of all, he was obvious about his deep affection for their producer. As protective as they all were of each other, that alone would have endeared him to them. By the end of the evening, Barrie noted, even Heath had mellowed.

"He hasn't called me a cretin once," Michael whispered triumphantly to Barrie when they were alone in the kitchen sipping cups of coffee.

She looked at him incredulously. "You knew he'd called you that?"

"Of course."

"Kevin, I suppose."

"A network executive never reveals his sources."

"I thought that was reporters."

"Them, too." He nuzzled her neck. "Do you suppose these friends of yours would be offended if I suggested it was time for them to leave?"

"Probably."

"What about if you told them?"

"Why would I want to do that?" she taunted impishly.

"So you can run your hands over my incredible thighs," he murmured with a wicked gleam in his eyes.

Barrie's mouth dropped open, and she flushed with embarrassment. "You know about that, too?"

He nodded.

"I think I'll order a closed set first thing Monday morning."

"Won't work," he told her seriously. "My spies are everywhere."

"Danielle again," she muttered in disgust. "What am I going to do with her?"

"Treasure her. She's a terrific friend."

"I'm not so sure."

"Who's a terrific friend?" the woman in question inquired tartly, sticking her head in the door.

"You are." Michael confirmed, just as Barrie responded "Nobody."

Danielle gazed from one to the other, her sharp eyes missing nothing. Barrie knew that she had witnessed their growing closeness, measured it and approved wholeheartedly. She also guessed she would connive to encourage it. Her next comment proved it.

"I just wanted to let you know that I've nudged everyone

else out of here," she announced proudly. "They all said thanks and good-night."

"See what I mean?" Michael murmured, nibbling on Barrie's ear. "She's a jewel."

"Notice that she hasn't left yet," Barrie reminded him significantly.

"I'm on my way. See you two on Monday," she said breezily. She winked at Michael. "Have a wonderful night."

"Goodbye, Danielle," Barrie said firmly.

"What about me?" Michael inquired when they were alone. "Do I go or stay?"

"What do you want to do?"

"You know the answer to that."

"Then I'd say you should follow your instincts."

The rest of the weekend passed in a wonderfully tender, sensual blur. It was a time for new discoveries, for more talk, long walks on the beach and passionate lovemaking. This time Barrie did not pull away afterward. Instead she hugged Michael to her and held on, delighting in this new-found excitement that rocked her senses, the tenderness that touched her heart, the matching of wits that brought them ever closer.

By Tuesday, though, the memory of those moments of mental and emotional intimacy had dimmed, replaced by new concerns over *Goodbye, Again*. When the ratings for the premiere came in during the week, Barrie felt shell-shocked as she stared at the national Neilsen numbers. She had anticipated problems because of the time slot but nothing like this.

Better to confront Michael about this head-on, she decided. She was just reaching for the phone to call him when it rang.

"Hello, dear. It's Mrs. Hastings. Mr. Compton would

like to see you, Mr. Donaldson and Miss Lawrence in his office."

"When?" Barrie asked with a sense of dread, wishing she'd had a chance to initiate the meeting on her own terms.

"As soon as you can get here."

"We're in the middle of a rehearsal."

"I know, dear, but I think he wants you here now, anyway." She paused, and Barrie thought she could hear Michael's voice in the background. When Mrs. Hastings came back on the line, she confirmed it. "He said immediately, Miss MacDonald."

Barrie sighed. "Okay. We'll be right there."

This was not going to be pleasant. If Michael hadn't even called her himself, he must be in quite a state of agitation. Whatever doubts he had had on Saturday night must have been solidified by the low ratings. Quickly she rounded up Heath and Danielle, and they walked across to the executive tower together. Barrie had a rough idea of what it must have felt like to walk to the guillotine.

"You don't suppose he'd cancel us after just a week," Danielle said, anticipating the worst.

"Of course not," Barrie said with far more conviction than she felt. "I'm sure he just wants to try to figure out some new game plan. Maybe he'll even see how right we were about the time period and move us."

"Don't hold your breath," Heath muttered, his defensiveness back in place.

Once they were in Michael's office, Barrie knew that her optimism had been unfounded. Michael's expression teetered somewhere between serious and ominous. To top it off, he hadn't even glanced in her direction, as though he found the idea of a direct confrontation with her over this too uncomfortable after all they had shared over the weekend.

"We have a problem," he announced without preamble.

Barrie took a deep breath and plunged in before he could go on. "Michael, I'm sure if we just give the show a little promotional push, it will begin picking up," she said with bravado. "I've already talked to the PR department, and they're going to set up some interviews for Melinda. On-air promotion says they'll get some spots on during football. That's always good exposure for a new series."

"That's all great, but it's not the answer."

"And I suppose you have one," Heath murmured belligerently. "Are we back to that blasted sheepdog again?"

Michael chuckled. "No, no sheepdog. But I think we are going to have to make some changes in the show, do a little fine-tuning with the characters." When Danielle started to interrupt, he shook his head. "Nothing drastic," he said soothingly.

For the next few minutes he outlined possibilities and asked for their input. For the most part, Barrie found little to disagree with. His comments were incisive and proved that he not only understood what they were trying to do, but that he knew the audience, as well. Heath and Danielle at least seemed relieved by the tone of the conversation. Barrie wasn't quite so certain. She had a feeling the worst was yet to come.

"Now let's talk about Karen," he said at last.

"Karen!" Barrie's voice rose as though the falling ax had just made contact with her neck for the first time. "Karen is just fine."

"No, she isn't," he said adamantly. "She needs to be softer, more vulnerable."

"Forget it," she retorted equally adamantly. "We're not changing Karen."

"Do you want the show to stay on the air?" he asked bluntly.

Barrie blinked and stared at him in amazement. "You would kill this show if I don't agree to let you change Karen's character?"

"Karen is central to *Goodbye, Again*," he said. "Would you agree with that?"

"Of course."

"Then fixing her is critical to making the show work. Without the changes I'm suggesting, you have nothing. You, not I, will be killing the show."

Barrie sank back in her chair in temporary defeat. "What did you want to do?"

"I told you. Make her more vulnerable. I want the audience to care about her. The way she is now, she's too glib, too sophisticated and certain of herself. That must be toned down to make her more appealing."

Suddenly Barrie couldn't take another word, another criticism of the woman who was her own alter ego. She was on her feet, her brown eyes flashing sparks. "Do you think I'm too tough? Too independent?" she demanded, as Danielle murmured a hasty excuse, urged Heath to his feet and practically dragged him out of the room. Barrie wasn't sure whether to bless or curse her for leaving her to deal with Michael alone.

"Of course I don't think you're too tough," Michael responded, clearly perplexed. "What does that have to do with anything?"

"Am I loveable?"

"Don't be absurd. You know how I feel about you. I

find your strength, your spunk very appealing. How did we switch from Karen to you?"

"I am Karen. This show is all about me. You know that. You even said it yourself."

"Barrie!"

"No, wait. Every time you chip away at it, every time you want to change something, it's as though you're stripping away a little more of me."

"Is that what all the defensiveness has been about? You think I've been criticizing you?"

"Well, haven't you? You were the one who cut that scene in the premiere because it didn't match what was happening with us. You obviously compared me with Karen yourself."

"I compared the situation and, yes, I suppose I realized that you and Karen had certain similarites. But I had no idea that you identified with her so strongly. I certainly didn't think you'd be so subjective about a character that you'd think I was attacking you."

"Would knowing that have made any difference?"

"In my decisions? No," he said honestly. "But I would have handled this better. I would have tried to make it clear that my comments were not personal in any way, that I was only trying to make the show work."

He sighed deeply. "Sweetheart, we may not always agree on what's best for the show or what an audience will accept at eight o'clock, but that's only a difference of opinion. It's certainly not a reflection of my feelings for you, any more than it would be if I preferred red wine and you preferred white."

"I do prefer white."

A soft smile curved his lips. "I can live with that," he said lightly. His voice became huskier. "In fact, I would like to live with you."

Barrie's mouth fell open. "You can't be serious."

"Of course I'm serious."

"You picked a very strange time to suggest that sort of a step for us."

"I've been thinking about it for weeks now. Hell, I've been thinking about it since the day we met."

"Do you actually think I would live with you when you're in the process of carving my future to bits?"

"Barrie, don't you understand yet? That's professional, not personal."

"Then I guess I'm just not all that liberated. I don't see how you can separate the two."

To her utter chagrin, his blue-green eyes were sparkling with amusement. "Karen could," he suggested pointedly.

"Well, I'm not Karen," she flashed back.

"That's not what you said a minute ago."

Barrie felt as though her world were suddenly spinning crazily. "You...you... Oh, why don't you just get out of here?"

"It's my office," he countered, infuriating her with his low chuckle and damnable logic.

"Then I'll go."

He shrugged. "If you must," he taunted. "Just think about what I said."

"I will not live with you, and I will not change Karen," she repeated firmly. "Not in a million years."

As she flounced out of the office, she heard him murmur softly, "We'll see."

Chapter 10

Barrie spent the next couple of days thinking about Michael's taunting comment. He was right. Karen would live with someone if she cared about him as deeply as Barrie was beginning to realize that she cared about Michael. She would accept the relationship for what it was, rejoice in it for however long it lasted, then blithely say goodbye again when it was over. Thanks and no hard feelings. Wasn't that the way modern relationships ended?

When Barrie had developed that easygoing style for Karen, it had seemed so simple and straightforward. It had been based on her own background of honesty and a complete lack of guile, as well as her ability to recognize clearly her own motives and needs and to act on them without any thought of the future. Apparently she had not allowed for the complexity of emotions that surfaced in a relationship of any depth. Certainly, she had not considered the possibility that any opening of the heart, any prolonged contact with a man of substance and sensitivity such as Michael, would create a natural vulnerability.

Based on her own past experience, she had thought a wise contemporary woman could remain aloof and uninvolved even in the most intimate relationship. She realized now what a short-sighted fool she had been! The men she'd known before had made it easy to stay objective and cool, had encouraged it, in fact. But they weren't at all like Michael. They had lacked his depth and certainly had lacked his desire for more serious involvement.

What now? she asked herself more than once. There was no point in denying that she was deeply involved with Michael, more than she had ever been with any other man. But how did he really feel about her? He never said that he loved her, only that he wanted to live with her. Was that enough? According to the standards she'd set for Karen, yes. But what about for her, especially now that she knew she was falling in love with him?

The more she thought about it, the more she realized that the only answer seemed to be to go along with his suggestion, to live with him and see what happened. Hadn't she just resolved to follow the relationship wherever it led? Was she ready to forget that resolution so quickly?

After all, despite her doubts, perhaps they could make it work. They could even discover their true feelings together. As Danielle had noted, Michael was everything she had ever claimed to want in a man. She hadn't often allowed herself to dream of an ideal mate, convinced that such dreams were futile. But during those sleepy late-night conversations she and Danielle had shared in college, she'd been pressed into describing someone who, in retrospect, had sounded very much like Michael. Strong, secure in his sense of himself, supportive, sensitive and funny. Now that she'd found someone like that, did she dare to risk losing him through her own indecision?

The answer was an emphatic no!

Bravely she picked up the phone and dialed Michael's office. "Okay, hotshot," she announced before her confidence could waver. "Let's give it a try."

"Give what a try? The changes?"

"No. Living together."

Michael practically choked, which was not exactly the delighted reaction she'd counted on to reassure her that she'd made the right decision. It was not particularly heart-warming, either. She'd envisioned his eyes darkening with passion as he murmured something like "Oh, darling, you'll never regret this. We'll be happy together. I promise."

Instead he was saying lightly, "Excuse me, are you sure you have the right number? This is the office of Michael Compton, vice president for programming."

She winced. "Don't rub it in."

The teasing didn't let up. "Who is this?" he inquired, his voice filled with exaggerated puzzlement. "I recognize the voice, but the remark seems strangely out of character."

"Cute."

"Is this the woman who only a few short days ago told me to take a flying leap off a Malibu cliff when I suggested this very same thing?"

"I never said any such thing," she retorted defensively, miffed by his thoroughly unromantic attitude. He was making fun of her, treating the most momentous decision of her life as a big joke.

"Maybe not precisely, but words to that effect."

"So I've had a change of heart. I'm entitled," she said stiffly, wondering why she was even bothering to try to convince him of her sincerity. If he weren't interested any longer, her pride told her she ought to forget it, as well. But she couldn't do that now. Not without a fight.

"And you think we should live together?" he was saying with slow deliberation, as though allowing her time to reconsider.

With her heart thundering against her ribs, Barrie ignored his skeptical response to her overture and replied firmly, "Yes."

The word seemed to hang in the midst of a very deadly silence.

"Sorry, angel," he said at last. "I don't fool around."

Suddenly the ground seemed to drop out from beneath her, and her resolve crumbled. This bland disinterest was the last thing she had anticipated. Where on earth had it come from? Only a few short days ago the man had been practically begging her to make a stronger commitment to him. Now, when she'd swallowed her pride, called him and announced that she had come around to his point of view, he was acting as though she were the one trying to convince him.

"What do you mean?" she snapped with what she thought was perfectly justifiable anger. "Who's playing games now? This was your idea."

"True," he admitted. "But just like you, I've had second thoughts."

"Why?"

"Let's just say your turnaround seems a bit too sudden. I'm not convinced it's what you really want. I have a feeling you think it's something you should do, just to prove a point."

"And what point would that be?"

"That you're as liberated as Karen."

Barrie paled at the possibly accurate and distinctly uncomfortable charge but replied slowly, "I don't have to prove a thing to you."

"Certainly not that," he agreed. "Maybe you're trying to prove something to yourself. Why don't we get together tonight and discuss this again when we have more time?"

"You know very well that I have a taping tonight."

"Maybe I can get a ticket," he suggested dryly. Barrie could just imagine the smug, teasing glint in his blue-green eyes. The image made her go weak in the knees. If the mere thought of him could do that, it was no wonder his real-life presence had made her abandon all good sense. Good Lord, had she actually considered moving in with the impossible man? Clearly her mind had been warped by the stress of getting her first series on the air. She should have thrown herself onto the couch of a shrink, instead of into the arms of a thoroughly egotistical network executive. She should be grateful that he'd dismissed her surrender so easily.

She sighed. So why didn't she feel grateful? Why did she feel betrayed and lonely? She wasn't at all sure she wanted to know the answer to those questions. Had she been counting on living with Michael even more than she'd realized?

Despite the perversity of those feelings, she mustered her most casual tone and replied, "Give it your best shot, Compton, but I hear we're booked up."

"No problem. I'll stand backstage."

"You do, and I'll wrap an electrical cord around your neck."

"Why?" he asked innocently. "Will my presence make you nervous?"

"Of course not," she lied boldly. He was the last person on earth she wanted to see tonight, but she'd be damned if she'd admit that to him. "But we do have a rule about outsiders being backstage, and I don't intend to break it for you."

"I'm hardly an outsider," he reminded her tartly. "I'll see you tonight."

Predictably enough, considering the way the day had started, the evening turned into an absolute disaster. Michael arrived just as they discovered that too many tickets had been given out for the taping. A crowd of angry tourists was lined up outside the studio. Barrie was afraid they'd storm the door right in the middle of the show.

To top it off, once the show began, the cast performed as though they'd never had a minute's rehearsal. Melinda's timing was awful. Some of the actors were forgetting their lines, leaving the others to flounder helplessly. As a result, the studio audience was not laughing in the right places, which had Heath pacing frantically around backstage, muttering dire threats against each and every member of the cast.

When the sound system broke down, delaying the taping for over an hour, Barrie felt like abandoning the entire production and hiding in her office. Instead, torn between humiliation that Michael had been a witness to all this chaos and confusion and her very real need to have his admiration, she tried to maintain a cool, competent facade as she set out to deal with each crisis.

But before she could take control, in each instance Michael was one step ahead of her, promising the tourists tickets for another taping, calming the cast, bolstering Heath's spirits, even rolling up his sleeves and working alongside the technicians on the sound system. Barrie began to feel helpless and unnecessary. The more useless she felt, the angrier she got.

"Compton, get off my set," she finally said in a low, measured tone that was filled with barely controlled fury. His eyes widened as he looked up at her in astonishment from his place amid the cables that crisscrossed the floor. A hush fell over the backstage area.

"What's wrong?"

"You're doing it again," she snapped.

"Doing what again?" he said blankly.

"Taking over."

"I'm just trying to help," he protested.

"I don't need your help, at least not this kind. I need you just to be nice to me, to be supportive. Can't you pretend for a few minutes that you don't know a thing about television? Just pat me on the head and tell me everything will be okay, that I can handle it, instead of treating me like some kind of incompetent imbecile who's incapable of dealing with stress or running her own show."

"Is that what I was doing?"

"Of course it is. The minute things started falling apart tonight, you didn't wait to see if I could manage, you just jumped right in and started giving orders."

Michael took a deep breath, his expression thoroughly abashed. "I thought I was pitching in to help, but I can see how it might not seem that way to you," he said apologetically. "I'm sorry if you thought I was being patronizing."

Barrie sighed and ran her fingers through her hair. "No," she said at last, "I'm the one who's sorry. I know you're just trying to help. I'm being overly sensitive. I didn't want you to see things unless they were perfect. And tonight was far from perfect."

"Nothing ever goes as smoothly as a producer would like it to," he consoled her.

"Maybe not," she said wryly. "But I think tonight was a bit beyond the norm."

"You could have handled it if I'd stayed out of your way."

She grinned at him impudently. "I know I could."

"From now on, if you'd prefer, I'll stay away from the tapings."

"Promise?"

He gave her his most beguiling smile, and her heart flipped over. "Well, I might just peek in occasionally..."

"Michael!"

"I won't stay. I promise. You can handle each and every crisis on your own without any interference from me. Write that on a piece of paper, and I'll sign it in blood."

The tension finally broke, and she laughed at his solemn oath. "You don't have to go that far. I trust you."

"I'm glad," he said, gathering her into his arms and holding her tightly. He whispered into her ear, "Now what was it you were saying about wanting someone's shoulder to lean on?"

"Not here," she murmured as his hands caressed her back, sending a shiver of sparks cascading down her spine.

"Why not?"

"We do have a taping to finish," she reminded him. "This delay is going to drive production costs up."

His hands fell away from her immediately. She grinned up at him. "I thought that might get to you."

"Later?" he suggested.

"Later."

It was three hours before the taping finally ended, and by then Barrie was completely drained. Michael had been true to his word and had stayed out of the way for the remainder of the taping, but, perversely, there had been times when she wished he'd ignored her earlier warning and taken charge. By ten o'clock she was awfully tired of being competent and independent.

"You all set?" Michael asked when he found her sitting on the audience bleachers staring at the set.

"Almost."

He followed the direction of her gaze. "What's wrong?"

"There was something odd about the set tonight. Melinda kept bumping into things. I can't figure it out, I'm sure this is the way it was last week."

"No, it's not."

Barrie looked at him in surprise. "It's not?"

"Nope. You've moved the sofa off-center. It looks better, but it's not as easy for her to walk around it where it is now. The aisle's too narrow, and the desk gets in the way."

He walked onto the set and nudged the sofa about two feet to the left. "That's the way it was before."

"You're amazing."

He beamed at her. "That's me."

"Remind me never to try to sneak something out of your office. You probably know down to a tenth of an inch where each piece of paper is."

"I remember the symmetry, but I don't always recall the content."

"That's reassuring. I'll just have to replace what I take with another piece of paper."

"You sound as though you're planning a burglary in the near future. Wouldn't it be easier to ask for whatever you want?"

"Not in this case."

"Why not?"

She hesitated, then finally admitted in a rush, "I want those notes you made the other day on Karen."

He chuckled. "I think I see why you didn't want to ask. Are you ready to make the changes?"

"Let's just say I'm beginning to agree that there's room for some modification. She seemed a little strident tonight. I thought Heath and I could take another look at her."

He sat on the bleacher next to her and cupped her chin in his hand. "Thank you," he said softly. "I know how hard it was for you to admit that."

"I'm not promising we'll make any changes," she countered quickly. "Just that I want to go over what you had in mind again."

"That's a start." He leaned forward and kissed her, a hungry, urgent kiss that drew her into his arms and left her wanting more as her blood roared in her veins.

"That was quite a start, too," she murmured with a sigh. She grinned at him impishly. "You're turning into quite a tease, Michael Compton."

"Me? A tease?" he squawked indignantly.

"Yes, you. First you back out on living together. Then twice in one night you start something you apparently have no intention of finishing."

"Who says?"

"Well, then?"

"You mean now? Here?"

He was examining the hard bleacher warily. "I suppose it's possible."

"Oh, I think we can do better than this. Come with me."

"But my car is here. I'll follow you."

"No way. Your car will be here in the morning. The guards wouldn't dare let anyone steal it."

"Okay," he finally agreed enthusiastically, apparently determining that the wicked gleam in her eyes could only work in his favor. "Lead on, Miss MacDonald. I'm all yours."

"I wish," she murmured under her breath as they got into her car.

"What's that?"

"Never mind."

Barrie had always enjoyed driving as long as she wasn't competing with a bumper-to-bumper collection of maniacs, and at this hour the road was relatively free of traffic. As she zipped west toward the beach, she and Michael chatted easily about everything but television. Despite the casual, innocuous conversation, however, she didn't let him forget for a minute that she had something far more intimate on her mind. Each time she shifted gears, she allowed her hand to caress his inner thigh or left it resting gently on his knee, her fingers seeking an interesting little erogenous zone she'd discovered along the curve of his muscle.

After one of these none-too-casual assaults, Michael moaned softly, and she glanced over to find him leaning back in his seat with his eyes closed and a satisfied smile on his lips. She took her hand away.

"Uh-uh," he protested, grabbing it and putting it back, this time a little higher. Her pulse pounded. Her little game was getting out of hand. If she wasn't careful, they'd end up trying to make love in a gas station parking lot with a gear shift poking in her ribs. Somehow there was no romance in that particular image.

This time when she staged a more forceful retreat, he let her go, but she could tell from the grin tugging at his lips that he knew he'd gotten to her just as effectively as she'd stirred him. When she pulled the car to a stop and switched off the engine, he opened his eyes and peered outside.

"Where are we?"

Barrie shook her head. "For a man who only a short time ago could tell that a sofa was slightly out of place, you seem to have lost your powers of observation. That is the Pacific Ocean."

"I recognized that much."

"Well, then?"

"I suppose a more appropriate question might be: What are we doing here?"

She leaned over and brushed a tantalizing kiss across his lips, and her fingers nestled in the warm curve where thigh and hip met. "What do you think?"

Michael's eyes widened. "Here?"

"It's softer than the bleachers."

"It is also sandy."

"I have a blanket in the trunk."

"Were you planning this, or do you come here often?"

"I come here quite a bit."

"Like hell, you do," he growled.

"Alone, Compton. Alone," she said soothingly. "It's a good place to sit and think."

"Oh."

They took the blanket into a secluded cove and spread it out. While Michael stretched out, Barrie stood over him, bathed in moonlight, and slowly removed her clothes. As each item was discarded, his breathing grew increasingly ragged. When she'd tossed aside the last item, her lacy bikini panties, Michael reached for her, but she stepped just beyond his reach.

"Last one in has to fix breakfast," she taunted, racing for the water.

"Why you..." Michael sputtered as he tried to pull off his clothes while chasing after her. His pants tangled around his legs, and he fell, sprawling, into the sand. By then she was already waist deep in the water, laughing at his expression of pure frustration.

He stripped off the rest of his clothes then and stood, and suddenly the laughter died on her lips. With soft moonlight bathing him in a silvery glow, he looked like some sort of an impressive god standing on the shore, his athletic body trim, firm and very, very masculine.

"If I have to come in after you, you are in a lot of trouble, Barrie MacDonald," he warned in a low, provocative voice that sent a shiver racing through her.

"I'm not afraid of you," she retorted bravely, though with each step he took toward her, her racing pulse told her she ought to be. When he dove into the silver-highlighted darkness of the midnight sea and disappeared from view, she tried to gauge his approach to elude him. But it was impossible, and she knew it. She gasped when his hands glided up her legs, circled her waist and then brushed upward.

"Barrie MacDonald, I want you," he murmured in a husky growl that inflamed her, "I want to make love to you, to feel you come alive to my touch."

With great urgency and tenderness he scooped her up into his powerful arms and carried her to the blanket. Lowering her gently, he knelt poised over her, and Barrie felt a growing tension in her abdomen. Her body was ready for him, needed him. She held her arms up to him.

"Love me," she pleaded urgently. "Now."

He shook his head. "Not yet. We have all night."

His touches began then with her face. Gentle lips were followed by caressing fingers that teased and taunted until her skin seemed on fire. There was no part of her that did not receive his loving adoration, not one square inch of her flesh that had not felt the moistness of his tongue, the gentleness of his hands.

"Please," she murmured, her body arching toward him, seeking the fulfillment he withheld.

The unbearable intensity of the experience left them both breathless and seemingly speechless. They were wrapped in each other's arms, and it was a long time before Barrie finally murmured softly, plaintively, "Michael, what do you want from me? What is it you really want?"

He sighed deeply and held her tighter.

"Sweetheart, I don't have an answer to that," he confessed honestly. "At least not the definitive kind you're looking for. I know that I need you, that I care about you. You've brought something into my life that I hadn't even known I was missing. I just know that now that I've found it, I can't do without it. You are so special to me. You're warm and intelligent and feisty. You're incredibly sexy. Yet there's a vulnerability about you that makes me want to protect you. I want you with me, where I can keep an eye on you. I need you."

Want. Need. Barrie listened to Michael's words, tried to hear what he wasn't saying, as much as what he was. As much as she yearned to hear it, he wasn't saying he was in love with her. A couple of months ago that wouldn't have mattered to her. Moments such as those they had just shared would have been more than enough.

With each day that had passed, however, she had fallen more deeply, more hopelessly in love with him. Admitting that finally had been such a relief. Overcoming all those years of fearing heartbreak hadn't been easy. In fact, she doubted that a lesser man than Michael could have brought her to this point, and she was grateful to him for forcing her out of her emotional hiding place.

But now she desperately wanted his love in return. She sighed and curved her body into his, listening to the reassuring beat of his heart. Surely a love to match hers was there. He had only to find it.

Now she was the one who would have to wait patiently. And hope.

Chapter 11

A week later, Barrie and Michael were sitting across from each other at her desk, eating the take-out Chinese food he had brought over for lunch, when the phone rang. She wrinkled her nose in disgust at the intrusion.

"Not again," she moaned. "You're going to eat every bit of this fried rice before I get my first grain, if this blasted phone doesn't calm down."

"You could ignore it," he suggested, scooping more rice out of the container with exaggerated glee. "You know it's not your boss or your lover."

"Who says?" she countered wickedly as she picked up the phone and said in a pointedly low, seductive tone, "Barrie MacDonald."

"Hey, sweetheart, how've you been?"

She immediately recognized the voice of Jeff Taylor, a sweet, intelligent attorney with whom she'd spent several pleasant but unexciting evenings. She grinned to herself.

Perfect. She would teach Michael Compton a thing or two about smug overconfidence!

"Jeff, sweetheart, how are you?" she said enthusiastically, noting that Michael's brows lifted quizzically, and his interest in the conversation seemed to pick up dramatically at the mention of a male's name. His chopsticks were poised midway to his mouth, and the shrimp and rice were dribbling back unnoticed onto his plate. She practically groaned out loud. Men! What predictable, territorial creatures they were.

"I'm terrific. I've been away on business for the past month."

"Really. Anyplace interesting?"

"Hawaii. One of my clients was having some problems with his properties over there."

"Nice work, if you can get it. I wouldn't mind being sent to Hawaii on business," she said, looking pointedly at Michael. He made a face at her.

"Now that I'm back, I thought maybe we could get together. I have tickets for a play tomorrow night. Are you free?"

Barrie had expected such an invitation from the moment she recognized Jeff's voice. She'd certainly known that he wasn't calling to chat about the weather or his trip to Hawaii. Still, she had no idea how to answer him. Certainly she was free enough. Michael hadn't made any plans with her for tomorrow or the rest of the weekend. He rarely planned much in advance for their evenings together, seeming to take it for granted that she would be available. Nor had they made any commitments to see each other exclusively since their disastrous discussion about living together.

So why was she hesitating? Only because he was sitting

right there in front of her? No. She'd be torn by indecision even if he were well out of sight.

Common sense told her there was absolutely no reason to turn down a date with another attractive man. Her gut told her she'd have a lousy time and that she'd spend the whole evening comparing Jeff with Michael, to the attorney's tremendous disadvantage. Common sense and his current reaction to a mere phone call told her it might do Michael even more good to realize he was not the only man in her life interested in taking her out. Her gut told her it would be a game, and it was childish to start playing it now.

"Barrie? Are you still there?"

"Sorry. I'm here, Jeff. I was just checking my calendar." She flipped the page over and looked at the vast emptiness on Saturday and Sunday.

Michael was no longer even making a pretense of eating, and he was scowling at her with an expression that would have kept even Romeo and Juliet apart. She ignored him and debated her response.

"And?" Jeff said hopefully. "Don't say no, Barrie. I've really missed you."

The sincerity in his voice, more than anything else, clinched it. It would hardly be fair to go out with a man who'd just admitted to missing her, when she hadn't given him a thought since their last date over a month ago.

"I wish I could go, Jeff, but I'm busy," she said at last. To her amazement, Michael breathed what sounded like a sigh of relief at her polite rejection.

"Another time, then."

"Sure. Another time," she said, knowing that that time would never come. "You take care, Jeff. It was good to hear from you."

"Who was that?" Michael growled before she could even put the receiver back into place.

"A friend."

"Were you serious about him?"

"Why do you put that in the past tense?"

"Because I assume you're no longer serious about him."

"Don't assume anything, Mr. Compton," she taunted. "It makes one too complacent."

"Very cute," he muttered as he glanced at his watch and jumped to his feet. "I'm late."

So much for concern about his competition. It seemed to have vanished in a puff of renewed self-confidence. Barrie glared at him and wished she'd kept him dangling a little longer. She sighed. It was too late now. He had already surmised that the faceless Jeff was not important in her life.

"See you later," he announced casually.

"Oh, really?" she asked innocently, hoping to stir some new doubts. The man was definitely getting to be too sure of himself. She glanced pointedly down at the blank page of her calendar again. "Did we have plans?"

"We do now," he said, kissing her thoroughly before rushing out the door. On his way out he practically crashed into Heath and Danielle, who were so embroiled in yet another heated argument about the latest script for *Goodbye, Again* that they barely acknowledged him.

"What's the problem this time?" Barrie asked them resignedly, picking hungrily at the little mound of fried rice not ravaged by Michael.

"I say Karen should go out with another man, even though she's involved with Mason," Heath explained.

Barrie's head jerked up as she was struck by the strangest sense of déjà vu. The show was mirroring her life again.

"I mean, why not?" Heath continued, glowering at Danielle. "There's no commitment. She hadn't made any promises to him, and this other guy is pursuing her."

"Is she attracted to him?" Barrie asked curiously, wondering if her lack of interest in Jeff Taylor physically had played a role in her refusal of his invitation.

"The guy is a hunk. Of course she's attracted to him. That's what it's all about."

"But is that kind of attraction alone enough for her to risk hurting Mason?" Danielle demanded skeptically. "I don't think so. It makes her seem shallow and callous."

"No. It just shows she has a strong sense of her own sexual needs. She'd think Mason could—or should—take it, just the way women have been accepting it for years that unless they're married to a guy, he's got the right to roam."

Danielle turned to Barrie for support. "What do you think?"

"I don't know," Barrie admitted finally. "A month ago I'd have said let her go. Mason can stand up for himself. But now it seems wrong." Just as it had seemed wrong to her only moments ago to accept a date with Jeff Taylor simply to make Michael jealous. She appealed to Danielle, tears glistening in her eyes. "What's happening to me?"

Danielle's face was instantly full of concern. "Sweetie, it's just a television show. Why are you so upset?"

Before she could explain, she realized that Heath was staring at her as though she'd betrayed him. "I thought you were the liberated woman, just like Karen. What's good for the goose is good for the gander, and all that sort of thing."

"Your sense of timing is lousy, Donaldson," Danielle growled. "Can't you see that? Get out of here."

"But we haven't settled this."

"We'll settle it later."

When he had gone, Barrie admitted to Danielle that

her own emotional turmoil was forcing her to rethink the character she'd created, as well. The Karen she'd created wouldn't have thought twice about dating a whole string of men, even if one of them happened to care very deeply for her and she for him. There would have been emotional safety in a crowd, protection from a commitment that could go painfully awry.

"But I can't play it safe that way anymore," she confessed. "It wouldn't do any good, anyway. I'm in love with Michael."

Danielle raised her hands in a victory gesture. "At last," she said triumphantly. "Are you going to marry him?"

Barrie quirked a brow. "Who said anything about marriage? He won't even live with me, and he's certainly not in love with me."

"Oh, posh-tosh. Who says?"

"I do. I practically asked him point-blank, and he avoided using those words as if they were missing from his vocabulary. He said everything else but that. He cares. He wants me. He needs me. But love? Forget it."

"Honey, I've seen the look in that man's eyes. He's not about to let you get away, and I don't think he'll settle for anything less than marriage, no matter what he does or doesn't say. Give him some time." She grinned at Barrie. "Don't you think those incredible thighs are worth waiting for?"

"I'm more interested in his mind."

"Uh-huh. Of course you are," Danielle said dryly.

"A man's legs are not a great basis for a marriage."

"Maybe," Danielle retorted without conviction. "Think of it this way, then. You'll never have to explain to him what a demographic is or how a rating is determined, *and* he has great thighs. Where would you ever find another man with those credentials?"

Barrie winced. "Don't even mention ratings. Every time I look at ours, I get this sick feeling in the pit of my stomach."

"They'll get better."

"And if they don't?"

"If they don't, you can just remind yourself that it was *Goodbye, Again* that brought you and Michael together."

"It may be the thing that drives us apart, too," she countered candidly.

"I love your optimism."

"I'm just trying to be realistic."

"The reality is that Michael Compton is crazy about you, and I refuse to listen to any more of your silly doubts."

"I thought that's what I paid you for."

"No. You pay me to direct a television show. Being your friend is something I do out of the goodness of my heart and because of my insatiable curiosity."

"Curiosity?"

"Of course. Ever since I realized you intended to set the world on its ear, I've wanted to stick around and see how it turned out."

"How am I doing so far?"

"You're getting better every day. Now plan something spectacular for tonight, something dear old Michael won't be able to resist."

"Any idea what that might be?"

Danielle feigned shock. "My dear, I don't know the man *that* well." She winked at her. "But you sure do."

When Danielle had gone, Barrie tried to think of something wildly romantic and impetuous that would set Michael Compton on his ear. She ticked off every fantasy she'd ever had, every tale she'd heard of other crazy, fun-filled flings. When the perfect idea finally struck her, she couldn't wait to put her plan into action. She made several phone calls, had a hurried conference with Danielle about that night's taping, then raced out of the studio to take care of several errands. At four-thirty she walked into Michael's office unannounced.

His head was bent over the papers on his desk, and a frown of concentration knit his brows. He was so engrossed in his work, that he didn't even glance up at her entrance. She cleared her throat loudly.

"Just put them over there," he muttered without looking up.

"Put what over where?"

His head came up then, and he stared at her in surprise. A slow, sensual smile transformed his face. Barrie smiled back. So far, so good. He hadn't tossed her out on her ear.

"Busy?" she asked, perching on the edge of his desk.

"Not too busy to see you. What's up? Has something happened since I saw you at lunch?"

"Can you take a break?"

He dropped his pencil and leaned back. "Sure. I'm all yours."

"Good. Come with me."

He shook his head. "I said I could take a break. I didn't mean I could get away from the office."

"Sure you can," Barrie countered confidently.

"I have appointments yet this afternoon."

"Not anymore."

He stared at her blankly. "What do you mean?"

"I mean they've been cancelled."

"Who cancelled them?"

"I did."

His expression altered to one of shocked disbelief. "Barrie, how could you do that? They were important."

"Not as important as what I have in mind. I checked with Mrs. Hastings just to be sure," she said firmly. "Now get your jacket and come on."

He sighed and relented finally. "When you get that determined little gleam in your eye, I suppose it's pointless for me to refuse."

"Do you really want to?"

He looked from her to Mrs. Hastings, who was standing in the doorway beaming at the two of them with maternalistic satisfaction.

"You're involved in this conspiracy, aren't you? You know what's going on?" he demanded of her.

"Yes, sir," she replied dutifully.

"Would you mind telling me?"

She grinned at Barrie, then looked back at him with an expression of pure innocence. "Sorry. I've been sworn to secrecy."

"But you're my secretary," he reminded her, then added pointedly, "For now."

"I am also a woman who loves surprises," she retorted tartly. "And don't you go threatening me, young man. I was here before you came, and I daresay I'll be here after you're gone. Now you just run along and have a good time. Don't be such a stuffed shirt."

"Stuffed shirt?" Michael's eyes widened, and he shot Barrie an accusing glance. "Are you proud of yourself? It's your fault that my secretary called me a stuffed shirt."

"And well she should," Barrie commented dryly. "I've never seen a grown man so terrified of a little surprise."

"The last time someone tried to surprise me I walked into a room filled with 300 of my nearest and dearest friends, all of whom had been celebrating so long before my arrival that they barely noticed me."

"That must have been a blow to your ego," Barrie commented, grinning at him.

"If it will help, I guarantee you that I'll notice you," she promised seductively. "In fact, I won't take my eyes off you."

He threw up his hands in a gesture of surrender. "Okay. When you put it like that, I don't dare refuse. Lead on."

Outside, Michael's limousine was waiting with the driver standing smartly at attention.

"What's he doing here?"

"It's part of the surprise."

"You ordered my limousine?"

Barrie shook her head. "Of course not," she denied indignantly. "Mrs. Hastings did."

"Thank goodness," he chuckled. "I see. Is there any point in my asking where we're going?"

"None."

"I don't like this," he said as they entered the limo.

"You don't like not being in control. Relax."

"I'm virtually kidnapped out of my own office in the middle of the afternoon, and you tell me to relax. You're the kidnapper. Why should I trust you?"

"Because I'm entirely trustworthy."

"That remains to be seen."

Barrie reached into her purse and extracted a white scarf. Michael eyed her doubtfully.

"What's that?"

"A scarf."

"I know that. What's it for?"

Barrie took a deep breath. This was going to be the hard

part. She groaned. Who was she kidding? It might very well be the impossible part.

"It's a blindfold," she offered casually.

Before she'd completed the sentence, Michael was already shaking his head. Decisively. "Uh-uh. No way. I draw the line at blindfolds."

"Michael," she said sweetly, curving herself into his side and running her fingers down his chest. She could feel his heartbeat speed up. "Remember how much fun we had when you talked me into getting onto the swing?"

He eyed her warily. "What does that have to do with anything?"

"Remember how pleased you were that I was willing to take a risk on that?"

"Yes," he said slowly, his eyes narrowing distrustfully. "But I am not wearing that blindfold," he repeated adamantly.

Barrie stared directly into his eyes and waited. Their gazes locked, held. "Please."

Michael moaned. "Barrie," he pleaded.

"Michael." Her tone was soft, cajoling.

"Oh, okay. Give me the damn thing."

She smiled at him brightly. "Thank you."

As soon as the blindfold was in place, she reached back into her purse. "Now, hold still a minute."

"What the hell are you doing now?"

"Ear plugs."

"What!" Michael's shout reverberated through the limousine, and Barrie noted that the driver's glance in the rearview mirror was thoroughly amused. "Forget it!"

"Please, Michael. Don't spoil my surprise."

"Dear Lord, woman, what are you up to?"

"It's just for a little while. I promise."

When the earplugs were in place, Barrie sat back in satisfaction and held tightly onto Michael's hand. Her grip was intended to keep him from ripping off the blindfold and tearing out the earplugs even more than it was to feel the warmth of his touch. She had a feeling his compliance with her odd demands would be very short-lived. Fortunately she only needed another half hour or so.

They completed the ride in silence, and when the car stopped, Michael immediately reached for the blindfold with his free hand. Barrie nabbed his hand in the nick of time and removed one ear plug.

"Not yet," she said and quickly put the plug back in place.

With the assistance of the driver, she led Michael from the car, across the pavement and up a long flight of stairs, ignoring his angry mutterings and the amused grins of everyone they passed. When they reached their destination, she pushed him down into a seat, thanked the driver and sat down next to him. By now he was thoroughly docile, though she had a feeling that at any minute he would rise up and rebel. When she heard the engines roar to life, she breathed a sigh of relief.

And when the plane began taxiing down the runway, she reached over and removed the ear plugs and blindfold.

"Where the hell are we?" Michael immediately grumbled, looking around. His eyebrows shot up in amazement. "We're on a plane."

He couldn't have looked any more stunned if he'd found himself on a spaceship. "What are we doing on a plane?"

"Going to dinner," she announced casually, picking up a magazine and thumbing through it. He snatched it from her.

"Look me in the eye and say that again."

"We're going to dinner," she repeated, staring him straight in the eye.

"Where?" He sounded shaky.

"Hawaii."

Once the full impact of what Barrie had done sank in, Michael burst out laughing, much to her relief.

"You're incredible!" he announced, giving her a kiss that literally took her breath away.

She regarded him closely. He seemed happy enough. "You're not angry?"

"How can I be mad at a beautiful woman who is taking me to dinner in one of the most romantic places in the world?" He paused. "You are taking me, aren't you? Or is part of the surprise that I'm paying for all of this?"

She grinned at him impishly. "Well, Mrs. Hastings did make the arrangements. She was sure you were too much of a gentleman to let me pay."

"Right," he said dryly.

"I did offer."

"I'm sure you did. Mrs. Hastings is a very generous woman...with my money." He reached up and pushed the call light for the stewardess. "I think I could use a drink."

Barrie watched him warily. The last thing she'd wanted to do was get the sweet, very cooperative Mrs. Hastings into trouble. "Don't be mad at her," she begged. "After all, this was my idea."

"I know that," he said. "She'd never dream this one up on her own."

"You're not going to fire her, are you?"

"Good heavens, no. Didn't you hear her say she'd be around the network long after I was gone? She knows where all the bodies are buried. She could blackmail every one of us."

"Mrs. Hastings would never do that!" Barrie replied indignantly. "She is the kindest, sweetest, most loyal secretary in the world. She adores you."

"Don't you ever tell her, but I think she's pretty terrific, too. Though I think I'll remind her that the next time some liberated woman wants to fly me across the Pacific for dinner, she should keep my credit card numbers out of it."

"If we talk about the show, you could charge it to your expense account," Barrie suggested slyly. "Would you feel better about that?"

Michael's eyes widened. "My God! The show! It's Friday. You have a taping tonight."

"Don't worry about it. Danielle's handling everything. The rehearsal came off last night without a hitch. Tonight will be a breeze."

"What happened to that noble producer who kept telling me that she was part of a team and that she'd never abandon them?"

"I'm not abandoning them. I'm letting them try out their wings. Everyone can use a little independence, you know," she told him nonchalantly.

"Are you sure Heath won't rewrite the script and put in a passionate love scene just to get even with us for leaving?"

"If he does, we can just edit it out again," she soothed. "Now stop worrying."

He chuckled suddenly. "It's nice to see you finally loosening up."

"What is that supposed to mean?"

"That the woman I met a few weeks ago would never have walked away from her television show for a mere dinner date."

"Love, this is no *mere dinner date*, as you call it," she

retorted, adding with dramatic emphasis, "We are having a romantic fling."

His smile widened, and he put his arm around her. "Tell me more," he murmured softly into her ear. "This is sounding better and better."

Chapter 12

Dinner on the terrace of a suite overlooking the ocean and Diamond Head had been sheer perfection. Soft breezes filled with sweet tropical scents touched their skin with a lover's gentleness, and the swaying of palm trees created an island music. A basket of fresh Hawaiian fruit, a bottle of chilled champagne and orchids on the pillows had provided the romantic finishing touches. But it was Michael's tenderness, his exquisite caresses, his whispered words that had filled the evening with romance.

Barrie lay by his side at dawn and watched him, her body sated, her heart filled to overflowing with a love more powerful than she had ever dared to dream of. She had hardly slept, not wanting to miss a moment of this beautiful time together. She couldn't seem to get enough of the sheer joy of looking at him, at his broad chest with its masculine shadow of hair, at his flat stomach, his curved bottom and those thick muscular thighs that seemed to symbolize exactly how powerful and virile he was.

As she stared at his sleeping form, a smile tilted his lips.

"You know, Mr. Compton, you're pretty amazing," she whispered, filled with wonder at this unexpected relationship.

He stirred. "Only with you sweetheart. Only with you."

"I hope that's true," she said, unable to keep a note of wistfulness out of her voice.

He looked at her closely. "Do you doubt it?"

She remembered all the advice she'd ever read about not admitting to doubts. And she recalled yet more sage counsel that honesty in a relationship was the best policy. She opted for honesty. "Sometimes, yes."

"Don't ever doubt it," he soothed, cupping her face and forcing her to meet his eyes. "I may not know how to say it right, but you are the first woman I've ever cared about this way. The feelings we share are completely unique in my experience, and I don't ever want to lose that."

"You won't have to," Barrie said, her heart suddenly lighter and filled with song. A love song. They might not have been a proposal or even an obvious declaration of love, but his words contained a powerful commitment nonetheless, and she rejoiced in what he had said.

He brushed a kiss across her lips. "I'm glad to see the smile back." He stacked the pillows at the head of the bed and pulled himself into a sitting position, then settled Barrie in his arms.

"Now tell me something."

"What?"

"Now that we've had dinner...and breakfast, is there more to this surprise of yours?"

Barrie's brow creased in a tiny frown. "I never thought

beyond last night," she admitted. "Isn't that ridiculous? I guess I just assumed we'd have to fly back this morning."

"Don't you think that would be a terrible waste of such a lovely room and idyllic setting?" he asked.

"Now that you mention it," she replied breathlessly.

"What shall we do about it, then?"

"I think you're on the right track."

"I thought so too."

For the next twenty-four hours they never left the room, sleeping only when they were so exhausted they could no longer talk or make love, ordering room service in the middle of the night when fresh pineapple and flat champagne were no longer enough to sustain them. Barrie knew that if she lived to be one hundred she would never again meet anyone who could bring her such joy, who could satisfy her so completely on so many levels. And when, just as she fell asleep, she thought she heard Michael murmur that he loved her, she was sure her heart would explode with happiness.

When they returned to Los Angeles late Sunday night, she was also certain that they were committed at last and that it would only be a matter of time before Michael said those three vital words aloud in broad daylight and followed them with a marriage proposal she knew she would accept. She had absolutely no fears any more about the future or about their ability to sustain their love for a lifetime. Michael had given her freedom from the past.

But as the next few weeks flew by, that incredible feeling of a perfect harmony with her mate was tempered by her concern over *Goodbye, Again*. She grew to dread the beginning of each new week, when the national ratings were announced. *Goodbye, Again* had crept up a bit its second week on the air but then slid right back down to the bottom. The cast and crew were demoralized, and there didn't seem to be a thing she could do. Pep talks were no longer nearly enough. Although she knew that Michael had been right about the show's tone, that had been fixed, and she was certain now that the real problem was that horrible Saturday night time slot over which she had absolutely no control.

"Dani, I don't know what to do. I feel so helpless," she said late one Tuesday afternoon after looking at the latest ratings. "I've tried talking to Michael about it, but it's getting more and more awkward."

"When do you try talking to him?"

Barrie looked at her oddly. "What do you mean? I talk to him whenever I get the chance."

"Like late at night? In bed?"

She began to see where Danielle was headed. "Okay. Yes. I suppose that's not the best place."

"That's the understatement of the year. You're the one who's been saying all along that having a business and personal relationship confuses things. Maybe you should try separating them again. Make an appointment and talk to the man in his office. That's where he makes his business decisions."

Barrie grinned at her. "And here I'd always heard the president got some of his best advice for running the country at home in bed."

"Maybe so, but the first lady is on his side. In the case of *Goodbye, Again*, you and Michael may be members of opposition parties."

Danielle was right, and Barrie reluctantly admitted it to her. "Okay, you win. I'll call over there right now and see what his calendar looks like for this afternoon."

Unfortunately, according to Mrs. Hastings, Michael's calendar looked crammed for the next week.

"He's flying to New York this afternoon, and I'm not sure when he'll be back."

"He's going this afternoon?" Barrie said incredulously. "He never mentioned a trip. Was it sudden?"

"No, dear. I don't think so. I made the arrangements several days ago."

"Oh," Barrie's voice was flat. "Well, never mind, Mrs. Hastings. I'll set up something when he gets back."

"That will be fine, dear," she replied, then added kindly, "Don't be upset about his trip. I'm sure he meant to tell you. He's been terribly busy and distracted lately."

"Sure," Barrie agreed without conviction. "Thanks."

"What's wrong?" Danielle asked the minute the receiver was back in place.

"He's leaving town this afternoon, and he never said one word to me about it."

"Maybe it slipped his mind."

"Dani, the man has been at my house practically every night for the past month. Surely he could have found a minute to mention that he had to go to New York. Was he just planning on not showing up tonight and calling from the East Coast later to announce, 'Oh, by the way, I won't be over later. I'm 3,000 miles away'?"

"Barrie," Danielle said warningly.

"Barrie what?"

"You're working yourself into a snit over nothing."

"Nothing?"

"At this moment, it is nothing. Give the man a chance."

"You're awfully generous. Aren't you supposed to be on my side in this?"

"I am. That's why I'm trying to get you to calm down before you blow up and say something you'll regret."

"I won't regret it when I give him a piece of my mind."

"Wanna bet?"

"I never indulge in useless regrets," she replied stoutly.

"You'd be better off if you didn't indulge that sharp tongue of yours."

"Thank you very much."

"You're welcome."

Michael did call from the airport to let Barrie know he was on his way out of town. And she did keep her mouth clamped firmly shut except to say goodbye and wish him a pleasant trip, but she didn't like it. As she told Danielle later, "I'd have felt a whole lot better if I'd let him have it."

The next morning, when she picked up the trade papers on her way into the studio, she was even sorrier that she'd restrained herself. The headline on page one of both papers referred to the cancellation of several fall television shows. Prominently mentioned in each story was the "promising comedy" *Goodbye, Again.*

"Despite being a personal favorite of network VP Michael Compton, this show suffered from anemic ratings from the start," one writer noted. "Not even his bias could save it in the end."

Barrie read the articles with her fists clenched. By the time she'd finished, she was gritting her teeth. If Michael had been in his office across the parking lot, she would have marched over there and punched him squarely in that sexy, dimpled jaw of his. How dare he! How could he make love to her night after night and then have the audacity, the absolute gall to publicly cancel her television series without saying a single word to her personally? She'd had to read it in the paper. No wonder the man had gone to New York. He'd wanted to be far out of her reach when she exploded.

She began muttering under her breath in graphic detail precisely what she planned to do to him when she got her hands on him. Mincemeat. That's what she'd make of him. He, not she, might have earned a reputation as someone who'd casually dissect his enemies without a second thought. But when she got through with him he'd look more innocent than Tom Sawyer by comparison. She was not about to let him make a fool of her and get away with it. She'd have his hide first! She picked up a lovely cloisonné paperweight he'd given her and threw it across the room for emphasis. It crashed against the door, just as Danielle opened it and peeped in.

"I take it you've seen the stories."

"You bet I've seen the stories," Barrie thundered, following up with a ten minute spiel of obscenities that would have made a sailor pale. Danielle winced but came in and sat down cross-legged on the sofa to wait her out. She finally sputtered to a halt.

"Finished?" she asked cheerfully.

"Not by a long shot. That man is an arrogant, selfish, cruel son..." She started all over again.

"You're going to have a stroke if you don't calm down," Danielle observed casually at last, only barely interrupting the flow of furious words.

"Besides," she noted, "you're wasting all the good stuff on me. If you have to use such foul language, save it for Michael."

Suddenly tears filled Barrie's eyes, and she buried her head on her desk. "How could he?" she mumbled brokenly. "Dani, how could he do this without even telling me himself? Good Lord, I thought he loved me."

"Sweetie, maybe that was the problem."

"What do you mean?"

"He knew what this would do to you. Maybe he couldn't bring himself to tell you in person."

"Michael's not a coward."

"He's not cruel either, is he?"

"I never thought so before," she sniffed, hating herself for breaking down.

"Then there must be some explanation."

"There isn't an explanation in the world good enough. Michael could talk from now until hell freezes over, and I will never accept this as anything other than the worst possible kind of betrayal."

When the phone rang on her desk, she flatly refused to pick it up.

"What if it's Michael?" Danielle argued.

"Let him put whatever he has to say in a memo. He seems to enjoy that."

"You're not being very professional."

"I'm not feeling very professional. I'm feeling like a woman who's been stabbed in the back by the man she loves."

The shrill ringing finally stopped, only to start again. "I can't stand it," Danielle said with a shudder, jumping up and snatching the phone off the hook. "Barrie MacDonald's office."

Though Barrie wanted to pretend disinterest, she couldn't help listening to see if it was, in fact, Michael.

"Yes, she's in, but she's not available just now," Danielle said coolly. "No, Michael. I'm not sure when she'll be available."

Danielle was quiet for several minutes, then said at last, "How do you think she feels? She's miserable."

She nodded. "Okay, I'll tell her, but I don't think she'll listen. Bye."

"Tell me what."

"That he's sorry. That there's an explanation. That he loves you. I think that covers all of the major points."

"Right," Barrie retorted sarcastically.

"He's calling back in five minutes, and he expects to talk to you."

"I won't talk to him."

"You might as well talk to him and get it over with. I have a feeling he's not giving up."

"And exactly what is he going to do to make me listen to him when he's 3,000 miles away."

"Okay. So he can't very well tie you down long distance, but you're only postponing the inevitable. He'll be back sooner or later."

When the phone rang again, Barrie glared at it. Resignedly Danielle picked it up.

"Nope. She's still not talking." She watched Barrie as she listened. "He says you're a coward if you don't get on the line."

Barrie yanked the receiver out of Danielle's hand. "Who do you think you're calling a coward?" she demanded. "I'd say you have the market cornered on that. To think that I trusted you."

"Barrie, what can I say? I'm sorry," he began apologetically. "I wanted to tell you myself, but the word leaked out yesterday before I had a chance. We weren't planning to make the announcement until next week when we'd firmed up the replacement shows."

"Were you planning on calling from New York, or were you going to send a telegram?"

"I was going to tell you in person the minute I got back. I would never handle a cancellation this way, no matter who the producer was, and I certainly wouldn't have done this to you, if I'd had any choice in the matter."

"Oh, you had a choice all right. You just made the wrong one, and now you're trying to weasel out of it."

"That's ridiculous. I love you. I would never intentionally set out to hurt you."

Barrie didn't know whether to laugh or cry. How she had longed to hear him say that he loved her. Now he was saying it in practically every other sentence, and she didn't believe him for a minute.

"Your timing is lousy, Compton. You never did understand how to write comedy."

"I'm not trying to be funny. I want to marry you."

"That's ludicrous. You've just destroyed my career. If you think I'd marry you after that, you're crazy. Marriage is no substitute for a career. A career won't betray you the way you betrayed me."

"I've hardly destroyed your career, I never meant to betray you, and I am definitely not offering marriage as a substitute. I'm proposing because I love you and I think you love me. Don't be stubborn and throw away our chance for happiness."

"Forget it," she snapped. "But I must say that line's really not too bad. Save it for your next melodrama."

"Barrie…"

She cut in curtly. "How long do we have?"

"Barrie, listen to me, please."

"How long?" she repeated adamantly.

Michael sighed wearily. "You are officially out of production now."

Barrie felt the sharp sting of tears in her eyes. "Fine. I'll be out of my office by the end of the day."

"You know that's not necessary."

"Yes," she said firmly. "It is. Goodbye, Michael."

"Barrie, wait. Please."

"Goodbye... Again."

Chapter 13

As soon as Barrie slammed the receiver emphatically back into place, she looked at Danielle and said abruptly, "Call everyone together. I might as well get this over with."

"Are you sure you want to talk to them now while you're this upset?"

Barrie's expression was tight-lipped, but her voice was perfectly controlled. "I don't want to do it at all, but I owe it to them. I can't just sit here and sulk all day. Come back and get me as soon as everyone's here."

Danielle nodded. "Okay, sweetie. Whatever you say."

Her voice had been quietly sympathetic. Too sympathetic. As soon as she had gone, Barrie's facade of bravado slipped and she blinked away a fresh cascade of tears. Hearing Michael's voice on the phone and listening to him declare his love and ask her to marry him had ripped her apart inside. She had expected those long-desired words to be almost magical when they were finally spoken and to bring her lasting happiness. Instead she felt only empty, alone and utterly devastated.

The cancellation would have been bad enough. At least the ratings had foreshadowed that for weeks now, and she had been almost ready for it. But nothing could have prepared her for the devastation of hearing about it secondhand. Michael had obviously made the decision days ago, and surely he had owed it to her to give her some warning. No matter what sort of fluke had allowed the word to leak out prematurely, Michael should have told her himself the moment he knew there was a risk of it appearing in print.

She sighed. Well, it was too late now. As soon as she had spoken with the cast and crew, she would gather her things and leave. With any luck she would be moved out of her office long before Michael even returned to Los Angeles.

When Danielle finally tapped on her door, Barrie took a deep breath and walked back to the set with her. From the long faces and red-rimmed eyes, she could tell that they were all taking the news as hard as she had, though for very different reasons. They had not just lost a series but had also lost their jobs. She had lost all that and her lover, too. All in all it had been quite a morning.

She stood before them, determined not to let them see the extent of her own private pain. She clenched her hands together behind her back and fought to keep her voice under control.

"I asked Dani to gather you all together for a few minutes so I could tell you personally how proud I am of each and every one of you," she said, as Melinda sniffed and tears rolled unchecked down the cheeks of several others. Even Dani, who had remained calm for her sake earlier, was now misty-eyed. Barrie's voice almost broke, but she quickly regained her composure and spoke from her heart.

"We tried to do something special with *Goodbye, Again* and I think we accomplished what we set out to do. I'm only sorry that more people didn't see it, that the network didn't give us a chance to prove ourselves.

"I don't want any of you to regard this as a failure. Creatively, *Goodbye, Again* was the very best it could be, and your individual contributions made it that way. As you all know, this series was very special to me, and I will miss working on it. I will miss working with each of you."

She tried a wobbly smile. "But you all know television by now. We may be back together in a few months with something else even more exciting and challenging. I hope so. But whatever happens, I know that you all will go on to do great things. You're much too talented not to."

Her voice broke then and, despite her most valiant efforts, tears streamed down her face. "Thank you. I love you," she managed at last and then turned and walked briskly away. Someone started to clap behind her, and then they were all clapping. The swell of sound followed her as she went, sobbing, into her office and closed the door.

The memory of that moment of heartfelt love and support sustained her for the next few days as she sat in her apartment or walked alone on the beach to try to decide what she wanted to do next. Although her answering service had given her message after message from Michael, she had ignored them all. There was nothing he could say now that could possibly make a difference.

Only Dani had been allowed to disrupt her self-imposed isolation, and Barrie nearly regretted it each time she allowed her to visit. Not that she could have stopped her.

Once Danielle started on a crusade, it would be like trying to halt a runaway freight train. Now her friend had the uncomfortable habit of bringing Michael's name into every conversation, ignoring her pleas to pretend that the man had disappeared off the face of the earth.

"He hasn't gone anywhere," Danielle retorted. "He is very much alive and, unless I miss my guess, very much in love with you."

"He had a charming way of showing it."

"The man made a mistake."

"I'll say."

"Barrie, you know what they say about forgiveness."

"That it's divine? I'm not feeling very divine right now. How can you even suggest that I just pretend this never happened?" she demanded. "The man ruined my life."

Danielle picked up a stack of messages, most of them from network officials and other producers, all seeking a meeting with her to talk over new projects. "It doesn't appear to me that your life is ruined. There are probably a dozen solid offers waiting for you right now. You told the cast they had a future in this business. So do you."

"I'm not interested."

"What are you interested in then? You're not eating. You're not sleeping. You're not even seeing anyone but me…"

"Which I occasionally regret."

"Go ahead. Be rotten. But I'm not leaving you to work through this alone. I'm going to stay right here nudging you until you decide to get on with your life."

Barrie threw up her hands. "You are impossible."

"I am your friend. Now tell me, what are you interested in?"

"I'm thinking about moving to Des Moines and opening a dress shop. I think that's about as much excitement as my psyche can handle from now on."

Danielle nodded wisely. "That certainly makes a lot of sense. You hate cold weather. You've never been to Des Moines, and you have absolutely no idea how to run a business."

"If I can bring a television show in on schedule and under budget, surely I can pick out a few nice dresses, hang them on racks and sell them."

"And be bored to tears in the process."

Barrie gave her a smug grin. "Not when I am married to the man of my dreams."

"Oh? Is there something you haven't mentioned to me? Is Michael retiring to Des Moines, as well?"

"No. But surely there's some nice, quiet, sane man who'd be willing to take me on. I was thinking along the lines of the strong, silent type. Maybe a history professor who wears tweed jackets with those nice suede patches on the sleeves. It would be wonderful if he smoked a pipe. They smell good."

"Ah, I can see it now. Long evenings in front of the fire, watching nature shows on educational television. Long walks in the snow."

"No snow," Barrie said adamantly. "I hate snow."

"Then you'd better rethink your plan and move to Phoenix. Unless you plan to spend several months of the year indoors."

"Okay, okay," Barrie grumbled. "So Des Moines is a lousy idea, but I want something like that. I can't take any more of this glitzy roller-coaster existence out here."

"Sweetie, you thrive on this roller-coaster existence. You couldn't wait to get your first show so you could climb on."

"And now I've had it, and the ride was not all it was cracked up to be."

"The ride was exactly what you knew it would be," Danielle corrected her. "Bumpy, but exhilarating. Michael Compton is the real problem. He was the wild hairpin turn in the track you hadn't counted on. And you can run to Des Moines or Beijing, for that matter, and you won't be far enough away to escape from that memory. The man has a hold on you, and you might as well admit it."

Barrie stared at her helplessly. She knew that what Danielle had said was true. As furious as she was with Michael, she hadn't been able to banish him from her mind. His face taunted her every time she closed her eyes. Even her morning shower could not provide safe harbor. The water gliding over her body reminded her of his gentle touch and aroused in her an aching memory.

"Is he back yet?" she asked at last.

"He's due in tonight."

"My, my. You've certainly kept abreast of the latest developments. Do you have his complete itinerary?"

"Nope," Danielle responded cheerfully, refusing to take offense at the taunt. "Just the salient points. Since you refuse to talk to him, I seem to be the next best thing."

"Perhaps you should go out with him, then," Barrie suggested, though a twinge of jealousy made her practically choke. "You seem to get along well enough, and you're obviously more forgiving than I."

"Sweetie, I'm not about to be second best in anybody's life. And you ought to be thanking your lucky stars that a man like Michael, who is so absolutely perfect for you, seems to think you're better than rum-raisin ice cream."

"I should hope so," Barrie retorted with a grimace.

"I like rum-raisin ice cream."

"Your taste buds have been warped."

"That's beside the point. When Michael gets back here, you ought to see him. The two of you can still work things out, if you'll keep that stubborn pride of yours in check."

Barrie sighed. "We'll see."

Danielle beamed in satisfaction. "Progress at last. I'd better get out of here while I'm still ahead for the day."

"Good idea."

Barrie spent the rest of the day walking the beach under a gray sky that perfectly suited her mood. Danielle had been right about one thing—probably more than one, but it would never do to give her too much credit—she couldn't go on like this. She was not only miserable, she was already bored. She needed to get back to work, and a dress shop in Des Moines or anyplace else was no answer. Deep down she knew that, though the idea had seemed attractively safe and serene for a few fleeting minutes in the emotional aftermath of the cancellation.

Back in her apartment, she pulled out the file cards on which she jotted notes to herself about possible new shows. Sometimes it was only a character description, sometimes a setting, sometimes a business that seemed like a unique backdrop for some crazy characters. As she sorted through them, she began making more notes, chuckling to herself at some of the possibilities, discarding others.

After an hour of examining all the cards several times, she kept coming back to one. The show would feature a successful workaholic father and a career-oriented mother. Their independent teenage kids would be in the throes of rebellion over having spent their entire adolescence cutting grass, cooking dinner and doing the grocery shopping.

And, she thought with a wry chuckle, there might be room in this one for a sheepdog.

When the doorbell rang, she was just envisioning the fluffy beast on the kitchen floor as the kids tried to wax around him. Or maybe even tried to use him as a mop. Her heartbeat seemed to stop as the doorbell chimed again. There wasn't a doubt in her mind about who it was. Michael's timing was always impeccable. She was about to create a show with a blasted sheepdog, and he couldn't wait to get his hands on it.

When she opened the door, she stood staring at him silently for a moment. He looked terrible. He was drawn and pale, his eyes red-rimmed from lack of sleep, his cheeks shadowed with the beginning of a beard. Even the dimple in his chin seemed downcast. Despite his appearance, her heart readily flipped over.

"Rough flight?" she asked tartly.

"No. The flight was just fine," he responded wearily, brushing past her. "We have to talk."

"Don't you think we're having this conversation about a week too late?"

"Probably. But the fact remains that since we didn't we're going to have it now." Barrie watched in amazement as he poured himself a glass of Scotch. He must be nervous. She'd never seen him drink anything much stronger than wine.

"For a man who's trying to worm his way back into my good graces, you're being awfully dictatorial," she taunted lightly. "You might want to revise your tactics."

His lips twitched with a tiny smile. "A week ago I was more than willing to be contrite and apologetic. A few days ago I was ready to be charming and win you back. Now I'm too frustrated to bother with all that. I made a lousy mistake of timing, and the one person I care most about in the world got hurt in the process. I'm sorry. I've told you that. I don't know how else to say it. By the time I realized those stories were going into print, it was too late."

"You could have told me when you first made the decision."

"That's just it," he said, running his fingers through his hair nervously. "I didn't make the decision. It was made in New York. I was flying there to try to talk them out of it. I wanted to move the show and give it another chance. I thought the changes you had made..."

"We had made," Barrie murmured distractedly as she focused on what he had just said. It hadn't been his decision at all. He had wanted to save the show. Knowing that suddenly seemed to make all the difference.

"Whatever. I thought they were working and that the show was finally on the right track. I thought a new time slot would bring in a new audience to sample it."

Barrie sat down next to him, her heart lighter. "You were really going to do that?" she said softly. "You were going to bat for us?"

"I wanted to. I was overruled. And before I could talk to them about the revised schedule I had in mind, the stories broke. By then it was too late."

"Why didn't you tell me that before?"

He stared at her indignantly. "How was I supposed to do that? Leave a message with your answering service?"

"You could have told Danielle."

"I did."

"She never said a word."

"I asked her not to. I told her because I needed her on my side, but I wanted to be the one to tell you myself."

Barrie threw her arms around Michael's neck and hugged him, her lips brushing a kiss across the stubble on his cheek. "Thank you."

"For what?"

"For believing in *Goodbye, Again*."

"I told you from the beginning that I believed in it, just the way I've been telling you that I believe in us."

Barrie took a deep breath and said softly, "You said something like that on the phone the other day. Did you mean it?"

Michael grinned at her wickedly. "You didn't give me the chance to say much. What especially are you referring to?"

She poked him in the ribs. "You know very well what I mean. Don't make me say it."

"Why not? I think you owe me that much for you evident lack of faith. What did I say?"

"Blast you, Michael Compton. You're taking all the romance out of this."

"Out of what?" he taunted innocently.

"Your damn marriage proposal. You asked me to marry you."

"I did? Gee, I must have been in a daze."

"Are you in a daze now?"

"No."

"Well, then?"

"Okay," he relented at last, cupping her chin in his hand and tilting her head until he could look directly into her hopeful brown eyes. "I love you, Barrie MacDonald. Will you marry me?"

She sighed and smiled contentedly. "Yes," she promised. "On one condition."

Michael's brows flew up. "My God, is this going to be anything like negotiating a contract?"

"Something like that."

"Should we call your agent?"

"Oh, I think I can look out for my own interests on this one."

"So what's the condition?"

"That you will never, never say goodbye again."

He grinned at her. "That's going to make it tough to leave for work in the morning."

"Don't go," she suggested, her fingers exploring the inside of his thighs until he moaned softly. "I can keep you occupied."

"We'll be poor."

"We'll be happy."

"We'll be bored."

She looked at him askance and intensified her touch. "Oh, really?"

He groaned. "Forget bored."

"Is it a promise? You'll never leave me again."

"I will never leave you again," he vowed solemnly, his lips hungrily capturing hers.

When his tongue teased against her lips, then dipped inside for a taste of honeyed sweetness, Barrie groaned, too, and melted into Michael's arms. But when his touch became increasingly more intimate as his fingers explored her shoulders, the tips of her breasts, her already throbbing abdomen, she couldn't resist pulling away to note in a prim, shocked tone, "Michael, it is barely eight o'clock. Don't you think you're getting a little carried away for this particular time slot?"

"You're sophisticated enough for what I have in mind

at any hour," he retorted dryly. "Besides, we're not on television."

"Thank goodness," Barrie replied, moving back into his embrace.

"Thank goodness," he echoed.

* * * * *

Also by Lee Tobin McClain

Love Inspired

Rescue Haven

The Secret Christmas Child
Child on His Doorstep
Finding a Christmas Home

Redemption Ranch

The Soldier's Redemption
The Twins' Family Christmas
The Nanny's Secret Baby

Rescue River

Engaged to the Single Mom
His Secret Child
Small-Town Nanny
The Soldier and the Single Mom
The Soldier's Secret Child
A Family for Easter

HQN

The Off Season

Cottage at the Beach
Reunion at the Shore
Christmas on the Coast
Home to the Harbor
First Kiss at Christmas

Safe Haven

Low Country Hero
Low Country Dreams
Low Country Christmas

Visit her Author Profile page at Harlequin.com,
or leetobinmcclain.com, for more titles!

THE SOLDIER
AND THE SINGLE MOM

Lee Tobin McClain

To Porter,
the real-world model for Spike. Rescue pets rule!

Therefore if any man be in Christ,
he is a new creature: old things are
passed away; behold, all things are become new.
—*2 Corinthians* 5:17

Chapter 1

It was 2:00 a.m. on a mild March night when Buck Armstrong saw his dead wife walking toward the town of Rescue River, Ohio, carrying their baby on one hip.

He swerved, hit the brakes and skidded onto the gravel berm. On the seat beside him, Crater—his chosen companion for the night—let out a yip.

Buck passed his hand over his eyes. It wasn't real—couldn't be. He'd made similar mistakes before, when he was tired, when the war memories came back too strong. Tonight, driving home from assisting in an emergency surgery out at the dog rescue, he wanted nothing more than to keep driving past the turnoff to the liquor store, lock himself in his room and shut it all off until morning.

He looked again, squinting through the moonlit fog.

They were still there. But they were running away from him, or rather, his wife was. Baby Mia was gone.

Where was the baby? He scrambled out of the truck,

leaving the door ajar. "Stay!" he ordered the dog automatically as he took off toward his wife. "Ivana! Wait!"

She ran faster, but Buck had gotten back into military shape since he'd quit drinking, and he caught up easily. Was relieved to see that the baby was now in front of her, in some sort of sling.

His hand brushed against her soft hair.

She screamed, spun away from him, and he saw her face.

It wasn't his wife, but someone else. A complete stranger.

He stopped, his heart pounding triple time. Sweat formed on his forehead as he tried to catch his breath. "I'm sorry. I thought you were—"

"Leave us alone," she ordered, stepping away, one arm cradled protectively at the back of the baby's head, the other going to her oversize bag. "I have a gun."

"Whoa." He took a couple of steps back, hands lifting to shoulder height, palms out. A giant stone of disappointment pressed down on him. "I don't mean you any harm. I thought you were... Never mind."

A breeze rattled the leaves of a tall oak tree beside the road. He caught the rich scent of newly turned earth, plowed dirt, fields ready for planting. Up ahead, a spotlight illuminated the town's well-known sign, kept up and repainted yearly since Civil War days: Rescue River, Ohio. All Are Welcome, All Are Safe.

Ivana had been so proud of their hometown's history as a station on the Underground Railroad, its reputation for embracing outsiders of all types, races and creeds.

The good people of Rescue River had even put up with the damaged man he'd been when he'd returned from war, until he'd repeatedly broken their trust.

"Go back to your truck," the woman ordered, hand still in her bag. Now that he could see her better, he realized she was sturdier than Ivana had been, with square shoulders and a determined set to her chin. Same long tawny hair, but fuller lips and big gray-blue eyes that were now glaring at him. "Do it. Back in the truck, now."

He should do what she said, should turn around right now and get on home before the memories that were chasing him caught up.

Should, but when had he ever done what he should? "What are you doing out here in the middle of the night, ma'am? Can I give you a ride somewhere?"

She laughed without humor, shaking her head. "No way, buddy. Just drive away. We'll all be better off."

He had to admire her courage if not her common sense. There was no good reason for a woman with a baby to be wandering the countryside, but she was acting as if she owned the whole state.

"Sure you don't want me to call someone?" Truth was, he felt relieved. He could go home and crash and try to forget that, just for a minute, he'd gotten the crazy hope that Ivana and the baby were still alive, that he'd get a second chance to love them the way they deserved.

"We're fine." She ran a hand through her hair and patted the baby who, somehow, still slept against her chest. He caught sight of wispy hair, heard that sweet, nestling-in sigh of a contented little one.

Pain stabbed his heart.

She did seem fine, perfectly able to defend herself, he argued against the faint whisper of chivalry that said he shouldn't let a woman and child stay out here in the middle of the night. After all, he wasn't much of a protector. He'd lost as many people as he'd saved in Afghanistan. And as for Ivana and Mia…

The sound of a mournful howl silenced his thoughts.

Crater. "It's okay, buddy," he called, and the scarred rott-weiler bounded out of the truck's cab. As Crater jumped up on him, Buck rubbed the dog's sides and let him lick his face and, for the first time since seeing the woman, he felt his heart rate settle.

"Let's go home," he said to the dog. But Crater had different ideas, and he lunged playfully toward the woman and baby. Buck snapped his fingers and the dog sank into a sitting position, looking back toward him. The deep scar on the dog's back, for which they'd named him out at the rescue, shone pale in the moonlight.

"That's a well-trained dog." The woman cocked her head to one side.

"He's a sweetheart. Come on, boy."

The dog trotted to his side, and as they started back to his truck, Buck felt his heart rate calm a little more. Yeah, his shrink was right: he was a prime candidate for a service dog. Except he couldn't make the commitment. As soon as he'd paid off his debts and made amends where he could, he was out of here, and who knew whether he'd end up in a dog-friendly place?

"Hey, hold on a minute." The woman's voice was the slightest bit husky.

He turned but didn't walk back toward her. Didn't look at her. It hurt too much. She was still a reminder of Ivana and all he'd lost. "What?"

"Maybe you *could* give us a hand. Or a ride."

Buck drew in a deep breath and blew it out. "Okay, sure," he said, trying not to show his reluctance to be in her company a moment longer. After all, he'd made the offer, so courtesy dictated he should follow through. "Where are you headed?"

"That's a good question," she said, lifting the baby a little to take the weight off her chest.

He remembered Ivana doing that very same thing with Mia. He swallowed.

"What kind of a town is Rescue River?"

"It's a real nice town." It was, too. He'd consider staying on there himself if he hadn't burned so many bridges.

"Think I could find a cheap room? Like, really cheap?"

He cocked his head to one side. "The only motel had no vacancy, last I saw. My sister's renovating what's going to be a guesthouse, but it's not open for another few months..."

"Does she have a room that's done, or mostly done? We don't need much."

Buck wanted to lie, would have lied, except he seemed to hear Ivana's voice in his head. Quoting Scripture, trying to coax him along the path to believing. Something about helping widows and orphans in their distress.

This woman might or might not be a widow, but to be out walking the rural Ohio roads in the wee hours surely indicated some kind of distress.

"She's got a couple of rooms close to done," he admitted.

"Do you think she'd let me rent one?"

He frowned. "I don't know. Lacey's not the most trusting person in the world. A late-night guest she isn't expecting won't sit well with her."

The comment hung between them for an awkward moment. It was the simple truth, though. Or maybe not so simple. The fact that the pretty stranger had a baby would disturb Lacey. A lot.

The woman gave him a skeptical look, then straightened and turned away. "Okay. Thanks."

Squeezing his eyes shut for just a second, he turned and tried to head back toward his truck. She wasn't his responsibility. He had enough on his plate just to keep himself together.

Nope. Like a fool, he turned around. "Hey, wait. Come on. We'll try to talk Lacey into letting you stay. At least for the night."

"That would be wonderful," she said, a relieved smile breaking out on her face.

Wonderful for her, maybe. Not for him. The last thing he needed was an Ivana look-alike, with a baby no less, staying one thin wall away from him.

"My name's Gina, by the way." She shifted the diaper bag and held out a hand.

"Buck Armstrong." He reached out, wrapped his oversize hand around her soft, delicate fingers and wished he'd driven home another way.

Gina Patterson climbed into the backseat of the handsome stranger's extended-cab pickup, her heart thudding. *Please, Lord, keep us safe. Watch over us.*

Don't let him be a serial killer.

But a dog wouldn't be that friendly with a serial killer, and a serial killer wouldn't act that loving with a dog. Would they?

"Air bags," she explained when he looked over his shoulder, eyebrows raised. "Can't sit in front." Technically, she shouldn't even bring Bobby into the truck, not without a car seat, only she couldn't figure out what else to do. She couldn't give Buck the keys to get her car seat from her out-of-gas SUV, and she certainly couldn't leave Bobby with him while she walked the three miles back to her vehicle.

They were safer in the backseat, she figured, safe from him as well as from any kind of car accident. If he tried to kidnap them, she could at least hit him in the back of the head with her shoe.

She was ready to drop with fatigue after three long days of driving, and it was getting colder by the minute. Buck's arrival had to be the blessing she'd prayed for. Although he seemed pretty gruff for a rescuer.

"Right, I knew that. It's less than a mile," he said, and his dog panted back over the seat at her, smiling in the way happy dogs did. It made her miss her poodles, but she knew her best friend back home would take care of them.

She scratched the dog's ears for a minute and then let her head sag back against the seat, thanking God again for keeping her and Bobby safe during their journey.

Well, mostly safe. She'd been foolish to leave her bag on the sink while she'd changed Bobby's diaper. Who'd have thought there'd be a purse thief in a rest area in rural Indiana? Fortunately, she'd filled her tank just before the theft—with cash—so she'd kept going as far as she could, leaving the interstate so there'd be less of a trail.

The debit card she'd kept in her jacket pocket might help in the future, once things back home cooled down, but she didn't dare use it now.

After the theft, she'd gotten scared and timed things all wrong. She'd thought she could make it to a hotel she'd seen advertised in a larger town up ahead, but the SUV was a gas hog and had sputtered to a stop a few miles back.

At which point she'd realized she didn't have enough cash for a hotel, anyway.

"All set?" Buck looked back at her and Bobby, brows raised over eyes the color of the ocean on a cloudy day.

Man, those were some haunted eyes. "We're set. Thank you for helping us."

She studied the back of him as he put the truck into gear

and drove into the town. Broad shoulders, longish hair and stubble that made him look like a bad boy.

What had *he* been doing out at 2:00 a.m.? The question only now occurred to her, now that she and Bobby were safe, or seemed to be. "Excuse me," she said, leaning forward, "but you haven't been drinking or…partying, have you?"

His shoulders stiffened. "No. Why?"

Whew. She hadn't smelled alcohol on him, but alcohol wasn't the only thing that could mess you up. Her husband had been an old hand at covering his addiction to cocaine, right up until he'd lost control on a California mountain and skied headlong into a tree. The drugs had shown up in the autopsy blood work, but when he'd left the ski chalet an hour earlier, she hadn't even known he was impaired. Yet another mistake her in-laws had laid at her feet.

Her throat tightened and she crammed the memories back down. "Just wondering."

So maybe she'd done the right thing after all. When Bobby had started to cry, she'd decided it was better to risk walking than to stay with her vehicle. She'd scraped together change from the floor and found her emergency twenty in the bin between the driver's and passenger's seats. So at least she could get Bobby some food. At ten months, he needed way more than mother's milk.

Hopefully, she could find a church that would take her in, because calling in her lost wallet might put the police on her trail. She chewed on her lower lip.

How had she ever gotten into this situation? She tried to tell herself it wasn't her fault. While she'd committed to stay with her husband, she hadn't married her in-laws. Once he was gone, so was her obligation to them. When

Bobby was old enough to know the whole story, he could choose to reconnect in a safe way if he wanted to.

"Guesthouse is right up there." Buck waved a hand, causing Gina to look around and realize that Rescue River was a cute little town, the kind with sidewalks and shops and glowing streetlamps, a moonlit church on one corner and a library on the other. The kind of safe haven where she might be able to breathe for a little while and figure out her options.

Except that, without ID and with just a twenty and change, her options seemed very limited. Worry cramped her belly.

The stranger pulled up in front of a rambling brick home. The outdoor light was on, revealing a porch swing and a front-door wreath made of flowers and pretty branches.

"I'll have to wake up my sister. You can wait here in the truck or out front." He gestured toward the house.

Well, okay, then. No excess of manners.

Except that, actually, she was the stranger and he was doing her a service. "I'll wait on the porch. Thanks."

He seemed able to read her mind as he came around to open the truck door for her. "Sorry to leave you outside, but my sister is sort of touchy," he said as they walked up the narrow brick walkway. "I can't bring a stranger in to set up shop without asking permission. It's her place." He paused. "It's a very safe town, but I'll leave Crater out here if that will make you more comfortable."

"It will, thanks." It had been the dog, and the stranger's reaction to the dog, that had made her decide he was a reliable person to help her.

That, and the fact that she was desperate.

In her worst moments she wondered if she'd done the right thing, taking Bobby away from her in-laws' wealth and security. But no way. They'd become more and more possessive of him, trying to push her out of the picture and care for him themselves. And she kept coming back to what she'd seen: her mother-in-law holding Bobby out for her father-in-law to hit, hard, causing the baby to wail in pain. Her father-in-law *had* started to shake Bobby, she was sure of it, despite their vigorous denials and efforts to turn the criticism back on her.

Once she knew for sure, she couldn't in good conscience stay herself, or leave Bobby in his grandparents' care.

When she'd first driven away from the mansion that had felt increasingly like a prison, relief had made her giddy. She'd not known how oppressed she had felt, living there, until she'd started driving across the country with no forwarding address. Realizations about her dead husband's problems had stacked up, one on top of the other, until she was overwhelmed with gratitude to God for helping her escape the same awful consequences for herself and Bobby.

As she'd crossed state lines, though, doubts had set in, so that now her dominant, gnawing emotion was fear. How would she make a living? What job could she get without references and with few marketable skills? And while she worked, who would watch Bobby? She wouldn't leave her precious baby with just anyone. She had to be able to trust them. To know they'd love and care for him in her absence.

Inside the house, a door slammed. "I've about had it, Buck!"

She heard Buck's voice, lower, soothing, though she couldn't make out the words.

"You've got to be kidding. She has a baby with her?"

More quiet male talk.

The door to the guesthouse burst open, and a woman

about her age, in a dark silk robe, stood, hands on hips. "Okay, spill it. What's your story?"

The woman's tone raised Gina's hackles, whooshing her back to her in-laws and their demanding glares. The instinct to walk away was strong, but she had Bobby to consider. She drew in a breath and let it out slowly, a calming technique from her yoga days. "Long version or short?"

"I work all day and then come home and try to renovate this place. I'm tired."

"Short, then. My purse was stolen, I'm out of gas and I need a place to stay."

The woman frowned. "For how long?"

"I…don't know. A couple of days."

"Why can't you call someone?"

That was the key question. How did she explain how she'd gotten so isolated from her childhood friends, how she'd needed to go to a part of the country where she didn't know anyone, both to make a fresh start and so that her in-laws didn't find her? "That's in the long version."

"So…" The woman cocked her head to one side, studying her with skepticism in every angle of her too-thin frame. "Are you part of some scam?"

"Lacey." Buck put a hand on the woman's shoulder. "If you're opening a guesthouse, you need to be able to welcome people."

"If you're serious about recovery from your drinking problem, you need to stop pulling stunts like this."

Buck winced.

Gina reached up to rub her aching shoulder. Great. Another addict.

The woman drew in a breath, visibly trying to remain calm. "I'm sorry. But you're blinded by how she looks like

Ivana. Stuff like this happens all the time in big cities. We have to be careful."

Bobby stirred and let out a little cry, and as Gina swayed to calm him, something inside her hardened. She was tired of explaining herself to other people. If she weren't in such dire straits, she'd walk right down those pretty, welcoming porch steps and off into the night. "You can search me. All I've got is this diaper bag." She shifted and held it out to the woman. "It's hard to run a scam with an infant tagging along."

Buck raised his eyebrows but didn't comment, and scarily enough, she could read what he was thinking. *So you don't have a gun in there.*

Of course she didn't.

The woman, Lacey, took it, set it down on the table and pawed through.

Gina's stomach tightened.

Bobby started to cry in earnest. "Shh," she soothed. He needed a diaper change, a feeding and bed. She could only hope the trauma and changes of the past few days wouldn't damage him, that her own love and commitment and consistency would be enough.

"Look, you can stay tonight and we'll talk in the morning." With a noisy sigh, the woman turned away, but not before Gina saw a pained expression on her face. "*You* settle her in," she said to Buck. "Put her in the Escher." She stormed inside, letting the screen door bang behind her.

Buck felt tired, inescapably tired, but also keyed up to where he knew he wasn't going to sleep. "Come on," he said to the beautiful stranger.

But she didn't follow. "This isn't going to work out. I'll find something else."

"There's no place else." He picked up her bag and beckoned her inside, with Crater padding behind him. "Don't worry, Lacey will be more hospitable in the morning." Maybe. He knew what else had bothered Lacey, besides the fact that she'd rescued him one too many times from some late-night escapade: Gina's little boy. Just last year, Lacey had miscarried the baby who was all she had left of her soldier husband. Seeing someone who apparently wasn't taking good care of her own child had to infuriate her.

He wasn't sure his sister's judgment was fair; Gina might be doing the best she could for her baby, might be on the run from some danger worse than whatever she'd be likely to face on an Ohio country road.

He led her through the vinyl sheeting and raw boards that were the future breakfast room, up the stairs and into the hallway that housed the guest rooms. "Here's the only other finished one, besides mine," he said, stopping at the room called the Escher. He opened the door and let her enter before him, ordering Crater to lie down just inside the door.

Gina looked around, laughing with apparent delight. "This is amazing!"

The bed appeared to float and the walls held prints by a modern artist Buck had only recently learned about. The nightstand was made to look like it was on its side, and the rug created an optical illusion of a spiraling series of stair steps.

"Lacey was an art history major in college," he explained. "She's hoping to coordinate with the new art museum to attract guests."

"That's so cool!" Gina walked from picture to picture, joggling the baby so he wouldn't fuss. "I love Escher."

He felt a reluctant flash of liking for this woman who could spare the energy for art appreciation at a time like this. He also noticed that she knew who Escher was, which was more than he had, until Lacey had educated him.

His curiosity about Gina kicked up a notch. She appeared to be destitute and basically homeless, but she was obviously educated. He scanned her slim-fitting trousers and crisp shirt: definitely expensive. Those diamond studs in her ears looked real.

So why'd she been walking along a country road at night?

She put the baby down on the bed and pulled out a diaper pad. "Sorry, he needs a change."

"Sheets and towels here," he said, tapping a cabinet. "There might even be soap. Gina already let one couple stay here for a honeymoon visit."

She turned to him, one hand on the baby's chest. "I can't tell you how grateful I am."

"No problem." Though it was. "I'll be right next door if you need anything."

She swallowed visibly. "Okay."

Unwanted compassion hit him. She was alone and scared in a strange place. "Look, Lacey is a real light sleeper. She'll wake up if there's any disturbance. And… I can leave Crater here if you want a guard dog."

"Thank you. That would be wonderful." She put a hand on his arm. "You've been amazing."

He didn't need her touching him. He backed away so quickly he bumped against the open door. "Stay, boy," he ordered Crater and then let himself out.

And stood in the hallway, listening to her cooing to her baby while a battle waged inside him. He wanted a drink in the worst way.

He reached down, but of course, Crater wasn't there to

calm him. He took one step toward the front door. Stopped. Tried to picture his recovery mentor.

Wondered whether the bar out by the highway was still open.

Ten minutes later, after a phone call to his mentor, he tossed restlessly in his bed. It was going to be a long night.

Chapter 2

A hoarse shout woke Gina out of a restless sleep.

Instinctively, she reached for Bobby. She found him in the nest she'd made with rolled blankets and towels. Thankfully, he slept on through more shouted words she couldn't distinguish in her sleepy state.

Sweat broke out on her body as she lay completely still, just as she'd done so many nights when her husband had come home drunk or high. Hoping, praying he'd sleep downstairs rather than coming up in the mood for some kind of interaction, whether affection or a fight. None of it ever ended well when he'd been using. Sometimes, his rage took physical form.

A knock on the door made her heart pound harder, but then she realized it came from the next room. She heard the clink of an old-fashioned key in a lock. A woman's murmuring voice: "It's okay, Buck. It's okay. You had another nightmare."

It all came clear to her: the guesthouse. The unfriendly landlady. Buck's haunted eyes.

Sounded like he'd had a nightmare and his sister had come to wake him out of it.

She drew in a breath and rubbed Bobby's back, comforted by the steady sound of his breathing. She'd landed in a safe place for the moment. The edges of the sky were just starting to brighten through the window, but she didn't have to deal with her day just yet. She could sleep again.

There were more murmurs next door. A hall door opened and closed. A toilet flushed. Then silence again.

Surprisingly enough, she did drop back to sleep.

"Good morning!" Gina walked into the kitchen the next morning with Bobby on her hip. He'd woken up hungry, and she'd nursed him and fed him her last jar of baby food. It was time to figure out her next step.

"Hey." Lacey's voice sounded unenthusiastic. She wore scrubs and sat with a cup of coffee in front of her. Her eyes were puffy and underlined by dark shadows.

No wonder, given last night's drama.

Lacey obviously wasn't going to make conversation, so Gina soldiered on. "Thank you so much for giving me and Bobby a place to sleep last night."

"Sure." Lacey glanced up from her newspaper and then went back to reading an article on the local news page.

"You headed to work?" Gina asked. "What do you do?"

The woman tried to smile, but it was obviously an effort. "I'm a CNA. Certified Nursing Assistant. And yeah, I leave in half an hour." A large orange cat wove its way between her legs and then jumped into her lap, and she ran her hands over it as if for comfort.

"You want me to fix you breakfast?"

That made Lacey look up. "What?"

"I'm a pretty good cook. If you're going to work, you need more than coffee."

Lacey let out a reluctant chuckle. "Is that so, Mom?"

Buck walked into the room, stretching and yawning hugely. He wore a plain, snug-fitting white T-shirt and faded jeans.

Gina swallowed hard. Okay. Yeah. He was handsome. At least, if you didn't look into the abyss that seemed to live permanently behind his eyes.

"How's everyone this morning?" he asked in a forced, cheerful tone.

Lacey pointed at Gina with her coffee cup. "She offered to cook breakfast."

"Sounds good to me," Buck said. "I've got comp time at the clinic from last night, so I'm gonna work on the house today. Could use some fuel, for sure."

Lacey waved a hand toward the refrigerator and stove. "Knock yourself out," she said to Gina.

Gina shifted Bobby and walked over to Lacey. "Any chance you could hold him? His name's Bobby, by the way."

Lacey scooted away so fast that the chair leg scraped along the freshly polished wood floor, leaving a raw scratch. "No, thanks. I… My hands are full with Mr. Whiskers."

Buck was there in a fraction of a second, concern all over his face. "I'll take him."

Gina cocked her head at the two of them, curious. She'd never met a woman who wasn't charmed by her son, especially when he was newly fed and changed, cooing and smiling.

Buck, on the other hand, held Bobby like a pro, bouncing him on his knee and tickling his tummy to make him laugh.

Gina rummaged in the refrigerator and found eggs, some

Havarti cheese and green onions. It was enough to make a good-tasting scramble. Thick slices of bread went alongside, and she found some apples to cut up as a garnish.

When she placed the plates in front of the two of them a few minutes later, they both looked surprised, and when Lacey tasted the eggs, she actually smiled. "Not bad."

"I like to cook." Gina cleared her throat. "Is there any work you need done today? I have to find a way to get some gas out to my car, but other than that, I'd love to spend a few hours working around here in exchange for your letting me stay last night."

Lacey waved a hand. "Don't worry about it. This breakfast is payment enough."

"Truth is," Gina said, her face heating, "I might need to impose on you for another night. So we could consider it advance payment."

The other woman studied her thoughtfully. "Can you handle an honest answer?"

"Of course."

"I have a hard time trusting someone who can't afford a hotel but can afford shoes like that." She gestured at Gina's designer loafers.

Gina looked down at the soft leather and felt a moment's shallow regret. She wouldn't be wearing shoes like this anymore, that was for sure.

"She could work this morning while I'm here," Buck interjected. "We need cleanup help, and anyone could do that. And this afternoon, she can work on getting her car and whatever else she needs to do."

Gina gripped the edge of her chair for courage. Asking for favors wasn't her favorite thing, not by a long shot, and she hated pushy people in general. But for Bobby, she'd do whatever was necessary. "What do you think about our staying tonight?"

Lacey's jaw hardened. "I'm not going to throw you out into the street right away," she said, "but you need to figure things out. Surely there's people you can call, things you can do. I don't want this to become permanent. The last thing either Buck or I needs is a stranger with a baby around here. You're poison to us right now."

Gina recoiled, shocked by the harsh words.

Buck held up a hand. "Lacey—"

"What? You know that's why you had a nightmare last night. Because she looks like Ivana and she's got a kid. It's too much for either of us."

"I'm sorry," Gina said, her heart going out to them. Underneath Lacey's brusque exterior was real pain that kept peeking through.

As for Buck, he'd looked down at his plate, but the set of his shoulders told her he wasn't happy. Something had happened to him, maybe to both of them, and Gina couldn't help wondering about it.

"I'll help this morning, if you'll allow it," she said, "and then work on doing what I can this afternoon with my car so I can move on. Maybe there's a police officer who can run me out to where it is. I'll need to take some gas."

And she'd need to rely on God, because twenty dollars wasn't going to buy much gas or baby food, and it was all she had.

Buck heaved a sigh as he put the last stroke of paint on the breakfast-room wall. Having Gina here was even more difficult than he'd expected.

She worked hard, that was for sure. She'd single-handedly cleaned one of the guest rooms that had been finished but a mess. Carried out vinyl sheeting and masking tape, swept up nails, scrubbed the floor on her hands and knees, polished the bathroom fixtures to a shine. Now she was removing the tape from the area he'd painted yesterday.

The only time she stopped working was when Bobby cried. Then she'd slip off, he assumed to nurse the baby or to change his diaper. She'd put together a makeshift play-pen from a blanket and pillows, and he crawled around it and batted at a couple of toys she had in her diaper bag.

She was resourceful, able to compartmentalize in a way few women he'd known could do. Certainly, in a way Ivana hadn't been able to do.

Unfortunately, in other ways, it was way too much like having Ivana around. Some of their best times had been working around the house together with the baby nearby. They'd felt like a happy family then.

So having Gina and Bobby here now brought back good memories, but alongside them, a keen, aching awareness of all he'd lost. All he'd thrown away, really.

He shook himself out of that line of thought. He had a mission, and he needed to stick to it. *Find out what you can about her*, Lacey had told him.

He was curious enough that the job didn't rankle. Not only would they find out whether she could be trusted to stay in their house another night, but he could maybe get rid of the crazy impression that this woman was just like Ivana.

"Do you want me to help with the trim?" She came in now, a little out of breath, with Bobby on her hip. "Or I could work on the kitchen cabinets. I noticed they need cleaning out."

"I'd stay out of Lacey's stuff. You'd better work on the cabinets in here. Do you know how to use a screwdriver?"

"Sure."

She set Bobby up in the corner of this room and went to work washing the cabinet fronts, removing the handles, humming a wordless tune.

It was a little too domestic for him. "So, how are you gonna punt here?" he asked, his voice coming out rougher than he'd intended. "You got a plan?"

She looked up, and her eyes were dark with some emotion he couldn't name. "I thought I'd try the churches in town first," she said. "Where I lived before, some of the churches had programs for homeless families. Just until I can get on my feet and figure out what to do next." She paused. "I'd prefer finding work, but I don't know what's available."

So she thought of herself as homeless. That suggested she wasn't just traveling from point A to point B. Something else was wrong. And it was weird, because she did have that rich-girl look to her. Her clothes were stylish and new, her haircut and manicure expensive looking. But she also looked scared.

"Not sure if you'll find anything formal around here, but the churches are big on outreach. I can take you to ours. And then…you mentioned talking to the police about your car?"

"They'll want to get it off the road as much as I do." She frowned. "I just hope they won't put my name in some kind of system."

"You hiding from someone?" he asked mildly.

Her eyebrows went together and her eyes hooded. "I… Yeah. You could say that."

"Boyfriend? Husband?"

She shook her head. "I'd rather not talk about it."

That figured. A woman as pretty as she was had to have a partner, and Bobby had a father. Had someone abused her? "I'm not asking you to tell me everything, but I can help you better if I know your situation."

Her cheeks flushed with what looked like embarrassment. "Thanks." She wasn't saying more, obviously.

"Where were you headed, originally?" he pushed on as he finished painting the crown molding.

She didn't answer, so he repeated the question.

"I don't know," she said finally. "Anywhere. It didn't matter. I just had to leave." She studied the cupboard she was sanding, one of the old-fashioned and charming parts of the breakfast room, according to Lacey. "I wouldn't mind finding a place to settle for a while. As long as it was safe."

Not here, not here. He didn't need any complications in Rescue River, and this woman seemed like a complication. "Safe from what?"

She shook her head. "Too long of a story." Her voice sounded tense.

"Okay, then, what would you like to work at? What are you shooting for, jobwise?"

"My line of work was being a housewife, but obviously I need to find something else."

Hmm. From the little she'd told him, he'd guess she'd been abused. And the last thing he and Lacey needed around here was an angry husband looking for his wife and child. She didn't show any bruises, but maybe they were hidden. "What are you good at?"

"Organizing things. Raising kids. Planning parties." She shrugged. "The type of thing housewives do."

He'd have said that housewives washed dishes and cooked meals. He had a feeling about what kind of housewife she'd been—not an ordinary one. With that breakfast she'd cooked, he could imagine her catering to some wealthy husband, giving brunches for country-club ladies.

So it was very interesting that she'd run away.

* * *

Gina was bone tired after her short, broken sleep and a morning of physical work, and stressed out about the eleven messages she'd found on her phone, her in-laws demanding that she return Bobby to them immediately. Of course she'd disabled the GPS on her smartphone, but she was still worried her in-laws could somehow find her.

But Buck had offered to drive her around and, tired or not, she needed to seize the opportunity. Once she had her vehicle nearby with some gas in it, she'd feel better. She'd have an escape route and she wouldn't be quite so dependent on the kindness of strangers.

When she went out to Buck's truck, he was leaning in through the rear door, adjusting something.

"Wow, where'd you get a car seat? That's wonderful!"

He cleared his throat. "It was sitting around here." He reached out and took Bobby from her arms without meeting her eyes, then settled him into the infant seat and expertly adjusted the straps.

Mr. Tough Guy continued to surprise her.

They stopped first at the grocery store, a small, homey market a quarter the size of the superstore she'd shopped at back home. The aroma of rotisserie chicken filled the air, and bushels of produce, labeled as locally grown, stood in rows just inside the front door. Gina held Bobby in his sling, facing out so he could see the people passing by, which he loved. Buck waved to a cashier and pounded a bagger on the back as they walked toward the baby aisle.

When they got there, she picked out six jars of the cheapest baby food available. She looked over at the diapers and bit her lip, hoping the single one remaining in the diaper bag would last until she got to the box in the SUV.

Buck held a plastic basket for their purchases and studied

the shelves. "Look at this stuff. Turkey with pears. What self-respecting baby would eat that?"

"I know. We used to see the weirdest baby food at World Gourmet. Avocado risotto, vanilla bean with spinach..." But that was a lifetime ago, when she'd been able to shop at the most expensive healthy foods emporium in her California town.

"Buck Armstrong, is that you?" came a woman's husky voice.

They both turned. There in the food aisle of the Star Market was the most beautiful woman Gina had ever seen. Tall, super skinny, with high cheekbones and long shiny stick-straight black hair.

A little intimidated by the woman's breathtaking looks, Gina could only offer a smile.

"Amy Franklin?" Buck reached out and hugged the woman, then held her shoulders to look at her, a genuine smile on his face. "It's been a lot of years. Welcome home!"

"It's nice to be back. Kind of." The woman wrinkled her nose. "And this must be your wife and baby! I heard you'd married. He's adorable!" She reached out to tickle Bobby's chin.

"No, I'm not—"

"No, this isn't—"

They both broke off. Bobby reached out to grab for the woman's gold necklace.

"No, sweetie." Gina loosened his fingers from the shiny chain and took a step back. "I'm just a friend he's helping," she said to the woman.

"Oh! My bad." The woman looked apologetic. "I have a little one, too," she said, turning her attention to Gina. "I'm raising my nephew, Tyler, and he's about this one's age. Maybe we could get together for a playdate sometime."

"That would be great. I'm..." She paused, wondering how to describe her uncertain status. "I'm just in from California and I don't know anyone. Well, except Buck and his sister."

"I'm originally from California, too! We should definitely get together!"

Gina felt a surge of warmth. The idea of making mom friends on her own, rather than having acquaintances who were part of her wealthy in-laws' power network, was just what she hadn't known she was hungry for. "That would be great! Where's your nephew now?"

"Oh, I'm trying out a babysitter, so I came to the grocery to give her an hour alone with him. And it's killing me! I should go back, but give me your phone number and I'll be in touch."

They punched numbers into each other's cell phones, and then the woman gave Buck a quick wave and left.

"Wow, is this town always that friendly?" she asked Buck.

He nodded and tried to smile, but his eyes were hooded and lines bracketed his mouth.

"Buck?" She touched his shoulder.

He shook his head very quickly a couple of times. "We done here?"

"Um, sure. I think so."

"Let's go." He turned and walked toward the checkout, rapid but stiff.

She hurried after him. "What just happened?"

"Nothing. I think I'll go ahead on out, wait in the truck."

"But why?"

He stopped so quickly that she ran into him. "You look a lot like my wife. My dead wife. People who don't know me well and don't know what happened are going to think you're her."

"Ooh." Realization dawned. "And your baby? What happened to your baby?"

"Dead in the same car accident." His words were clipped, toneless. "Let's go."

It was what he didn't say that haunted her through the checkout and the ride to their next stop, the church. She longed to ask him more about it but didn't dare push the issue.

Obviously, his pain was raw. And having her around was like salt in the wound.

Too bad, because she was really starting to like Rescue River.

Chapter 3

When they arrived at the church on the edge of town, Gina was captivated. Its white steeple shone bright against the blue sky, and the building was surrounded by a grassy lawn. A creek rambled alongside the church, and several long picnic tables stood under a shelter. It was easy to picture small-town church picnics on that lawn.

Gina hoisted Bobby to her hip and followed Buck toward the church. As they walked up the steps, the door opened and several men came out dressed in work clothes, followed by another in a police uniform. Everyone greeted Buck, and the police officer tickled Bobby under his chin, making him giggle. That close, Gina could see the name tag that indicated he was the chief. Her stomach tightened. For the first time in her life, she felt like law enforcement officers were her enemies, not her friends.

Buck introduced her and briefly explained her story,

even though Gina was willing him to be quiet with all her silent might.

"Car broke down, eh?" Chief Dion said. "SUV? White?"

"That's the one," she said faintly.

"Saw it this morning. Ran the plates."

Gina's heart thudded like a doom-filled drumbeat. Had her in-laws reported her car missing?

"Our computers aren't communicating too well with those in California, so I couldn't get any information," he said. "Glad to know it's got an owner. Need any help getting back on the road?"

"It's just out of—"

"We might," Buck interjected. "We're headed out there in just a few minutes."

"Call me if there's any problem," Chief Dion offered. "In fact, I might be able to meet you out there or have one of our officers meet you. Make sure everything's okay."

"Sounds good."

As soon as Dion was gone, she turned to Buck. "Why'd you tell him we might need help? It's just out of gas. And I'd...rather not have police involvement."

"Oh? Why's that?"

"It's complicated." He'd been very helpful, and yet she couldn't fully trust him. She'd yet to meet the person who couldn't be swayed by her in-laws' money and power. The police detective she'd consulted privately about their unnecessary roughness had brushed aside her concerns and seemed more interested in how to get the wealthy couple to donate even more money to the local police department.

No, it was her and Bobby against the world. She headed on into the church, welcoming the dark, cool air.

"Come on—pastor's this way." As he took the lead, his shoulder brushed against her in the narrow hallway. An awareness clicked into her, something she hadn't felt since well before her husband had died. Whoa. What was *that*?

As they approached a doorway marked Pastor's Study, a middle-aged man stood up from behind the desk and came out to greet them, shaking Buck's hand heartily and then turning to her. "What a pleasure! Buck, we don't see you here often enough these days. You just missed the men's prayer group, fixing up one of the elementary classrooms. What brings you here?"

"This is Gina," Buck said. "She's looking for some help. Gina, meet Pastor Ricky."

Heat flushed Gina's face. She hated being in this position: helpless, homeless, asking for what amounted to a handout. *It's for Bobby*, she reminded herself.

The pastor invited them in, and Gina sat down, cuddled Bobby to her chest and explained their situation to a minimal degree. Homeless, purse stolen, looking for work and a place to stay.

The pastor nodded sympathetically. "The church isn't really set up for that," he said. "When we need places for people to stay, we usually ask families to put them up. In fact, Lacey, Buck's sister, has helped us out a few times."

"It would work better if she stayed somewhere else," Buck said.

Ouch! Gina had been an interloper back at her in-laws' place, where she'd been tolerated because she had given birth to the heir to the empire. But that feeling of always being on the outside, a burden, was a part of what she'd been fleeing.

The last thing she wanted was to feel that way at Lacey's place, but Buck was making it obvious that he didn't want her there.

"Let's see. There's Lou Ann Miller, but I think she's

away visiting her sister. Maybe Susan Hayashi? Except her mom and brother are here visiting, and they're doing some renovations on Sam's house. Getting ready for the wedding, you know. Such a nice couple." He looked at Buck's impatient expression and waved a hand. "But you don't need to hear about all that. You're sure Lacey's place isn't an option?"

"Like I said, somewhere else would be better."

"Sure enough. I'll ask around. And I'll check the balance in the emergency fund." The pastor studied Buck with a level expression, obviously wondering what was going on. "I'd take you in myself, except we have a houseful of teenagers for the Artists for Christ Concert over in Mansfield. Not very quiet for your baby."

As if on cue, Bobby wiggled hard, trying to get down to the floor, and she gave the place a quick check for hazards and then set him down. "Do you know of any jobs?" she blurted out before she knew what she was saying. And wondered when Rescue River had become a viable place to live. "I don't want charity—I want to work, and I'm willing to do anything. I'm good at decorating, cooking and event planning, and I'm really organized. And I have most of a college degree." Her voice cracked a little on the last word. She'd been thinking about her job skills ever since she left her in-laws' place, and figuring out how to package her housewife background into something more impressive. Still, it was hard to brag about herself.

"Hmm. Again, we're a very small town, so I don't know of much. But what about Lacey? She's doing all that renovation. Surely she could use some help…"

"That's not going to work." Buck's words were flat, firm and final.

And that irked Gina. She scooped Bobby back up into

her arms. "I'm sorry I remind you of your ex. I'll get out of your hair as soon as I can. But I have to do my best for my son. Why are you so against my working for Lacey, if I can talk her into it?"

He lifted an eyebrow, clearly trying to play it cool. "Because you're on the run and we know nothing about you." He rubbed the back of his neck with one hand. "And...look, Lacey's not as strong as she acts. Let's leave it at that."

What could she say? She nodded, feeling like there was more to the story.

The pastor put a hand on each of their arms. "Let's take it to the Lord," he suggested, and Gina felt ashamed she hadn't done more praying about her situation. She'd been too tired and too worried, but that was exactly when she needed to turn it over to God. Buck and Gina bowed their heads, and the pastor uttered a short prayer for Gina to find shelter and work and for everyone to get along. Something like that. Though she felt too upset and flustered to focus on the words, the pastor's heartfelt prayer offered a tiny sense of peace.

At the gas station, Buck pulled out a couple of five-gallon gas cans. "We'll fill both of these," he said to the attendant who came out to help, even though they were at a self-serve pump.

Gina touched Buck's arm, embarrassed. "Um, could we just fill one? About halfway? That should do me until..." She trailed off, her face heating. Never in her life had she been completely broke, not able to afford more than a couple of gallons of gas at a time.

He waved a hand. "Don't worry about it. We'll fill both."

"No, I'd rather just do what I can afford."

"I said don't worry about it."

"Trying to get me as far away as you can, are you?" She

was half joking, and then she saw on his face that she'd guessed exactly right. "Fine, fill both." She slammed back into Buck's truck, feeling unaccountably hurt.

There was no particular reason why Buck should like her or want her to stay. Just because he'd rescued her last night, he didn't have responsibility for her future or Bobby's. That was solely on her shoulders.

The thing was, as she rode around Rescue River, even now as she watched the gas-station attendant clap Buck on the shoulder and help him lift the heavy gas cans into the back of his pickup, she *liked* this place. She could picture herself and Bobby playing in the park and attending the church and getting together with other friendly people. She could imagine herself a part of this community.

On the other hand, the idea of the man beside her resisting every moment of her presence was disconcerting. She hated not being wanted. She'd grown up feeling that way, and she'd married into a family where she felt like an outsider. Was she continuing her same sick pattern?

Rescue River was where the Lord had led her. It seemed like the perfect place to stay, at least for a while.

She just had to convince Buck not to block the whole idea.

Buck helped Gina fill the gas tank on her loaded, late-model SUV, continuing to wonder what her story was, continuing to get distracted by the lemony scent of her hair. Dion was there, too, helping and subtly questioning, observing everything.

It was early evening, but Buck could still hear the steady *chink-chink-chink* of a rotary tiller off in the distance. Probably Rob Richardson, trying to get his field finished before the rain came on. Sun peeked through a bank of dark clouds, illuminating the freshly plowed acre beside them. Buck inhaled the sweet, pungent zing that indicated a storm was headed their way.

Gina thanked them both politely, strapped Bobby into the car seat and headed back to the guesthouse. Buck was about to climb into his truck when Dion gestured to him. "Stay back a minute, would you?"

Buck turned toward the police chief. "Sure. What's up?"

It wasn't like he was eager to get home. He was half hoping that Gina, now that she had a tank of gas and some baby food, would hightail it to the next town. Or the next state.

Then again, what would she do if she left Rescue River? Alone without money and with a baby to care for, what were the odds that she'd survive, let alone do well?

He didn't want to worry about her, because being around her disturbed him on so many levels. Her resemblance to Ivana evoked all kinds of feelings he'd had during his marriage. That initial attraction. Anger at how Ivana's love for him had cooled. Fear that he'd made a lifelong mistake in marrying her, and guilt that he'd let his feelings show.

Horrible guilt about how everything had ended. And with that, the way his drinking had spiraled out of control.

"We have a little bit of a problem," Dion said.

"With the car?"

"More so with the baby. Did you notice the bandage on his arm?"

Buck nodded. "She said it's a scratch."

"Mmm-hmm. Have you seen any other marks on the kid?"

Buck stared at Dion as the puzzle pieces started moving into place. "You're thinking...what? That somebody abused the baby?"

"Could be." Dion nodded, not looking at Buck, staring out over the fields. "Could be her."

"No." Buck reeled back against that accusation. "I've seen how protective she is. She wouldn't do anything to hurt him. I more got the impression that she's running away."

"That's my gut instinct, too, but she's a pretty woman and a mother, so guys like us can be a little distracted. Keep your eyes open for it, would you?"

"Did you find out something against her?"

Dion frowned. "Not officially. But I have a few friends in law enforcement on the West Coast. Apparently, someone tried to report the car stolen, only to find out that it's not even eligible for unlawful use for another four days."

"Unlawful use? So…"

"So she took a car that belongs to a family member or friend. Maybe she had permission to use it, but not to take off in it."

"What are you saying? What do you want to do?"

"I'm thinking she's either a woman in trouble, or she's trouble herself. Either way, that baby's the victim."

"So we should…"

"We should try to get her to stay in Rescue River, is what I'm thinking." Dion frowned, rubbed a hand over his chin. "No, it's not exactly our problem, and we can't make her stay, but it would be a good thing for her to stick around here until I can make some phone calls, find out what her story is. It's safe here, and I can monitor the situation, make sure she's not the abuser and maybe prevent those who are from finding her."

Something primal raised the hairs on the back of Buck's neck, and he gave Dion a narrow stare. "You like her, don't you?"

They weren't exactly friends. Dion had pulled Buck out

of a couple of fights in his role as a cop, when Buck was drinking. Nowadays, Dion was more likely to evangelize him, which was almost worse. But at least it meant that Dion didn't think he was unredeemable, like so many in town did.

Maybe they had the beginnings of a friendship, but it wasn't enough to quell Buck's irrational twinge of jealousy at the thought of Dion liking Gina.

Dion's eyebrows came together. "What're you talking about, man? I don't even know her. I just see a Christian duty, and a judicial one, to watch out for her. And to watch her. Asking for your help as a citizen."

Buck chuckled, feeling relieved. "That's a first. You asking me to help you on the right side of the law."

"People change." Dion gave him a level stare. "Remember that, my man. People change."

Buck pondered that thought all the way home, and it gave him a spring to his step as he trotted up the guesthouse stairs, trying to stay ahead of the rain that was starting to fall. People changed. Maybe even him.

Just before he touched the door handle, he saw a movement on the far side of the porch.

Gina. Rocking gently on the porch swing, pulling a blanket over her shoulder, probably to shield Bobby from the sound of Buck's footsteps and the flash of lightning.

He walked quietly toward them, mindful of what Dion had said. He wanted to watch how she handled Bobby with Dion's questions in mind. If Gina was in trouble, he wanted to help her somehow. He couldn't push her away, no matter how disturbing it was to be around her. She could be in real danger.

"Hey," he said, keeping his concerns out of his tone. "You made it back okay? Vehicle's running well?"

She nodded. "Yes, and Lacey said we can stay one more night. Only one, though. Then we have to be on our way." She sounded sad.

"Do you...want to stay more?"

She adjusted Bobby with a tender care and private, loving smile. Then she looked out at the rainy twilight. "I like it here, and it feels safe. Like a good place to get my bearings."

"That's the town's history and reputation," he said. "Rescue River's always opened its arms to those in need."

"It feels welcoming." She shot him a glance. "Well, mostly."

Buck decided to be honest. "I feel for your situation, but..." He trailed off as she adjusted Bobby again, and he realized exactly what she was doing.

She was nursing him.

He stood up quickly. "Whoa, I'm sorry to intrude. I didn't realize..."

"It's okay," she said, chuckling. "It's a natural thing and I know how to cover up. I've fed Bobby in all kinds of places."

"That's...pretty cool." He'd never been one of those guys who was turned off by nursing or pregnancy or childbirth. Just the opposite, in fact. He'd never loved Ivana more, never felt closer to her, than when she was in the height and glory of womanhood, pregnant with his child or feeding little Mia from her own body. The whole thing amazed him. God's creativity in action.

Rain was pounding hard now, bringing with it a fresh, clean-washed smell and cooler air.

He felt himself looking at Gina in a new light. His heart

warmed toward her in a visceral way: that ancient male re-action to a mother and child in need. Yes, having her here was disturbing, but he thought he could handle it, at least for a short time.

And after all, he wouldn't be here for long himself. He was putting every penny he had into making restitution, repaying money he'd borrowed, getting back on his feet. Living here with Lacey rent-free in exchange for his reno-vation work. He didn't have the means to leave town, not yet, but he would soon.

"I like it here, Buck," Gina said. "I think God may have sent me and Bobby here for a reason. I'm thinking, maybe, I'd like to stay."

His ambivalence must have shown on his face, because she cocked her head to one side and spoke. "That bothers you, doesn't it? How come? Is it about my resemblance to your wife?"

"Somewhat." Actually, he was starting to wonder how he'd ever mistaken her for Ivana. She had a plucky strength and determination, a set to her chin, a way of holding her-self that were completely her own. Still, he had questions.

She frowned and looked down at Bobby, who was start-ing to show signs of being done nursing. She turned a little away and wiped his mouth.

"Want me to burp him?" he asked before he could stop himself.

She quirked an eyebrow. "Can you?"

"Sure." He leaned down and picked up the baby boy and held him against his shoulder. He was sturdier than Mia had been. Gina had mentioned that Bobby was ten months. Mia had made it only eight.

But propping a baby with one hand, flipping the burp

cloth over his shoulder, patting the baby's back, that all came right back to him. Like riding a bike. You didn't forget.

He pulled Bobby a little closer, breathing him in, cherishing the feel of the baby, pretending he was Mia. Pretending his little daughter was still alive and well and happy. That he hadn't driven Ivana from their home in a moment of anger and desperation.

If only none of it had happened.

"Look," she said, "I'm sorry if I bring up memories for you. Maybe I'll get on my feet quickly and be able to get out of here. But meanwhile..."

"Meanwhile what?" He was holding her baby in the rainy twilight, looking at her and finding her beautiful, and feeling like he might be stepping into the biggest mess of his life.

And then, as he adjusted the sweet little bundle in his arms, Bobby's pajama leg came up and he saw it.

A bruise the size of a beer coaster. Or a man's fist.

"If it were just me, I'd leave for your sake," she said. "But this looks like the perfect safe place for Bobby, and I have to put him first."

He concealed his reaction to the bruise and stroked the baby's downy hair, his heart pounding. "Of course you do."

"But I don't know why I'm even talking to you about it. Your sister's the one who's determined to get rid of me." She was looking up at him with troubled eyes as the wind blew a strand of hair in front of her face. "I don't know what to do."

He could see that it cost her to admit that, to ask for advice. She'd do it, though, for her son. He could already tell she was that kind of woman.

He didn't think she could possibly have injured Bobby,

which meant that someone else had done it. Someone she was running from?

And if so, what right did he have to push her away? Especially if it resulted in this little one being hurt again?

He patted Bobby's back until a loud burp made them both laugh. Then he sat down in the rocker across from the porch swing, still holding Bobby.

"Want to tell me about Bobby's father?"

She drew in a breath and let it out again, slowly, seeming to consider. Finally, she spoke. "Hank was…smart and handsome. And rich."

He smiled. "Bodes well for Bobby."

"Yes. I just hope he doesn't inherit a couple of the other genes."

"Like?"

"Like the addiction-prone one."

"Oh." Buck looked away, feeling ashamed. Addiction was considered genetic by some, but more of a character flaw by most. And it was a flaw he shared. "Did your husband ever do AA or anything like that?"

"He was more into cocaine," she said, "but sure, he did NA. Plenty of times."

"It never took?" That was discouraging. "You're talking about him in the past tense. Is he dead?"

"He died not long after Bobby was born. Ski accident."

"Drugs?"

She nodded. "Yes. He was high, skiing one of the most dangerous double black diamond slopes in California. He didn't have a chance."

"I'm sorry." Why did a guy do drugs when he had a wife and baby who needed him?

Then again, why did any addict do what he did?

"So that's not who you're running from."

She shook her head. "No. It's...my in-laws."

"Your husband's family? What's the problem there?"

She sighed. "Abuse, if you must know. I don't want to talk about it."

Buck's pulse rate shot up. There it was. He'd like to get his hands on those people. "If they abused you or Bobby, they should go to prison."

"They should, but they won't," she said with complete certainty.

"They're that powerful?"

"They're that powerful."

The sky was black velvet now, the air cooling more. She huddled under the blanket she'd been using as a nursing cover. She looked so pretty. So vulnerable. So in need of protection.

As was the little baby now sleeping in his arms.

He wasn't going to let anything happen between him and Gina, no way, but he had to let her stay. Dion had asked him to, and he had a lot to report to the police chief. And maybe, just maybe, it was a way for him to get over Ivana, move on. Maybe this was part of the restitution he was trying to practice in his recovery.

He was to make amends for wrongs he had done. Well, he was doing that with bar owners around town, with friends he'd borrowed from. With Lacey, who'd had to put up with a lot from him during his two-year drinking spree.

But the people he'd wronged the most were dead.

Could he make restitution through Gina and Bobby? Give something to them, and that way right the balance with his wife and child, who were beyond earthly help?

And once he'd made his restitution and saved up a little money, he'd leave. Leave, with a clean slate, and start over somewhere where nobody knew his past. It was what he wanted. All he wanted. All he was working for.

The wind blew the cool farm air toward the house, fragrant with fresh-plowed earth. Crickets sang out in a chorus. Streetlights flickered on down the block, where the shops were.

He slid one hand away from the baby and into his pocket where he carried his recovery coin. Six months sober. He could handle this new challenge.

"I'll talk to Lacey," he said gruffly. "Try to get her to let you stay awhile. And you can work on the renovation with me."

Chapter 4

Later that night, Gina had just closed her eyes when her phone buzzed. She grabbed it, not wanting to risk waking Bobby.

When she saw it was her friend Haley, back in California, she sat upright. "Hang on," she whispered and slipped a robe over her lightweight tank top and shorts.

Grabbing her phone, she hurried down to the small alcove on the landing of the stairs. It was one of the few public areas in the guesthouse that was finished, with lace curtains and a braided rug. She settled into the window seat, pulled her feet up underneath her and leaned back against comfortable cushions. She could see the half-open door of her room at the top of the stairs, so she'd notice if Bobby stirred.

"Okay, I can talk," she said quietly. "How are you? I miss you so much!" Ever since she and Haley had shared a room on the maternity floor, their babies born within hours of one another, they'd been close friends. Haley was the only person in whom Gina had confided about her plans to leave town.

"I miss you, too, but that's not why I called."

"Are the dogs okay?"

Haley laughed. "They're bad, and spoiled, but you know I love them. No, that's not the problem."

"Did you find anything out?" She was hoping, though not expecting, that Haley had figured out a way she could gain access to some of the money she should have inherited as Hank's widow.

"It's not good news." Haley cleared her throat and went into business mode, not a problem for her since she worked in a bank. "I've been nosing around, and it sounds like assets in probate can be tangled up for a year, eighteen months if the estate is complicated."

"Which it is." Hank's parents, seeing the mess Hank had made of his life after Bobby was born, had put most of his inheritance in trust. Gina even suspected that they'd gotten Hank to sign some CDs over to them when he was high.

"I talked to my manager—in confidence, didn't identify you—and she said that because there wasn't a will, there's no way around this long process. I'm so mad Hank didn't protect you and Bobby!"

"I know." Gina's chest ached, as it always did when she thought of Hank. He'd been so much fun when they'd first met; he'd swept her off her feet, had loved her madly. In the first two years of their marriage she'd realized his partying went further than it should—sometimes much further—but they'd still had a base of love and care for each other.

Bobby's arrival had changed everything. The responsibility of fatherhood had overwhelmed Hank, and Gina, sleep deprived and cranky, hadn't been as understanding as before. He'd gone off the deep end, dug into his bad habits and made the leap from recreational drug user to addict.

"He wasn't thinking straight," she said to Haley and left it at that.

"The good news is, within a few years, when it's all straightened out, you and Bobby should be okay." Haley's voice didn't sound all that reassuring, though.

"It sounds like there's a *but* in there somewhere."

"There is." Haley's voice sounded shaky. "Gina, there's a big problem."

"What? Tell me." Gina's heart felt like a stone. She wanted to start a new life, for herself but even more, for Bobby. But right now, it seemed like she'd never get free.

"It's your in-laws. When I saw Hank's cousin this morning, she told me they're going to report your car as stolen."

"What?" From the downstairs kitchen, Gina heard what sounded like an argument and lowered her voice. "That car's mine! Hank gave it to me!"

"But is the title in your name?"

Gina squeezed her eyes shut as if she could block out this unwelcome news. "No. It was in Hank's name."

"And since the estate's stuck in probate…"

Gina leaned her head back against the window, staring up at the ceiling. If they'd reported the car stolen, she was essentially a common criminal.

"Gina? Honey?"

Gina blew out a breath. "I'll be tracked down for sure, then, because the police department here has my vehicle information. What am I going to do?" Her voice broke on the last couple of words, and she swallowed hard, determined to maintain control.

"I've already thought about that. You've got to give it back, that's all."

"Give it back? When I'm here and they're in California?"

"Yep, and I've figured out how. You use one of those driving services. They load your vehicle on a truck and drive it across the country. It's done all the time."

Gina was still wrapping her mind around the facts: that her car wasn't her car, and that she was a wanted criminal. "It's got to be expensive," she said finally. "I'm almost out of money."

"Didn't you say you had a debit card?"

She did. "But it's not safe to use it." It wasn't as if there was a lot of money in the old joint account—Hank had drained most of it away in the months before his death— but there was something. Something for Bobby's future, if they could make it through the first couple of months.

Haley sighed audibly. "No. No, it's not safe, especially now that you're a wanted person. The police could track you to where you are."

Gina felt a sharp rush of shame that she had no savings of her own. If only she hadn't acquiesced to staying home with Bobby... She glanced up toward her room. No, she couldn't regret that decision. They'd both agreed that since they had the means, it would be best for her to spend Bobby's early years at home with him.

She shoved open the window, letting the rain-soaked breeze soothe her hot face.

"We've got to hire you a transportation service, have you send back the car. The way I see it, you don't have a choice." Haley cleared her throat. "I talked to Josh. We... we can pay for it."

"No." Gina couldn't let her friend do that. She and her husband had tons of student debt and no family money. Although they both worked, the high cost of living in their part of the state made it so that they barely scraped by every month.

And yet Haley was right. Staying out of trouble with the law was a bigger priority even than a financial safety net.

"Look, what if I mail you my ATM card? That way you can take the money out of my account, and if it's traced, it'll be local, not here." Gina couldn't believe how quickly she was able to flip into criminal mode when it was Bobby's safety in question. "If I do that, can you set it up for me? Do we just send the SUV to them? I'm afraid they'll find out where it came from and track us down."

"Nope. Overnight the card to me, and I'll get it all set up right away. As soon as the SUV arrives, I'll drive it over to your in-laws' place and leave it."

"How? In the middle of the night?"

"Maybe. Or maybe I'll figure out some explanation." She paused. "I really want this to work for you, Gina. I miss you, but you did the right thing. Bobby comes first."

"Thank you so much. You're an amazing friend." Her throat tight, she chatted for a couple more minutes and then ended the call.

How was she going to manage without a vehicle? And yet, what choice did she have?

She looked out the window at the streetlights of Rescue River. The main street glistened with today's rain. She could see the market, the diner, the library.

She could see them, which meant she could walk to them. She looked up at the stars. "You knew what You were doing when You put me here, Father," she murmured in a low voice.

She let out a sigh and slid her feet down to the floor... only to shriek at the sight of a large figure standing a couple of steps down from the landing. When she recognized Buck, her heart rate settled a little.

He flicked on the hall light. "Sorry to startle you. I was talking to Lacey about your situation. Coming upstairs to my room." Unnecessarily, he gestured toward the upper floor. "I didn't mean to eavesdrop."

She remembered the raised voices she'd heard. "Let me guess," she said. "Your talk with Lacey didn't go well."

"I'm afraid not." He sat on the other end of the curved window seat, his face barely visible in the glow of a streetlight. "She's just not comfortable having you here. She said you could stay for a couple more days, through Monday, Tuesday if you really need to, but that's all."

The weight of her responsibilities pressed down on Gina. She couldn't stay, then, not unless she found another job. But she couldn't go, not with her transportation being taken out from under her.

"Hey, I'm sorry." He reached out a hand and patted her shoulder.

Surely he meant it as a friendly touch, but to Gina, the warmth of his large hand made her want to hurl herself into his arms. He seemed so strong and competent and kind.

And she couldn't give in to that desire to be rescued. "Thanks for trying. With God's help, I'll figure out something."

Rather than nodding and moving away, he gave her shoulder another pat and looked into her eyes. "When I met you, I thought you were one of those ladies who lunch, someone who never had a problem. But that's far from the truth, isn't it?"

"Miles away." She couldn't handle the compassion in his eyes, but she couldn't look away, either.

"If I wasn't knee-deep in problems of my own, problems

of my own creation, I'd try to help you more." He squeezed her shoulder once and then pulled his hand away.

"Thanks." She actually believed him.

"One thing I *can* offer," he said, "is an invitation to church tomorrow. Nine o'clock. It's a great community church, the one we stopped by before, and who knows, maybe someone is hiring or can put you up." He sounded doubtful. And she couldn't tell whether he wanted her to stay or not. Probably not.

He was offering her solace, and shamefully, church didn't seem like a lot of help right now. But it was what she had, and she knew, intellectually at least, that God was big enough to handle any problem.

And she also knew that staying here in the dim moonlight, talking to a very handsome and compassionate man, wasn't the solution to anything. She stood and turned toward the stairs. "I'd love to go. Thanks for asking."

Minutes after Gina went into her room and closed the door, Buck trotted downstairs. He was putting on his coat when Lacey came out of the kitchen, holding her orange cat in her arms.

"Where are you going?" she asked. "It's late."

"Need some air." The conversation with Gina had thrown him off balance in more ways than one, and he knew he wouldn't sleep anytime soon.

Not to mention he was worried about the baby. Earlier tonight, when Gina had gone inside to fetch his binky, Buck had snapped a photo of Bobby's bruise to show Dion.

His sister cuddled the cat closer and studied him, her forehead wrinkled.

"It's just a walk, Lace."

"You're sure?"

"Yes!" Then, ashamed of his sharp tone, he put an arm around her shoulders and gave her a gentle squeeze. He shouldn't be mad at her when she'd bailed him out of so many problems. Between her own tragedies and his bad behavior, his waiflike younger sister had been forced to grow stronger than any woman should have to be. "I won't be out long and I won't do…what I used to do."

"I know." She leaned into his side. "I just got in the habit of worrying about you, know what I mean?"

"I know. But I'm fine."

At least, he *hoped* he was fine, he thought as he stepped out the door. In the past, he'd have for sure gone on a bender just because he felt mixed up about that encounter with Gina.

He was worried about what he'd overheard, but that wasn't all of it.

Turned out God had a sense of humor. He was *attracted* to the pretty, maternal stranger.

Buck blew out a sigh and strode through Rescue River's small business district. A farming community to the core, the town shut down early. The diner and the shops all had doors closed and lights off.

Clouds scuttled over the moon and a breeze rattled the tree limbs. Buck pulled his coat closer around him. Ohio weather. Yesterday had been springlike, but tonight it felt like a front was coming through.

There *was* one business still open, one place where light and happy noises indicated life: the Ace Tavern.

Buck straightened his back and told himself to keep walking. And he did. He walked past.

Behind him, the door of the tavern opened. Could he be blamed for turning back? Any combat vet worth his salt had it ingrained: know what's going on behind you.

A long-haired woman came out, alone. Wearing a jacket that didn't look too warm, skintight jeans and ridiculously high heels. There was a click, a flash, and she got her cigarette lit, then looked up and saw him. "Hey, handsome, come buy me a drink," she said. Then she squinted and leaned toward him, catching herself on the bar's wooden outside wall. "Well, if you ain't a sight for sore eyes. Buck Armstrong."

He stepped closer and recognition dawned. "Hey, Heather, how's it going?" He reached out to grasp her hand and ended up steadying her. "Been a while." Heather was at least fifteen years older than Buck, but they'd been good drinking buddies. Heather was one of the few people in town who'd been able to match Buck shot for shot.

The thought of that brought a tight feeling to his throat.

A glass of whiskey, he knew, would take that feeling away. Warm him right up, too.

"Gonna finish my smoke and then go back in. C'mon, have a cold one and let me know what you been up to." She spoke slowly and carefully but still tripped over a few of the words. Did he used to sound like that?

"You planning on driving home tonight?" He knew Heather lived out in the country, had been to a couple of parties at her place.

"Sure, yeah. Why, want to come out my way?"

"No, not tonight, thanks."

"Your loss." She turned to go back into the bar and stumbled.

Catching her, Buck blew out a breath. He knew well enough what falling-down drunk looked like, and Heather was falling-down drunk. And he needed to make sure someone would take care of her. Holding her elbow, he steered her inside.

The bar wasn't crowded. A couple of guys playing pool, a man and woman talking intently in a booth, and three or four of his old acquaintances at the bar. Regulars, people who didn't have much family. Whether they hung out at the Ace because of that, or whether their drinking had pushed loved ones away, they didn't have another place to go, and the bar served as home to them.

"Hey, Armstrong!" Word circled around the place, and it was like he'd never left. Guys clapping him on the back, Heather clinging to his arm, proud to have brought in a popular old friend, the bartender turning over glasses, shot and a beer, his old favorite.

"Not tonight, Arnie," he told the bartender, leading Heather to a table and then extricating himself from her grasp.

Mild catcalls of disapproval greeted his refusal. Everyone here knew he was in AA and probably didn't want to tempt him too badly, but they'd welcome him back into the fold in a minute. His choice.

He stepped over to the bar and handed Arnie a couple of bills. "Get someone to take Heather home tonight, could you? She shouldn't be driving."

Arnie pocketed the money with a smile. "I'll take her myself."

"Thanks." *Get out of here, now.* He looked around at the beer signs, the glittering rows of bottles, ran a hand over the scarred wooden bar. This place had been here forever. A classic.

Get out now.

He turned toward the door.

"Sure I can't get you a drink? My treat." Arnie held up a glass.

Get out. Buck fingered his sobriety coin, squeezed it

hard until the edges dug into his palm. Looked up at the ceiling, made a plea.

"No. No, thank you." Somehow, he got his mouth to form the words and got his feet to start marching. Like marching during wartime, when you'd been up twenty-four hours and more and didn't think your legs could carry you. One step at a time.

A moment later he was out of the bar and leaning against the wooden front of it, breathing hard. He pulled out his sobriety coin and, in the light from the bar's window, read the serenity prayer printed in tiny letters on the back. Or pretended to read it; actually, he knew it by heart. *God, grant me the serenity to accept the things I cannot change, the courage to...*

In front of him, a police cruiser stopped, and he was still enough of a drunk that his heart raced before he remembered he hadn't done anything wrong.

Dion stepped out and walked over, stood a little closer than was polite. Undoubtedly trying to tell if Buck smelled of liquor. "In trouble, my friend?"

"Just got away from it." He held up his coin.

Dion narrowed his eyes, studying it, and then the light dawned. "Your recovery coin. Close call?"

Buck nodded, his heart rate settling back to normal. The fresh, cold air braced him. He could do this.

He hoped.

"Want to grab a cup of coffee? I'm done with my shift."

He *wanted* a drink. But no. He didn't intend to go back there, not ever. "Thanks—coffee sounds good," he said and got into the cruiser.

He'd definitely have something to share at tomorrow's AA meeting.

When they reached the truckers' restaurant out by the

highway—the only nondrinking place open at this hour—
the owner hurried toward them. He was a short man in a
white shirt with pants pulled up high on his ample belly,
and his hand was raised like a stop sign. "You're welcome,
Chief, but him I won't serve."

Heat rose in Buck's face. He dimly remembered some
late-night, postbar confrontation, some shouting, a few
shoves.

The smells of coffee and fried food wafted through the
air. A couple of uniformed waitresses stood near the cash
register, watching. They probably remembered Buck, too,
and not in a good way.

He turned to go.

"He's my guest," Dion said. His voice was quiet, but he'd
drawn himself up tall. He was a big man, and command-
ing, and the restaurant manager visibly cringed.

"Well, all right, if you'll take full responsibility. But if
there's any trouble…"

"If there's trouble, I'll handle it, my friend."

The manager nodded and stepped aside, and Dion led
the way to a booth in the restaurant's back corner.

Once they'd both ordered coffee, Buck let his head sink
onto one fist and stared down at the none-too-clean table.
"I'll never get out from under my reputation. I've got to
leave Rescue River. Repay my debts and leave."

Dion shook his head, slowly. "You're a new creation.
Did you think that was just words?"

"The outside looks the same, and no one around here
believes in the change. It's dangerous," he added for clari-
fication, remembering Arnie holding up the glass.

Instead of responding to that, Dion studied him. "What
was it had you out walking so late?"

Buck looked at Dion's dark eyes, eyes that seemed to

hold a depth of thought and wisdom beyond most of the people Buck knew. "Did you ever meet a woman you really liked, but you knew she was out of reach?"

Dion's mouth twisted a little and he looked out across the restaurant. "In a manner of speaking."

Daisy Hinton, the town's pretty blonde social worker, sprang into Buck's mind. He'd heard the rumors about her and Dion but didn't know whether there was any substance to them.

Dion rubbed the back of his neck. "What are we talking about here? You got a crush on someone unattainable?"

Buck sighed. "It's Gina. I like her."

"The new lady in town?" Dion lifted an eyebrow. "Back up, my man. What have you heard? How's the baby doing?"

"The good news is, Bobby is doing fine. Gina couldn't possibly be the one who was abusing him. He's thriving, and she's real gentle with him."

"Good." Dion sipped at his hot coffee. "What's the bad news?"

Buck hesitated. Should he tell Dion what he'd overheard, possibly getting Gina into trouble? But if he didn't tell Dion, and something happened to her that could have been prevented...

"I can tell you know something," Dion said, "so why don't you go on and tell me."

Buck shook his head. "Man, I feel sorry for your kids, if you ever have any. You're going to read them like a book."

A strange expression crossed Dion's face so quickly that Buck decided he must have imagined it. He stirred sugar into his coffee. "It was just a little something I overheard. One-sided phone conversation."

Dion lifted an eyebrow, waiting.

"She was talking about whether she and Bobby could

be hunted down here. Something about mailing an ATM card to a friend so the withdrawal couldn't be traced." He paused, then added, "She also sounded worried about the fact that you have her vehicle information. And it sounds like she's going to ship her car back to California."

Dion's eyes narrowed. "So the vehicle *was* stolen."

"I thought so, too. But she seems to want to give it back."

Dion shook his head, a mirthless chuckle escaping. "That's what they all say."

"She wasn't saying it to make an impression. She was talking to a friend."

"And…there's nothing illegal about shipping a car. But if she doesn't have the registration or title or some identifying paperwork, no legitimate shipper will take it on."

"So we could just wait and see. If she's able to ship the car, that means she's got the rights to it."

"Or something." Dion frowned. "Tell you what. I'll do a little digging, but I'm not going to bring a lady in for wanting to ship a car. What I *am* going to do is to keep a pretty close eye on her."

Buck nodded. Dion had to do his job. And thinking of that reminded him of the photo he'd taken. "Look at this," he said as he pulled out his phone and brought up the image. "Zoom in on the baby's leg."

Dion's eyebrows rose. "Is that a bruise?"

Buck nodded and held up a hand. "After seeing her with the baby, there's no way she could be at fault. She's very protective of him. Protective like someone who's escaping an abuser, not someone who's an abuser herself."

Dion's brows drew together. "Maybe."

"Give her a chance," Buck said. "She could be a new creation, too."

"Touché, my man. But my job is to clean up the messes

people make along the way." He leveled a pointed gaze at Buck. "And your job is to stay sober and help your sister. Not to get overinvolved with a pretty possible criminal passing through town."

"You warning me?"

"Let's just say we're not that far removed from the days I had to pull you out of that bar and toss you in jail to sober up. Worst thing a former drinker can do is to get involved with the wrong company."

Buck nodded, but he couldn't truly agree with Dion. He had the distinct feeling that he, with his miserable track record, was the wrong company for Gina. Not the other way around.

Chapter 5

Gina found the next day's church service renewing and refreshing, and afterward, friendly people talked her into attending the church luncheon and meeting to plan the Freedom Festival. After a quick check on Bobby, who was loving the church nursery, she found her way to the fellowship hall.

Amy, the tall, gorgeous woman she'd met in the grocery store with Buck, hurried over. "Hey, they're just finishing up the general meeting, and everyone's going to eat before breaking into committees. You should come sit next to me and we can talk about getting our babies together."

"That would be nice." Although she feared she wouldn't find a way to stay in Rescue River long enough to build real friendships, Gina was grateful to be able to sit with someone other than Buck and Lacey. She didn't want to impose on them.

After she'd gotten her plate of meat loaf, mashed potatoes and green beans, she headed over to where Amy was gesturing. And sighed. Amy was next to Buck and Lacey at a table full of people. So Gina ended up sitting with them after all.

Conversation focused on the upcoming festival. Apparently, it had been going on for years, celebrating Rescue River's history with the Underground Railroad and the arrival of spring, which had meant easier travel for those seeking freedom.

Lacey was more animated today, talking about the guesthouse. "There's a room in the basement and another in the attic that were kept available for fugitive slaves. Apparently, at one time there were thirty people staying at the house."

"You should get a historic-landmark designation!" Gina said. "It's a lot of paperwork, but with a history like that, I'm sure you'd be approved."

Lacey didn't seem to hear her, speaking instead to Amy about how hard it was to get the renovation done while working full-time.

"I could help you with it," Gina offered when there was a break in the conversation. "At least to get it on the National Register of Historic Places, which is easier. I've helped a couple of organizations do it."

Lacey gave her a look, one Gina could read. It was the same look she'd gotten when she'd tried to connect with the popular girls back in high school. *You don't belong*, it said.

Gina bit her lip. "Look, I know I won't be here much longer, but I could print out the paperwork for you and give you some advice tonight. It's well worth doing. And it'll draw a lot of people to your guesthouse when it opens."

"I don't want to get the word out too soon. It's going to take a long time to finish, with the hours Buck and I work."

"Hey, hey," said a man sitting across from Amy. "Don't

blame me. Buck has worked so much overtime that he could do half days for the rest of the year and be okay." He looked at Gina. "I'm his so-called boss, Troy Hinton," he said, reaching out to shake her hand.

"Yeah, but I can't take time off, and the work we need to do now, like hanging wallpaper, requires two people," Lacey said. "I'm working extra hours myself, just to try to raise enough money so I can quit my day job and focus on the guesthouse when it opens. *If* it ever opens."

"I've hung tons of wallpaper." For Bobby's sake, Gina forced herself to persist. "I could just stay a little while and help—"

"No!" Lacey's voice cracked, causing conversation around the table to pause momentarily. "Not happening."

Gina felt her face heating with embarrassment.

Buck leaned toward his sister and spoke to her rapidly, and Lacey's eyes filled with tears.

One of the people who'd just come to the table, a pretty Asian American–looking woman who'd been introduced as Susan, shoved her plate away and came around the table to Lacey's side just as Lacey stood and murmured a broken apology to Gina.

"Come on," Susan said. "I'll take you home."

"Sorry about that," Buck said to Gina after Lacey and Susan were gone and conversation had resumed. "She has issues related to some stuff that's happened to her. She miscarried a baby, and quite honestly, I don't know if she'll ever recover. Lacey's strong in some ways, but she takes things hard."

"Oh, no! How awful!" Being a mother was the best thing that had ever happened to Gina, and she could only imagine how losing a baby would feel. "I'm so sorry I upset her."

"Not your fault."

It wasn't, but how sad. Gina sighed and distracted herself by looking around the room at the tables full of people eating and talking. Up by the stage, a group of kids tossed around a couple of sponge balls, their laughter and shouts contributing to the general noise. Near the pass-through to the kitchen, women were cutting and serving pie, and the scents of cinnamon and nutmeg made Gina's mouth water. It smelled like the home of the girl she'd most envied back in her grade-school days, a girl who'd come from a big, warm family.

Behind her, she heard the sound of a baby crying, and she stood and turned at the same moment as the man who'd spoken about Buck being able to take time off. In the doorway of the fellowship hall, one of the nursery workers scanned the room, holding a crying Bobby. When she saw Gina, she waved, indicating that she'd bring Bobby over.

"Oh, yours, not ours," Troy said, sitting back down.

"Woot!" The woman next to him gave him a gentle high five. "We actually get to finish our meals. I'm Angelica, by the way," she said to Gina.

"Yeah, until Xavier gets too wild and we have to rein him in." Troy put an arm around Angelica, looking at her with warm possessiveness. "I have to fight for adult time with my wife."

The loving look she gave him back made jealousy knife through Gina's heart. Would she ever have a relationship like that, or was she doomed to repeat past failures?

Shaking off the jealousy, Gina thanked the nursery worker and pulled Bobby into her lap, cuddling him close. He was what was important, not her own romantic longings.

"He's adorable!" Angelica said. "How old is he?"

"Ten months." Gina nuzzled Bobby's head and wiped his tears.

"He's a big boy!" Angelica leaned forward to tickle Bobby's arm, making him chortle. "My Emmie is nine months, but she's nowhere near this one's size."

"Mom!" A boy of seven or eight hurtled into Angelica's side and then looked curiously at Bobby. "Who's that baby?"

Another little girl, a year or two younger, hopped into Angelica's lap. "Xavier took my dancing bear, Aunt Angelica."

"I just hid it, Mindy. It's behind the curtain." Xavier gestured toward the stage and leaned forward to tickle Bobby's knee.

Mindy stuck out her tongue at him, slid off Angelica's lap and ran toward the stage. At which point Gina realized that the little girl was missing a hand.

"Be kind to your cousin," Angelica scolded her son gently. "Go play with her."

"But she wants to play dumb games."

"Listen to your mother," Troy said, his voice stern, and Xavier stuck out his lower lip, then nodded and ran toward Mindy.

As people watched and chuckled and asked to hold Bobby, Gina felt a sense of homecoming unlike anything she'd ever experienced before. She loved it here. She wanted to raise Bobby here.

An elderly woman approached their table, pushing a rolling walker. "Are you going to finish putting my house back together before the festival?" she asked, pointing a bony finger at Buck.

"Um, I don't think so, Miss Minnie."

"Why not?"

"Too much to do and not enough time to do it, with Lacey and me both working."

Amy explained. "The guesthouse belonged to Miss Minnie until recently."

"Was it in your family a long time?" Gina pushed her mostly empty plate aside, too interested to finish her meal.

"Since before the Civil War," the woman said. "And to think that I would be the one to let it go out of the family…"

"Do you have any records, letters, stories?" Gina asked, fascinated as always by living local history.

"I certainly do, young lady. A whole trunk full of them. And you are…?"

"I'm sorry." Gina stood. "Would you like to sit down? I'm Gina Patterson. I'm…" She glanced around. "I'm just passing through, I guess. But I used to volunteer at the historical society where I lived in California. I hope those documents will be able to stay with the house."

"First time anyone's shown any interest," Miss Minnie grumbled.

"Sit down and join us, Miss Minnie," Buck said, standing too and holding a chair for the woman.

"No, sirree. I have more people to visit." And she was off, pushing her walker with surprising speed.

"Sure would be great if Lacey could open the house in time for the festival," someone said.

Let me help. Gina had to press her lips together to keep from saying the words out loud. "What kind of guests come to town during the festival?" she asked instead.

"Last year, we got over three thousand visitors." Troy had his arm around Angelica, unconsciously stroking her hair as he spoke. "City people, mostly, from Cleveland and Pittsburgh and Columbus. People who like the small-town scene."

"People with money?" Amy asked.

A pretty, plump blonde woman lifted an eyebrow at Amy. "You planning to pick pockets?"

"Daisy!" Angelica shook her head. "Be nice to Amy. She's newly back in town."

"And no," Amy said, laughing, "I'm not picking anyone's pocket. I'm hoping to take the visitors' money, but honestly. If I stay, I might open up a shop."

Gina opened her mouth and then shut it again.

"What?" Angelica asked, and Buck looked curious, too.

"It's just…you couldn't *pay* for the kind of advertising Lacey would get if she could have an open house during the festival. Even if it was just partially done, a few rooms. The people who come to town are already looking for the small-town experience. They're perfect customers."

"For sure," Buck said. "Just don't see how we could get it done in time."

Angelica looked at Gina. "Could you help them? Because this might be a God thing."

"I… Yeah, I could."

"How?" Buck asked sharply.

"It's not just the historical-society work and the fact that I've done a lot of decorating. I also majored in marketing in college."

"So you know how to showcase a place like the guesthouse to make it shine, right?" Angelica asked, smiling as if she already knew the answer.

"Yeah," Gina admitted, "I do. The place would be booked for months in advance even before it officially opens. Especially if there aren't a lot of competing guesthouses and B and Bs here."

"There's just the one other motel," Buck said, "and it's very basic." He looked thoughtful, as if he were really considering the possibility of having Gina stay and help.

"You and Lacey should totally hire her," Angelica said.

"Well, but it would mean having Bobby around a lot." Now that Buck seemed to be considering the idea, all the reasons against it flooded into Gina's head. "And we'd have to stay there. If we could stay, your sister could pay me pretty minimally."

"I can take Bobby some," Angelica said unexpectedly. "I'm at home with Emmie, and it would be fun for her to have a playmate."

"I couldn't pay much for child care," Gina warned, feeling uncomfortable with the need to economize. But she was determined to learn—or relearn—to live without the easy wealth she'd gotten accustomed to during her marriage.

Angelica waved a hand. "You wouldn't need to pay. It could be our contribution to the guesthouse. Rescue River needs it badly."

"No, I'd find a way to pay. But that would be great. There are fumes in some parts of a renovation, and that wouldn't be good for him. Would it, sweetie?" She reached out her arms for Bobby, who was snuggling now in Buck's arms.

"I'll hold him—it's fine," he said. "All of this is a good idea for Rescue River and for Lacey. But I have my doubts about whether..." He broke off, looked down at Bobby and then back at Gina, his face bleak. "Like I said, having a baby around would be hard on her."

And on you, Gina thought.

Around them, clattering dishes and bustling footsteps announced that the meal was coming to an end, but at their table, everyone was watching Buck.

Abruptly, he handed Bobby back to Gina and lifted his hands like stop signs. "All right, all right. I'll talk to her again. But I can't make any promises. I doubt she'll agree to anything of the kind."

As for Gina, she wondered whether Buck would present a fair case. He seemed almost as set against her staying as his sister was.

On Monday and Tuesday, Buck busied himself with work at the vet clinic. His boss, Troy Hinton, took in every animal who had a need, whether the owners could pay or not, so there was plenty of work.

Midafternoon on Tuesday, Buck was washing up after a procedure when there was a sharp click and then someone crowded behind him.

Adrenaline surged. Buck spun, wet hands up, and grabbed for his assailant's throat.

"Hey, hey!" His boss's surprised voice and familiar face made Buck drop his hands and step back, heart racing.

He looked away and drew in a couple of deep breaths, like they'd taught him at the VA.

"You okay?" Troy's voice was mild as he put away a pair of surgical forceps and started washing his hands at the other side of the sink.

"Yeah. Sorry, man."

"I should know better than to sneak up behind you." Troy dried off and then sat down at the computer.

It was a great thing about working for Troy Hinton: he was calm, an old friend, and he'd known about Buck's PTSD—and his other flaws—when he'd hired him.

His heart still racing, Buck stepped out the back door of the clinic for some air...and heard a whining, scratching sound at his feet.

There was a closed cardboard box, a couple of feet square, with holes punched in the sides and an envelope on the top. Uh-oh.

He picked up the box and carried it inside. "Drop-off,"

he said to Troy and set the box down on the floor. He handed the envelope to Troy, then grabbed a pair of forceps and used them to open the box gingerly. No telling what he might find. Could be something wild and scared, even rabid.

But when he got the box open, a dirty white mop flung itself out and planted front paws on Buck's leg. When he bent to pat what looked like its head, the little dog licked his hand, barking and whining.

He squatted down. "Okay, buddy. It's okay." He stroked the matted, dirty fur. "What's in the envelope?" he asked Troy.

Troy squinted at a sheet of notepaper and then read aloud. "'I'm sick, can't take care of Spike no more. My kids want to put him down. Please help.'"

"Spike?" Buck brushed back the excessive hair on the little dog's head and looked into anxious dark eyes. "You're a tough guy, huh?"

A couple of bills fluttered to the floor, and Troy picked them up, a five and a single. "Six dollars." He shook his head. "Guy probably went without something to leave that."

"Got room for him at the rescue?"

"I'll make room. Better check him out first." Troy got a small biscuit out of the jar they kept on the desk and whistled, and the mop waddled over to him. "Hey, big guy. How long were you out there?"

The little dog's whole body wagged.

"Sit," Troy said, and the mop sat down and held out a polite paw. When Troy offered the biscuit, the dog grabbed it and ran off to the corner of the room to eat. "He's hungry."

"Somebody trained him, though. Can't figure why anyone would want to put the little guy down." Buck stood. "Want me to do an exam?"

"No. I want you to take afternoons off like you're sup-posed to and go work on your sister's guesthouse. Why are you even here, come to think of it?"

Buck shrugged. "I meant to, but..."

"But what? What's going on?"

Buck blew out a sigh. He'd told himself he was needed here, but the truth was more complicated.

"Avoiding Gina and Bobby?" Troy sat down in the roll-ing chair and crossed his arms.

"Might be." Of course he was. He'd convinced his sis-ter to give the new situation with Gina a try, and now he wasn't sure it had been the right thing.

"How come? You gotta deal with stuff, man, not let it slip under the rug."

And this was the bad thing about working for Troy: he was a little too insightful. "She's kicking up some memo-ries, and not just for Lacey."

"Go home," Troy ordered.

"You're sure—"

"I'm sure."

So that was how, the next morning, Buck found himself just outside a smallish bedroom, listening to Bobby's baby chatter and Gina's murmurs.

He was almost wishing he hadn't talked Lacey into al-lowing Gina to stay and help. "Until the Freedom Festival and not a moment longer," Lacey had said.

Even that amount of time might be too long.

He, Lacey and Gina had talked last night, figuring out a plan. Lacey would open half of the house for the Freedom Festival, so people could see the progress and get excited about coming to stay, and then work on the rest of the house throughout the summer and possibly into the fall.

And right now, his role was to work afternoons—and possibly evenings—with Gina to finish the three rooms. Mornings, when he was working at the clinic, she'd be figuring out the historical-landmark paperwork and setting up a website to publicize the guesthouse.

Bobby was on hands and knees next to a table Gina had set up in the middle of the room. As Buck watched, the sturdy baby grabbed the leg of the table, hauled himself to his feet and then fell right back down on his diaper-clad behind. Undaunted, he reached for the table leg and began to repeat the process.

Gina bent over a book that lay open on the table. She tucked a lock of hair behind her ear and looked from the book to a can of something—paint, maybe—and then back at the book again.

Man, she's pretty. Buck's heart kicked up to a faster rate. Ignoring that, he tapped on the door frame.

"Hey." Gina smiled when she saw him, eyes sparkling, and his heart rate jumped up another notch. "I thought we'd start with the simplest project," she said. "Come see what I…I mean, we…have planned."

Calm down, buddy—she's not for you. He walked into the room, deliberately not focusing on Gina.

It was a corner bedroom with windows on two sides, and Gina had opened them. Birds chittered madly outside and a fresh breeze cooled his face.

"It's a little chilly in here, but I figure we'll get warm as we work. I like having the windows open, because we're going to be using primer today and I don't like him breathing it." She looked down at Bobby, her face curving into a smile, and Buck realized that the baby had pulled himself up again and stood, banging on the table leg, grinning.

"The fresh air is no problem. If you want to work on filling nail holes and doing repairs, I can do the priming in a different room from where you and Bobby are."

"I've already done that. And I cleaned the walls. So now, it's down to whether you prefer doing the edges with a brush or rolling." She held up a paintbrush and roller.

"Rolling is more fun for sure, but let's both work on the edges a little. That takes twice as long."

"Great."

While Buck opened two cans of primer and stirred them up, Gina brought out a pack-and-play. She put Bobby inside, along with a stack of plastic blocks and vinyl-covered books. "That'll keep him for a while, and when he gets bored, maybe he'll take a little nap." Gina bit her lip, her forehead wrinkling.

"You're short of toys for him."

She shrugged. "He's used to having a lot more stuff to entertain him, but it's okay. It'll develop his imagination."

"I know where you can get a bunch of baby stuff, free." He hadn't known he was going to offer until it happened, and the moment the words were out of his mouth, he regretted it.

Her forehead smoothed out. "I would love it, if you're serious. It's a challenge to entertain an active baby in the workplace."

"You've been doing fine." Maybe she'd decide she didn't want the loan.

"I'm fortunate that Susan Hayashi brought over the pack-and-play and a few toys. Apparently, they belonged to her fiancé and were just stored in his basement."

"I'm sure Sam Hinton had nothing but the best for Mindy. He's a pretty wealthy guy." But Buck didn't envy the CEO of Hinton Enterprises for his millions. The man had lost his wife and had struggled for a couple of years to deal with issues related to his daughter's disability and reaction to losing her mother. He'd only recently started looking happy and energetic again, since Susan Hayashi had come into his life last summer.

"So, where's this cache of baby toys?" she asked as she turned on the radio. "Is it your old stuff? GI Joes?"

"No...though I did have my share of those, and don't you dare call them dolls." He was hoping to distract her, and it worked.

"You grew up here in Rescue River, right? What did your parents do?"

Buck dipped his brush and started to paint a careful edge, finding the meticulous work soothing. "Yeah. Dad sold cars and Mom..." He paused, thinking how to explain it. "Mom taught piano when she could."

"Sounds like a story." Gina knelt to apply primer around a window frame.

"Yeah." Buck let out a mirthless chuckle. "It's a real old story. When Lacey and I were little, she just had a couple of cocktails before dinner. By the time we were teenagers, it was pills to get going in the morning and wine with lunch."

"Oh, I'm sorry." Gina glanced his way, compassion in her eyes, and shook her head. "That's so hard to deal with."

"Your husband had similar issues, right?"

She nodded, but didn't bite at the change of subject. "Is your mom still living?"

"No. Died when I was twenty-one." He was so used to saying it that he felt just a twinge of sadness, nothing more. Mom had been too talented for a small town, and too East Coast for Ohio, and actually, she'd been absent to him and Lacey for several years before her death.

The quick squeeze of his shoulder surprised him. "I'm sorry for your loss. And for having to grow up that way."

Quickly, Buck shook his head. "It wasn't like that. Lacey and I were blessed. Dad's a great guy. Everyone in town loved him. And his parents—my gram and gramps—they filled in the gaps when Mom wasn't doing well. It was hard on Lacey, not having a mom who could help her with the girl things. But for me, it was a real good childhood."

"So how come you started drinking?"

Just like that, Buck's easy mood shattered into pieces. Bobby was standing in the pack-and-play, waving his arms, and Buck put down his brush and went over to pick the boy up, craving the comfort. "Drank a little during the war. And a lot after. It would've taken a better man than I am to do two tours in Afghanistan without drinking."

She nodded, moving over to the next window frame and running the paintbrush along it with easy skill.

The fact that she wasn't looking at him, and the comfortable feel of Bobby in his arms, made him go on. "Got worse when I lost my wife and child. They say there's a genetic factor with alcoholism, and it looks like I inherited it." Gently, he set Bobby down in the playpen and, when the boy started to fuss, located his binky and popped it into his mouth. Then he pulled out the stepladder that had been lying along one wall and set it up. "What about you? Did you grow up in California?"

"Yes. Sacramento."

"What do your parents do?" He wondered why she hadn't gone to them when she'd had the trouble with her in-laws.

"I never knew my mom," she said. "And Dad...well, he's got his own life. He's homesteading in Alaska with a group of friends. Kind of a back-to-nature thing."

She said it carelessly, similar to the way Buck talked about his own mother. "I didn't think homesteading even existed anymore."

"It doesn't, not the way it used to be, land for work. They're subsistence farming on public land. No electricity, no cell phones… It's pretty basic."

"Does he know you're in trouble? Can he help you?"

Gina just shook her head a little, a smile curving her lips. "Dad's not the type to rush in and save his daughter. He's a dreamer, always broke. I'm actually just glad he's got these friends to stay with. That way, I don't have to worry about him."

Interesting. Gina was in a tight spot herself, but she talked about her father like the man was another child, not someone she could turn to. "Have you been up there to visit?" He was wondering if it would be a viable place for Gina to go and stay with Bobby for a while. She seemed to want to hide.

The thought of her leaving Rescue River, though, put a very alarming pressure on his heart.

"I surprised him on his fiftieth birthday. Took a bunch of books and supplies. It was kind of fun."

"What was it like?" For whatever reason, he wanted to keep her talking. Her voice was low for a woman, a little husky, and the sound of it sent a pleasant sensation rippling down his spine.

"Well, fishing for our dinner was an adventure. And hauling water really is good exercise." She flexed her arm, making a muscle, and tossed a saucy grin his way.

The air whooshed out of his lungs. She was, quite literally, breathtaking when she smiled that funny, relaxed smile.

"But there was a downside." She wrinkled her nose. "I really prefer indoor plumbing, especially when it's cold outside."

"I can imagine. And it doesn't sound like a good place for a baby."

"No. I never even considered it." Gina stretched her back and shoulders, flipped her ponytail and returned to work.

Which Buck needed to do, too. He didn't need to think about how lively and pretty Gina was, how her attitude toward what sounded like a pretty neglectful dad wasn't bitter. How she saw the humor in a situation that some would have resented.

Bobby had been pulling himself up at the edge of the pack-and-play, and now he started to climb. He fell back and immediately tried again.

"It's just a matter of time until he figures out how to escape," Gina said, watching him. "If you were serious about finding him some other toys, sooner might be better than later."

"Um, sure." *Be a man*, he told himself. But dread filled his heart.

Chapter 6

Buck really, really didn't want to do this.

And if he had to visit the place he'd avoided for a year and a half, he didn't want an audience. "Are you sure you want to come along? I can do it myself," he offered again as his stomach knotted tight.

"No, it's fine. I'd like to come. I know what kind of stuff Bobby likes, and if he has an outing now, he'll settle down better later on. We haven't gotten out much since I sent away my SUV." She was fastening Bobby into his car seat as she talked. Then she climbed into the passenger seat of the truck.

Which left Buck no choice but to get in and drive. He turned on the radio so he wouldn't have to talk.

All too soon, they approached the little cottage, set back from the road with a big grassy yard, a garden on one side. He looked away from the house and the memories.

Tightening his jaw, he drove down the rutted driveway

to the garage, took his time about turning the truck around so it would be easy to load things into the back.

Then he couldn't postpone getting out any longer, so he cut the engine and opened the door.

The sound of the rushing creek and chirping birds filled his ears, and the smell of earth rose up to him. He couldn't help but glance at the garden, notice it was turned over. The tenant must be eager to get to gardening.

Like Ivana had always been.

"Who lives here?" Gina asked as she freed Bobby from his car seat and set him down, holding his hands so he could toddle. "See the bird?" she asked, kneeling and pointing to a robin that was hopping through the shining green grass.

"A single mom," he said noncommittally. "Couple of kids, I think."

"Don't you have to talk to her first?"

He paused, hand on the garage door handle. "It's my place. She rents the house, but not the garage."

He didn't look at her, but he heard her soft "oh."

The sooner he raised the garage door, the sooner he could get done and get out of here. "It's a mess," he warned and slid the door open.

He stared at the ground for a minute, not wanting to look. Not wanting to kick up the memories of the day when he'd cleaned out their house, alone, in a drunk frenzy of pain. He felt ashamed, now, of how he'd thrown everything in here. He'd probably broken some stuff that would have been perfectly useful to someone in need.

"It's actually kind of neat." Gina walked past him to stand in the doorway of the garage, squinting to see, and he looked up and realized she was right. Toys were stacked along one wall, alongside some labeled boxes. Furniture and more boxes lined the rest of the garage.

There was a sound behind them, and they both turned. A pretty redhead stood there with a couple of kids behind her, one probably first grade, the other littler, maybe three. "Hi, I'm Cassie. And you must be Buck Armstrong? I hope you don't mind. Your sister and I straightened everything out a couple of months after I moved in. We were afraid it was a fire hazard."

"It's fine." He introduced himself and Gina, welcoming the distraction. Then Gina introduced Bobby and showed him to the little kids, doing that instant bonding thing women—especially women with kids—were so good at doing.

Ivana hadn't been that good at it, and she'd complained about feeling left out at the playground and swimming pool. It was part of the reason they'd chosen to live out here: she'd been more of a loner.

"Would you like me to take Bobby into the backyard for a little bit, so you can focus?" Cassie asked. "It's fenced in and we have some fun climbing toys."

"Um…" Gina hesitated, obviously reluctant to leave Bobby with a stranger. "I wouldn't want to inconvenience you."

"Just bring him over if you'd like." Cassie started walking back toward the play area in the backyard, surrounded by a white picket fence.

He'd put in that fence himself, so Mia could play safely as she grew.

He clenched a fist and forced that thought away. "She's safe. A nice lady. Lacey checked her references."

"It would be so good for Bobby to be able to climb and play with her kids. And I can watch him from here… Okay. I'll be right back."

Grimly, Buck strode into the garage and pulled out the

two biggest boxes labeled Toys. He was going back in for more when Gina returned. "Go ahead and look through the boxes," he said as he pulled out a high chair. Mia's high chair. He put it down and turned to Gina. "Take whatever you think he'd like. We should do this quick."

She glanced up at him speculatively. "Look, I didn't realize... I totally understand if—"

"It's fine." It had been almost three years. He could deal with this. To prove it, he knelt beside the nearest box and started pulling stuff out randomly.

There were some toys he didn't even remember, a shape-sorter thing full of triangles and squares, a little phone, some dolls. Stuff that looked new. Gifts, probably, meant for when Mia got older.

Gina pulled an empty box out of the truck and sat down beside him on the grass. She started inspecting the toys he'd gotten out, murmuring almost to herself. "This one's got some little parts—better not take that. But he'd love that light-up ball. He doesn't play with dolls, not yet, but I think it's fine for boys to play with dolls. Maybe if there's a boy one..."

Her words soothed him. He was doing fine. He was handling this.

He pulled out a bucket and shovel, and an image of the week they'd spent at the beach came back to him. Sitting with Mia in the sand, showing her how to dig, watching her giggle as the water touched her toes. Ivana hurrying over with an umbrella, scolding him, but mildly. They'd gotten along great that week.

"Go ahead and take anything." He got up quickly and walked back into the dark garage.

He found the ExerSaucer he'd had in mind when he'd first proposed this harebrained idea. Beside it was a little seat on cables, and he remembered that it was a door jumper Mia had loved. He swallowed and grabbed that, too.

As he came out of the garage into the sunlight, Gina looked his way and her eyes lit up. "Oh, wow, that'd be so great if we could borrow the ExerSaucer!"

This was worth it, to see that happiness in her eyes, to find a way to lighten her burden.

And then he saw what she had in her hand.

Mia's pink elephant. Her lovey. The toy she'd slept with every night and nap time. She'd just started insisting that they take it everywhere, a new phase, when she and Ivana had disappeared that last, fateful time. When he'd seen it lying on the couch, he'd figured they'd be right back, had stopped worrying about them.

Mia hadn't even had her lovey in those scary, horrible final moments.

Without realizing he'd moved, he had the elephant in his hands. He turned it over to look at the toe she'd always sucked on. Held the slightly dirty-looking creature to his face.

When he smelled it—smelled *Mia*—everything he'd been trying to forget came rushing back.

He could feel her in his arms, could hear her cry. He remembered what it had been like to walk the floor with her, bouncing her gently, helping her calm down. Feeding her a bottle. Tickling her into a good mood.

Putting her down in her crib for a nap. And when she'd reach up her arms to him, wanting to be held when she really needed sleep, he'd put Pinky into her arms and she would sigh and cuddle her elephant.

Somehow, he found his way over to the side of the garage where he could be alone. He squatted down, his back against the wall, drawing his arms and legs in while physical pain racked his chest. His throat and eyes felt swollen and he could barely breathe.

He let his head drop to his chest, held the little pink elephant to his face and fell apart.

Gina steered the truck into its parking space at the guesthouse and looked over at Buck.

He was staring straight ahead, his whole body rigid.

Guilt washed over her at having been the catalyst for all this pain. She'd known plenty of grief herself, losing her husband, but the loss of a child was unimaginable. She opened the door and extracted Bobby from his car seat, held him close and looked at Buck.

Who could never hold his baby close again. She swallowed hard. "Do you want to…? Can I do anything for you? Call someone? Do you want to talk?" She was babbling, asking too many questions, but it seemed better than letting him deal with all of this alone.

She'd seen men cry before. Her dad had wiped tears when he'd learned that his sister had passed away. And her father-in-law had gotten a little choked up at Hank's funeral.

But to see this big, tough veteran truly break down… Whoa. That was a first. Even after she'd given him some privacy, had loaded the truck and gotten Bobby into his car seat, the sight of Buck hunched there, shoulders still shaking a little, had made her cry, too. She'd had to grab a handful of tissues and pull herself together before she could help him to his feet and drive him home. Because this wasn't about her; it was about him.

"No. I'm… Let's get this stuff unloaded. Got to do a couple errands." He opened the car door and got out, moving mechanically to the back of the truck.

"You don't have to…"

"I got this." He lifted the box and the couple of big toys out and carried them up to the house.

Unsure how to help, she followed him, carrying Bobby.

He had the things in her room before she'd gotten halfway up the stairs. "Can I have the keys?" he asked, his voice expressionless.

And then he took them from her and drove off for parts unknown.

A couple of hours later, when he came back, Gina deliberately gave him his space, staying in her room with a book she'd checked out from the Rescue River library. But when Bobby woke up hungry, and she heard voices downstairs, she decided she had to come out of her room.

Shifting Bobby on her hip—man, was he getting heavy!—Gina walked down the curving wooden staircase and into the large, old-fashioned kitchen.

Buck, pouring coffee at the counter, didn't turn around. But at the table, three curious faces turned her way, and two older gentlemen stood. "You sit down right here, sweetheart," said the one with an impeccable comb-over, a dress shirt and expensive-looking slacks and shoes.

"Don't be ridiculous, Hinton. My seat is closer." The other man, shorter and stocky, dressed in a flannel shirt and work pants, held the chair he'd been sitting in, at the end of the table.

Feeling like she was walking into something she didn't quite understand, Gina sat in the closest chair and set Bobby down beside her. "Thank you both. I'm Gina Patterson, and this is my son, Bobby."

"Pleased to meet you," said the slender, gray-haired woman at the table, holding out a hand to grasp Gina's. "I'm Lou Ann Miller, and this is Elias Hinton and Roscoe

Camden. And you two men can sit down. Honestly! There are plenty of chairs."

Buck brought over cups of coffee, a sugar bowl and a creamer, waving off Lou Ann's offer of help. "You sit," he said. "The water's almost boiling for tea, if you'd rather have that."

Lou Ann held out for tea while Gina and the men accepted coffee.

"What brings you to Rescue River?" Mr. Camden asked bluntly. "We've been hearing different stories at the Senior Towers."

"Leave the woman alone," Mr. Hinton ordered. "You shouldn't listen to all of the tall tales over there."

"That place *is* a hotbed of gossip," Lou Ann said. "There's no need for you to fill us in on your personal business, dear."

"Thanks." Gina smiled apologetically at Mr. Camden. "It *is* somewhat personal, but I'm hoping to stay awhile. It's a lovely town."

"Quite a history, too," Mr. Hinton said. Bobby was holding on to the leg of his chair, looking up with curiosity, and Mr. Hinton reached down and picked him up, handing him a teaspoon to bang on the table.

"The house's history is just what I'm interested in." Gina seized on the topic. "I'm helping Lacey apply to put this house on the National Register of Historic Places, and I'd like to learn more about the background of the house and the area. Do you all have any ideas where I could find out more?"

Buck chuckled as he sat down at the table, pushing a teacup toward Lou Ann and dunking his own tea bag. "You've just opened a big can of worms. These three know everything about the town. From three very distinct viewpoints."

Fifteen minutes and a rousing argument later, Gina had appointments to meet with all three of them, and the elders made their departure.

When Buck came back into the kitchen, Gina raised an eyebrow at him as she gathered up the coffee cups. "Why do I feel like I've been through a war?"

"Longest-lasting love triangle in Rescue River."

Buck looked at Bobby, who was chanting, "Up! Up!" He reached down and swept the baby into his arms.

A tingle of awareness passed through Gina's chest at the sight of her son against the rugged veteran's broad chest. A few teaspoons slipped out of her hands and clattered on the floor.

Instantly Buck was across the room, sliding Bobby to his hip and kneeling gracefully, helping her to pick them up.

The tingle intensified.

It wasn't just his physical grace or his good manners. It was what she'd learned about him this afternoon. Somehow, the fact that he had the capacity for that much emotion had made Buck twice as appealing to her.

Gina ducked her heated face away from him and deposited the spoons in the sink. "Thanks. Clumsy of me."

He rose lightly, his white teeth flashing in a smile. "That's not the word I'd think of to describe you."

Their gazes held for a beat too long.

"Listen," Gina said, "I'm sorry to have opened up old wounds earlier today. Are you okay?"

He nodded. "Embarrassed. You think you're over something and then it hits you."

"That's grief," she agreed. "Don't be embarrassed. It's natural."

"I guess." He blew out a breath. "I don't mean to be rude, but could we drop the subject?"

"Oh, sure! I'm sorry."

He touched her chin. "Don't take it personally. At all. I needed to do that, I guess, but now… I feel like I've been hit by a truck. I can't handle getting run over again today."

"Makes sense." Gina tore her gaze away and rinsed dishes while Buck carried the rest of the dishes to the sink, still holding Bobby. "I guess I'll have to take a little time off from wallpapering to talk with the folks who were just here, but I hope that won't be a problem. I know you have to spend some time at the clinic, too. And we don't always have to be working together. There's some stuff I can do alone, or you can. A lot of stuff, actually." *Stop babbling, stop babbling.*

While she felt flustered, Buck seemed perfectly composed. "Time away from the house isn't a problem. We're not punching time cards here, just trying to get the work done."

"Hey, Gina." Lacey's voice, behind them, provided a welcome respite from her worries. "I came home for…" She saw Buck holding Bobby and swallowed visibly. "For an early dinner," she said, her voice quiet.

Gina's heart ached. She and Bobby didn't mean to, but they kept causing pain. "Sit down and I'll fix you something. Fix all of us something. We may as well eat before we go back to work," she added to Buck.

"No. Hey, I think I'll just head on back. I don't have much time." Now Lacey's voice sounded choked. Her cat, Mr. Whiskers, meowed loudly, and she picked him up and held him close to her chest. "Hey, buddy, where's your wife, huh? Where's Mrs. Whiskers?"

Gina shot Buck a glance, the same one he was sending to her. Again, that something arced between them. She took Bobby out of his arms, opened the fridge and grabbed a bowl of mashed potatoes and peas from last night's dinner. "On second thought, I think I'll feed Bobby first," she said as she headed for the porch.

She'd give Buck a chance to talk to his sister, give Lacey some space in her own house.

And meanwhile, she'd remind herself not to pay attention to the occasional sparks between herself and Buck. She needed to remember she had bad judgment with men. Just look at the mistake she'd made in her marriage.

Anyway, Buck had mentioned leaving Rescue River. He seemed to fit here, but he'd said he was moving on soon.

She looked down the street toward the library and restaurant that marked the beginning of the town's small business district. It was unusually warm for this time of year, and despite its being a weekday, lots of people were out. She saw two mothers walking along with babies in strollers. A small group of older people clustered on the benches in front of the Senior Towers. And a group of teenagers stood talking in front of the library, their excited voices floating to her on the warm breeze.

This was where she wanted to raise Bobby, God willing. She wanted to take him to the library and show him off to the seniors. To shop at the little market.

And this was where Buck *didn't* want to be. Another reason not to get involved.

Through the screen door, she heard Buck's rumbling voice and Lacey's quiet one. Good. That was what Lacey needed, to talk to her brother.

That, and not to have a baby in her face every moment.

Gina breathed in the smell of the earth, thawing in the weak sunshine of early March. A few daffodils were pushing up beside the porch steps, and she set Bobby's food down and carried him into the yard to let him crawl in the grass. She wished she'd thought to put a jacket on him, but she'd been rushing to escape.

She needed to do something different about Bobby if she was going to stay here and help with the renovations. His presence was causing Lacey pain, and while it was inevitable that he should be around Lacey sometimes, the woman ought to be able to come home for a peaceful dinner without getting her wounds, whatever they were, ripped open.

Bobby had crawled over to the fence, and as she watched, he pulled himself up to stare out between the slats. It wasn't good for him to be trapped in the house with paint and renovation tools and overbusy adults. The new toys were great, but he needed more stimulation, more attention.

She pulled her phone out of her back pocket and found Angelica's number. She was just finalizing the arrangements to have her care for Bobby three days per week when Buck came out onto the porch.

When she ended the call, Buck lifted an eyebrow. "You're taking Bobby somewhere?"

"To Angelica's," she tossed over her shoulder, jogging to get the baby before he figured out that the front gate was open. She swept him up and blew on his belly, causing him to chortle gleefully. Then she hugged him close and climbed back up the porch steps. "He's going to stay with her three days per week. That way, I can focus better on work."

"And Lacey won't see him as much." He gave her a half smile. "Thanks for that."

She nodded, holding Bobby, as the March sun tried to warm her back. His eyes warmed her more and she drew in a quick breath, unable to look away.

But all at once his face seemed to close and he turned. And that was good, she told herself firmly. She busied herself settling Bobby on her lap and spooning potatoes into his mouth, getting a little inside him before letting him try with the spoon, which would lead to a mess.

Best to remember that Buck had his secrets, his reasons to keep a distance. As did she. A little front-porch attraction didn't add up to anything in the lives of two people whose pasts were all too complicated.

Chapter 7

Two days later, Buck held the door so that Gina could walk ahead of him into Love's Hardware. He tried not to notice the fruity smell of her shampoo.

They'd dropped Bobby off at Angelica's and now were picking up some supplies before another day of renovation.

He was spending too much time with her. The pink of her cheeks, the light smattering of freckles across her nose, the gentle sway of her walk—all of it held far too much of his attention.

"Wow." Gina stood staring at the crowded array of garbage cans, lamp oil, electrical cords, gutter spouts, hammers and pipes. "It's truly everything but the kitchen sink."

"We have those, too," said a voice above them. "Back left corner of the store."

At the sound, both Buck and Gina looked up.

As Buck had suspected, the voice came from Harold Love, the wiry, white-haired African American store owner, who stood at the top of a tall stepladder. He was sliding a large box from the high shelf above the store's sales racks.

"Hey, Mr. Love, it's Buck Armstrong," he called, knowing the old man's vision wasn't the best.

"I was just praying for a little help here. Buck, son, if I drop this down, can you catch it for me?"

"But that's huge—" Gina's eyes widened.

"Right here." Buck stepped forward, feeling an absurd desire to impress her with his strength.

Mr. Love dropped the box, and Buck caught it easily. It was light, probably containing some type of paper product.

Gina touched his arm and nodded over at Mr. Love, who was now climbing down the ladder, slow but steady. "Is he okay?" she whispered.

Buck set the box down on the floor and nodded. "Don't worry about Mr. Love. He's been doing this for more than fifty years." All the same, he took a step closer, ready to help the man if needed.

"Grandpa!" A pretty, heavyset young woman came bustling from the back of the store. "Did you climb up there yourself after I told you not to?" She turned to Buck and Gina. "His vision is getting worse. He's not supposed to do things like that."

"Now you just let me be, Aliyah." Mr. Love reached the floor unassisted and smiled in their general direction. "Thank you for the help, young man." He headed back toward the counter, using his hands to unobtrusively guide himself, moving confidently. He seemed to have an inner picture of every item of stock and every inch of the store, so his visual impairment wasn't obvious to most people. He liked it that way, Buck knew.

Buck had renewed his old acquaintance with Mr. Love

when he'd started working on Lacey's house, and he valued their friendship. It was all about nuts and bolts, paints and primers, plumbing and wiring. Unlike most of the other people in Rescue River, Mr. Love knew nothing of Buck's alcoholic antics, or at least, he hadn't been affected by them. The eightysomething man was a nonjudgmental, easy part of Buck's past.

Aliyah scolded Mr. Love a little more before heading toward the back of the store, shaking her head.

Gina's phone pinged. She pulled it out, looked at it and frowned.

Curiosity tugged at him. Was she starting to make friends in town?

But whoever was texting her, it wasn't Buck's business. Deliberately, he focused on the familiar sights and sounds of the store. From hidden speakers, the sound of Smokey Robinson filled the air; it was all Motown, all the time here at Love's Hardware. A grinding sound in the back of the store told him a key was being made. The faint, acrid smell of lawn products permeated the very bones of the place.

Buck walked toward the counter, gesturing for Gina to follow along. "How's business today?" he asked the older man.

"Just fine, just fine, now that you've come in." Mr. Love patted his arm. "As soon as I heard it was you, I knew you wouldn't mind giving me a hand. Just like old times, eh, son?"

"That's right."

"Now, let me just carry this cleaning solution over to Miz Miriam's cart and I'll be right back to help you. Don't let anyone else take care of you. I want to help you myself. Aliyah and all the young folks want to put me out to pasture and I'm not having any of it." The old man hustled away, carrying the heavy jug of cleaning solution.

Buck saw Gina's raised eyebrows. "My first job when I was in high school. Mr. Love was a tough boss, but fair. He taught me a lot."

She smiled, and then her phone pinged again. Her face tightened, just briefly, but she didn't pull out her phone. Instead, she crossed her arms over her chest and looked around. "What an amazing place."

Mr. Love, returning to the cash-register area, heard her. "This hardware store has been in my family since 1901," he said proudly. "Now, what can I do for you people? Buck, son, you still working on Miss Minnie's old house?"

"That's right—trying to get some rooms open in time for the Freedom Festival."

"And we're looking to get it onto the National Register of Historic Places," Gina added. "If you've been in the area and familiar with the house for a long time, I might like to talk to you as I'm doing the paperwork."

"Have you talked to Miss Minnie yet?" Buck asked.

"We're supposed to meet soon. She's a busy lady."

"That she is." Mr. Love smiled. "I'd be honored to help. That house is a very important place to a lot of people in this town. *Very* important."

"How do you mean?" Gina asked. "If you have time to tell us about it."

Mr. Love perched on the high stool behind the counter. "Falcon Station was the stop before our place on the Underground Railroad."

"I knew the guesthouse was a stop," Gina said, "but I didn't know there were others nearby. Is yours still standing?"

"Standing, but not much more than that. The house is

gone, but the old barn where travelers hid is still around, about ten miles up the road. Has a rose painted on the side that you can barely make out. Served to let folks know it was a safe place."

"I've seen it." Buck remembered driving by during some high-school carousing. A couple of older boys had warned him that any spray painting, egg throwing or sign shooting should steer clear of the Old Rose Barn. In turn, he'd passed along the message to younger boys when he was a senior.

"Could it be made into a national landmark, too, I wonder?"

Mr. Love beamed at Gina's interest. "I don't know about that. It's just one of those weathered, falling-down barns, though I've taken the kids and grandkids up there and told the story."

"Maybe we could see it sometime, too."

"You surely could," the older man said, "but the Falcon home has plenty to keep you busy exploring. Have you looked for the secret treasure in the cellar?"

"Treasure?"

"Or something hidden, anyway. Never saw it for myself, but that's the story."

Gina's eyes lit up again, and she gripped Buck's arm. "Have you explored the basement?"

"No way. It has a dirt floor and nasty cobwebs."

"Wimp," she said, scoffing at him. Her hand was still on his arm, her eyes full of fun. "Tell you what, soldier hero. I'll protect you if you'll go down there and explore it with me."

He lifted an eyebrow. "Will you hold my hand?"

"If you're good." Her lips quirked up at the corners. *Wow.*

Her phone pinged again, and the smile faded from her

face. She took it out, read the message, frowned and shoved it back in her purse, hard.

"Something wrong?" he asked as Mr. Love turned to assist another customer.

"Nothing. No big deal." She turned toward the rest of the store, straightening her shoulders, back to business. "Do you have a list?"

"It's all up here," he said, tapping the side of his head.

She rolled her eyes. "Great. Let's see how much you remember."

They headed to the drawer pulls and wall anchors they'd come for. Buck made his selections, and when he turned back toward Gina, she stood transfixed in front of a rack of gardening supplies, rakes and hoses and shovels. She was holding a packet of seeds in her hand.

He approached her. "You like gardening?" he asked.

"Just think what could be done with the little yard in front of the guesthouse."

He wasn't much for flowers, but he could imagine they'd look nice. The question was, if Gina planted flowers now, would she be around to see them blossom? Would he?

"I wonder why they called it Falcon Station?" she asked him.

"Miss Minnie's last name is Falcon." He lowered his voice. "Rumor has it that Mr. Love has been sweet on Miss Minnie for years."

She lifted an eyebrow. "The elders in this community are very…"

"Social? Romantic?" He grinned. "Something in the water, maybe."

Her phone pinged in her purse. And again. And again.

She squeezed her eyes shut for a moment, then pulled out her phone and looked at it. Her hand flew to her mouth.

"What's wrong?" Buck stepped closer, wanting to protect her from whatever was making her look so scared.

"They're cutting off my phone," she said faintly. "What am I going to do without a phone?"

"Who?"

"My in-laws. Bobby's grandparents." She shook her head back and forth, her expression despairing. "What am I going to do? They're going to…" She trailed off and squeezed her eyes shut.

Buck's eyes narrowed. "They have some kind of control of your account?"

She pressed her lips together and then nodded. "I didn't think about it, but yes. I'm on their plan."

"Does your phone have a GPS?" he asked immediately.

She shook her head quickly. "I disabled that right away, as soon as I left. And I blocked them from being able to see my call log and turned off location services. I just… I guess I wasn't thinking about how they could cut off my phone. And it's not like I'm a phone addict or anything, but I need Angelica to be able to contact me about Bobby. I need that phone for emergencies."

"Ma'am?" Mr. Love's voice came from behind them. "We have some of those no-contract, prepaid cell phones."

She turned. "You do?"

"Right over here." He felt his way along the shelf to where a display stood. "Take your pick." He put a wrinkled hand on Gina's arm. "And if you're ever in trouble, you're more than welcome to seek refuge here at the store. We have a sitting room in the back with a refrigerator and coffeepot, and more than a few people have stayed a few days there over the years."

"Thank you so much!" Gina's eyes went shiny. "I appreciate your kindness." She fumbled at the phones in the display, picking up one, putting it back without looking at it and picking up another.

"This one's good. I've used these before." Buck identified a simple phone and pulled it off the rack.

"All right." Her voice was faint.

He was surprised that someone as competent and calm as Gina would get this upset over a piece of technology. "Look, it's just a phone," he said gently. "We can manage this."

"It's not just a phone!" She spun on him. "They're threatening... They want to..." She broke off, shook her head. "It's not just a phone," she repeated, her voice flat and dull.

"Here. We'll pay for it all together." But as Mr. Love rang up their purchases and Gina bit her lip, and her phone buzzed repeatedly, Buck was worried. So far, her former in-laws had taken away her transportation and her communication. What was next? Did they have no shame about mistreating the mother of their grandchild?

After a day of trying to drown her worries in work and avoid Buck's concerned glances, Gina hated to have to rely on him for a ride to pick up Bobby.

She'd realized a few days back that driving without a license could get her in trouble. Her license had been stolen along with her money, and she couldn't order a replacement without kicking all kinds of search engines into play. So when Buck and even Lacey offered her the use of their cars, she had to decline.

She disliked the lack of independence, would have tried hard to find a babysitter in town, except that Angelica's situation was so ideal: she was caring for her own baby and one other—gorgeous Amy Franklin's nephew—in a big, comfortable farmhouse. More important, Angelica was warm and loving and so, so good to Bobby.

Her own humiliation as she approached Buck, who was putting away plastering supplies, had to take a backseat to Bobby's well-being.

"Ready to go?" he asked, sparing her the need to ask. He was thoughtful that way. He seemed to anticipate what she might need and offer it, making it seem less of a burden and more of a friendly favor.

Still, the dependency rankled. "Yes, whenever you're ready, and thank you."

"No problem."

But when they arrived at the dog rescue farm, Buck stopped her from emerging from the vehicle with a hand on her arm. "I feel like you're uncomfortable with accepting help. But that's what we do around here—we help each other."

She twisted her hands on her lap. "Why are you doing so much for someone you barely know?"

He opened his mouth and closed it, his eyes snagging with hers.

"What?" Her heart was pounding.

"You're worth it. I don't know who made you think you're not, but you deserve to be helped and treated well."

Those words were like a balm to Gina's soul, but she didn't completely trust them. "I'll go in and get Bobby and be right back out," she said, her breath coming fast. "Unless you want to come in? It's up to you."

"I'll come in and say hello." He was out of the truck and around to her side to help her before she could climb down herself.

They walked into an idyllic scene. On the floor of the living room, all three babies sat, surrounded by toys. Amy's little one, Tyler, was shaking a rattle. Angelica's Emmie banged a truck on the floor, calling, "Ah-ah-ah." And Bobby sat up straight, staring at Emmie, the monkey in a circle toy in his hand forgotten.

On the comfortable couch, Amy and Angelica sat, keeping a relaxed eye on the babies.

Bobby saw Gina and waved his arms, a huge smile breaking out on his face. She picked him up and snuggled him to her. Even though this situation was obviously good for Bobby, it was hard to be away from him all day.

"Hey, Buck! Have we got a proposal for you!" Angelica glanced over at Amy and they both laughed.

"Why do I feel like I'm about to get talked into something?"

"We're having a girls' night," Amy said.

"And we want Gina and Bobby to stay."

"And we can drive them home after."

"So, thanks for bringing her out here, but—"

"We'd invite you to stay, but—"

Buck lifted his hands, palms out, and started backing away. "Hey, I get the message. I know when I'm not wanted."

At that moment, an ancient bulldog stood slowly from the dog bed where it had been resting and limped over to Buck. "See, Bull likes me even if nobody else does," he joked, squatting down to scratch behind the dog's ears.

Gina tried to feel upset that they hadn't even consulted her, just assumed she would stay, but truth to tell, she liked it. Liked feeling wanted, liked being around other women with babies. Liked having evening plans and something that felt like friendship.

Buck, though, noticed the omission and beckoned her

over to where he was squatting beside Bull. "You want to stay or come on home? I'm fine either way."

"I'll stay." She felt absurdly conscious that she was planning her evening with him the way you would with a husband. "If that's okay with you, I mean, you drove me out here. But they said they'd bring me home…" She was babbling. She needed to stop babbling. She focused on Bobby, settling him back down on the floor beside the other babies.

"All right. See everyone later." With a final pat to Bull, Buck was gone.

Turning to face two women she didn't know well, Gina felt a moment of shyness, thrown back into a high-school world where, because of her dad's eccentric lifestyle and lack of money for stylish clothes, she hadn't fit in well with other girls. But Angelica stood and took her by the hand, tugging her toward the couch. "Here, hon, sit down. I'm just going to check on the salmon, and then we can pick up where we left off. You know Amy, right?"

"We're already friends," Amy said, and Gina's heart warmed. "Bobby's so adorable." She tickled his chin. "Wow, how many teeth does he have?"

"Five, and I think he might be cutting another. He was super fussy last night."

"I hear you. That was us a week ago."

"You guys are having salmon? If I'd watched three babies all day, I'd barely be able to order pizza." Gina sat down on the couch next to Amy.

"She claims it's easy. And low calorie. And if we're good at dinner, we can eat the chocolate mud cake I picked up at the Chatterbox before I came out here."

Gina's mouth watered. "I am so there. I love chocolate. But what's the occasion?"

"Actually, we're second choice. Angelica was cooking

for Troy and Xavier, but he'd forgotten to let her know they'd rescheduled a game for tonight. Basketball," she clarified. "Troy coaches. So she called me and asked if I'd bring dessert. I stopped by the café for three pieces of cake, and presto…it's a party. I think she tried to call you, too, but couldn't get through."

That comment punctured Gina's pleasure. She pulled out her phone, looked at it. "I sent texts earlier today. In fact, I sent you a text, to see if we could get together this weekend."

"Didn't get it," Amy said. "Did you forget to pay your bill? Because when that happened to me once, I could text, or it seemed like it, but nothing sent and I couldn't receive messages or calls."

She'd sent the texts after the exchange with her in-laws, when they'd threatened to cut off her phone. So they had actually done it. That fast, she was severed from her old life. Suddenly, the salmon didn't smell so good. Her stomach churned.

The old bulldog came over and nuzzled at her hand, and she scratched his ears distractedly, trying to look on the bright side. She was actually slightly relieved that she wouldn't be getting texts or calls from her in-laws anymore. And she could give Angelica the number from her new, no-contract phone.

She could do this.

The only thing that worried her was, if they'd cut off her communication so quickly, would they come for Bobby next, as they'd threatened to do?

Amy was still looking at her quizzically, but Gina turned away, unsure of whether she could reveal any of her problems to these women she didn't know well. Fortunately,

Angelica called them into the kitchen and they picked up the babies and went in.

"You have three high chairs?" Gina asked, surveying the neatly set table with chairs alternating with high chairs.

"I'm married to a Hinton," Angelica said wryly. "They have everything."

The farmhouse kitchen was warm and comfortable, even sporting a couch in the corner. They served themselves and chopped bits for the babies, and soon they were all digging in, talking like old friends. The kids babbled and guitar music played quietly in the background, and Gina felt her worries slide away.

"So," Amy said, turning to her purposefully, "I have an idea."

"What's that?"

"I want to rent a little space in downtown Rescue River, maybe start a craft and yarn shop."

"Wait a minute," Angelica said. "You're staying in Rescue River for sure?"

"It's a good place to raise Tyler, and I can't go back to New York." Amy didn't explain why. "With this craft shop, I'd like to link it in with the town's history. You're helping to restore Lacey's house and you know all about the historical-landmark stuff. Wonder if we could reclaim one of the old buildings in downtown and get grants to renovate it?"

Gina's eyebrows lifted. "That's an interesting idea," she said. "I've always dreamed of opening a shop for interior decorating, but I have no money to start something like that."

"That's why we need grants," Amy said. "I don't have a lot to invest, either, but I would guess a couple of the buildings on the edge of downtown are dirt cheap. Some of them may have historical significance. Isn't it worth checking them out?"

"Probably." Gina started to say more and then broke off. Could she be honest about her fears and limitations with these women?

She wanted so much to belong. To have true friends, not just acquaintances impressed with her fancy home and car.

But the more people who knew of her situation, the more likely someone would let slip some information that would lead her in-laws to Bobby.

She couldn't take that chance.

"I... Everything about my life is up in the air right now. I don't know how much help I can be." To avoid the pain of the cold shoulder that would inevitably follow, she turned to Bobby and helped him spoon up some food.

To her surprise, she felt a hand press her arm. "I understand problems," Angelica said. "When I came back to Rescue River, my life was pretty messed up."

From her other side, Amy sighed. "We all have issues. I don't know if I'll ever be able to be open about what happened to me in New York."

"Even if your problems are too big for you, they're not too big for God," Angelica said gently. "That's what I had to figure out before I could really be happy. Really open my eyes to what was around me, all the good stuff."

"Good stuff like Troy?" Amy teased gently.

"Exactly."

Gina felt some of the tension leave her shoulders. These weren't judgmental high-school girls; they were real Christian women, who weren't going to let the fact that someone didn't have a perfect life push them away.

Yet another reason she was glad she'd landed in Rescue River.

"Speaking of men," Angelica said, "what's going on between you and Buck?"

"You saw that, too?" Amy said to Angelica.

Her cheeks warming, Gina grabbed a wet cloth and focused on wiping off Bobby's hands and face. "Saw what?"

"It's not so much what I saw as what I felt," Angelica said.

"Vibes," Amy agreed. "Major emotional vibes between the two of you. And I was glad to see it. Buck's a nice guy."

"How long have you known him?" Angelica asked, and there was something in her voice, some guardedness that made Gina curious.

"We were in school together," Amy explained. "All through, from kids' birthday parties to high-school track to his goodbye party when he went in the service. Knew his family, knew Lacey. Loved his dad."

Angelica nodded. "From what I heard, everyone loved his dad."

"Didn't you know Buck, too?" Gina glanced up from putting Bobby's sock back on. "You went to school here, right?"

"I was a year younger and on the outside of the main group in high school, but he was always nice to me."

"He's a good guy." Amy lifted her baby out of the high chair and took him over to the sink to wipe him down. "His mom had a pretty bad drinking problem, but Buck's dad and Buck and Lacey were so well liked, someone usually stamped down the gossip before it got too bad."

"It had its impact on Buck, though," Angelica said quietly. "Well, that and the war."

"So I hear." Amy came back to the table and sat down, holding Tyler on her lap. "I haven't been around for a few years, but wowie! The stories of his drinking reached me all the way in New York City."

"It was pretty bad." Angelica leaned back in her chair and looked at Gina, the skin between her eyebrows pleated. "One time before Troy and I got together…"

Gina lifted an eyebrow, waiting, her heart sinking.

"It's just… Buck and I were going to go out. He came out here—I was staying at the bunkhouse with Xavier. Anyway, he came to pick me up and he was really drunk. Too drunk to drive, so Troy and I called Lacey to come get him. He got pretty belligerent."

"I heard there were a lot of incidents like that," Amy said. "After he came back from Afghanistan, right? Substance abuse is a huge problem for vets. A way for them to cope with the things they saw and had to do."

Amy's choice of words—substance abuse—reminded Gina of how careful she needed to be. No judgment. She had absolutely no judgment where men were concerned.

She'd fallen for an addict before, and she was doing it again.

Angelica reached out and put a hand on Gina's arm. "I don't want to gossip, and I really like Buck. I'd just… I saw how you two were looking at each other, and I worried… Just be careful, okay?"

"Well, but he's in recovery, right?" Amy rocked Tyler gently. "That can really work. I saw it dozens of times out in California. And shouldn't we try to help him, not judge him?"

"Of course, and I feel for Buck—I really do. He's had so much to deal with." Angelica frowned. "It's just…sometimes recovery programs don't work. And families are devastated."

Gina knew about that firsthand. She nodded, her thoughts chaotic.

"I would never tell you what to do," Angelica said. "I'd just suggest you be careful. With Bobby and all."

Gina nodded. "I will." Restless, she stood and paced, Bobby on her hip.

On a built-in shelf beside the sink was a photograph in a wedding frame. Troy, Angelica and Xavier, all dressed up in wedding clothes, with the ripe harvest fields behind them.

Her throat closed. She remembered her own wedding day, the hopes, the promises. She'd thought that the biggest decision of her life was over and done. And done well.

There was so much she hadn't known on that day. So much suffering in the future.

But for someone like Angelica, who'd chosen the right man, the future *was* bright.

Amy and Angelica were still talking about Buck. "I just don't think he can handle a lot of stress. It's likely to push him back into drinking."

"That's so sad, but you're probably right."

"Troy says he plans to leave Rescue River as soon as he's repaid the debts he incurred during his drunk phase."

Gina gripped the edge of the sink as she listened and stared at the picture. No matter her romantic dreams, she and Buck weren't going to get together. There wasn't a potential relationship. She wasn't going to be saved by him.

She had to save herself…and leave Buck alone.

Chapter 8

"So, why have you been avoiding me?"

The moment Buck asked the question, he wished he hadn't. He and Gina had to work together this whole evening—they'd set it aside to wallpaper after Bobby was in bed. She'd just come downstairs and into the front guest room. Lacey was away, working her third double shift this week.

"I haven't been avoiding you. We've been working together every day!" She stood by the table they had set up for spreading paste, her hand on her hip.

"Working together, yeah, but no talking. Did I do something wrong?"

He figured he knew the answer. It had started after her evening with Angelica and Amy. No doubt she'd been told some of the details about him and his past escapades.

She opened her mouth like she wanted to say something and then shut it again.

"Are you going to tell me or not?" He didn't know why he was pushing; it was like he'd lost control. Like when he'd been drinking, only he wasn't drinking. And he probably shouldn't make a big deal of it, but it was bugging him. The way she acted toward him mattered.

He definitely needed to discuss this with his sponsor.

She looked down, then lifted her eyes to his again. "It's just... I don't want you to get the wrong idea. We can't... you know."

He nodded, defeat blasting his heart. "You heard the truth about me." And he knew it, knew he had to get out of Rescue River for just that reason, but never had it discouraged him so much.

"It's not exactly that." She wasn't entirely denying it, he noticed, because she was honest to the core. "It's just... there *is* a spark." She lifted her eyes to his, looking troubled.

Heat rose in him at her words. "On your side or mine?"

She looked down, color staining her cheeks.

Was that because she felt the spark herself or because she didn't?

When she didn't answer, that told him everything. She'd noticed that he was attracted but she didn't feel the same herself.

In awkward silence they worked together to paste, lift and spread the wallpaper. The moments in between, while they were waiting for the paste to permeate the paper, felt uncomfortable. And when they got to the big break, when they had to let the whole room dry before putting the moldings back up, the silence was excruciating. He was just about to get up and go to his room when she spoke up suddenly. "Let's go explore the basement."

"What?"

"There's supposed to be a secret room or hiding place. Let's go try to find it."

Great. It was the last thing he wanted to do, the only way of breaking the silence he'd much rather have said no to.

But she was already out the door, and a gentleman couldn't let a lady go into the dark alone.

They made their way down the house's wooden cellar stairs. There was no railing, and a single bulb hung down to illuminate the old stone walls.

Something brushed his leg and he kicked out, barely restraining a yell, heart pounding.

An indignant yowl sounded, and the reclusive Mrs. Whiskers ran past him up the stairs.

Gina had grabbed a flashlight and she shone it around, but the darkness was so heavy that the light barely penetrated.

A sick feeling rose in him as they reached the low-ceilinged, dark main room, but Gina wasn't affected the same way; she was giggling, grabbing his arm at the scuttling sound of some little creature, shuddering openly. To her, it was obviously a trip through the fun house.

Sweat trickled down his back. He tried to focus on her and not on the memories.

"I wonder what's here. Have you even been down here before?"

"No." He could hear the hoarseness in his voice and wondered if she could, too.

"We'll go over the walls, see what we can find." She shone the light around, scanning the stone walls, exploring.

He took deep breaths of cold, dank air and told himself he was fine. He was in a basement in Ohio, not a cave in Afghanistan.

Still, when a rock she was fiddling with came out of

the wall and fell to the floor with a thump, he grabbed her shoulders, heart racing, and pulled her back. "Come on. Let's get out of here."

She tried to move out of his grip, but he held on. "Come on!"

"Buck. Hey, Buck!" She twisted away but kept hold of his hand, shining the light in his direction. "Hey, what's wrong? You look awful."

He blew out a breath and drew in another lungful of musty cellar air. "Bad memories."

"Memories of what?" She tugged him over to where they could sit on the stairs.

Light came in from the open door above, illuminating an escape route. His breathing calmed a little. "Afghanistan. There were...lots of caves."

"And you had a bad experience in one." It wasn't phrased as a question.

"Yeah." He took another minute to breathe, feeling his body steady, his heart rate settle. He was cold from the sweat, but he no longer felt sick. And since he'd already wimped out on her, and since she didn't have any romantic interest in him anyway, he might as well tell her. "A buddy and I got ambushed in a cave. Separated from our unit, and we didn't know the country near as well as our enemies did. It got ugly." He ran a hand over his face.

"But you got out okay, in the end?"

"I did." A bleak sense of failure overwhelmed him.

"And your friend?"

He shook his head. "He didn't make it." And that was the shame of it. He should have been able to save John, but he hadn't. They'd made a plan to run for it, knowing they couldn't cover each other, but he should never have agreed to it, because John had gone down. And he'd never forget the misery of walking down off that mountain without his buddy.

"That must be hard to deal with." She'd never let go of his hand and now she gripped it tighter. "I can't imagine. Wow."

And then she just sat with him, quiet.

Her simple acceptance of how bad it had been, her comforting silence, surprised him. He hadn't told anyone—outside of his shrink—about that particular failure. He'd worried that he'd be condemned. Thing was, no one could condemn him more harshly than he condemned himself.

She was kicking at the bottom of the stairs and a loose board fell down. She picked it up and studied it.

"Look at that," she said.

"Is that a keyhole?" he asked at the same moment.

She squatted down and shone the flashlight under the stairs, and he had to marvel that she seemed to have no fear of mice or spiders or whatever other nasty thing could be down there.

Instead, she pulled out a wooden box, deteriorated, rotten on one side.

Her eyebrows lifted. She looked at him and then held it out.

He met her eyes and then, slowly, lifted the lid.

Inside was a tarnished silver cross necklace.

She studied it. "Wonder who this belonged to?"

"I don't know. Maybe there's some information in Miss Minnie's paperwork."

"Or maybe Mr. Love would know something."

He put the necklace back into the box and closed the lid. "We didn't find a secret room," he said, "but we found something interesting."

"There could be an amazing story behind this. We can display it in the guesthouse!" She sounded excited.

"You did the right thing, dragging me down here."

She looked at him and their eyes held. Hers sparkled with the excitement of their find and then darkened. Her tongue flicked across her lip.

It took everything in him not to kiss her.

"Buck?" she said faintly.

"Yeah?"

"It wasn't one-sided."

He lifted an eyebrow, wondering if she meant what he thought she meant.

"That...spark. I...I felt it. *Feel* it."

What was a man supposed to do when he'd faced his fears and found a treasure? How was he supposed to remember to do the wise thing?

He put a hand on either side of her face, reading her expression, trying to figure out whether she'd mind. Her eyes were wide, but not afraid.

He pulled her closer and lowered his lips to hers.

Being in Buck's arms, immersed in his sweet but intense kiss, Gina felt like she was floating. Never in her life had she experienced anything like this.

His lips were firm. He definitely knew what he was doing, kissing her. She sighed and settled into the strong, warm circle of his arms.

He lifted his head to look into her eyes, and she couldn't hide her dreamy satisfaction. He nodded and dipped down for another kiss, his hands stroking and touching her back, but not straying anywhere that made her uncomfortable.

He was careful, protective. He was looking out for her

rather than going for anything he could get. That alone set him apart from most men she'd known.

And the closeness she felt wasn't just physical. He wanted to know about her, to help her; he cared. More than that, tonight he'd let her know him more. What he'd revealed, his vulnerable side, made something burst free in her heart, a seed that could grow.

And then, through the baby monitor she'd left in the kitchen, she heard mild fussing.

"Bobby's crying," she told Buck.

He dropped his arms immediately. "Better check on him," he said, and she stood, steadied herself and then turned and hurried up the stairs, the little wooden chest still in her hand.

As she trotted up two flights, the euphoria of kissing Buck faded and doubts rushed in.

He's an alcoholic!

He's too vulnerable to take on the mess of your life!

He's leaving Rescue River!

She reached her room and found Bobby tossing, face red, half-asleep. He'd gotten himself into the corner of his crib and was too sleepy to find a more comfortable position.

She moved him and patted his back until he settled down.

Touching her baby brought her back into line with her goals. She needed to remember them.

She was here to take care of herself and Bobby, to protect her son from harm, and find a safe place to raise him.

She wasn't here to get involved with another risky, dangerous person.

The door creaked. "Is he okay?" Buck asked, coming up behind her, putting a hand on her shoulder.

A hand that felt possessive. And although everything inside her wanted to curl toward him, to feel his arms around her again, her responsibility for Bobby overcame it.

She braced herself. "That can't happen again," she said and looked up at him.

Hurt flashed across his handsome face, making her remember that he wasn't a carefree, blustering addict like Hank had been. He was a man who'd fought for his country and bore the emotional scars from it. A man who'd lost a wife and child.

She closed her eyes for just a minute, confused.

When she looked at him again, his mouth and eyes had gone flat. "All right. If you're both okay, I'm going to turn in."

His words were flat, too. When he walked away, his shoulders looked stiff.

Her mouth opened to call him back, and she pressed both hands over it to stop herself. It hurt to nip this thing between them, but it was best to do it now rather than ripping apart a full-grown love affair.

And it had to be stopped. It was best for Bobby. Ultimately, it was best for Buck, too.

But what about me? What about what I want? She wrapped her arms around her middle. She felt like she was breaking apart.

When you were a parent, you made the decisions that were best for the child. That, she knew.

Doing the right thing was hard, but in the end, it would lead to less pain.

She walked over to her bed and sank down on it, arms still wrapped around her middle. She tried to pray, to cry out to God, but rather than finding comfort, she saw Buck's hurt face before her eyes.

Why did she have to hurt someone else to do the right thing by Bobby?

Why did she have to hurt herself?

No answers came. So, slowly, she closed the door to her room and got ready for bed. Went to check one last time on Bobby and saw the wooden box she'd been clutching in her hand when she'd run upstairs.

There was the cross. But now, studying the box in brighter light, she saw that it should be deeper than it was, suggesting that it had a false bottom. She tried to pry it up, and when her fingers wouldn't do the job, she found a metal nail file and slid it between the bottom of the box and the side, prying upward until the old piece of wood gave way.

Inside was a slim leather book filled with careful, old-fashioned handwriting.

Immediately, she thought of telling Buck. She wanted to share this with him. And she would, but not tonight—they were both too vulnerable, too hurt.

She flattened the pages out and began to read.

Buck paced the guesthouse, feeling like a caged dog. He picked up a magazine and then threw it down again. Started to straighten up the wallpapering supplies and then realized they'd just need to get them out again tomorrow. There was nothing to do now, and no way he was going to sleep.

He'd opened himself up to Gina, had experienced her sweetness and the hope of some more substantial connection with her.

But she'd shut him out.

He slammed a hand into the wall of the downstairs hallway and relished the pain of it. She'd responded to him; he was experienced enough to know that. Her breathing, her quickened pulse, her dark, lidded eyes told him that she'd enjoyed the kiss. And he hadn't pushed it too far; he'd been careful to respect her boundaries. He knew what kind of woman he was dealing with. Gina was a lady, through and through.

No, it was worse than that. When she'd gotten away from him and had had a moment to think, she'd realized she didn't want anything to do with him. What had she said? *No more of that.*

Maybe she'd had time to think about the drawbacks of a man who was afraid of small dark places. Or a man with a bad history everyone in town knew about. Or a man from a modest background, rather than the wealth she was accustomed to.

Or maybe it was just something about him.

For the second time this week, he thought back to his marriage. Not the loss of Ivana and Mia, but the months leading up to it, when he'd heard repeatedly about his failures and inadequacies as a husband.

He hadn't had it all together when he'd come back from Afghanistan. He'd needed counseling, time to figure out the right professional direction. The fact that he hadn't been sure of himself, combined with Ivana's weariness as a new mother, had made for stressful times.

It wasn't that he hadn't tried. He'd practiced listening skills he'd learned in counseling, brought flowers and gotten sitters so they could go out on dates. But none of it had worked.

You're not the man I thought you were. Those words, the ones he'd stuffed down and tried to forget, came ringing into his brain now.

He'd like to rip that brain right out of his skull. He could feel himself going down.

What did it matter if he had a drink, or ten? His life

was never going to get any better. Work, sleep, try not to drink. Always alone.

At least at the bar, he'd have companionship. Not the kind he wanted, but something was better than nothing.

He paced some more. Looked up at the ceiling, where he could hear Gina moving around.

Was she upset, too? Uncomfortable hearing him roam around the house? Ambivalent about pushing him away?

Maybe she was, but she'd sounded sure of what she was saying. She'd made a decision.

Just for a moment, he'd thought he might get the girl. He'd thought that life could open up for him again, that he could have the companionship he craved. Not just someone to hold in his arms—although Gina fit beautifully there—but someone to talk to, someone who understood.

He had to get out of here.

Grabbing his jacket from the hook beside the door, he ran to his car and drove.

Twenty minutes later he was parking beside the big, dark barn out at the dog rescue farm. When he opened the door of his truck and slammed it shut, all the dogs started barking. Only then did he realize he needed to text Troy and Angelica, who lived with their kids in the adjacent house, to let them know he wasn't an intruder.

It's just me, out at the barn.

You okay? came the text back from Troy.

Yeah. Just forgot something.

He went inside, breathing in the familiar smells of hay and sawdust, feed and dogs. Rather than put on the main light, he just turned on the lamp on the desk near the door, found a flashlight and headed back.

The dogs continued barking, of course, and he got drawn into petting some of the needier ones. When he saw Spike, the Maltese mix from the alley the other day, he opened his crate, picked him up and carried him around. He'd turned out to be healthy enough, just your average senior, overweight dog with bad teeth. But with most of his matted hair shaved off, he was a little guy. He didn't fit in with the bully breeds that made up most of the population at the rescue.

"But somebody loved you, huh?" He rubbed behind the dog's ears, thinking of the note and the money.

The dog licked his face gratefully.

"Your breath smells worse than a garbage dump," he chided the old dog.

Yeah, he was talking to a dog. Which might mean he was crazy, or might mean he was sane.

Finally he got to the kennel he'd been seeking. There was Crater, in the back of it, licking his paws. When the dog saw Buck, he came bounding forward.

Buck opened the kennel awkwardly, still holding the Maltese. "Hey, buddy," he said. "Want to come home with me tonight?"

He only did that on the bad days. Lacey hadn't bargained for a big, clumsy dog in her house. But she knew he needed the company sometimes.

Crater trotted confidently beside him, mouth open, tongue hanging out. He seemed to laugh at the other dogs, still in their kennels.

When they got back to Spike's small crate, Buck bent down to put the little guy in.

Spike struggled, looking up at him with big, dark eyes, letting out pitiful cries.

"I don't even like small dogs." Firmly, he shut the crate and headed for the door.

Above the noise of the other dogs, he could hear Spike's high-pitched howl.

All the dogs were barking. All of them needed a home. He was giving one of the unadoptables an outing, that was all. He reached down to rub Crater's head and the dog stared up at him adoringly.

That high-pitched howl again.

Buck groaned. Stopped. Started walking again.

Crater looked at him quizzically.

His steps slowed. He turned around. Then he jogged back to Spike's cage, opened it and swept the fat Maltese into the curve of his arm. "One night on a real bed. Just one, you hear?"

Twenty minutes later, as he let himself into the guesthouse and went upstairs—Crater beside him and Spike in his arms—he realized he hadn't even considered taking the turnoff for the bar.

Chapter 9

A scratching sound tugged at Gina's consciousness. Was Bobby scratching, or was it Buck? Someone was in a box and she needed to help him get out of it, she knew that, but she couldn't make herself move.

More scratching, and then vigorous, high-pitched barking.

Barking?

And then an indignant yowl, some growling and more barking.

Gina sat up in bed, her eyes barely able to open. When she saw the bright daylight outside her window, she jumped up. How late had she slept?

Automatically she checked on Bobby, but he was sleeping through the sounds of an animal fight right outside their door. She shrugged into her robe and went out to see what was going on.

Buck was coming up the stairs at the same time, already dressed and covered with a fine white powder, like he'd been plastering.

"Hey." He snapped his fingers and the big dog, Crater, bounded over. Buck pointed at the floor, and Crater sat.

The orange cat, Mr. Whiskers, and his reclusive lady friend perched on a high, built-in ledge. They both glared disdainfully at a small, fat white dog who continued to bark furiously at them.

Gina bent down and picked up the little dog. It quieted down and licked her face before twisting toward the cats.

She wrinkled her nose. "Dog breath, wow!"

"His teeth aren't the best. That's Spike."

"Spike?"

"Uh-huh."

"Okay." She studied the ten-pound dog doubtfully. "These guys weren't here when I went to bed."

"I needed company," he said gruffly. "Sorry they woke you."

His words brought back the night before, and she immediately thought of their kiss. Her face heated and she started to touch her lips, then cuddled the little dog closer instead.

He'd needed company. Why had he needed company? Because she'd hurt him?

She remembered the old journal she'd found and opened her mouth to tell Buck about it when Bobby called. He was always hungry in the morning.

She pressed the little dog into Buck's arms and went to her son.

As she changed him and prepared him for the day, she heard Buck whistle to Crater and go back downstairs. Good. And she'd keep Bobby with her today, maybe do some paperwork instead of working beside Buck. They were making good progress on the renovation, and it looked like there would be several rooms ready to display for the festival if they all stayed on task. It was time to figure out a publicity plan.

And it was time for her to spend a day apart from Buck. Exactly what she *didn't* want to do, because the thought of working with him, beside him, filled her with longing. Made her want to share another sweet kiss.

But she couldn't reopen that wound. It was kinder to be cruel.

After feeding Bobby some breakfast, she went out onto the front porch. She sat on the steps and put a blanket and toys in the yard for Bobby. As he banged plastic together and plucked at grass, she updated the marketing plan.

At one point, Buck opened the door to let the little dog out and saw her there. "Will it bother you if Spike hangs outside with you? He's getting into everything." Buck's voice was toneless, exquisitely polite.

"No problem. I like him. C'mere, Spike."

Normally they'd have laughed together about the ill-fitting name. He'd have told her the dog's story. But today, he just nodded.

He was turning away when Bobby started shouting. "Buh! Buh!" He waved his arms at Buck and started to crawl toward him.

Buck looked back, and a muscle twitched in his jaw. He stepped inside and closed the door.

Pain twisted in Gina's chest. She didn't like being estranged from him. Didn't want this coldness. Didn't want Bobby to get sad from rejection, although truthfully, her son had spotted a robin and turned toward it, easily distracted.

If only she could be distracted that easily.

It's better this way. She tugged the little dog closer to her side and determinedly went on writing out her plan.

An hour later, she heard the sound of a camera clicking and looked up to see Amy, phone in hand, snapping photographs. "You just look so cute, with Bobby and that little dog," Amy said. "I'll send these to you. You working hard?"

"Yeah. Getting some paperwork done."

"For the national-landmark thing?"

She nodded as Amy opened the picket fence and let herself in. "Some of that, and I'm working on marketing. We need to send out some blasts on social media, get the word out about the guesthouse and how it'll be open for the festival."

"I can help with that," Amy offered. "You think you're going to make it, then?"

"It's looking good." Then it came together for her. "Hey, we need to take a bunch of pictures of the renovation. We can post them, and the fixer-upper crowd will think it's awesome."

"That's for sure. Want me to take a few more of the outside?"

"The inside, too, if you're willing. I'm a terrible photographer. But where's Tyler?"

"Out at Angelica's. Why isn't Bobby there today?"

"He's only there three days per week." Gina didn't add that she needed the comfort of keeping her son close today.

They went inside and Amy walked around snapping photos. In the kitchen Gina put Bobby in his high chair, placating him with dry cereal while she fixed a tray of fruit, cheese and crackers for an early lunch. She made a separate plate for Buck to find when he was ready. She and Amy could sit outside to eat, away from him.

She could hear Buck and Amy talking, but she stifled her desire to listen. It didn't matter. Wasn't her business.

The voices came closer, and then they both walked into

the kitchen. When Buck saw her, he stopped in the middle of a sentence. He stammered something, turned abruptly and left.

Amy frowned after him and then looked at Gina. "Why's the tension so thick in here?"

Gina so wanted to tell her. She was suffering from a serious shortage of girlfriend consultation.

But what could she say? *He kissed me and I liked it and then I cut him off? It'll never work for me because of who he is and who I am? I'm crazy about him?*

She blew out a sigh. "Grab those glasses, will you? I'll carry the pitcher and we can have some lunch outside."

Once they were settled on the porch, Gina rocked Bobby and held him against her, and just as she'd hoped, he relaxed into sleep. After he drifted off, she ate some snacks with one hand and held him, and then Amy made a nest for him and they laid him down.

"You're still not off the hook. What's going on between you and Buck?"

Unable to think of a real excuse, Gina settled for half the truth. "We went forward a little bit in our…friendship. And then we…I…decided not to go further."

"Why?" Amy poured another glass of lemon-infused water for both of them.

"Because Bobby comes first," Gina said firmly.

"And? Is Buck somehow anti-Bobby?"

"No, he's great with him. It's just…men mostly aren't reliable, and Buck…well, you heard what Angelica said that one night. He's got a drinking problem, and I—"

"He's in AA, right?" Amy interrupted. "Have you ever seen him drink?"

"No, I've never seen him drink. But still…"

"Why did you say men mostly aren't reliable?"

Man, Amy was like a bloodhound on the scent. But Gina didn't know whether to get into talking about her dad. "Just…past history."

"But Bobby's a boy. It would be nice if he had some male role models in his life."

"That's true, and yet…" She sighed. "I don't know." She leaned over to check on Bobby, hoping Amy would take the hint and get off this line of questioning.

But no chance of that. "What was your childhood like?" Amy pressed. "Was your dad in the picture?"

"Yes." Gina thought of her dad, and as always, the shaggy, smiling image of him brought a fond feeling. "He was my only parent. My mom passed on right after I was born."

"Good relationship with him, I assume? Because you're smiling."

"I'm smiling because I love him to pieces," Gina said. She was about to stop there, to brush it all off as she usually did with inquiries about her childhood, but Amy's understanding face, her receptive silence, made Gina feel like she could share a few details. "But my childhood was a little different."

"Different?"

Wondering how to explain, Gina thought back, and a memory flashed into her head. "Once when I was about seven," she said, "I invited a couple of girls to come over after school. We all got notes from our parents and they rode home on the bus with me." She put her elbows on her knees and leaned forward, remembering. "When we got off the bus, we were running up toward the house, but one of the girls stopped. She wanted to know why my house was so little, and why the porch roof was sagging, and why the driveway was made of dirt, not asphalt."

"You grew up poor," Amy guessed.

"Yeah. I explained it away, and we went inside. And there was nobody home."

"Your dad was gone?"

She nodded. "I was used to being alone, but they both got scared and started to cry. They wanted their moms."

"What did you do?" Amy asked.

"I fixed us all a snack. Showed them how to put butter and sugar on white bread, and they loved it. And then I told them stories until their moms came to get them."

Amy nodded, looking sympathetic and nonjudgmental. "Sounds like you were pretty mature. Did the moms find out?"

"My dad rolled in just as they did, and somehow, he smoothed it over. He really was handsome back then, and super articulate. There wasn't a woman within miles who couldn't be charmed by him." She sighed. "But of course, the girls weren't allowed to come over again, and they spread the word. Pretty much nobody trusted my dad to do what he said he'd do."

Amy nodded. "And so you don't trust men," she said. "Makes sense, with that background."

Gina hadn't really put it together like that before, and she wasn't sure she bought it. "I got married, though. I was happily married." For a while.

"And what was he like? Your husband."

Gina thought. "He was the playmate I never had," she said, her eyes filling with tears. "When we were first dating, and when we first got married, we had so much fun together. He really *was* like a little boy, and I got to be a kid again with him, too."

"That sounds good," Amy said, "but it also sounds like

you married your father. Someone else irresponsible, you know? How did he do when Bobby came along?"

Gina frowned. "Not well. I couldn't party anymore, and he couldn't cope with responsibility, and..." She blew out a sigh. How to explain the disaster their marriage had become? How to explain the issues with his parents, who'd morphed from kindly caregivers to monsters with the arrival of Bobby?

She pushed her plate away. "I should probably get back to work. I'm sorry to do all that talking."

"It's okay," Amy said. "I was the one asking all the nosy questions."

"I'm glad you came over." And she was. Gina hadn't had much girl talk since she'd been here, aside from a couple of phone calls with Haley back in California.

They hugged, and then Amy held her shoulders. "Remember," she said, "the past doesn't have to determine the future. Buck isn't your dad. And he's not Bobby's father. Give him a chance, okay?"

Except he was all too much like them, Gina thought as she settled back down to work. And though she'd put her trust in two men who hadn't repaid it, she wasn't going to make the same mistake a third time.

She watched her baby's chest rise and fall with his sleep breathing. No mistakes. Not this time. The stakes were too high.

After lunch, Buck changed into scrubs and headed out the front door, Crater trotting behind him.

Gina still sat there, working on Lacey's laptop. Bobby slept beside her and the little Maltese pressed against her side. In the spring sunlight, she looked so pretty that his throat hurt.

He swallowed. "C'mon, Spike. Time to go back to jail."

"Do you have to take him?" She put a protective hand on the dog.

"We're not set up for a dog here." He looked around, anywhere but at her. "No little-dog food, no dog bed..."

"I know, but he looks so sad!"

As if to prove her point, the dog peered up at him from beneath shaggy fur, his dark eyes pleading.

"I know—that's why I brought him home. But Lacey..." His sister hadn't okayed it. She also was never home these days; she was working double shifts at the hospital, ostensibly to earn extra cash, but really, probably, to stay away from the painful memories Bobby evoked.

"Oh, of course. I wasn't thinking." She sat up straighter, scooped the dog off the wicker couch beside her and deposited him into Buck's arms.

The dog whined and struggled to get back to Gina.

"Hey, come on, buddy." He scratched behind the dog's ears until it settled into his arms as if confident he'd do the right thing.

Gina was watching him expectantly, too.

"Okay, look, I'll work on it. But no promises."

"Of course!" She was beaming. "Thank you!"

Buck would do just about anything to make her smile like that again. Which was really bad.

It was almost like he was falling in love with her.

Stuffing down that very disturbing thought, he spun away and hurried down to his truck.

Out at the rescue, after Buck had put Crater and Spike back into their kennels, he and Troy did a couple of procedures, working together like a well-oiled machine. Buck prepped and assisted, grateful for the distraction from his troubled thoughts.

One of the local farmers brought in a goat that had gotten tangled in some barbed wire, and Buck cleaned and bandaged its leg. In town, Troy's practice was mainly small animals, but out here, they did what was needed.

Spike barked and whined every time he walked by, so when they hit a lull and were doing paperwork in the office, he brought the Maltese out and let it run around. After a cursory sniff of the room, the dog settled beside Buck's office chair.

"What's up with that?" Troy asked, nodding toward Spike. "Thought you went for bigger dogs, like Crater."

"Yeah. He's just so..." Buck trailed off and reached down to scratch the shaggy little guy's ears.

"Needy?"

"Yeah."

Troy nodded and changed the subject abruptly. "How are Gina and Bobby doing?"

"Great, I guess." Buck focused on the intake form in front of him, filling in the details.

Troy leaned back in his office chair and put his hands behind his head. "You guess? Thought you'd know."

Buck shook his head and kept on writing.

"I thought something was heating up between you."

"No." Buck looked up to meet Troy's assessing gaze. "Can't."

"How come?"

Impatiently, Buck gestured toward himself. "Look at me, man. I'm a mess. Not a good choice for anyone."

"I don't know about that. Your life is more stable than hers."

Stable wasn't a word Buck had applied to himself, ever. But if he thought about how he lived now, he realized, it was accurate. He stayed with his sister, went to work at one or the other of his jobs, came home, went to bed. Got up and did it all again. Even went to church on a regular basis, and got something out of it.

But he'd seen the expression in Gina's eyes after that night she'd gotten together with Angelica and Amy, and then again after they'd kissed. She'd heard things. She had doubts about him, and understandably so. "I have a history, and it keeps wanting to chase me."

"People see you changing," Troy said mildly. "You're not chained to your past."

Buck stood, restless. It was what Dion had said, too, but he and Troy were both looking at life with rose-colored glasses. The past *did* come back to bite you. "I gotta get back, do a little more work tonight." He paused then, fingered his sobriety coin and made an abrupt decision. "Hey, listen. You know I'm working the steps in AA."

Troy nodded.

This was never easy. "One of the steps is making amends, and I need to do that with you."

Troy tipped back in his chair. "You're doing great now. That's all that matters."

"No." Buck forced himself to stand there and go through with it. "I was a jerk in a number of ways, but a day I remember in particular, I came in to assist with surgery when I'd been drinking. Started to botch things up, and you had to kick me out and finish it all yourself."

"I remember. I think I had a few choice words for you."

"I deserved them. I put the dog you were working on at risk, and I'm sorry." As soon as he said that, a weight he hadn't known he'd been carrying lifted off his heart. "I'd like to find a way to make that up to you."

Troy let his chair fall forward with a gentle bang. "You don't owe me anything. But—" he waved an arm toward the dog area "—you might owe something to those guys. Or, at least, to one of them." He looked down at the Maltese that stood patiently at Buck's feet. "Think about it."

"I will." He shrugged into his jacket and headed for the door. Spike trotted confidently after him. When he started to go outside, the dog ran out and jumped at Buck's truck.

Afternoon sun heated Buck's back, and a cardinal sang its "Birdie? Birdie? Birdie?" from the top of a bare-limbed tree. Buck took a minute to breathe in the spring air.

Troy stood in the barn's doorway, watching as Buck walked to the truck, opened the door and lifted the little dog in.

"Hey," Troy called. "The half-drunk guy who used to stumble in here wouldn't have given that dog a second glance," he said. "You're changing, whether you know it or not."

"He's crazy, right?" Buck said to the little dog as he put the truck in gear.

The dog propped its front legs on the door to look out, making nose smears all over the side window. Buck sighed, lowered the window a little so the dog could at least catch a whiff of springtime and drove back to the guesthouse at a sedate pace that wouldn't knock the Maltese down.

Troy was right. On days like this, Buck barely recognized himself.

Chapter 10

Two days later, Gina was drinking a glass of lemonade on the porch, trying to muster the energy to either cook dinner or take Bobby to the park, when a shuffling sound drew her attention to the street.

Miss Minnie Falcon was approaching the house, pushing her walker. She stopped in front of the gate and shaded her eyes with her hand, looking up toward the house.

"I'll get it, Miss Minnie," Gina called. She hoisted Bobby to her hip and hurried down to open the gate. "Would you like to come up and sit for a while?"

"I would, thank you. I'll just leave my trusty steed here." She parked her walker beside the porch steps.

Gina laughed, helped her up the steps and into an upright rocking chair and then brought her a glass of lemonade.

Bobby crawled over and pulled up on Gina's leg, looking curiously at Miss Minnie.

"Why, look at him stand right up!" the older woman said. "Is he walking yet?"

"So far, he likes crawling better. It gets him around faster." Gina replaced the baby gate at the top of the porch steps and handed Bobby the colorful roll-and-crawl ball they'd gotten from Buck's stash. Bobby batted it, chortling when a tune started to play and then crawling after it. "I feel like he's ready to walk. He cruises all around holding on to things, but he just hasn't done it by himself yet."

"Everything in its own time. Once he starts to walk, you won't be able to hold him back." Miss Minnie leaned forward and took a sip of lemonade. "My, this is delicious. Thank you, dear. I won't bother you for long."

"It's no bother. Truthfully, I'm glad for the company." Gina meant it, too. Not only because she'd been feeling a little lonely, but because it was mostly the older generation who shared her fascination with history. "In fact, I'd love it if you'd tell me something about this house. Were you born here?"

Miss Minnie nodded and relaxed back into the chair. "Oh, yes. I was born here and lived my whole life here. My parents wanted to fill it with children, you see, but there was only me. I did have a lovely childhood, though. Right here in the middle of town, everyone stopped by."

"It's a perfect location," Gina agreed.

"Everyone from all the farms would come to do their Saturday shopping in town, and of course, they came Sunday for church, so we always had something going on." Miss Minnie looked off into the distance as if she were able to see the past. "Father passed when I was in my twenties. But Mother lived to be quite old. Almost as old as I am now." Miss Minnie looked down at herself and chuckled, then shook her head. "I'd bring her out onto the porch every day and we would have a little tea before dinner. She loved to watch the people go by."

Gina smiled and nodded, hoping the older woman would continue. "Has Rescue River changed much?"

Miss Minnie gestured toward town. "The Chatterbox Café has been here for as long as I can remember. Lyman's Tailors and Sadie's Stout Shop are gone. But Love's Hardware, that's still there."

"I met Mr. Love last week."

"Oh, that man." Miss Minnie shook her head with a little smile.

Gina suddenly remembered Buck's comment that Mr. Love was sweet on Miss Minnie. "He seemed charming," she said, lifting an eyebrow.

"Indeed he is." Two high spots of color appeared in Miss Minnie's cheeks. "Now, that's enough about me. Tell me, child, are you planning to stay here in town?"

Gina looked around at the sunny street and sighed. "I love it here. But I only have my job of helping with the renovation a couple more weeks, until the Freedom Festival." Something about Miss Minnie's inquisitive, sparkling eyes made Gina want to confide. "It's hard for Lacey, having Bobby here. He reminds her of all she lost." Although to be fair, Lacey had been trying to get comfortable with Bobby, asking Gina questions about him and even, a time or two, offering to hold him.

"Of course." Miss Minnie shook her head. "That poor child, she's had so much heartache. As has her brother."

"But…it's strange. Buck seems to like babies, even though he lost his daughter."

"Men and women are different." Miss Minnie set down her lemonade and rocked gently. "Although I never had children myself, I know how women hold on to things. And then Lacey's husband..." She rocked faster for a moment, shaking her head. "Well. I'm not about to spread gossip." She looked at Gina with curiosity. "Some folks seem to think you and Buck Armstrong make a good couple."

Heat rose to Gina's face, revealing too much, and she laughed weakly. "Oh, well..."

Miss Minnie's face crinkled into a smile and she patted Gina's arm. "Let an old woman give you some advice. Life is short, and the things you think will always be there one day are gone." She looked around at the porch and the house, her chin trembling a little. "One day, everything's gone."

Gina's throat tightened. Not sure of what to say, she reached out to squeeze Miss Minnie's hand. "I'm so glad you came over. I'd like to hear more about the house and its history."

Buck's truck pulled into the driveway, and a minute later, he trotted up the stairs, holding the little white Maltese that had made its way into Lacey's heart by now, as well as Buck's and Gina's. "Hey, Miss Minnie, how's it going?" he asked cheerfully.

"Well, I declare, this house is Grand Central station." The elderly woman's voice was cheerful again. "And my mother would turn in her grave to know there were dogs living here."

"He's just a visitor," Buck said, "but if I remember right, you and your mother were all about cats." He opened the door and whistled, and the orange tabby walked out, tail high.

"Now, is that Mister or Missus?" Miss Minnie asked.

"It's Mister. Can't you tell he's a tough guy?" Buck picked up the cat in his free hand, chuckling, and deposited him in Miss Minnie's lap.

After they'd visited a few minutes more, Miss Minnie petting the purring Mr. Whiskers, the older woman headed back to the Senior Towers.

Gina fixed a quick dinner and they made short work of the dishes. Gina settled Bobby in his crib and then, feeling more comfortable with Buck for the first time since their kiss, came back downstairs. "Do you have time to look at something?" she asked Buck.

"Sure." He looked surprised but not unhappy that she'd reached out to him.

She showed the box and the journal to Buck. "This journal was in the box we found."

He studied the first pages. "Who wrote this? One of Miss Minnie's relatives?"

"I read the whole thing," Gina said, "and I think it was written by a young fugitive woman who stopped here on the way north."

"Really?" Buck examined the pages with more interest. "That's some history."

"Read it!"

She watched as Buck turned slowly through the old pages, deciphering the spidery handwriting, getting as caught up as she had herself at the tale of Minerva, a young fugitive who'd fallen in love with Abraham Falcon, the eighteen-year-old son of the Falcon family.

He looked up at one point, shaking his head. "He proposed? And gave her a fancy ring? That must have raised some eyebrows pre–Civil War."

"Apparently so. Especially since she was expecting a baby. But the people who were most upset were those she'd escaped with. They didn't think Abraham—or any white man—could be trusted."

"Understandable." He read a little more. "So they tried to talk her out of it and she wouldn't listen."

"Right, and wouldn't come along as they were getting ready to go to the next station."

"Which was the Old Rose Barn, I guess? Mr. Love's family place?"

"It must have been. It's not very far away, but I was reading that stations were pretty close together in this area." Gina was glad Buck was as interested in the story as she was. "Apparently, she didn't trust Abraham completely, because she concealed the fact that she could read and write. When he found out, he was angry she'd concealed it, and she was angry that he couldn't understand why."

Buck whistled. "*I* can understand it. Teaching a slave to read and write was a crime in the old South. She'd probably had to conceal her ability for years."

"Anyway," she said, too impatient to wait for him to read the whole journal, "they had a big fight. Minerva got mad and gave the ring to her sister as she was leaving. She told her sister to use it to get to freedom. But her sister said no, she'd hide it in the roses for Minerva to find when she got over being angry."

"If she was that mad at Abraham, why didn't she go along with the others?"

"She said she knew it would slow everyone down. She was near her time of giving birth."

"So did they make up, Minerva and Abraham?" Buck had given up all pretense of reading the diary for himself.

"They did. The last entry is about how happy she is that they've come to understand and trust each other even better than ever before."

"The last entry? So we don't know what happened?" His forehead wrinkled as he turned to the last page. "It just stops. There was no ring with the journal, no description of a wedding?"

She shook her head. "She must have started another journal, or else been busy with the baby. At least, I hope that's what happened. I hope she didn't have to give up on marrying him."

Buck nodded. "Totally understandable that her friends didn't want her to trust Abraham."

"But she believed in him."

A curious expression crossed Buck's face and then was gone. "I wonder what roses she's talking about. Where her sister hid the ring, and whether Minerva and Abraham ever found it."

"She said she'd hide it in the roses. I wonder if that was around here? The roses couldn't still have survived, I don't think."

"I don't know," he said. "There's a rose garden right by the sign coming into town..."

"Oh, there are a million possibilities, and this journal is really old. We probably wouldn't find anything now." Gina felt disappointed. "At any rate, mementos like the journal should be preserved."

"Since Abraham is one of her ancestors, Miss Minnie may know what happened to them, whether they got married," Buck said. "Or maybe Mr. Love will. He's also familiar with the town's history." He studied the ragged, leather-bound book again. "This reminds me of hunting for treasure when I was a kid."

"Hey, I have an idea," Gina said without thinking it through. "We should go digging."

"Are you asking me out?" he shot back. And then he blew out a breath. "Sorry. I know you're not."

She looked into his eyes and read the confusion there.

She was confused, too. She'd made the decision that he should not be in her life, and she hadn't had a moment's happiness since. "You don't need to be sorry."

"No. I *am* sorry. We can't go there. I'm leaving, and you're focused on Bobby. It's fine."

The thought of him leaving crushed her happy feelings. She was lonely, plain and simple. Bobby was wonderful, but he was a baby. She was starting to make some friends, but that didn't fill the gap in her.

"Tell you what," he said. "After Bobby goes to sleep, and Lacey's home in case of any problem, let's go out searching."

"You mean it?" If they were going to be apart, a little time together wouldn't be bad. Would it? Especially if there was a mystery involved?

And the idea of a mystery sparked another thought. "I wonder if we could also look at Miss Minnie's old materials about the house," she said. "We might find answers there. And we might find some stuff that would make awesome decorations for the guesthouse. We can have cases and shadow boxes. Guests will love knowing more about the history of the place."

He was looking at her, smiling. "You don't do things halfway, do you?"

She flushed. "Just stop me. I'm getting carried away again."

"No need to stop. I like it."

High-pitched barking from the ground broke their gaze. Spike, wanting attention.

"Hey, buster, don't be jealous," Buck said to the concerned little dog. And then to Gina: "Meet me here after Bobby's asleep?" He touched her hair, pulled his hand back with a wry grin and then disappeared up the stairs, Spike trotting behind him.

* * *

When the doorbell rang around eight o'clock that night, Buck was knee-deep in plaster supplies, but he wiped his hands off and tried to get downstairs before whoever it was rang again. This was about the time Gina put Bobby down, and Buck didn't want to wake him up.

Didn't want anything to interfere with their plans for later. Idiot that he was.

But when he got there, Gina was already at the door.

She listened, opened the door to take a business card and then opened the door wider to let the person in.

Danny Walker.

Local banker and resident womanizer.

"Come on in the kitchen," she said. "We can talk in here." She led him toward the kitchen, only belatedly noticing Buck standing there in the hallway, clothes a mess compared to Danny's nice suit.

"Hey!" Danny held out a hand and pumped Buck's. "I heard you were living here, working on the place. That's just great, what you and Lacey are doing here."

"Thanks. What's up?" In his not-that-friendly voice was the question *Why are you here?*

"Got some business to talk over with Gina here," he said easily.

Buck cocked his head.

Gina lifted an eyebrow at him. Her message was plain: *not your affair.*

And she was right. It wasn't. He stomped back upstairs and applied plaster with extra energy, then did some repairs downstairs until, finally, he heard Danny leave.

It took him about thirty seconds to think of an excuse to go into the kitchen. And then he wished he hadn't, because Gina was smiling.

"What did he want?" he asked.

"He wants my business," she explained happily. "He'd heard about my interest in possibly starting an interior-decorating place, and he wanted to talk about loans and options."

Buck frowned skeptically. "Do you really think it was your *business* he was after at eight at night?"

"What else?" She looked puzzled.

"Maybe…to hit on you? You're a beautiful woman."

Gina didn't seem to love the compliment. "So the only thing I have going for me is my looks? Nobody would want my ideas or my creativity or the work I can do?"

"I didn't mean that. It's just… I know Walker. He has a track record."

"Thanks a lot for undermining my confidence." Gina shoved back her chair and started noisily putting dishes away. "He was totally respectful and businesslike. I'm meeting him for coffee next week to talk more about it."

"There you go. He was after a date and he got it."

"It is *not* a date! Every outing isn't a date!" She came closer and stuck her finger in his chest. "And what's more, I don't appreciate your stomping around upstairs, or pounding nails in the next room, when I'm trying to have a business meeting!"

It had been obvious, then. And even though he knew that Danny wouldn't have called on a homely woman with such alacrity, he still felt bad. "I'm sorry. I guess I'm jealous."

She'd turned away with a flounce, but at his words, she spun back. "Jealous? Of what?"

Now he was truly and deeply in it. He studied the toe of his work boot, scraped it across the floor. "Of a guy who might be hitting on you. Wanting to date you."

"We've already discussed how nothing can happen between us, Buck!" She crossed her arms over her chest, looking exasperated. "So even if I *did* want to go out with this Danny guy—which I don't—I don't see where you'd have a leg to stand on, being jealous."

"I know," he said miserably. "It's true. I'm sorry."

She had opened her mouth to say something, but now she shut it. "You're sorry?"

"I was wrong," he added. "I shouldn't have come in here or asked you anything about it. Or banged around while you were talking to him."

She laughed and rolled her eyes. "When you apologize so well, how can I stay mad at you?"

It was like the sun came out again. "So, you still up for hunting treasure?"

"As soon as Lacey gets home, as long as she agrees to keep an ear open for Bobby. He shouldn't wake up—he was exhausted, but there's always a first time. She can call me and we won't be far away."

Lacey came in the door just then, wearing scrubs, looking tired. "Hey," she said, waving to them. "You two look like you're up to something."

Gina explained about the journal and showed it to Lacey, quickly explaining their quest. Watching them together, Buck was guardedly optimistic. Lacey seemed to have come around to where she liked Gina, and she was doing better with Bobby, paying him a little bit of attention, giving in to his cute ways.

And now Lacey said she was willing to listen for Bobby, even asking Gina to put her baby monitor in her room. "Because I'm just grabbing a sandwich and going to bed. I want to make sure I hear him."

So the women organized that while Buck got cleaned up. He and Gina both emerged from their rooms at the same time, and Buck was absurdly pleased that she'd put on a pretty skirt and sweater. He'd worn khakis himself, something different from his usual scrubs and jeans.

All of a sudden, holding the door for her and walking down the porch steps beside her, Buck felt like he *was* on a date. Even after all their discussions to the contrary.

They strolled through the darkened downtown, gently lit by old-fashioned streetlights. There was a March chill in the air, belying the day's earlier springlike weather. A family headed into the Chatterbox Café. Someone emerged from Love's Hardware, and then the illuminated sign clicked off.

Gina shivered and pulled her jacket tighter, and Buck wanted to put an arm around her and pull her close. Wanted it so much that he pressed his arm tight against his side to make sure he didn't slip up and do it.

When they passed the Ace Tavern, it served to remind him of why he shouldn't make any move toward a relationship with Gina.

As they got to the edge of the town, traffic thinned out, pedestrian and vehicular. Finally they reached the Rescue River sign, on a little garden spot with a bench and some bushes, and Buck pulled out the canvas bag of gardening tools he'd brought.

"I remember when I first saw this sign," Gina said. "It seemed like a fantasy, that I'd ever be welcome and safe. But I do feel that way now."

"I'm glad," he said and risked taking her hand to tug her over to the bench. "We'd better wait until full dark. I doubt digging up the ground around the town's welcome sign is smiled upon."

She hesitated and then sat down beside him, and this time, he couldn't resist putting an arm along the back of the park bench. It was there, for her to lean into or not.

She did, and nothing felt so natural as to tighten his arm around her.

They sat and talked as the stars peeked out and the moon rose, its silvery light casting shadows. When she shivered, he pulled her tighter against him, but the way her closeness tugged at his heart, the confusing little sigh she let out, made that seem like a bad idea. "We should dig," he said, forcing briskness into his tone. "We don't have all night. You'll get frostbite."

She laughed but stood and walked around, looking at the little plot of land. "If I were hiding a romantic memento, I'd hide it...here."

"Under the sign?"

"Yep. According to Miss Minnie, there was always a little garden here, welcoming people to town."

"But the sign wasn't here back in the day," he argued, just for the sake of talking to her, hearing her voice. He knelt down where she'd indicated, though, pulled out a shovel and started to dig.

"It should be under the rosebush, if that's a rosebush," she said. "Are you finding anything?"

"I don't... Wait. I'm hitting something, but it's probably just a rock."

He dug a little more and was about to pull a giant stone out when headlights illuminated them.

Gina clutched his shoulder and he stood quickly, stepping in front of her. Adrenaline surged in him, but not the crazy kind. This was Rescue River, not Afghanistan.

"Not the criminals I expected." It was Dion's deep voice. Behind him was his black-and-white police car.

"Hey, man." Buck reached out to grasp the chief's hand. "Thanks for not using the siren on us."

"What are you two doing?"

"We're trying to solve a mystery," Buck explained. "Show him the diary, Gina."

She fumbled in her purse and brought it out, encased in a large plastic bag, and they took turns telling the big police chief an abbreviated version of the story it contained.

Dion shone his light down on the book, looking thoughtful. Then he turned the flashlight on the hole Buck was digging. "You find anything?"

"We thought we might find the ring her sister hid. It was supposed to be among the roses." He shook his head. "Hit something down there, but I'm pretty sure it's a rock."

"Are we in trouble?" Gina asked at the same moment.

Dion chuckled. "As crimes go, this isn't the worst. I might let you off with a warning if you fill up the hole all nice."

"You never heard about anything hidden here?"

Dion frowned. "I've been in Rescue River a long time. I've heard a few things, but not about here."

"Where, then?"

He studied them thoughtfully as if trying to decide whether to tell them. Finally, he nodded. "You ever been to the old cemetery?"

"The one by the church? That's the only one I know about," Buck said.

"No. There's another one. I'll show you."

After they'd filled in the hole and replaced the sod, Dion drove them out one of the country roads to a tumbledown church. Behind it was an overgrown yard with multiple depressions and a few stones. "This is a cemetery?" Gina asked, stepping closer to Buck.

"It's the AME cemetery," he said. "Not used anymore, but some folks still have kin buried here. And look." He led them across the rutted ground and to a stone bench that backed up against the woods. "Know what that is?" he asked, touching a tangle of vines that grew as tall as he was.

Buck shook his head.

"Is it…a rosebush?" Gina guessed.

"That's exactly what it is. I wonder if what's referred to in your journal is buried here."

Buck studied the bench and the bush. "Could be."

"Have a look around, but don't dig. We don't want to disturb anyone's remains."

Gina knelt in front of the little bench, looking at the rosebush, its buds just starting to come out. "What a lot of history is here," she whispered, touching the carving there.

Dion shone his powerful flashlight on a couple of stones next to the bench.

"'A friend loves at all times,'" Buck read from one of them. "Proverbs 17:17."

"Look at this," Gina said, kneeling to trace the inscription on a nearby headstone. "Minerva Cobbs. She didn't write her last name in the diary, but could this be her grave? How many Minervas could there be in a town the size of Rescue River?"

"Are there dates?"

"No. And if this is her grave, she didn't change her name to Abraham's." Gina bit her lip. "I did an online search for Minerva Falcon and nothing came up. I really wonder what happened."

They looked around a little while longer but didn't find a ring or anything else that would help fill in the blanks of the story, a story Buck was getting curious about himself. Or maybe he just wanted to keep that interested sparkle in Gina's eyes. "How are we going to find out the rest of it?" he asked her.

"Talk to the old folks," Gina said promptly. "They're more likely than anyone to know. Are you in?"

Dion raised an eyebrow, his mouth quirking a little at one corner.

"I'm all in," Buck said. Right or wrong, he wanted to spend every moment he could with this woman. Every moment he had before leaving town.

Chapter 11

The next week went by in a flurry of renovations. They worked hard to get the first floor ready for the Freedom Festival, and when the Monday before the festival arrived, Gina could look around the guesthouse and feel assured that what she'd promised Lacey would come to pass. They'd be ready.

She and Buck had postponed their meeting with Mr. Love and Miss Minnie, but this morning, as they returned from dropping Bobby at Angelica's place, they settled on the next day.

"Should we take them out to lunch?" Gina asked. "I know Miss Minnie likes to go to the café."

Buck turned down the road into town. "If we want to look at Miss Minnie's materials, maybe we should meet at the Senior Towers."

"Great. If you can pick up Mr. Love, we'll meet there

right after lunch." They were driving through downtown. "Speaking of the Chatterbox, can you drop me off there?"

"Sure." He pulled up beside the place, and Gina told herself she didn't need to provide Buck with an accounting of her day, where she was going or whom she was with.

At the same time, they'd gotten in a rhythm of working together. "This shouldn't take long," she said, "and I'll be back at the house to work on that crown molding."

"Take your time," he said, his voice expressionless. "There's your breakfast date, right there."

"It's not a date!" She gathered her purse and briefcase and slid out of the truck without waiting for Buck to get the door for her. Nonetheless, he got out and stood beside the truck, for all the world like a protective father. She rolled her eyes.

"Gina!" Danny greeted her happily. "Come on—I've got us a table." He nodded at Buck and escorted Gina inside, a hand on the small of her back.

When Buck did that, she liked it. But when Danny did it, it felt…creepy. She walked faster to get some distance from his touch.

As they sat down to discuss more details about a possible loan, Gina felt uneasy. Why *did* Danny need to meet with her again? And why were they doing it at a restaurant instead of at the bank?

She didn't have much experience with men; she'd been awkward in school, and then soon afterward she'd gotten attached to Hank. She wasn't the flirtatious, frequent-dating type. So she couldn't tell what vibe Danny was putting out. Did he want to date her? Couldn't he read her lack of interest in him?

As she got out her notes and ordered coffee, she cast a glance in the direction where Buck had roared off and frowned. Why had he put this insecurity into her head? Why couldn't he accept that women could be businesspeople, meeting with other businesspeople? That it wasn't always about dating?

"We're really looking forward to working with you," Danny said after their coffee had arrived. "Have you thought any more about what your business might entail? Had the chance to look at any storefronts?"

"Not really, Danny. I've been totally occupied with getting Lacey's house ready for the festival."

"How's that going?" he asked, and she told him about what they were doing. "That's great, great," he said. "But let's focus on your business as soon as that's over."

She frowned. "Can I ask why you're so interested in working with me? I'm not a high-capital investor, believe me."

"Oh, we like to help small-business people in Rescue River. It's a community outreach kind of thing. Keeping the downtown strong."

She nodded, studying him without making it obvious. He just didn't seem sincere. "I have to give all of it some thought."

She wished Buck were here so she could ask him his opinion, learn more about Danny's background. If only he weren't so touchy about her having coffee with another man! With concern, she realized that Buck was the person she most trusted right now, most wanted to share the details of her life with, big and small.

When did *that* happen?

"You're staying in town, though, right? You'll be here through the festival and beyond?" He looked so eager that, against her better judgment, she was flattered. Even though she wasn't going to pursue a relationship with him, it was nice to have a man show interest.

"I'm planning to stay, at least for a while," she said. "Rescue River is a wonderful place. So warm and safe and welcoming."

An odd expression flashed across his face and then was gone. "Right," he said smoothly. "Rescue River *is* a safe place."

And as they parted ways, she wondered again why Danny was so interested in her business, even though she'd been open about the fact that she didn't know how long she'd be able to stay.

That afternoon, Buck drove Gina out to pick up Bobby in a thoughtful mood. As he waited for them in the truck and then headed back to Rescue River, he considered his own progress.

In the past, he would have been royally mad that Gina had had coffee with Danny against his advice, to the point where he couldn't have had a reasonable discussion. He remembered, with some embarrassment, a couple of occasions when he'd gotten jealous about Ivana. Both had led to huge fights. But today, he'd managed his feelings with just a little mild argument.

And out by the Rescue River sign last week, when Dion had flashed his lights, he hadn't freaked out. Yeah, he'd been startled, but he hadn't grabbed Gina and taken her to the ground or some crazy move like that.

Counseling and AA and prayer must be starting to have an impact, even on a hardheaded creature like him.

Gina cleared her throat like she'd been trying to get his attention for a while. "Hey," she said. "If this is too much trouble, I can start asking Angelica to bring me home."

"What?" He glanced over at her and was surprised to see her lower lip out and her eyes blazing. "It's no trouble. What are you talking about?"

"You've been completely silent during this whole drive. You didn't even say hi to Bobby!"

"Well, excuse *me*." Was he supposed to put on some kind of show for her? He paused, took a breath. *She's a woman. She has different needs.* "I'm sorry. I didn't know I was acting weird."

"You're not sulking about my having coffee with Danny Walker?"

He frowned, thinking. "I'm not thrilled about it. I don't trust the guy."

"So you *are* mad." There was the satisfaction of being right in her voice.

"No." He shook his head. "You're an adult. And...although I feel a lot for you, we're not a couple. I don't have the right."

They were driving through Rescue River now, getting close to the guesthouse, and he didn't want to leave things like this. On an impulse, he pulled over beside the town park. "Look, since I neglected Bobby before, how about we take him to the playground for a little bit?"

He turned off the truck and looked at her. There were two vertical wrinkles between her eyebrows, and her lips pressed together.

"We don't have to," he said. He put his hand back on the keys, waiting for the put-down that might be coming. You never knew with women.

But then she smiled, her cheeks going a little pink. "Okay. Sure. That would be great."

Happiness flooded him. He'd been able to get her from upset to happy. He *was* learning, maybe at a slow pace, but still. He came around to her side of the truck, opened the door for her and helped her out.

Her hand was soft, delicate. He pulled in a breath.

She shot a glance at him and then got very busy unhooking Bobby from his car seat in the back.

He shouldered the diaper bag while she carried Bobby, wiggling with excitement, on her hip.

"I have to say," she said as they headed toward the play area, "I *was* uncomfortable with Danny this morning."

"What did he do? Did he make a move on you? Do you want me to talk to him?"

"No, no!" She laughed a little. "I just… Well, I question his motives."

"I can tell you his motives," Buck groused.

Her laugh rang out like a bell. "I love this park," she said, waving her hand around. "We didn't have this kind of friendly-feeling place in my neighborhood in California."

"I used to play sports here as a kid," he said, accepting the change of subject, "And do less wholesome things when I was in high school."

"You're such a bad boy." She rolled her eyes and then looked wistful. "This must have been a great town to grow up in."

"It was." And for a second, Buck got a hard, hot yearning to stay, to raise a family here like had been the plan with Ivana and Mia.

They reached the playground, and Buck set the diaper bag down on a bench. A couple of moms on the other side of the colorful play structures stood talking while their kids climbed the taller one, yelling out their after-school joy. Off in the distance, someone was stringing lights and people were unloading something from a truck, probably getting ready for the festival at the end of the week.

Gina carried Bobby over to a bucket-style swing and eased him into it, and then stood in front while Buck pushed it gently from behind, making Bobby giggle each time he swung toward his mom. A light breeze rattled the still-bare tree limbs and the sun warmed the back of Buck's shoulders.

When Bobby tired of the swing, Buck lifted him out and helped him toddle over to a play structure. Bobby pulled himself up and climbed through an opening, landed on his hands and then pulled himself through. Immediately, he turned around and did the same thing again.

"He is *so* close to walking." Gina squatted down and reached into her pocket, then looked at the basic flip phone with disappointment. "Oh, man, I wish I'd brought my other phone to take a picture!"

So Buck pulled out his phone and snapped a bunch of photos and a video—of Bobby, mostly, but also of his pretty mom. She'd be happy to have memories of herself and Bobby together as he grew.

He sure was a cute kid. As cute as Mia had been, though in a different way. Sadness and nostalgia washed over him, but gently, a spring shower rather than a storm.

He could think about Mia now. And yeah, it hurt, a lot. That was only natural. Losing her and Ivana would always be the biggest sadness of his life.

He glanced up at the sky, pale blue with fluffy white clouds scudding by. Mia and Ivana were with Jesus now. And he didn't know what heaven was like, but he was sure that mother and daughter were together and happy. Maybe there was a big swing set somewhere up there.

His throat tightened. He swallowed, then focused on Bobby. "Come on, little man. Ever gone down a slide before?"

* * *

Gina watched as Buck lifted Bobby halfway up the plastic slide, then whooshed him down. As Bobby laughed, Gina's heart melted a little.

Buck was so kind. Even when they were arguing, even when she'd been a teeny bit unreasonable, he didn't blow up or sulk. Instead, he tried to make things right.

She was starting to trust that Buck had her best interests at heart, that he wasn't trying to manipulate her the way Hank—and, yes, her father as well—used to do.

Moving to the bottom of the slide, she knelt down so Bobby could glide into her arms, safely guided by Buck. A couple more trips, and he wanted to wander over to a low play table. She helped him, and he stood banging the table like a drum.

"Sit down over there," Buck said, pointing to a smooth stretch of rubberized play surface. Then he lifted Bobby and set him down a few yards away, holding him by his shoulders. "Walk to Mommy," he said.

Gina's mouth dropped open. "Do you think he can?"

"Call him," Buck said. "I won't let him fall."

So she held out her arms to her son. "Come on, sweetie."

Bobby chortled and lifted one awkward leg after the other, staggering unsteadily toward her. Buck was supporting him—and then he wasn't.

Never taking his laughing eyes off her, Bobby toddled into her arms.

"Oh my word! His first step!" She was laughing and crying at once as she pulled Bobby to her and hugged him tightly. Such joy. And such sharp pain that Hank wasn't here to see it.

A movie of memories flashed through her mind, the good ones this time: Hank in the delivery room, flourishing the scissors as he fearlessly cut the cord. The way he'd insisted on taking Bobby to visit every friend he had, the moment the pediatrician had okayed it, just to show off his brand-new son. How he'd swept her into a huge hug when they'd seen Bobby's first smile.

Hank hadn't been perfect, not by a long shot, but he had loved his son. And he would have loved to see this milestone.

Buck knelt beside her and wrapped both her and Bobby in his arms.

Tears flowed down Gina's face even as she laughed and kissed Bobby. "I'm happy and sad at the same time," she said to Buck.

"Me, too." His voice was a little choked.

She looked into his eyes and realized it was true. He'd lost as much as she had. More.

She tightened her arms around both of them—Buck, who'd seen so much, and Bobby, who was only beginning to explore the world. Closed her eyes and lifted a wordless prayer.

Bobby struggled free, used Buck's arm to pull up to a standing position and then looked from her to Buck expectantly. "Go!" he demanded.

"Has he said words before?" Buck asked, laughing as he scooted a few yards away and held out his arms for Bobby.

"Not that clearly." Gina wiped her eyes and steadied her baby and let him go, lurching from leg to leg with undeniable independence.

The next day after his lunchtime AA meeting, Buck stopped by the hardware store as planned. He picked up a few needed supplies while he waited for Mr. Love to finish giving detailed instructions to his granddaughter, who'd run the store alone in his absence.

"I got this, Granddad," she said good-naturedly. "You can take an hour off to do some visiting!"

Reluctantly, Mr. Love headed out the door. Buck crooked his arm for the older man and alerted him to curbs during the three-block walk to the Senior Towers.

"Now, see," Mr. Love said, lifting his face to the spring sunshine, "isn't this nicer than riding in a car? Not that I didn't appreciate the offer. But any chance to be active and outside, I take it."

"A good philosophy." Buck listened to the birds singing in the trees, just beginning to offer a few buds, and smelled the earthy scent of spring. He'd like to share in that feeling of new life, but truthfully, his insides were in turmoil.

He'd spent more time with Gina and Bobby during the past week than during any of the previous weeks since she'd arrived in town. They'd worked long hours, and tag teamed on child care and cooking and dog walking, since Crater and Spike were now established residents of the guesthouse. They'd shared conversations about their pasts, argued amiably over final paint colors and finish details, and generally made a great team.

They'd shared Bobby's first step.

Passing the Chatterbox Café made him think of Gina meeting Danny. He shouldn't begrudge her starting to establish other friendships, and he didn't—as long as the friendships were female. But Danny Walker's obvious interest in Gina bothered him.

Danny was too slick for Gina, and he didn't think them a good match, but then again, he had no right to comment on or criticize her choices. What say did he have?

"What's got you bent out of shape?" Mr. Love asked.

"Who says I'm bent out of shape?"

"It's more than obvious. You're wound up tighter than a drum. And I'm a fast walker, but you're rushing me here. Cut me a break. I'm eighty-seven!"

"Oh, man, sorry!" He slowed down. "And…you're right—I'm a little uptight."

"Woman problems?" Mr. Love asked.

"Now, why would you jump to that conclusion?"

Mr. Love chuckled. "I couldn't help noticing the attention you paid to that young lady in the hardware store. Gina? Is she going to be there today?"

"She'll be there." Buck debated denying everything, but Mr. Love had known him a long time. "And yeah," he said. "I like her. But she's got issues, especially with addicts and drunks. And I'm leaving town. *And* someone else is after her."

"You've got problems." Mr. Love nodded. "Serious problems, but there's one thing—you're not defined by being a drunk. Kid I knew, who worked so hard in the store, he wasn't a drunk."

"I've changed."

"Yes, you have. More than once. A man can be forgiven for going a little crazy after the losses you had, but that doesn't mean you'll be crazy forever. You seem kinda sane to me right now."

"Maybe."

"And why are you leaving town? Rescue River is your home!"

Buck shook his head. "Burned too many bridges. Bad reputation. I need to start fresh."

"Like my mama used to say, no matter where you go, there you are. You think your problems won't follow you into another town?"

Buck guided the man around a broken section of sidewalk. "That's exactly what I think. In another town, they won't look at me like the criminal who busted up a restaurant or got his license taken away."

"You're going to give up your woman just so you don't have to have hurt feelings?"

The question echoed in the air, and Buck wondered: Was that what he was doing? "Sounds kind of cowardly," he admitted.

"Yes, it does. And you've never struck me as a coward."

Buck blew out a breath. "Speaking of women…anything you want me to do to promote your case with Miss Minnie Falcon?"

"Hey, hey now." Mr. Love held up a hand. "Show respect for your elders."

Buck chuckled. "You can dish it out…"

Mr. Love bumped a fist into Buck's upper arm. "We almost there? I'm getting tired of talking with you."

"As a matter of fact, we are. But I've got my eye on you." Buck was grinning, satisfied with having turned the tables on the old man.

When they walked into the homey, plant-filled lobby of the Senior Towers, Gina and Miss Minnie Falcon—and a whole cadre of Miss Minnie's friends—were waiting for them.

"Trust a man to be late," Miss Minnie said, leaning forward to check the grandfather clock. "No sense of time."

Buck took a breath, but Mr. Love squeezed his arm, communicating nonverbally not to respond.

"They're right on time," Gina soothed, "or maybe a few minutes late is all. Should we head up to your apartment, Miss Minnie?"

"We should. I've got everything all ready."

After a few words with the other women in the lobby, the four of them went upstairs and were soon looking through the trunk of materials Miss Minnie had saved or inherited over the years.

"We're looking for something from 1850 or thereabouts," Gina said, her face flushed with excitement. "How much do you know about what's in here, Miss Minnie?"

"I surely do wish I could see better," Mr. Love said wistfully.

"There are letters from some of my ancestors," Miss Minnie said. "And drawings, jewelry, even some early photographs. A good deal of family history."

"We'll respect your privacy," Gina said. "Are you sure it's okay with you if we go through it?"

Buck loved that about her, that she was sensitive to the older woman's concerns. Gina hadn't had an easy life, and maybe that was how God was using her trials: to make her kinder than the norm.

"It's perfectly fine. I'm so old now, I don't care who knows my business."

"I know exactly what you mean, Minnie," Mr. Love said.

Miss Minnie blushed. "Look for a pair of daguerreotypes in a brown leather case. From what you've told me, they'll be very interesting to you."

Buck and Gina knelt in front of the trunk and opened the lid. Inside was a jumble of letters, a blue military uniform, jewelry in worn velvet cases and pewter candleholders.

Gina sat back on her heels, very close to Buck. "Wow, Miss Minnie, this is awesome! It belongs in the historical society for sure!"

"If we had one, I'd gladly donate it to them."

Buck carefully picked up a brown leather case. "Is this the one?"

"I believe," Miss Minnie said, "that those photographs are images of the couple in your old diary, Abraham and Minerva."

Gina's eyes sparkled as she studied the images: on one side, a beautiful African American woman in an elegant wedding dress; on the other side, a handsome white man in a formal suit, including a vest and short tie. "So they did get married!" She practically glowed with excitement.

Miss Minnie shook her head. "No, dear. Those photographs were taken weeks before the wedding was to happen. You'll notice the style of dress conceals her pregnancy."

"I imagine any pictures had to be taken in secret, given the times and her status as a runaway," Mr. Love said.

"Wait—I'm confused." Buck was studying the photograph. "Did she have Abraham's child?"

Miss Minnie shook her head. "It wasn't Abraham's child, you see. She arrived pregnant. She'd been assaulted by a plantation owner down South."

"How awful," Gina breathed, glancing over at Buck.

"I respect the fact that he was willing to marry her in that circumstance," Mr. Love said. "It must have been quite unusual back then."

Miss Minnie nodded. "What happened to her was awful, and yet if she hadn't found a safe place to bear her baby, I wouldn't be here."

"You're a descendant?" Buck looked up from the trunk. He'd known Miss Minnie for years, ever since she'd been his Sunday-school teacher, but he hadn't known that she had a slave ancestor.

"That's right. Miss Minerva Cobbs was my great-grandmother."

"Wow. You were named after her," Gina said.

"Yes, young lady, and proud to be. Since that day, there has always been a Minerva in the Falcon family."

Buck was impatient to hear the end of the story. "You said they didn't marry. Did she decide to move on with the others headed north?" Buck was remembering his Ohio history. "Because the Fugitive Slave Act would've put them at risk, right?"

"The rest of the group wanted her to come with them. They were worried Abraham would take advantage of her, that he wasn't serious about marriage, but they were wrong."

Gina moved a little closer, her shoulder brushing Buck's, and he felt his blood pressure rise. Did she know what she was doing to him? He leaned back against the couch and put up a pillow for her back, and she scooted back and sat right next to him, the side of her leg burning into his.

He shot up a prayer for calmness.

"Tell us what became of them," Gina asked, seemingly unaffected by their closeness.

Miss Minnie shook her head, looking sad. "Like many women of those times, she died in childbirth. But Abraham and his parents raised her son, Ishmael, as their own and gave him their last name."

Mr. Love whistled. "Even despite his mixed race."

"They were staunch abolitionists and strong Christians. They believed all people were equal."

"Wow." Buck tore his attention from the woman beside him to focus on the story. "There are people nowadays who could learn a lesson from your ancestors."

"They very nearly made a full-time job of assisting fugitives to freedom. It's said that eight hundred people came through the Falcon home." Miss Minnie smiled proudly.

"That's amazing!" Gina was practically rubbing her hands together. "We have *got* to tell this story."

"Miss Minnie should be the judge of that," said Mr. Love. "She may not want it known that she has some mixed blood."

She inclined her head at him. "My father was one of Ishmael's five sons, the youngest, and he inherited the house. And while he didn't advertise his ancestry, he didn't hide it within the family, nor in Rescue River. He always encouraged me to be proud of my great-grandmother, and I am."

"And you should be." Gina gripped the older woman's hands. "But what do you think about making it public? There's no pressure to do that."

"It's not widely known," Miss Minnie admitted. "In fact…" She trailed off and looked at the floor as if lost in thought.

"Are you okay, Miss Minnie?"

"I've never married," the older woman said. "But I was engaged. When my fiancé discovered my background, he broke off the engagement."

"For racial reasons?" Gina asked. "That's awful."

She nodded. "I'd left this area, gone away to school. People in other places weren't as open as those in Rescue River."

Mr. Love shook his head. "My, my. I always wondered why a fine-looking woman like you didn't have a husband. You had plenty of suitors as a schoolgirl."

Miss Minnie chuckled. "I did make a few conquests, didn't I?"

"Hearts were broken, right and left."

Buck didn't ask, but he wondered whether Mr. Love's heart had been one of those broken, or at least bruised, by a younger Miss Minnie.

"And so you stayed single," Gina said.

"Don't feel sorry for me, young lady. I've had a wonderful life in this town. And it may be that I don't have the temperament for marriage. I always did have strong opinions of my own, and when I was young, not many men could tolerate having a wife on an equal plane."

"Not many men in your circle had any sense," Mr. Love said. "Why, I would have…" He shook his head. "But times were different then."

"Yes, they were."

As the two elders began sharing stories of people they'd both known in years past, Buck glanced at Gina to find her watching them, her face a study in care and concern. As if in common accord, they moved to the trunk and started sorting through the items now brought to life by the story they told.

Ribbons and photographs and letters. "Where do we begin to sort these out?" he asked quietly.

"We start small," she said. "I think we should find just enough to make a display for the Freedom Festival. And if Miss Minnie is feeling up to it, maybe we could ask her to come talk to visitors."

"Mr. Love as well," Buck suggested. "He's done presentations for the festival before." He looked up to ask Mr. Love about it, but he was talking intently to Miss Minnie, their heads close together.

He turned back to Gina and found her lifting an eyebrow at him. "Senior romance?" she whispered.

"Love is beautiful at any age," he said, and Mr. Love's example gave him courage to reach out and touch Gina's shoulder, gaze into her eyes. "We may have barriers, Gina, but it's nothing like people faced in times past."

She looked from the old diary in her hand to him and then back again, color rising to her face.

He touched her chin. "No pressure," he said, "but maybe, when things settle down, you'll give this a little thought."

She looked at him, her eyes darkening. "Give *what* a little thought?" she almost whispered.

He let his hand caress her soft cheek and tangle in her hair. "Us," he said. "Give *us* some thought."

That night, Buck was going into the Star Market just as Dion was coming out.

"Any news about the mysterious buried treasure?" Dion asked, grinning.

Buck filled him in on the conversation they'd had with Mr. Love and Miss Minnie.

Dion whistled. "I had no idea. Definitely need to record them telling their stories, and sooner rather than later. Did she know anything about the ring you were hunting for?"

"You know, in the midst of all the storytelling, we completely forgot to ask."

"Makes sense."

Buck was about to turn away when he thought to ask Dion about Gina's California in-laws. "Hey, any news about Gina's situation?" He knew Dion had been monitoring the police airwaves and had also contacted colleagues in California to keep updated.

Dion lifted his hands, palms up. "It's strange," he said. "According to my friend in California, there was a ton of inquiry and investigation for the past couple of weeks. But yesterday, it stopped."

"Stopped?" Buck tilted his head to one side. "What do you make of that?"

Dion shrugged. "Maybe they've given up."

"Maybe," Buck said.

"Or maybe… I don't know. Let's keep our eyes open."

"Will do," Buck said, an uneasy prickle crawling up his neck.

Two days later, Gina finished the dishes, strolled toward the sitting room and looked in. Buck was there, leaning back in a big chair with Bobby on his lap, turning the pages of a board book. In front of the fireplace, Crater and Spike nestled on a folded blanket, and Mr. and Mrs. Whiskers curled up together on the back of the couch. Pretty lamps stood on end tables, and paintings of local landscapes graced the walls. They'd all worked late last night, dragging furniture out of storage, to get several of the rooms finished.

She stopped in the doorway to survey the scene, her heart swelling with happiness.

Her son was thriving here, that was the main thing. He got all the attention he needed, and even though he had a case of the sniffles, Buck was cuddling him close. He treated the boy like kin.

She took pride in the beautiful room. The walls were a light chocolate shade, set off by white moldings, and this afternoon they'd put up the ornate chandelier she'd found in a local antiques shop. Heavy gold draperies added weight and warmth, and the chesterfield sofa and wing-back chairs gave the room the look of an old library.

At that moment, Buck looked up and saw her, and the light in his eyes sent warmth all the way to her toes. Maybe they had a chance after all.

"Ready?" he asked. They were planning to do the finish work on the final room tonight, in preparation for the start of the festival tomorrow.

"I'm ready. But you two look comfortable."

"We are. He's a little stuffy." Buck studied Bobby and brushed his wispy hair off his forehead. "Almost asleep. Can he stay down here with us?"

Touched by the big veteran's care for her son, she scanned the room. "We'll be right next door. He can rest in here." She folded a couple of blankets, put them on the floor and set up the baby monitor.

They worked in the connected room as the sun slanted low and golden, making hazy squares on the polished wooden floor. Gina painted baseboards with glossy white enamel while Buck put a door back on its hinges.

Buck set his phone to play quiet contemporary music. They chatted a little as they worked.

Gina's heart was full to breaking. After tomorrow, this interlude of renovation would be done. Lacey could find someone else to do the work, or she and Buck could do it themselves at a more leisurely pace.

And whether Gina stayed in Rescue River or moved on, her time of working closely with Buck would likely come to an end.

She didn't want it to; she wanted to go on working with this man. Her attachment to him was growing daily, and her fears about his past were lessening. She was starting to think that maybe, just maybe, she'd fallen for a winner this time.

But he wouldn't be around. He had a plan and knew what he needed. And that was, apparently, to leave Rescue River.

She finished her painting and tapped the lid back on the can, then stood to survey the room.

"Penny for your thoughts," he said, coming up behind her.

She looked over her shoulder at him. "This has been

fun, renovating the place," she said, surveying the room. "I'll miss it."

"You're talking like it's over."

"You know what Lacey said. Only until the festival— no more."

"Okay," he said, "but you'll stay in Rescue River. Right?"

"I don't know. I'd like to stay, hire out as a historical renovation consultant or open a shop for interior decorating, but I'm not sure it would be wise to take that on." She sighed. "It's a lot of responsibility, being a single parent, you know?"

She felt him nod behind her. And then he put his arms around her and pulled her back against him. "Whatever happens," he said, "I hope you know you've got a friend."

But, oh, she wanted more. "Is that what we are? Friends?"

"What do you think?" he asked, his breath warm against her ear.

The feel of his arms enfolding her, warming her, circling her, set her heart pounding. She felt him nuzzle her hair. The music swelled and the light was dying and the poignant contentment made her close her eyes. "I think I could stay like this forever," she whispered.

His arms tightened, and for a moment, they just breathed together, their whole bodies in sync.

Suddenly, the dogs went crazy, Spike's hysterical yip combining with Crater's deep growl.

And then, before she could step away from Buck to investigate, she heard a sound and saw a sight she'd hoped never to experience again: her former mother-in-law, holding Bobby, standing in the connecting doorway. "How nice," Lorna said. "You're cozying up to a derelict while our grandson rolls around on the floor with the dogs."

Chapter 12

Buck took in the situation instantly.

"Art! Lorna!" Gina's voice was a breathy gasp. Based on her stricken expression and the well-coiffed older couple's words, these had to be Gina's husband's parents.

The sight of that fist-size bruise that had marred Bobby's leg when he first arrived came back to Buck. Bobby's grandparents. His *abusive* grandparents.

Two long steps put him directly in front of them. "Bobby needs to go to his mother. Now."

He reached for the baby.

The older woman turned away. "Step back, young man," she said, her voice scornful, but also a little scared. "Don't you dare touch me or this baby."

"I don't want to touch you," he said, "but if you don't give Bobby back to his mother right now, I will."

He'd commanded men to do things they'd never have risked on their own. He'd frightened macho Afghan militants into backing down. Dead drunk, he'd glared down punks with guns in the seediest parts of Cleveland.

Never had his powers of intimidation felt so important.

Gina seemed to draw from his strength; she came and stood beside him and held out her arms.

The older woman looked sulky, but then some kind of nonverbal signal passed between her and her husband.

She handed the baby to Gina.

Gina seized Bobby, pulled him close against her shoulder and stepped back. Her face was white. "How did you find us? What are you doing here?" She ran her hands over Bobby's arms and legs as if she was worried that they'd already hurt him.

The man, Art, stepped between Buck and his wife and turned his back, effectively excluding Buck from the conversation. He was probably six feet tall, his sports jacket stretched across his shoulders, his khaki-clad legs planted wide. He crossed meaty arms over his chest and glared at Gina. "Did you think we couldn't find you, with our connections?"

She swallowed visibly and clutched Bobby closer. "You don't have connections in Ohio," she said in a hoarse voice.

The woman cackled. "We know people everywhere. We aren't like you, a nobody from nowhere."

Buck mentally scanned through everyone he knew in Rescue River, wondering who would run in these folks' elevated social circles. Sam Hinton, maybe? But Sam would swallow glass before he'd betray a woman and child in need.

"Our friends Bernice and Jerry Walker just happened to see their son's post about a new guesthouse on social media," the woman said. "They thought the woman and baby looked familiar. They got in touch with us, and we spoke with their son."

Gina gasped. "Danny Walker. And those publicity pictures Amy was taking that one day. I never even thought—"

"After he met with Gina and assessed the situation for us, he was concerned," Art interrupted. "He saw you getting involved with someone you shouldn't. Said that you and Bobby were practically homeless."

Betrayal was written all over Gina's face.

"And I must say," Lorna added, looking around the room, "he was right to be concerned. You're working as a common laborer."

"Place is dirty." Art brushed imaginary dust off his sleeve.

"And our grandson, lying on the floor unsupervised, with a couple of dirty, dangerous dogs. He could have been bitten."

"Or hurt on these nails and wood." The burly man nudged at a small pile of scraps with his toe.

"Art. Lorna. Come on. There's a baby monitor, and the dogs are perfectly safe," Gina said. But her voice sounded insecure.

Buck felt a quake of doubt, too. *He* was the one who'd suggested that Bobby stay downstairs with them.

But he'd trust Crater with any child, and Spike wouldn't hurt a flea.

Whereas these folks had already hurt Bobby. "You're trespassing in my sister's house," he said. "Get out."

"Door was unlocked," the man, Art, said. "Anyone could have walked in. You might want to think about that."

"It's a safe town," Gina said. "Or was, until the two of you came in."

Dion. Buck needed to call Dion.

He got out his phone and scrolled through his contacts, tapped Dion's name. "You need to get over to the guest-house," he said the moment Dion answered, not trying to hide his words from either Gina or Bobby's grandparents. "The people who abused him before are here. Gina needs help."

"Be right there," Dion said.

Lorna's penciled-on eyebrows lifted almost to her hair-line. "*We're* the danger? Us?"

The man pointed at Buck, thumb and forefinger out like a gun. "We know all about you, son. If anyone's a danger to Bobby, it's you."

"We talked to the nice people next door, in the Senior Towers," Lorna said, hands on hips. "They told us about *your* reputation. Drunk all over town, breaking places up, getting yourself arrested. Why, the very idea of our grand-son anywhere near you has us terrified."

"And not that she's treated us well," Art said, "but we'd hate to see Gina take up with the likes of you."

"Do you even have a job, aside from day work?"

"We heard you're in AA but that you were also seen at a bar recently."

"Once an alcoholic, always an alcoholic."

Gina was looking at him, her eyes stricken. "You were at a bar recently?"

"Not to drink," he tried to explain. "Not to drink."

But the words, true as they were, sounded false in his own ears. Like the excuses he used to make to Lacey. Like the lies every alcoholic knew exactly how to tell.

"You're a danger to both Gina and Bobby," Lorna de-clared. "We'll certainly take steps to keep you away from our grandson. And, Gina, what on earth were you thinking, leaving safety and comfort in California for this?" She swung a scornful arm around. "For *him*?"

The words went on, spoken by all three, an argument the older couple was clearly winning. It all started to blur together in Buck's head as he backed slowly out of the room and toward the guesthouse's front door.

What *had* he been thinking, getting so close to a nice woman and her innocent baby? Thinking he could have a normal relationship with them, be good for them, even?

He'd been the downfall of Ivana and Mia, and he was headed toward being the downfall of Gina and Bobby.

He opened the door and stepped onto the front porch. He had to get out of here. Had to make Gina and Bobby safe by leaving. But he couldn't go until she had another protector.

"If you think you'll be able to keep custody after this, you're wrong," he heard Art say through the screen door.

"When we go back to California, we're taking Bobby with us," Lorna added.

A police car squealed to a halt in front of the house, and Dion was out of it and up the porch stairs in seconds. When he saw Buck, he stopped. "Fill me in."

"The grandparents from California. Making threats, scaring Gina and Bobby." As if to back up his words, a loud wail came from inside the house.

Dion nodded and hurried inside, leaving the door open like he expected Buck to follow. When Buck didn't, he looked back, eyebrows lifted. "Come on, man."

But Buck knew what was best for everyone, and he wasn't it. He grabbed his wallet and keys. "You handle it," he said and headed out, bent on getting far, far away from here.

Gina survived the next hour of shouting and accusations by clinging to Bobby, soothing him, reminding herself to stay strong for him. She reeled from the force of Art and Lorna's hatred, her stomach churning with fear. Could they take Bobby from her?

Could she prevent them, with her complete lack of money and power?

Her mind darted in all directions, but it kept coming back to one question. Where was Buck? Why wasn't he here, standing by her?

Of course, it wasn't his problem or his obligation. She shouldn't feel betrayed. Still, she'd trusted him and felt he was a friend, if not more.

If not a whole lot more, if their sweet embrace was any indication.

But now, in her hour of need, he seemed to be gone. True, he'd gotten Dion here, for which Gina was incredibly thankful, but still. She'd expected something different from him.

Then again, if he'd been frequenting bars...

As Art and Lorna talked heatedly to Dion, heaping on accusations and innuendos, Gina shot up prayers for help and safety with every breath, her body cringing from the onslaught of lies and bitterness that seemed almost physical in its intensity. She didn't see how God could deliver her, but she tried desperately to remember all the biblical promises she'd ever memorized.

Dion was a force of calm and reason. Obviously sensing that she was near her breaking point, he pulled Art and Lorna aside for quiet moments of conversation while she took Bobby upstairs to calm down. As she let him nurse, she prayed hard, and bits of verses came back to her.

The Lord is my strength and my shield.

We are more than conquerors.

Thou preparest a table before me in the presence of my enemies...of my enemies...of my enemies.

She wanted to stay in her room, to shut out the hateful forces downstairs. But she needed to pay attention. She couldn't shrink away as she used to do.

She put Bobby down in his crib, but he fussed and lifted his arms, so she picked him back up and carried him downstairs, stopping in the doorway of the living room to listen to what was going on.

"You wouldn't understand," Lorna was saying in a patronizing voice. "You people are used to all that drinking and rough behavior."

Gina blinked. Had Lorna really said that? To *Dion*?

"Did you want to elaborate on just what kind of *people* you mean?"

Lorna hemmed and hawed.

"I didn't think so." His answer was quiet, with steel underneath. "Now, I suggest you go back to where you came from and leave the decent folks of Rescue River alone."

Art and Lorna both started talking at once, even as they backed toward the door. Phrases like *back tomorrow* and *with a warrant* and *custody hearing* and *abducted out of state* flew from their mouths.

Gina stepped out of the kitchen in time to see Dion take a couple of steps toward the couple.

They turned and left, slamming the door.

Gina sank down onto a bench in the entryway. "I'm so sorry about them," she said to Dion. "They're awful."

"I can see that." He leaned against the wall, looking through the window beside the door as a car engine started up outside. "But it's not your fault."

The sound of spitting gravel as the car sped away took

some of the weight off Gina's heart. "I caused them to come here and disturb your town."

He shook his head. "That was their decision. We just have to make sure they don't get access to Bobby."

"You knew about his bruises?"

He nodded. "Your in-laws aren't the only ones who have connections. Did you ever get a restraining order against them?"

"I tried. The officer I talked to advised against it." She paused. "They donate a lot to the local police fund-raisers."

Dion just shook his head.

Car headlights flashed through the window, and fear clawed at Gina's stomach. Had Art and Lorna come back?

Or had Buck? Now, after the trouble was temporarily over? She braced herself to yell at him, but truthfully, all she wanted was the protection and comfort of his arms.

But it wasn't Buck who came through the door. It was Lacey.

"Hey, guys, are we all set for tomorrow? I heard we're supposed to have record turnout at the festival…" She broke off, seeing Dion. "What's wrong? Where's my brother? What's he done now?"

Gina flinched. Lacey, who knew him so well, had made the automatic assumption that Buck had gotten into trouble.

The truth clicked into place, like pieces from a puzzle. His sister assumed he'd fallen off the wagon. He'd been seen at the bars.

She blew out a breath as her hopes and dreams about him shattered around her. She'd thought he was a great guy, wonderful. She'd even begun to dream of a future together.

But he is *a great guy!*

Yes, he was. Her husband had been, too, when he wasn't high.

But she knew where this road led. Despite the twists and turns, despite the promises and the calm periods, and, yes, the happiness, in the end, what you got was a couple of cops on your doorstep.

Ma'am, are you Gina Patterson? We have some bad news...

Her eyes filled with tears as disappointment congealed into a huge lump in her stomach. When would she ever learn? Why had she let it happen again? She had to understand that love wasn't meant for someone like her, too needy, too hopeful, too ready to look past fatal flaws when they came in the guise of a charming guy, someone like her dad.

She couldn't subject Bobby to that. But look at her—earlier tonight, she'd been ready to jump into Buck's arms, to make a commitment that she and Bobby would be his family.

She was a fool.

Dion and Lacey were talking quietly, glancing over at her. She heard Buck's name. And then they both took their phones out, punching in numbers. Waiting.

No answers.

Gina felt the same discouraged hurt that was written on Lacey's face, the same tight-lipped anger that flattened Dion's mouth.

Buck hadn't cared enough about her and Bobby to stay. The siren call of the bottle had been louder to him than Bobby's cries.

She knew it was an illness, that he couldn't help himself.

But he was helping himself! He was in recovery! You never saw him drunk, not even once!

But if he was well and whole, he'd be here now.

They all waited for another hour, drinking coffee, checking phones, talking a little. Gina took Bobby upstairs and put him to bed, then came back down. Too restless to sit, she cleaned up the little bit of remaining mess in the room she and Buck had been working on.

Before everything had gone straight downhill.

When she came out, Dion was shrugging into his jacket. "I've got to get back on patrol, but I'll make sure you're all locked down," he said. "We'll have frequent surveillance. And, Lacey, you stay here with Gina and Bobby, okay?"

Gina opened her mouth to protest, then closed it again. She didn't want to be an obligation. But Bobby's safety took precedence over her own embarrassment.

"Of course." Lacey moved to stand by Gina. "We'll be fine."

After Dion checked the locks and all the downstairs windows, he drove off with another promise of frequent patrols.

Gina turned to face Lacey. "I'm sorry to have involved you in all this. I know you didn't want us here, and that you've been working extra to avoid being around us, getting all your memories kicked up. As soon as I can find a way to keep Bobby safe, I'll be out of here and you can go back to life as normal."

Lacey took her hand and tugged her into the kitchen. She filled the kettle with water and put it on the stove. And then she came to sit across the table from Gina. "It may not seem like it," she said, "but you and Bobby have been a help for me. Forced me to face some things about myself. To get my thoughts and plans together." Lacey closed her eyes for a minute and then opened them again. "It's been painful. But I understand some things better now. I'm not going to *get* better, not completely."

"Oh, Lacey, with God's help—"

"I know." Lacey held up a hand. "I'm praying all the

time, looking for guidance, asking for forgiveness. And I realize I'm never…" She swallowed hard.

The teakettle whistled, and she stood and poured hot water over tea bags, brought two cups over to the table.

"We don't have to talk about this now," Gina said. "It's late. I'm sure you want to go to bed."

"Do *you* want to? This has to have been an awful, scary day. I don't know the whole story, but you must be exhausted."

"I'll never get to sleep. If you can distract me by talking about something other than my horrible in-laws, go for it. Please."

Lacey dunked her tea bag repeatedly, not looking at Gina. After a moment, she spoke in a low voice. "I realize I'll never be able to love a man and child again. Not like I loved Gerry, problems and all. And maybe that's why…" She broke off, opened her eyes wide as if that would make the tears stay inside. "That's why God made me infertile. Why I can't have another baby."

"Oh, Lacey." Compassion for the other woman flooded Gina's heart, making her own worries recede. "Are you sure?"

"Pretty sure. I just got results from a few more tests."

"And here I've been preoccupied with work and all my problems and never even thought of what you might be going through. I'm sorry. That must be so hard to deal with."

Lacey grabbed a napkin and started shredding it. "It's like I'm frozen inside. Maybe I'm going to stay that way. But when I get over this initial…hurt, I'll figure out what to do with my life as a single person. There's nothing wrong with being single."

Gina nodded. She needed to start remembering those ideas herself. "That's what the Bible says."

"Exactly. And maybe that's His mercy to me, stopping me from even trying to connect with a man and have a family. Because I can't." Her voice was quiet and bleak.

"Oh, Lacey, don't give up if that's your dream. There's all kind of medical advances, there's adoption, there's—"

"I know," Lacey interrupted. "I know, and I know it's not going to happen for me. But let's get off my issues. I feel like a rat, talking about this when your baby's at risk."

"I *want* to talk—"

"No." Lacey raised her hand like a stop sign. "Please. I can't... Look. I've got a burglar alarm, and Dion made me turn it on. The locks are great—Buck made sure of that. We'll be safe through the night. And things will look better in the morning." She blew out a breath and banged the table with a fist. "I just can't believe that brother of mine. I thought he was making such good progress."

"Me, too." Gina's voice broke a little and she pressed her lips together.

They finished their tea in silence and then hugged goodnight and went upstairs.

"Tomorrow is another day," Lacey said.

Gina nodded. *Another day when Bobby's at risk of being taken from me.*

Chapter 13

Buck didn't know how long he drove. It could have been minutes, or it could have been hours. Finally, when he couldn't outrun his pain, he pulled off the highway into a little rural strip mall's parking lot.

It looked familiar, and he figured he'd been here before. In his drinking days, he'd spent a fair amount of time traveling, doing odd jobs, letting whatever town he was staying in cool off.

There was a Chinese restaurant at one end of the strip mall, still open, and he thought about going in to get tea and something to eat. But since the place looked familiar, had he been here before? In what condition? He couldn't face another manager barring the door, another rejection.

The words of Gina's former in-laws rang in his ears.

Drunk all over town.

Once an alcoholic, always an alcoholic.

A danger to Bobby and Gina.

It was that last one that hurt his heart and scared the daylights out of him. Bobby and Gina meant the world to him. He loved them both—he knew that now. He wanted them to be his family.

Only, if he was a danger to them, then no dice. He couldn't put them at risk. If he were the cause of someone else dying, another woman and child...well, that would be unforgivable. Better to keep running and never come back than to harm them in any way.

He remembered his wife's words in their final bad days. *Terrible husband...don't know why I married you...disaster as a father.* He'd had enough counseling to know that words spoken in anger couldn't fully define who he was. At the same time, if the sources all agreed, then you'd come upon truth.

Even the people at the Senior Towers had condemned him. His old friends, the people who'd known him since childhood.

And Dion...his disappointed expression when he'd looked back and seen that Buck wasn't coming along. It was a killer.

The truck cab was getting stuffy, and he needed to move. He got out and leaned back against the side of the truck, looking around the small plaza. Yes, he'd been here before, had seen that dollar store, that gas station.

He knew without looking behind him that there was a bar across the street. His back actually tingled, as if the place were pulling him magnetically toward it.

He was far enough from Rescue River that no one was likely to know him there. He had money. He could easily go in and get a drink or a couple. No one from home would find out.

And even if they did, who cared? His reputation was already in the sewer.

Some part of his mind recognized the dangerous direction of these thoughts, and he fumbled in his pocket for his sobriety coin. But he was still wearing work clothes, and he hadn't put the coin in his pocket this morning. Had missed doing it a lot of days lately, in fact. He hadn't been thinking about alcohol.

He'd been thinking about Gina.

He blew out a breath and tried to latch on to what he'd learned in AA. He should call his sponsor. He reached back into the car, and only then did he realize he didn't have his phone on him. He'd left in such a hurry that all he'd grabbed was his wallet. His phone was on his dresser at home, turned off so it wouldn't wake the baby.

Bobby.

He looked heavenward. "I've tried, Lord. I've really tried here."

Of course, there was no answer. God wasn't on speaking terms with a loser like him. God was in agreement with all the good people of Rescue River.

He banged a fist against the top of the car, stupidly. It hurt, and he winced as he climbed back in and started the engine.

Washing his mind clean of any thought, he drove over to the little bar's parking lot, pulled up close, got out.

As he approached the door of the roadhouse, a light flashed next door. Curious, he looked over.

It looked like another bar beside the first one, only where the first bar flashed beer signs, this one had the message— Jesus Saves—along with a blinking cross.

He hadn't seen it the last time he was here. Lacey would have called it tacky.

Was it some kind of joke? But no, above the door was a small sign: New Country Church. Along the storefront windows were painted slogans and verses: "Sinners Saved by Grace" and "All Welcome" and "Because He Loves You."

Buck shook his head. Some crazy Christian, or a bunch of them, making a church along the highway. Trying to, anyway. He had to admire the effort, however futile. How would a church compete with a roadhouse full of light and color, with pulsing music, laughing people?

Whereas the little church...

Ridiculing himself for being a fool, he walked over to the door. A Thursday night, late—no way would it be open.

He tried the door.

It opened.

"Really, God?" he said out loud. Took one last glance back at the roadhouse. Then walked into the storefront church.

The next morning, Gina was already up and dressed after a restless night, feeding Bobby, when there was a pounding at the door.

Lacey didn't come down, and Gina wasn't sure whether or not she'd left for work. So she answered the door herself, Bobby on her hip.

Standing on the porch was Dion in full uniform, and Daisy, a woman Gina had met briefly at the church lunch.

But Daisy acted official rather than friendly as she shook Gina's hand. "Daisy Hinton. I'm a social worker, here to look into a couple of things for Children and Youth. Is this your son?"

Gina's heart pounded so fast she thought she might pass out. "Yes, this is Bobby," she said and clutched him tighter.

"May I come in?"

"Okay." Gina stepped aside.

"I'll leave you to it, then," Dion said to Daisy. "Call me if you need anything. I won't be far away."

In the hall, Daisy took off her coat. "We had a report of child neglect. I'm just here to ask a few questions."

Gina's knees went limp and she sank down on the hallway bench, clutching Bobby so tightly that he fussed a little. They'd done it. They'd reported her. She was going to lose her son.

He leaned his head against her and clutched her hair in stubby fingers, and she straightened her spine. No way would she let them win.

"You can't take him." Gina stood and gauged the distance to her car, wondering whether she could outrun this woman. No doubt Dion's presence and assurance that he was near was meant to forestall just that.

"No, that's not what this is about. Not at this point. Can we sit down and talk?"

Manners. Show her you're a good mom. Gina gestured the other woman into the kitchen. "I'm sorry—I'm a little upset. Would you like some coffee?" She looked at the high chair where Bobby had eaten his breakfast. Cereal was scattered over the tray and on the floor, and there was a smear of banana on the chair itself. Too late, she noticed that some of it was in his hair as well.

Why, oh, why hadn't she cleaned things up before answering the door?

"No coffee, thanks. Can you tell me a little about your routines with Bobby, where he stays while you're working, that sort of thing?" As she spoke, Daisy watched Bobby, not staring, just observant.

Gina blew out a breath and tried to speak, but no words came. She reached for her own coffee and lifted it, thinking it would calm her, but her hand shook so badly that she sloshed some out onto the table and banged it back down too hard.

"Hey," Daisy said gently, "it's okay. Take a minute."

The kind tone brought tears to Gina's eyes. Still, she knew she shouldn't trust it. Daisy was just trying to get her to open up.

Never had she felt so alone. Sure, she liked it here in Rescue River; she'd made a start at some friendships. But the reality was that she was new in town, not really a part of things. She was an outsider, and it was her word against two other outsiders, Bobby's grandparents, so much more wealthy and powerful than she was.

The one real friend she'd thought she had was notably missing: Buck. He hadn't come in last night, as far as she knew; he must be out carousing or else sleeping it off. She'd chosen the wrong person to attach herself to, as usual.

The loss of him, of who she'd thought he was, opened up a hole in her chest, so painful she almost gasped with it.

Bobby struggled to get down and she set him on the floor, then immediately wondered if that was the right thing to do. Lacey kept the kitchen clean, but the mat below the high chair held the remains of breakfast.

Daisy watched as Bobby pulled up on the chair and moved toward his race-car push toy. A couple of steps, and he fell forward onto his hands, then moved into his preferred crawling mode. Gina went over to make sure he didn't run into anything, and Daisy stood, too.

"Seems like his development is normal," she said. "What's he doing lately?"

That, she could talk about. "He's pulling up a lot and taking a few steps, like you just saw. He's not steady yet." Remembering how he'd taken his first step when Buck was watching, her throat tightened. She'd felt so close to Buck then. She'd trusted him.

Bobby pushed his car into the hallway and down, banging it into the doorway of the front room. He looked back at Gina. "Da? Da?"

"He wants the dogs," she explained, and then her hand flew to her mouth. "Is that bad, that I let him be around the dogs? They're gentle as lambs, but my former in-laws were upset…" She trailed off, not wanting to incriminate herself.

"Being around animals is actually good for babies. Helps them not get allergies."

"That's what I've read." Relieved, Gina opened the door and Spike and Crater cried to get out of the crates they stayed in at night.

She opened the crates, picked up Bobby and let the dogs go outside. "Sorry," she said over her shoulder. "Mornings, they need to get out and get fed."

"I understand. I'm Troy Hinton's sister, after all. I know rescue dogs, and I know Crater." She gave the large dog a head scratch as he bounded back inside. His tail wagging, Crater soaked up the attention and then ambled toward the kitchen, pausing to lick Bobby a couple of times. Bobby giggled and sat down hard on his diaper-clad behind.

Gina's adrenaline spiked again. Was that bad, letting a dog lick a baby? But it was too late to change it.

Spike tore in, barking, and ran in front of Crater to get to the kitchen. "He thinks he's the alpha," Gina explained. "And Crater lets him think so. Do you mind if I get them their breakfast? They'll settle down after that."

"I have all morning," Daisy said, "and this is actually great, to see your household, and your care of Bobby, in action."

Way to make me self-conscious, Gina thought as she

scooped dog food into bowls. But the daily routine relaxed her a little, as did Daisy's apparent friendliness.

Don't get too trusting, she reminded herself.

"So," Daisy asked, "while you're working on the house, where does Bobby stay?"

Gina tensed. "Sometimes we—I mean, I—I gate him in an adjoining room. Sometimes he's in his jumper, although he doesn't like it as much as he liked his jumper in California. He doesn't like to be confined." She looked down at Bobby, only to realize he was crawling rapidly out of the room. "Bobby!" She put down the dog food and hurried over to close the kitchen door. "Exhibit A," she said and pulled out a couple of pots and pans for him to bang.

"Do you have alternative care if you're doing something he shouldn't be around?" Daisy asked, so Gina explained about Angelica.

They walked around the house slowly, with Gina showing Daisy the places Bobby played, his toys, his crib. As they talked about his routines, Gina started to relax. Daisy just didn't seem like an enemy; she seemed fair.

After they'd gotten back to the kitchen, Daisy sat down at the table and pulled out her tablet computer. "I'm going to make a few notes here, if you don't mind," she said. "No guarantees, but I don't see anything that would warrant removing Bobby from the home."

Relief washed over Gina, and she offered a quick prayer of thanks.

Daisy typed rapidly on her tablet, and Gina started wiping down the high chair while Bobby pulled more pans out of the cupboards.

The kitchen door opened. "Hey," Lacey said. "I slept in a little, since I'm off today. Daisy, what's up?"

"Just looking into a few things." Daisy tapped away on her tablet.

"Like, professionally?"

Daisy nodded, still typing.

"The in-laws," Gina explained. "They filed a report against me and she's investigating."

"What?" Lacey stared. "You're the best mother I've ever seen!"

Gina's jaw just about dropped. "I…I have to say I'm surprised, but thanks."

Bobby had picked up a plastic bowl, and now he put it on his head, making them all laugh. Gina hurried to get it off so he wouldn't be scared, but they were still laughing when Art and Lorna flung open the kitchen door. Spike barked fiercely from behind Gina's legs while Crater walked out to stand, alert, in front of the intruders.

"Where's our grandson?" Art demanded.

"I don't recall inviting you into my home," Lacey said.

"We were given to understand a social worker would investigate. Can't you quiet down that dog?"

"I'm a social worker, and I'm investigating," Daisy said calmly, snapping shut the case of her tablet. "Come here, Spike. Good boy." She swept the little dog up onto her lap.

"But…but it looks like you all know each other," Lorna argued. "That's hardly a fair investigation."

"In this town, we all know each other," Lacey said.

"And we like it that way," Daisy added.

Gina swung Bobby to her hip and stepped forward, empowered by the other two women's presence. "And that's why I want to raise Bobby here," she said. "It's a warm, safe environment. A real community. He'll grow up happy here."

Lorna's hands went to her hips. "Once we get a *real* investigator in here, I'm confident that our home will be determined to be a better environment for him."

Gina's stomach dropped. Could they do that? She wouldn't have thought so, but she'd been surprised before at what their money could buy.

She opened her mouth to protest, but Lacey stepped forward and put an arm around Gina. "Since you're uninvited guests and this is my home, I'd like to ask you to leave."

Crater stepped forward with them, emitting a low, almost inaudible growl.

Lorna took a step back, but Art huffed and didn't move.

"I have the police on speed dial," Daisy said pleasantly. "Shall I call them?"

"Come on, Lorna. Once I make a few phone calls, they'll be singing a different tune." The older couple turned and walked out onto the front porch, and Gina followed to make sure they really left.

And there was Buck, trotting up the steps, looking much the worse for wear.

"You again!" Lorna sputtered. "So it's true you live here. We ought to have you arrested. A common drunk in the same house as our grandson!"

Dion's police car cruised slowly by, and Art hurried toward the street to flag him down.

"He's not..." Gina broke off. She didn't know *what* Buck was or wasn't. She couldn't deny the burst of happiness in her chest when she saw him, but she couldn't trust it, either.

"What are *you* still doing here?" He asked the question of Lorna, politely, but with steel in his voice.

"Getting ready to take custody of our grandson, if it's any of your business."

"No, you're not." Gina lifted her chin and glared her in-laws down. "I'm through putting up with your manipulation and…and abuse. Bobby's staying here with me, and that's that."

"Abuse? You've been watching too many trashy TV shows."

"I saw Art hit him." She narrowed her eyes at Lorna. "And you were holding Bobby still so he could do it. Don't even try to deny it."

"I do deny it," her mother-in-law said, her lip curling. "And no one's going to believe you over me."

"I think they will. Wait here. Everyone, please." Buck pushed past Lorna and into the house, giving Bobby a brief chin tickle that made him chortle, looking into Gina's eyes with something inexplicable in his own. Then he disappeared up the stairs.

Hearing some noise on the street, Gina stepped out onto the porch. Dion was walking toward the house with Art, but something off to the side made him stop and stare.

Gina looked, and then she stared, too.

From the direction of the Senior Towers came a parade of white-haired people, some striding, some using walkers and some being pushed in wheelchairs.

They appeared to be headed…here.

When they reached the gate in the front of the guesthouse, the clatter of canes and the scrape of wheels on concrete trailed off. The crowd parted to allow Miss Minnie Falcon to march to the front, her eyes blazing.

Instinctively, Gina went down to meet the older woman, holding Bobby on her hip. "What's going on, Miss Minnie?"

"I'll tell you what's going on." She stopped her walker and drew herself up, pointing a long, bony finger at Art, then at Lorna. "We were having breakfast this morning when word came around that you two are attempting to take little Bobby away from his mother."

"And that they're using things we said as evidence, which is just plain ridiculous," Gramps Camden contributed from the front of the crowd.

Behind Gina, the door of the guesthouse opened. She looked back as Buck hurried out, still in his bedraggled clothes, and then stopped. Crater stood at his side.

"For one thing, that young man," Miss Minnie said, gesturing at Buck, "is a fine, upright person, and any child would be safe with him."

Gina blinked at the vote of confidence.

Ninetysomething Bob Eakin, the Towers librarian, came forward, adjusting his Proud WWII Veteran baseball cap. "He may have had some troubles in the past, but who here hasn't?" he asked, his voice ringing out loudly. "Who will cast the first stone?"

Realization swept over Gina. She *had* been casting stones, had been believing the worst of Buck even against the evidence of her own senses. "Buck Armstrong is totally safe," she said. "I'd trust him with Bobby's life."

Buck descended the steps slowly, his forehead wrinkled. He opened his mouth as if to speak and then closed it again.

"And what's more," said Lou Ann Miller, who was pushing a wheelchair, "Gina Patterson is a wonderful mother. I've visited her and seen her with Bobby. There's no reason on earth to take that baby away."

Seeing the white heads nodding, Gina's throat tightened. When in her life had people ever stood up for her this way, taken her side?

Art made an abrupt, waving gesture, seeming to discount their words. "The truth will come out, and then we'll get custody."

Buck took an intimidating step forward, and despite his ragged clothes, his straight posture and steely gaze made everyone quiet down.

"The truth *will* come out. I had occasion to take a picture of Bobby right after he and his mother arrived in Rescue River," he said, holding up his smartphone. "And if you'll look where I'm zooming it in, you'll see the fist-size bruise on Bobby's leg." He looked at Gina. "I'm sorry to make your story public, but these people have to be stopped. The reason she left California," he said as he turned to the crowd, "is that these two were beginning to abuse their grandson. This bruise is just the outward mark of some pretty awful behavior."

Art and Lorna sputtered and looked at each other. Before they could formulate a response, Dion's voice boomed out. "Is that true, Gina?"

She cleared her throat so she could say it loud and clear. "They hit him and shook him. I was afraid for his safety."

A murmur came from the Senior Towers crowd, rising in volume. Indignant voices stood out.

"That's an outrage."

"They should be prosecuted."

"We don't tolerate that kind of thing around here."

Lorna's face was red and her eyes shiny with tears. Art looked apoplectic. "You haven't heard the end of this," he snarled at Gina. "It's not against the law to discipline a child."

Dion stepped toward the couple. "I'll be following up with my colleagues in California. Now, I'd suggest you get out of our town and don't come back."

Assenting voices came from the white-haired crowd.

Art and Lorna looked at each other, then turned and hurried down to their car, hunching away from the disapproving stares and comments of those watching. A moment later, their car pulled away.

Gina stood, dazed, as voices and activity swirled around her. Finally, a gentle hand patted her back. "I brought down a chair," Lacey said. "Come on—sit."

So she sank into an Adirondack chair, Bobby in her arms, and Lacey sat down beside her. Spike jumped up, licked her leg and Bobby's, and then squeezed in beside her, panting. And as people came up to express their indignation or sympathy, offering help and comfort, something long empty inside her started to fill. She was cared for. She was protected. She was home.

Chapter 14

It was now or never.

Buck hitched his duffel to his shoulder and walked out into the moonlight. He'd thought about it all day today, had prayed, had found moments between the busy festival activities to discuss things with Lacey.

He'd gotten his life and his sobriety back in Rescue River, had learned he could love again. He'd even, at the storefront church, come to see that he wasn't to blame for Ivana's driving off the road with Mia. But he was still some distance from being fully recovered, and he didn't know if he'd ever get there. The wise pastor he'd talked to last night had reminded him of what the Bible said about being single: it could be a blessed state, allowing a person to devote himself to God's work.

But Buck knew he couldn't get to that point while being in Gina's presence. He'd come to care too much. At the same time, he'd seen how she didn't trust him, might never trust him, because of her own past. The minute Art and Lorna had started lobbing accusations, she'd believed them.

He didn't blame her for that; he did have a past, and so did she. But he owed it to himself and to God to go somewhere he could make a difference and rebuild a life.

He'd debated over and over whether to talk to her before he left, but in the end, he'd decided that a quick departure would be less painful for both of them. He'd left a letter for her with Lacey, explaining why he was leaving.

He strode out the front door, intent on reaching his truck before he changed his mind.

"Where are you headed?"

The soft voice nearly shattered him. Slowly, he turned toward the source of it: Gina, on the front porch, bathed in moonlight and holding Bobby.

Nod and run! His brain made that very practical suggestion. But his heart and soul tugged him toward the pair, so he dropped his duffel by the rocking chair and walked over.

Gina smiled at him, looking relaxed. She'd always been gorgeous, but from the time she'd arrived in town, tension had tightened her face and haunted her eyes. Now that was gone, and the effect of her genuine, full smile was stunning.

"Wh-what are you doing out here?" he stammered, buying time.

"I finally got him to sleep." She nodded down at Bobby, relaxed in her lap. "But then he woke up again, all fussy. Sometimes fresh air and rocking helps him settle down."

"And you can relax now, knowing you're safe here," he said.

"Exactly. I never felt quite at ease bringing him outside at night. Silly, I know, but I worried that Lorna and Art would jump out and grab him."

"I don't think they'll be bothering you anymore." He

believed it, too. He'd followed them when they left downtown with their tails between their legs, had watched them check out of the motel at the edge of town and made sure they drove away. He'd spoken to Dion this afternoon, and the full force of the law had been in effect. Dion was in contact with the police in the couple's hometown and was working on a restraining order here. If a trial came, Gina would have to testify, but after his conversation with Lorna and Art, Dion was certain they'd stay away.

"Thanks for what you did with the picture," she said. "In the confusion afterward, I couldn't find you. I wanted to make sure to tell you, I think that's what turned the tide."

"Only after you spoke up and told the truth." He shrugged. "And Miss Minnie did a pretty good job of telling them off."

"She did, for sure. But it wasn't until the whole town—and Dion—saw that picture that we really got rid of them."

He looked up at the stars, breathed in the smell of night blossoms. Now that he was here with Gina, he might as well talk a little. Besides, it would take a while for his brain to regain control and make him leave. "I should have stayed with you when they first came. I had something to work out, but I shouldn't have left you."

"I was upset you did," she admitted. "Pretty mad at you, in fact, but it all turned out all right." She put a hand on his arm. "You're not perfect, Buck, but you're a good man."

Just like that, he was forgiven. He shifted and knocked a boot against his duffel and it tipped out into the middle of the porch floor. She looked at it, then at him. "You're leaving?"

He looked down at the duffel, then up at her. "Yeah."

"Again, without telling me?" There was hurt in her voice.

"I wrote you a letter. Lacey has it." He looked out across

the silvery, quiet street. Should he go into it with her? Would he be able to leave at all if he stayed here, talking with Gina in the moonlight?

Talking with the woman he loved?

The answer, obviously, was no.

He forced himself to stand up. To put his duffel over his shoulder. One step at a time.

Bobby stirred, then opened his eyes and saw Buck. "Buh! Buh!" he said sleepily, holding up his arms.

Buck picked the baby up, a lump in his throat. This inimitable little man had helped him to heal, and Buck hated to leave him. "Hey, it'll be okay," he said, jostling the sleepy boy.

Don't go, then, his heart mourned. *Stay!* "I could…" He started. Then stopped himself. *No. Don't reopen that door.* "See you," he croaked out, handing Bobby back down to Gina. And then he turned and walked slowly down the porch steps, feeling older than any resident of the Senior Towers.

Gina watched him go with a perfect storm of pain and confusion swirling inside her.

Why was he leaving? Because he *didn't* care for her, or because he did?

Because he was honorable or dishonorable?

"Buh," Bobby fussed, reaching toward the vacant spot where Buck had been.

Babies and dogs, they could sense who was a good person. And she could sense it, too. She hadn't trusted herself, and she hadn't made good decisions in the past, but she'd changed. Grown. Toughened up.

If Buck were a danger to her and Bobby, she'd let him go, no question. But she knew with every fiber of her being that he wasn't a danger, that he was, in fact, perfect. Not a perfect, flawless person, maybe—there weren't any of those—but perfect for her.

The sound of his truck starting pierced the darkness, and suddenly she was on her feet, clutching Bobby to her hip. She rushed down the steps to catch him. "Buck! Wait!"

But he was already pulling out in the street, his jaw square, face grim. He didn't look to the right or left, but only forward. And he drove away.

Despair gripped her heart. If he left, would he ever come back? Would he know she cared for him? That she loved him?

She walked out into the street, looking after him. She was wearing flannels and a T-shirt, fuzzy slippers on her feet, a robe billowing around her in the slight breeze. She looked like a fool.

Moonlight illuminated the shops, now dark and empty of people. The streetlamps cast a soft glow. She loved this town. But it wouldn't be home without Buck.

She started speed walking down the middle of the street, Bobby tight against her chest. She passed the Senior Towers, where one or two windows still glowed, and thought of the parade of helpers that had come to save Bobby today.

She wanted to stay here, to raise Bobby here. But she didn't want to do it alone.

"Buck! Come back! Come back!" She started running down the middle of the main street of Rescue River, the robe flying behind her like wings, chasing those two red taillights. Waving her free arm frantically. "Hey! Come back!"

The lights were getting dimmer. She slowed to a walk, straining her eyes.

She couldn't see the taillights. He was gone. She blew

out a sigh that ended in a sob and stood, holding Bobby in the middle of the downtown she loved.

"Come back," she whispered. "Please, come back."

But there was no sound except the rhythmic croaking of a couple of frogs in the creek. No sign of a truck turning around or coming back.

Bobby's fussing rose to a wail, and she felt like wailing, too. She couldn't—she had responsibilities—but she felt like it.

Despair made her shoulders hunch over as she carried her crying son back toward the guesthouse.

He had to do this. He couldn't look back.

He put on his turn signal, being careful even though there was no other traffic on the road. By the book, by rote—that was the only way he could force himself to leave Gina and Bobby behind.

He started to turn and glanced in his rearview mirror. He thought he saw something back in the middle of the downtown.

What was that? Billowy, floating, but half looking like a woman?

Memories slammed into him, of that first night he'd encountered Gina and Bobby on that lonesome road outside town. So much had happened since then. He'd relearned how to feel, how to love. He'd grown to where he could put aside his own past, his temptations, because that was best for the people he cared about. The two people he cared about most in the whole world.

The truck was coasting into the turn and he couldn't help it; he stopped and looked back, squinting through the darkness.

There was definitely someone there.

He'd better go back just to make sure it wasn't someone intent on harming Gina and Bobby. Some lowlife sent by her rich former in-laws to scare or threaten them.

He turned the truck around and headed back, slowly, trying to see.

Clouds skittered over the moon, throwing the street into darkness. He let the truck coast quietly, watching.

And then his heart gave a great thud. It was Gina, walking back, head down.

Walking slowly, as if she'd come out into the middle of the street.

As if she'd been chasing him.

If there were any chance at all…

He pulled the truck crookedly into a diagonal parking place and got out, not even bothering to close the door. "Gina! Wait!"

She turned. Her eyes widened. "Buck?"

"What are you doing out here?" He strode toward her. "I…I just had the thought…" He hesitated. And then realized he needed to put his pride aside and tell the whole truth. "Gina, if you have any interest in pursuing this thing we've got…"

Her free hand went to her mouth, her other arm around Bobby. Slowly, her eyes never leaving his, she nodded her head.

He was in front of them in two seconds, wrapping his arms around her right in the middle of Main Street. "Gina, I promise you, I've changed. I'm a new man, with a new life."

Her eyes got shiny, and as she stared up at him, a tear spilled out.

He reached down and thumbed the dampness from beneath her eye. "I know you've got baggage, and the Lord knows I do, too. But with God's help…"

That gorgeous smile spread across her face, and it was like the sun coming up. "With God's help, we just might make it work."

"You're willing to try?" He was laughing a little and yet his own throat felt tight. "Gina, I love you so much you wouldn't think there was any extra room in my heart, but there is, because I love Bobby just about as much as I love you."

She stepped into his embrace. "I love you, too," she murmured against his chest.

"Buh," Bobby said sleepily. "Buh. Buh."

They both laughed a little and cried a little. "Come on," he said, wrapping an arm around her shoulders. "Let's go home."

Headlights flashed behind them. Buck shepherded Gina and Bobby to the sidewalk.

A marked car pulled up beside them—Dion. "Everything okay here?"

"More than okay," they both said at the same time. Then laughed.

Dion gave them an assessing look. "You left your truck running, buddy, but I'll take care of it. Looks like you've got something better to do."

As they walked back to the guesthouse, Gina clutched his arm, making him stop. "But what about your reputation, the troubles you've had here?"

"I still have some reparations to make," he said, "but this community is forgiving. I figured that out yesterday, when the seniors all defended me." He smiled down at her. "When *you* defended me."

"We take care of each other here," she said.

"And you? You're okay being with someone who'll probably go to AA meetings for the rest of his life?"

"Absolutely," she said, moving closer to his side. "I trust that you've turned a corner."

He had turned a corner, Buck reflected as they climbed the stairs together. And he was sure glad he *hadn't* turned the corner out of Rescue River. Because this was the start of the new life he'd always wanted.

Chapter 15

The last day of the festival was drawing to an end when Gina came downstairs, having just gotten Bobby up from his nap. She carried him toward the front room, pausing to stand in the doorway.

Buck was there, and Gina's breath caught when he smiled at her. They'd spent almost every moment together since Friday night, talking and dreaming.

It was as if the Lord had taken away all her anxiety and stress, and she was able to accept that Buck loved her, that she was lovable and that this was God sanctioned and could work. Feeling his arm around her as they'd walked through town yesterday, taking in the festival, had been bliss.

At the front of the room, Mr. Love and Miss Minnie Falcon sat telling the story of their ancestors and how the house had served as one of the most prominent stations on the Underground Railroad. They'd held visitors rapt both days, and they were thriving on the questions and interest.

Bobby started babbling, so Gina backed away, not wanting to detract from the elders' storytelling. Lacey waved her over to the front desk. "Look at this," she said, showing Gina the computer screen.

"What am I looking at?" Gina leaned closer. "Are those...bookings?"

Lacey nodded, beaming. "Starting this fall, we're booked every weekend up until Christmas." She blew out a breath. "Which means we'll have to work like crazy to get this place done, but with all these reservations, I'm feeling confident enough to cut down to part-time at work so I can help, too."

"That's wonderful!" Impulsively, Gina hugged the woman.

"I owe it to you," Lacey said. "You believed in what could happen before I did, and your work and PR abilities are what tilted the balance."

Gina leaned back on her elbows, looking around. "It does look great. And what's happening in there—" she gestured toward the front room "—that's just serendipity. Good for everyone."

"It's good for me, seeing you and Buck together," Lacey said. "He deserves happiness." She looked wistfully into the room, where her brother was kneeling to help Mr. Love hold up the large door, with its tiny peephole, that had camouflaged the fugitives' hiding place in the basement of the Falcon home.

"Your time will come."

Lacey laughed. "I wouldn't go that far. I'm just glad to see my brother happy. And you. And those two crazy rescue dogs."

"Things are going to get even crazier when my California dogs come home. My friend Haley is driving them when she comes to visit next month." But it would work out. She had faith that everything would work out, now.

As the last group of guests filed out of the front room, Gina slipped inside. Mr. Love waved to the last visitors, and then he leaned over and said something to Miss Minnie.

"Why, Mr. Love," Miss Minnie said, her cheeks pink. "I hardly think that's appropriate at our age."

"I've buried two wives, and I'm not looking for another," he said calmly. "But there's nothing wrong with companionship. And a man is never too old to appreciate a beautiful woman." He patted Miss Minnie's hand.

"Except I know you can't half see," she complained, but a smile lit up her deeply lined face.

Mr. Love turned to Buck and Gina. "Miss Minnie and I, we've been talking, and she helped me look through some of the heirlooms we had out at the old farm. I found something pretty special, as this young man knows."

Gina looked at Buck and was alarmed to notice perspiration on his upper lip and a pale cast to his face.

"I've had an offer for this particular item," Mr. Love continued, "that I'm tempted to accept, but only if the buyer can put it to good use." He pulled out an old velvet box, just a couple of inches square. "The young couple who were going to use this more than one hundred and fifty years ago never got their happy ending. This has been in a cubbyhole in the Old Rose Barn ever since, waiting for the right time to be found."

"We can't help them," Miss Minnie said, "but maybe we can help to create some happiness right here and now."

"I'm hoping." Buck took the box from Mr. Love and walked over to Gina, drawing her toward the high-backed love seat. "Sit down a minute."

Gina's heart rate kicked up a notch, and she did as he asked.

The two elders watched, smiling, obviously in on some secret. Lacey was leaning on the doorjamb, smiling as well.

Buck knelt in front of her. "Gina," he said, "you know how I feel about you, and I want to ask you, will you marry me?"

"What?" Her voice rose to a squeal.

He opened the box, and there was a Victorian-style gold ring, its central diamond surrounded by small diamonds that formed the shape of a cross.

Gina's breath caught. "Minerva and Abraham's ring?"

Buck nodded. "You haven't answered my question." His hands shook a little, holding the ring box.

Joy rang through her like bells. "Of course! Yes, yes, yes!" She tugged him to the seat beside her.

"There's only one condition," Mr. Love said, "on my selling Buck that ring."

"What is it?" Gina asked.

"Anything," Buck said at the same time, so fervently that he drew a laugh from Lacey, still standing in the doorway.

"That the person wearing it has to stay right here in Rescue River." Mr. Love flashed a smile. "We don't want you going anywhere."

"Why would anyone want to live anywhere else?" Miss Minnie glanced over at Mr. Love, and a dimple appeared in her cheek.

Tears sprang to Gina's eyes. "I'll stay," she said, and then she couldn't get out any more words. She just nestled closer to her future husband's side.

The sound of barking came from the next room, where Spike and Crater had been confined to their crates, safely out of the way of the festival's guests. Lacey disappeared, then returned a minute later with the dogs bounding in beside her, in hot pursuit of Mr. Whiskers. Mrs. Whiskers, who'd been weaving through Buck's and Gina's feet, jumped up on one arm of the love seat, and Mr. Whiskers leaped onto the other arm. Both glared indignantly down at the raucous canines.

Buck chuckled, then touched Gina's chin, turning her face toward him for a kiss. And, safe in his arms, Gina knew that she and Bobby had found the home and family she'd always craved.

* * * * *

On Wednesday after work, Hannah drove toward home, the twins
in the back seat, and tried not to be nervous that Luke was in the
front seat beside her.

"I really appreciate this," he said. His car hadn't started this
morning, and he'd walked the three miles to Rescue Haven.

Of course, Hannah had insisted on driving him home. What else
could she do? It was cold outside, spitting snow, and he was her
next-door neighbor.

"I hate to ask another favor," he said, "but could you stop by
Pasquale's Pizza on the way?"

"No problem." She took a left and drove the two blocks to the
only nonchain pizza place in Bethlehem Springs.

He jumped out, and she turned back to check on the twins,
trying not to watch Luke as he headed into the shop. He was good-
looking, of course. Kind, appreciative and strong. And he had the
slightest swagger in his walk that was masculine and appealing.

But he was also about to go visit his brother, Bobby, if he kept his promise to his ailing father. And when she'd heard about that visit, it had been a wake-up call: she shouldn't get too close with him. The fewer chances she had to spill the beans about Bobby being the twins' father, the better.

He came out of the pizza shop quickly—he must have called ahead—carrying a big flat box and a white bag. What would it be like if this was a family scenario, if they were Mom and Dad and kids, stopping for takeout on the way home from work?

She couldn't help it. Her chest filled with longing.

He climbed into her small car, juggling the large flat box to make it fit without encroaching on the gearshift.

She had to laugh at the size of his meal. "Hungry?"

"Are you?" He opened the box a little, and the rich, garlicky fragrance of Pasquale's special sauce filled the car.

Her stomach growled, loudly.

"Pee-zah!" Addie shouted from the back seat.

"Peez!" Emmy added, almost as loud.

"That's just cruel," she said as she pulled the car back onto the road and steered toward Luke's place. "You're tempting us. I may have to order some when I get these girls home."

"No, you won't," he said. "This is for all of us. The least I can do is feed you, after you drove me around."

Her stomach gave a little leap, and not just about the prospect of pizza. Why was he inviting her to have dinner with him? Was there an ulterior motive? And if there was, would she mind?

Don't miss
Finding a Christmas Home *by Lee Tobin McClain,*
available October 2021 wherever
Love Inspired books and ebooks are sold.

LoveInspired.com

"I. Want. Ice. Cream!"

Tony looked around, wondering whether to pick Jax up and carry him back to the cottage or to let this spectacle play out on the street.

And then, like a vision, there was Kayla, dressed in workout clothes and a woolly red hat. Even though she probably couldn't help, since Jax hadn't warmed up to her or her class all week, it was good to see a friendly face.

Kayla veered off from the friend she was jogging with. "Jax! Tony!" She approached them like she was going to swoop Jax up and then stopped abruptly, looking at Tony. "Um, can I help?"

Tony sat back on his heels. "I wish you would," he said wearily. "He wants ice cream for dinner, and he didn't like hearing 'no.'"

"Ooooh." Kayla looked at the ice cream shop and then at Jax, whose cries had ever so slightly decreased in volume. She knelt and lightly rubbed Jax's arm. "Hey," she said, her voice quiet. "I can't talk to you and your uncle if you're so loud."

Jax paused, hiccuped and then resumed the tantrum.

"I can just take him home." Tony stood.

"Goody's does have real food." Kayla stood, too. "The crab cake sandwiches are to die for, and the fries are greasy, but really good."

Tony's stomach rumbled. "Should I give in, though? Won't that reinforce the bad behavior?"

Jax rubbed his eyes and sat up, still crying dramatically, but not so loudly.

"Maybe make a deal? If he goes in and behaves and eats real food, he could have some ice cream?" She smiled. "I have to recommend the chocolate milkshakes." She kissed her fingertips and gestured toward the shop.

Her pink cheeks and sparkly eyes took Tony's attention away from his nephew and his guilt and his aloneness. He smiled for the first time in a long time. "That good, huh?"

Their gazes held for just a moment too long.

She broke first, laughing a little, looking down at Jax. "He's listening," she said.

Tony knelt beside his nephew. "Okay, kiddo. Miss Kayla says they have healthy food here." If crab cake sandwiches and greasy fries could be considered healthy. "Come in and sit and eat your supper nice, no crying. If you do that, you can have ice cream for dessert."

Jax hiccuped, considering. "Miss Kayla, too?" Jax looked up at his teacher.

Tony caught his breath. It was the first sign of liking that Jax had made toward Kayla. Toward anyone outside his family, actually.

Kayla looked surprised and then gave Jax a big smile. "That's very nice of you."

Tony stood. "I'd be honored if you'd let me buy you dinner." Her cheeks got pinker, and Tony wondered if it had sounded like he was asking her out.

"Oh, well, I can work out anytime, but how often do I get to have dinner with Jax?"

Jax stared up at her, eyes wide, and then his face creased into a smile. He reached up and took her hand. It looked like the kid was getting a sudden crush.

Given that Kayla had rescued Tony from carrying a screaming four-year-old across town, he felt the same way.

Don't miss
First Kiss at Christmas, *the next book in*
Lee Tobin McClain's The Off Season *series!*

HQNBooks.com